OFF BALANCE SERIES

BALANCE

LUCIA FRANCO

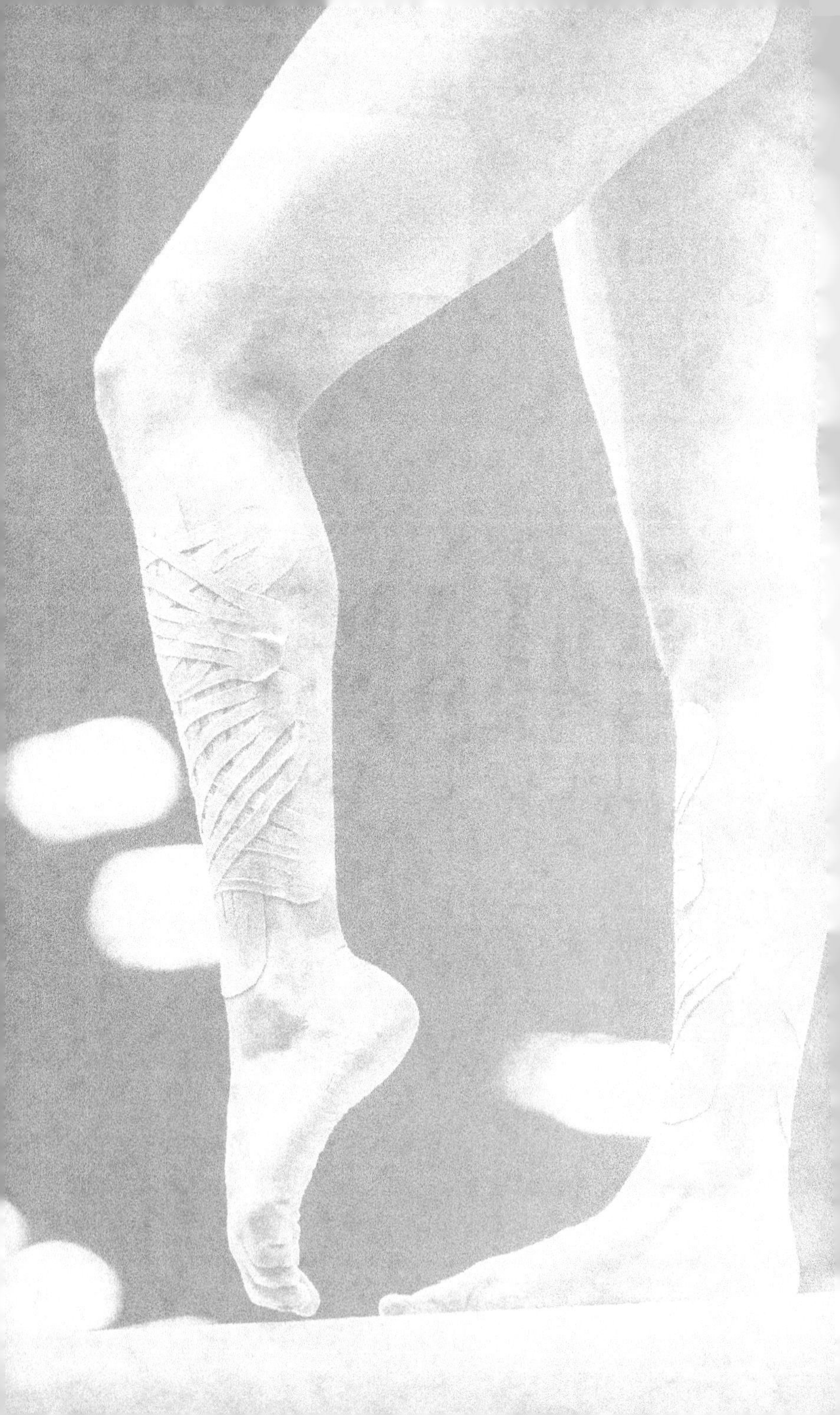

One toe off the beam and their forbidden desires could ruin everything they've worked for, throwing it all off balance.

OTHER TITLES BY LUCIA FRANCO

Dear Reader,

The Off Balance series is a continuation series. The novels must be read in order to follow the story.

This story is purely fictional and does not reflect real-life events.

Each novel in this five-part series follows a heavy May-December romance between a gymnast and a coach. If you consider this subject and any related content disturbing, then the Off Balance series is not for you.

Gymnastics is a hands-on sport that involves hours of close contact with a coach. My goal was to focus on the beauty of the sport in detail, show the emotional aspect of an athlete's dedication, and show how two people can cross forbidden boundaries and evolve together.

This story will push you, question you, and take you outside of your comfort zone.

The Off Balance series is intended only for readers 18 and older. Reader discretion is advised.

-Lucia

"Any coach who has been coaching for ten years and says he never fell in love; with an athlete or vice versa is lying."
  —Anonymous

GLOSSARY

All-Around A category of gymnastics that includes all the events. The all-around champion of an event earns the highest total score from all events combined.

Amanar A Yurchenko-style vault, meaning the gymnast performs a round-off onto the board, a back handspring onto the vault with a two and a half twisting layout back flip.

Cast A push off the bar with hips and lifts the body to straighten the shoulders and finish in handstand.

Deduction Points taken off a gymnast's score for errors. Most deductions are pre-determined, such as a 0.5 deduction for a fall from an apparatus or a 0.1 deduction for stepping out of bounds on the floor exercise.

Dismount The last skill in a gymnastics routine. For most events the method used to get off of the event apparatus.

Elite International Elite, the highest level of gymnastics.

Execution The performance of a routine. Form, style, and technique used to complete the skills constitute the level of execution of an exercise. Bent knees, poor toe point, and an arched or loosely held body position are all examples of poor execution.

Giant Performed on bars, a swing in which the body is fully extended and moving through a 360-degree rotation around the bar.

Full-In A full-twisting double back tuck, with the twist happening in the first back flip. It can be done in a tucked, piked, or layout position and is used in both men's and women's gymnastics.

Free Hip Circle Performed on the uneven bars or high bar, the body circles around the bar without the body touching the bar. There are both front hip circles and back hip circles.

Handspring Springing off the hands by putting the weight on the arms and using a strong push from the shoulders. Can be done either forward or backward, usually a connecting movement. This skill can be performed on floor, vault, and beam.

Heel Drive A termed used by coaches to inform the gymnasts they want them to drive their heels harder up and over on the front side of a handspring vault or front handspring on floor. Stronger heel drives create more rotation and potential for block and power.

Hecht Mount A mount where the gymnast jumps off a spring board while keeping their arms straight, pushes off of the low bar, and catches the high bar.

Inverted Cross Performed by men on the rings, it is an upside down cross.

Iron Cross A strength move performed by men on the rings. The gymnast holds the rings straight out on either side of their body while holding themselves up. Arms are perpendicular to the body.

Jaeger Performed on bars, a gymnast swings from a front Giant and let's go of the bar, into a front flip and catches the bar again. Jaeger can be done in the straddle, pike, and layout position, and is occasionally performed in a tucked position.

Kip The most commonly used mount for bars, the gymnast glides forward, pulls their feet to the bar, then pushes up to front support, resting their hips on the bar.

Layout A stretched body position.

Layout Timers A drill that simulates the feel of a skill, or the set for a skill without the risk of completing the skill.

Lines Straight, perfect lines of the body.

Overshoot, also known as Bail A transition from the high bar facing the low bar. The gymnast swings up and over the low bar with a half-turn to catch the low bar ending in a handstand.

Pike The body bent forward at the waist with the legs kept straight, an L position.

Pirouette Used in both gymnastics and dance to refer to a turn around the body's longitudinal axis. It is used to refer to a handstand turning moves on bars.

Rips In gymnastics, a rip occurs when a gymnast works so hard on the bars or rings they tear off a flap of skin from their hand. The injury is like a blister that breaks open.

Release Leaving the bar to perform a skill before re-grasping it.

Relevé This is a dance term that is often used in gymnastics. In a relevé, the gymnast is standing on toes and has straight legs.

Reverse Grip A swing around the bar back-first with arms rotated inwards and hands facing upwards.

Round-off A turning movement, with a push-off on one leg, while swinging the legs upward in a fast cartwheel motion into a ninety degree turn where legs come together before landing on both feet. The lead-off to a number of skills used to perform on vault, beam, and floor.

Salto Flip or somersault, with the feet coming up over the head and the body rotating around the axis of the waist.

Sequence Two or more skills performed together, creating a different skill or activity.

Stick To land, and remain standing without requiring a step. A proper stick position is with legs bent, shoulders above hips, arms forward.

Straddle Back An uneven bar transition done from a swing backwards on the high bar over the low bar, while catching the low bar in a handstand.

Tap Swing Performed on bars, an aggressive tap toward the ceiling in a swinging motion. This gives the gymnast the necessary momentum to swing around the bar to perform a Giant or to go into a release move.

Toe On Swing around the bar with body piked so much the feet are on the bar.

Tsavdaridou Performed on beam, a round-off back handspring with full twist to swing down.

Tuck The knees and hips are bent and drawn into the chest, the body is folded at the waist.

Twist The gymnast rotates around the body's longitudinal axis, defined by the spine. Performed on all apparatuses.

Yurchenko Round-off entry onto the board, back handspring onto the vaulting table and Salto off the vault table. The gymnast may twist on the way off.

CHAPTER 1

A bsolutely not!"

My father's harsh voice boomed around his home office.

"You haven't even heard what I have to say," I argued, not settling for anything less than his full attention.

"I don't care what you have to say. You can talk until you're blue in the face. You are not moving to New Hampshire. End of discussion."

"Dad, just listen. Gymnastics—"

"I've made my decision, and it's not changing." He picked up his pen and focused on the papers in front of him. "Now, please, I have work to do."

Devastation sucker punched me in the gut. I was surprised by how unreasonable he was in not letting me speak. New Hampshire was home to one of the best gymnastics facilities in the country, and I'd prove it to him. My weeks of research wouldn't be wasted. I would not give up. I just had to try harder.

"It's renowned for its coaching and athletes," I pressed on.

"No." He gave me his infamous look, the one capable of making a grown man flinch.

My future was at stake, and I had to fight for it. As much as I would miss my current gym, it was no longer useful. I could take only so many extra hours of conditioning and private classes. Advancement in this sport required proper training, and I couldn't get it at my old gym.

"Transferring to another gym isn't unheard of. A lot of families send their gymnasts to train at better facilities." I stood my ground.

"Adrianna Francesca Rossi!" His tone and anger bled into my frustration but didn't stop me.

"Just hear me out! Please," I pleaded, on the verge of tears. My mother would no doubt sniff them in the air and be on me like a bloodhound within seconds. Tears showed weakness, and a Rossi was never weak—at least according to her.

Dad didn't respond. Instead, he stared right through me.

Blowing out a loud, aggravated breath, I stood up and peered through the large window in his office which overlooked the expansive, lush lawn in our backyard. My gaze drifted over to the right, catching the beautiful colors of the late afternoon sun reflecting off the pool. We lived in one of the most elite neighborhoods on the prestigious Amelia Island. We had everything money could buy. Everything except a great one-of-a-kind gymnastics coach that could help push me closer to achieving my dream.

Turning back to my dad, I took in the flare of his nostrils and stiff jaw. He had become eerily still. The room grew cold, and goose bumps broke out on my skin. I knew this side of him, and it wasn't pretty. This was a side nobody dared to test.

I had pushed too far.

"Go," he said. "Now." His voice was quiet and calm, dismissing me to return to his work.

I fled his office and retreated to my bedroom, slamming the door just as the tears started to fall.

Gymnastics was everything to me—my heart and soul, the air I breathed. It was the one thing that allowed me to be me. To express myself creatively in the way I chose, not how someone else decided for me. I'd rotated between eating, sleeping, and flipping for as long as I could remember. The competitiveness, the challenge of mastering a new skill. The way I defied gravity—my heart soaring, the sound of applause, the gasp from the audience—made the sacrifice worth every bit of pain and manipulation my body went through. Nothing could take that feeling away.

It was the one place I could be free from the restraints my family's name had on me.

My name is Adrianna Rossi and I'm a competitive gymnast—elite gymnast, to be exact. Or I would be as soon as I had the right coach.

I had completed all levels required according to USA Gymnastics in order to move forward and test for elite. It was only a matter of time before I held the coveted rank. I trained day in and day out for this. My days consisted of four-hour training sessions in the gym, a tutor to homeschool me, and a private chef to prepare my calculated caloric meals.

As I fell onto my bed, devastation hit me hard. The rejection crushed my heart and it felt like my dreams were slowly being ripped away.

Like most hungry gymnasts, my ultimate goal was the Olympics.

If I graphed the training along with my age, I could compete in my first Olympic Games by the time I was twenty. While twenty was still considered youthful by normal standards, it was ancient in the gymnastics world. Though, it wasn't unheard of to compete in The Games at that age. One of my favorites, Svetlana Khorkina, competed in three Olympics by the age of twenty-five, her first at seventeen. Oksana Chusovitina, who competed in six Olympic Games, also started at seventeen. My goal wasn't entirely farfetched. I just needed the proper training. I was good, but I wanted to be great. And the only way to be great was to train with the best.

Though I was young, I wasn't naive. I knew what kind of mental and physical abuse my body would go through in order to reach the professional level. I needed a drill sergeant with a sharp eye.

I needed it and wanted it.

I didn't fully understand why my dad objected to me leaving. I knew he thought of gymnastics as a hobby, but he'd always done anything to placate me. He never told me no and usually threw money at whatever my heart desired. It wasn't as if he spent much time at home anyway. Frank Rossi was too occupied with expanding and maintaining his real estate empire. Rossi Enterprises was one of the top developers, with properties worldwide. He left my mom in charge of raising my brother and me, which was a joke.

When I first began gymnastics at three years old, my mother used to sit at my practices and attend my meets. It was all about appearances back then, but I was young, so she really didn't have much choice. However, the older I got, the less of an effort she made. I think the last meet she came to I was twelve years old. Mom was usually too busy with her charity work or trying to keep my older brother, Xavier, out of the media.

At first their lack of interest bothered me. I wanted them to *want* to be there, to watch me tumble and flip and balance on the beam.

To see me move up to another level or stick a dismount without wobbling. I craved my parents' attention as all children do, but after years of begging, I eventually gave up and learned to adapt to their indifference. Nowadays, Mom rarely came to practice, and neither of my parents attended many competitions.

Their actions forced me to be independent, something I quickly learned to value. That being said, I refused to give up. I wouldn't let anything, or anyone, take my end goal away from me.

I wasn't sure how much time had passed when I heard a faint knock on my door. I cracked my eyes open and was surprised by the darkness surrounding me. Another, louder knock sounded, and I prayed it wasn't my mom.

"Yeah?"

"Ana?" Relief coursed through me at the sound of my dad's voice. "Can I come in?"

A fatigued sigh rolled off my lips as I sat up on the edge of my bed. "Come in."

Dad opened the door, flipping on the light switch as he walked in. A quick glance at my reflection in the mirror on the adjacent wall had me pulling back in shock. My face was blotchy and swollen from crying. Hair lay stuck and matted to my face. I was a hot mess.

I squinted at my dad, trying to adjust to the light. The sorrow in his heavy eyes showed. It was clear he was remorseful over his decision and the way he reacted. The last time I'd seen him, he'd been dressed in a clean, crisp shirt and tie. Now the tie was gone, a few buttons were undone, and his sleeves were rolled up. He was disheveled and worn out, and I knew I was the reason. I'd acted like a spoiled brat and argued with him, something I always tried to refrain from. Usually it was my older brother who caused so much turmoil for my parents, not me.

"Yes, Dad?" I tried to lighten the tension. A soft smile charmed his face. I was a daddy's girl through and through, and he knew it.

"May I sit with you?"

I nodded, and he sat next to me, the mattress dipping a little. He moved the tangled hair from my cheeks and eyed me carefully.

"You look like you've been crying, which can only mean I'm at fault."

I flattened my lips and cast my eyes down. "I may have been."

"I apologize, sweetheart." He ran a tired hand down his face. "About the gymnastics…"

"Yeah?"

"Listen, it's not that I don't want you to do it. It's that I don't want you moving so far away on your own. You're still young, and the world is a dangerous place. What if something happened to you? I wouldn't be able to get to you fast enough."

My voice softened over his concern. "Dad, you're always traveling for work." My words caused him to wince, and I instantly felt terrible for stating the fact. But it was the truth, and I had to get my point across. "What would be the difference?"

He ran a hand through his salt and pepper hair. "You're right. I do travel a lot for work, and I'm sorry I'm not around enough, but the difference is I'm an experienced adult, and you're not."

I slouched in defeat. "I know. I was just hoping you'd give it some thought. It's not like I'd be completely alone. I'd live in a shared apartment with a den mom and other gymnasts."

"Not *your* mom, though. I don't even know those women, Adrianna. You're my daughter. I can't trust them with you."

I gave him a serious look. "Dad, we both know Mom isn't the kind of mother to do something like that for me." The kind of mother who gives and does anything for her children to see them thrive. Joy Rossi had more important things on her agenda.

My dad sighed. "You've put up a good argument and I've thought about it." I perked up. "I might have a compromise. I have a business associate in Cape Coral who happens to coach gymnastics. Let me give him a call and see what he says."

My eyes widened. "Where's that?"

"South. About two hours or so from here. It's right outside of Florida near the water."

I paused, pursing my lips together. "You have a friend who's a coach? How did I not know this?"

"You met him when you were younger, though you probably don't remember. He bought some real estate from me many years ago and we've stayed in touch. Every so often we'll flip a house together, or he'll ask for advice on property. His name is Konstantin."

The name didn't ring any bells. "What level does he coach?"

"That I don't know. I only know he's a former Russian Olympian and is good at what he does."

Hope sprouted inside of me to the point I couldn't contain my smile. Russians were crazy, their gymnastics training even crazier, which caused my stomach to flutter with anxiety. I wouldn't complain. I'd take what I could.

Beggars couldn't be choosers.

"I can't believe you didn't tell me this sooner."

"His past doesn't come up in our real estate transactions. I didn't know you weren't happy at your current gym," he countered. "If you'd told me your coaches weren't cutting it, Konstantin could've stepped in sooner."

Touché.

"When are you going to call him? Can you call now? Please?" Enthusiastically, I shook his arm and jumped, bobbing on my knees. "Dad!"

He chuckled at my eagerness, the light in his eyes returning. My dad and I had the same exact shade of green eyes. I resembled him the most. From my dark hair, thin straight nose, and skin tone, we were very similar. And just like my dad, when I got excited about something, my eyes turned a brilliant jade color. Although, I wasn't sure where the deep crimson tones in my hair or freckles came from.

He faked a sigh, restraining a smile. "Come into my office and I'll give him a call."

"Really?" I shrieked. When he nodded, I threw my arms around his shoulders and hugged him tightly. "Oh, thank you, Dad! Thank you! Thank you! Thank you!"

He patted my back lovingly. I jumped from my bed and trailed closely behind. Once we were back in his office, I plopped down into a studded leather chair in front of his desk. I placed my hands under my thighs so I didn't fidget while my father got situated.

And by situated, I mean pouring himself a glass of bourbon.

"All right, remind me again what level you are. What's the goal you want to achieve?"

Sadness crept inside me. I wish he knew without me having to remind him. The man could spout off twenty different business transactions from the top of his head, but he couldn't retain a few facts about his daughter.

"I'm a level ten, but I want to test for elite. Find out if he coaches elite first and if he has an elite program."

He nodded and dialed a number, enabling the speakerphone. The phone rang a few times until a deep voice picked up.

"Allo?"

My brows creased together. *A-low?*

"Konstantin, my friend, Frank Rossi here. How are you doing?"

"Frank, it is good to hear your voice. You are just the man I wanted to speak with actually." Dad mentioned he was Russian, and his heavy accent confirmed it.

"Is that so? Perfect timing, then. Did you get my Christmas gift? I sent a bottle of my favorite vodka to you and that pretty girlfriend of yours."

Konstantin paused, laughing lightly. "I will have to ask Katja when I get home. Her appetite for vodka is just as voracious as mine. I hope she did not drink it all without me." He chuckled, as did my dad. "Thank you in advance. That was very kind of you."

"How is Katja doing? Have you guys decided to settle down yet?" Dad asked, swirling his glass tumbler of bourbon. As much as I liked hearing him catch up with his friend, I was anxious for him to get to the point.

"Ah, not yet," he responded with a deep sigh. "It is not for her lack of trying. All in good time."

Dad chuckled, and my heart started to beat faster over his next set of words. "I have a question for you. Are you still coaching gymnastics?"

"Funny you should ask. I am, and I just happened to buy World Cup from the previous owners about a year ago. I was thinking about expanding it, but I wanted your expertise on whether it is worth it or not."

"Ah..." Dad's brows lifted, a sparkle twinkling in his eyes. I knew that look. It was his chance to dabble in something look. "How perfect the timing is, then. Do you recall telling me when my precious daughter was ready to switch to give you a call?"

He paused. Silence filled the air. My heart stopped. "I do."

"She came to me earlier asking to transfer to some gym in New Hampshire. Do you know of any gym over there?"

"Not one worth remembering."

Dad's eyes bore into mine. He raised a pointed brow. "Well, she said it's one of the best gyms on the East Coast." He let out a huff. "I can't imagine anyone being better than you."

Konstantin chuckled. "You flatter me. I had no idea your daughter was still training. Tell me, what level is she."

I held up two hands to remind him.

"She's a level ten, but she said her gym doesn't have an—"

"Elite coach," I whispered.

"Elite coach, which is what she's telling me she needs," Dad said. "Are you elite?" I cringed at my dad's question. *He* wouldn't be elite. He would coach elite.

"I do have an elite program and team of elite girls." The line goes silent, and I hold my breath. "Correct me if I am wrong, but is your daughter in high school now?"

"She is indeed. She'll be graduating soon," he added proudly.

"Hmm. That is quite old for an elite. Is she training for college now?"

"To be honest, I'm not sure what she plans to do or can do. I know she wants to train at an exclusive gym."

That hurt my heart like a knife to the chest. I'd just told him a few hours earlier what my plans for the future were.

"All right." He cleared his throat. "I have a dinner meeting I need to get to, so can I give you a call in the morning and we can go over this?"

"Perfect, sounds like a plan. I look forward to hearing from you. While we're at it, we can also discuss your expansion idea for your new gym."

"Even better."

When Dad hung up the phone, I didn't feel any better. I frowned. It didn't sound like a sure thing once he heard my age. I almost wished he hadn't been on speakerphone.

"Don't worry, sweetheart. There isn't anything I can't make happen now."

CHAPTER 2

Staring out the window, I couldn't see beyond my transparent reflection as we passed another mile marker.

My heart fluttered, and a small smile curved my lips thinking about how long I'd waited for this moment. I couldn't remember a time I'd been this happy...or impatient, edgy, and restless. I was a wheel of emotions. The knots in my stomach pulled tighter as anxiety swirled through me at breakneck speed.

I took a deep breath and rested against the cold leather seat, praying it wasn't much farther.

Two months ago, Dad had come through and gotten me into World Cup Academy of Gymnastics, which happened to be one of the top-rated gymnastic training centers in Georgia. With my heart set on finding the best gym, I had tunnel vision after a teammate had mentioned the one in New Hampshire. It never dawned on me to look anywhere else. From what I gathered, Dad made a generous donation to World Cup, allowing me to train at the facility. Being a struggling athlete, I was desperate to reach the next level. I didn't want to rely on my dad and his business relations, but if it helped get me closer to my dream, then so be it.

As my dad had always said, "You use your connections." I was ready to do whatever it took. This was the one—and only time—I was truly happy about coming from an affluent family.

I'd done some research and found out World Cup wasn't just any gym. Previously owned by former top-ranking coaches around the world, it was renowned for its training and ability to take athletes to a new level. The coaches were very particular, elite gymnasts were handpicked, and it took natural-born talent and dedication to be one of its members. Some of the best gymnasts had come out of this gym, trained by a group of intense coaches who pushed their limits with their level of training.

It seemed like hours had passed by the time we veered to the right, finally exiting the highway. Curving around and following the snake-like bend down the street, we pulled up to a gray building with dark-tinted windows a couple of minutes later.

"So this is what you want?" my father asked as he made his way around the Escalade. He placed his hands into the pockets of his expensive, tailored pants and surveyed the place as the wind billowed against him.

"More than anything," I replied, unable to hide the smile on my face. I'd been speechless while staring at the large structure before me. This was what I'd wanted for the past year, and now it was mine. Happiness surged through me fast and my smile grew larger.

My mother stepped out wearing bright red high heels with a matching red dress. Leave it to Joy Rossi to dress like the First Lady. She pulled her stark white jacket tight around her waist, her eyes skittering around, not a blonde hair out of place despite the wind's effort. Judging by the scowl on her face, you'd think we were in the dingiest place on earth.

"This is probably where muggers hide at night and bums come to sleep. Of all the gyms, I can't believe Konstantin picked this place. It looks...disgusting."

I couldn't tell if her shudder was from the breeze or the fact that she thought I had purposely picked some remote serial killer town with no running water or electricity.

"Joy," my father warned.

I shook my head, not agreeing with her judgmental attitude. How she came to that conclusion in two minutes was beyond me. Deep down, I knew Dad would never have agreed to this had he not done his own research and thought it was unsafe.

Glancing around, I could see commercial buildings nearby and hunter-green dumpsters placed sporadically outside. Obviously, it was a part of town where industrial businesses were located—a commercial area—not fancy, five-star restaurants where my mother was used to dining, or ritzy boutiques where they didn't sell anything that wasn't couture or in season. Unfortunately, she didn't see things my way. What she saw were dim colors with no life, and most importantly, a place where she would gain nothing.

I saw my future. I saw my dream staring at me from behind the concrete walls, daring me to get my ass moving.

Dad held his arm out, gesturing for me to lead the way, and I headed up the walkway toward the entrance. Grabbing the cold door handle, I pulled it open and stepped inside World Cup with my parents following closely behind.

The smell of chalk permeated the air, and my stomach quivered at the first intake of the aroma into my lungs. It was a distinct scent, and taste, to a gymnast, practically part of our food groups, difficult to explain to anyone not involved in the sport. Similar to baby powder but chalkier smelling. Muffled music blaring through the speakers, a spring board rebounding, and the sound of uneven bars ricocheting as they're released, grabbed my attention. It was music to my ears. The kind of sound that got my adrenaline moving and my pulse thumping, beckoning me to drop everything and wrap my hands around the bars or feel the spring floor beneath my bare feet.

Taking another deep breath, I exhaled, unable to hide my splitting grin. My heart was ready to explode. Finally, I was where I was supposed to be.

Glancing around the empty lobby, I wasn't sure where to go, but the window to my right showed a view of the huge facility. It was completely deceiving from the outside...cue the anxiety. Intimidation hit hard in that moment.

Gymnasts, both male and female, were scattered about, white chalk dusting their skin. I could see not just one, but two floors, three sets of uneven bars, and seven balance beams, along with two vaults. There was also a tumble track, various equipment for men, and a high bar with a foam pit and resi-mat, a huge mat on top of a foam pit used for practicing softer landings. Farther back were a bunch of doors. I had no idea what they were for, but I was curious to what they led to.

Even my parents seemed to be in awe of the gym if their wide eyes were any indication. A shiver shot down my spine and goose bumps coated my arms in enthusiasm as a rush of adrenaline began beating through my veins at the sight before me.

The sound of a slamming door from behind me shook me out of my trance, compelling me to look over my shoulder. My parents followed the sound and I spotted a tall, fit man. With his hands on his hips, his eyes surveyed the lobby and connected with my parents' before trailing down and locking with mine, his narrowing gaze holding me in place. All the air left my lungs. His powerful presence demanded attention, and without a doubt, he had all of mine.

Never in my life had I seen someone so unbelievably gorgeous. There was no other word I could use to describe him. His commanding eyes made me think it was possible he could be a coach, but no coach I'd ever seen had been so attractive. Come to think of it, none of them had ever been under the age of forty without a potbelly and receding hairline. This man was solidly built and full of muscle.

A silent breath escaped my lips as he stalked toward us with power and poise. My heart nearly hurdled into my throat as I stared like he was some sort of Adonis. Dark stubble dusted his square jaw, full lips that begged for attention, straight as an arrow nose. Combined with inky black hair, olive skin, and golden undertones. Sweet baby Jesus, the man was perfection.

Crossing the room, he extended a hand.

"Frank, it is good to see you again." His forearm flexed, the veins signifying the muscular strength he wielded. It was incredibly difficult to tear my eyes away as he gave my father a firm handshake. He was absolutely, drop-dead gorgeous. Avery would call him fucking hot. My best friend loved to add "fucking" to the beginning of everything.

"Kova."

This was my dad's friend, and he owned this place. Interesting. He looked like he was fresh out of college, no more than twenty-five max. Dad didn't have very many young friends I was aware of—I could count on one hand the friends I had met who were younger than him. They typically had graying hair, crow's feet, and over-worked, aging skin. The complete opposite of what was standing right in front of me.

So Kova was Konstantin. Where the nickname came from was beyond me, but the more talking they did, and the camaraderie I witnessed, the more I realized this was indeed the man my dad had told me about.

I remembered hearing the name Konstantin years ago in the gym-nastics circle. He was one of the most decorated gymnasts to date, bringing home more medals to Russia than any other male athlete. He'd competed in two Olympics and dominated each of them. He was supposed to try for a third Olympics but pulled out at the last minute due to unforeseen circumstances. Rumors circulated, some even saying steroid use was the reason he didn't compete, but to my knowledge he never publicly gave a reason for his absence.

"Welcome to World Cup Academy of Gymnastics."

That accent was most definitely Russian. For a gymnast, Kova was tall. At least six feet. Paired with his profoundly muscular shoulders and firm chest, evidenced by how tight his shirt stretched, he looked like the perfect package, if there ever was one.

My eyes drifted down, and my cheeks bloomed with heat. Oh, my God. Now, I was checking out his package!

"You remember my wife, Joy, and our daughter, Adrianna. Or Ana as we call her."

I internally rolled my eyes. My name was Adrianna, not Ana. I always hated the nickname. It made me feel like a child being reprimanded, yet they continued using it, knowing how much I detested it. Grin and bear it, I told myself. Grin...and bear it.

As Konstantin shook my mother's hand, I chuckled on the inside. Her hand was enveloped in his and I would bet she worried he'd chip her nail polish. It was a damn handshake for Christ's sake, yet she acted so fragile. Nothing was more annoying than when my mom acted like she was made of porcelain. I guarantee her dainty, cold fingers rested in his hand like they were dead, which only seemed to match her icy demeanor.

"Hello again, Kova. You have a nice...facility." She tried to say with sophistication, but I could see right through her bleached teeth and her pretentious personality. An air of money surrounded her and she wore it like a second skin. My mother and I couldn't be more opposite.

Konstantin turned my way and I nearly lost all common sense. His emerald eyes were encircled by a thick black ring with faint web like lines in the irises. Mesmerizing. They reminded me of a rainforest—beautifully alluring, uncharted territory without knowing what lurked all around. Framed between thick lashes, his gaze was penetrating, like he could read my deepest, darkest secrets.

"Ana, it is a pleasure to see you again. Last time I saw you, you barely reached my knees and ran around with pigtails. You have grown so much," he said.

Pigtails? I think I stopped with the pigtails around five. If that was the case, he was clearly over twenty-five.

"Adrianna." I emphasized my full name. The ends of his lips curved upward just a hint and my stomach tightened. I tucked a lock of hair behind my ear demurely and returned the smile.

"Are you sure you are ready for this? The elite program is completely different than level ten. Much more intense. I have already explained this to your father, but I want to assure you this is going to be nothing like your old gym. You are going to be exhausted, and probably bruised and sore until your body adjusts to the training. Just because your dad and I go way back, do not think for one minute I will be easy. I hope you are ready for that kind of conditioning."

The overwhelming urge to repeat his thick accent hit me with a vengeance. I wanted to throw my hands in the air, speak extra loud like a boisterous Italian, and repeat every word Konstantin had just said. The way he spoke was so sexy, and that whole intense demeanor thing he had going on worked in his favor.

"I am," I responded confidently.

Glancing back at my parents, Kova said, "How about we head into my office and go over some paperwork before taking a tour of the gym, yeah?"

CHAPTER 3

The next thirty minutes were spent reviewing the fine print and signing medical release forms.

My mother appeared as if she suffered from constipation no matter how hard she tried to look composed. Gymnastics, along with legal documents, were so out of her element. Pretending to be a concerned mother was not in her comfort zone. Charity fundraisers were more her thing, where she could dress up, plaster on a phony smile, and act like she gave a shit about something. It was hard to blame her as my own thoughts drifted around the room, taking in the various medals and trophies, quickly losing interest in the topic myself.

The paperwork didn't interest me. All I wanted to do was get on the floor and feel the carpet beneath my feet. Floor was my absolute favorite event, though I excelled at vault. It was where I felt free and could let go, flying through the air at my heart's desire. I loved tumbling, loved defying gravity, and secretly prayed to God I wouldn't land on my ass each time.

I despised beam with pure hatred. But that was another story entirely.

I looked over at my dad in deep conversation with Konstantin. He was interested in knowing more about my training, but then again, he liked reading the small print and knowing exactly what he was paying for. It was why he'd done so well with his own company. No one could nickel and dime him. He loved money and ensured he knew where every penny he made went. And it didn't matter this was a friend he should probably be able to trust, he'd still cover his bases. However, I wasn't stupid. I knew this was more about the business side of things for him than giving me something I loved and was passionate about. This was just another deal for him to analyze and negotiate over, rather than my future.

In the midst of explaining the forms and going over my strict training regimen, I heard the words 'dance class' and my attention snapped back to the conversation.

"Dance class?" I butted in.

Konstantin lifted a perfectly arched brow, his eyes narrowing as if just realizing I was in the room.

"I was mentioning to Frank that you will be taking ballet class, along with jazz."

My mouth gaped open. "Ballet?" I asked, annoyance thick in my tone. Please tell me this was a joke. There was no way in hell I'd take ballet. I hated ballet.

"Yes, Adrianna. Ballet. It helps with posture and grace on the floor. Not to mention, flexibility and core strengthening."

"I have grace and fluidity on the floor already. I don't need extra dance classes."

I never had to take ballet back home, so I was certain I didn't need to take it here. All these extra classes would take away from the one thing I came here to do, and I refused to let that happen.

Konstantin slowly placed his expensive looking, shiny pen down. It was unnerving how he stared at me and I wanted to look away, but I held strong. I kept my eyes trained on him, focusing on the black flecks glittering in his eyes, showing him I wasn't weak.

"I am going to make it easy for you. You play by my rules here. You either take the classes or you will not train at World Cup."

Easy. As if I was some moron who didn't comprehend complex words. My parents hadn't spent thousands of dollars a year on a private tutor for nothing. I'd had straight A's since the fifth grade. I was already taking Pre-Cal and college level courses, and he treated me like I couldn't spell D-I-C-K.

Slapping on a fake smile, I said in a sugary voice, "Ballet really isn't necessary. It'd be a complete waste of time. I've never needed it before and I don't need it now." I finished with a few rapid blinks and waited for his response. I liked to call this my "social event face" a skill mom taught me. Sweet, innocent, and full of shit, and if you lived in Palm Bay, it was considered a standard fashion accessory.

Konstantin paused and simply stared at me for a few heartbeats. Just when I thought I'd won, he pulled back the papers my dad had in his grip. Looking to my dad, he said, "I can see *Ana* is not ready for this kind of commitment, Frank. It takes dedication, hard work, and most importantly, *listening* skills. And until she understands it is my way—"

My chest heaved, blood pumping rapidly through my heart. He was rejecting me, saying I couldn't train here, but I refused to let that be an option. So I cut in before he could speak another word in that stupid Russian accent of his I loved only moments earlier.

"How many of these classes do I have to take?"

He looked back at me. "As many as you need."

I clenched my teeth and dipped my head slowly in surrender. Despite his good looks, he acted like a total ass, and that was something I wasn't used to.

Konstantin slid the papers back to Dad, but his gaze never wavered from mine. "I spoke with your old coach and asked about your current training, where you could use improvement. He said you lacked flexibility, which is where ballet comes into play—it helps open your hips, stretch your legs, and gives long lean body lines gymnastics often hardens. Contrary to what you believe, he also mentioned you could use more grace. Dance is an important element to have for balance beam and floor. We want you to flow, not come across as a robot. With that being said, an evaluation will determine your specific needs."

My blood pressure climbed and it took everything in me not to refute his statement. Just when I thought I was moving forward, I really took ten steps back. I was not a stiff robot on the floor like he insinuated. I knew how to move for fuck's sake.

"And all these extra dance classes—ballet and jazz—are included in her new gym schedule?" My dad piped in, and thank God he did. I was ready to blow a fuse. "She'll be doing two-a-day, along with training for a total of forty hours a week?"

Konstantin turned back to my dad. "Yes, she will have two days off. What she chooses to do with those days is up to her, but when she is here, she is under my supervision and the control of World Cup, along with the other coaches. As much as I want to put gymnastics first, school is more important, so we work around a schedule for all the gymnasts. Once it is set, she will have to take responsibility and balance it. Typically, there will be practice in the morning where we focus on strength and conditioning, break for school, then gymnastics in the afternoon. Dance will be on rotation." He took a breath and continued. "Most gymnasts here are in public school, so their hours are consistent. A few girls share an apartment to help keep their expenses low. I understand you have rented an apartment for her?"

Dad cleared his throat. "I've gone ahead and secured one of the top floor units at Cape Harbor for her. It's a two-bedroom condo across town in one of my gated communities. I also purchased an SUV as her own to drive when the time comes."

Now I wish I hadn't skipped out on getting my license when I turned sixteen like everyone else did.

"As you know, being a Rossi brings a lot of publicity, and I need to ensure Ana is safe. She appears much older than she is and has a strong head on her shoulders, unlike most girls her age. I know you'll be nearby if anything should happen, but I still worry about her being so far away. I took the necessary precautions before allowing her to move here. Ana doesn't want for anything, and anything she does need, she'll have so she can focus on gymnastics. My wife has even gone the distance to have her meals delivered to her condo and a tutor in place."

Stifling a groan of embarrassment, I chewed the inside of my lip instead.

Dad always managed to find a way to mention money and how much of it he had. It was humiliating and I detested the pompous manner he spoke about it, friend or not. It was mortifying, especially sharing the fact he ordered meals for me. He knew I was responsible enough to make wise decisions, unlike my brother who reveled in the Rossi name and money.

I stared at Konstantin, trying to gauge his reaction at the unnecessary shit my father elaborated on, but his face gave nothing away. His cold stare—the resting dick face—could rival my mother's. I stifled a chuckle. The way his presence demanded attention caused my heart to hammer against my ribs. As long as he didn't open his mouth to spew more ridiculous ballet suggestions, I couldn't help being drawn to him.

"All right, Adrianna, not only do your parents have to sign, but so do you." Another form? Enough already. Sell me to China, they have good gymnastics coaches over there. So what if they lie about their ages.

Konstantin handed me a stack of papers.

"The first is your commitment to the gym, your oath to train hard and give one hundred and fifty percent, and to not quit, not that I expect you to. However, should you decide to end your time here at World Cup before the year ends, there will be a hefty fee charged to your parents, just like I do with every teammate. I am sure you know this is not an easy gym to get into, hence the need for this obligation. This agreement is renewed every year."

Just as I was about to press the pen down to sign my name, naturally Mom had to get her two cents in.

"Ana, this is a very expensive endeavor. I'm sure more than most parents would be willing to spend. We know you're responsible and trust you to do the right thing, but your father and I would be very upset if we had to pay an unnecessary fee on top of it all," she warned with glaring eyes. "Are you sure you're committed to this?"

"More than anything in the world," I mumbled under my breath. If she wanted to test my resolve at the eleventh hour, she could throw any doubts out the window. I was looking my dream straight in the face, and a few more documents to sign would not get between my goals and me.

"Anything?" Her voice heightened her question. She had no idea how much this meant to me, or how dedicated I was to gymnastics.

"She gets it, Joy," Dad said, and then gave me a satisfied smile.

For whatever reason, my mom pushed me hard on just about everything. It was disconcerting and I wished she'd back off and encourage me instead.

Dad understood my dedication because he was the same way. Once we found something to pour all our sweat and blood into, there was no going back. Our devotion drove us.

"All right, the next document states you will not date anyone while you are under my authority and training," Konstantin said, eyeing me as he slid it across his desk. He couldn't be serious. I'd never heard of a coach doing this before.

"I know it sounds juvenile, but this is a very important piece of paper you will have to sign. I do not need you losing your focus. You will end up skipping practices and pissing me off. It could ruin your career and it will only waste my time. My time is precious. I expect, and deserve, your focus and determination, not anyone else."

"I understand."

I scribbled my name without reading and pushed it back. Konstantin held my gaze. "You should always read the fine print before you sign anything," he said quietly, sounding disappointed.

He peered down at my signature, his eyes moving as he read. "Right here states," he said, pointing, "you will be under my supervision during gym time." Konstantin handed a paper to my father and said, "This is basically the same agreement I gave your daughter. Since there is no parental supervision, she will be under the supervision of World Cup while training in the facility. Anything she does after she steps out of the gym is not my responsibility; therefore, neither I, nor World Cup will be held accountable for her actions. All the gymnasts living on their own while training here must sign it."

Dad read over it silently then looked at me and said, in an unyielding voice, "I hope you realize how much faith and trust we're putting in you to be responsible, young lady. This is no joke."

Wide eyed, I nodded. "I understand completely, Dad."

Dad signed the agreement and Konstantin stacked the papers together, bound them with a paper clip and set them aside. Kova crossed his arms firmly across his chest, leaned back in his leather chair, and looked directly at me.

"My training is unconventional, it is tough and brutal. There will be days when you will not be able to stand the sight of me. It is intense and exhausting. I am not here to be your friend, I am not here to pat your back when times get rough, I am not here to coddle you. I am here to be your coach and help get you to the next level. I come from Russia with some of the strictest coaching around. I have learned from the best, and just because you are your father's daughter does not mean I will go easy on you. You will forget everything you were taught in the past and relearn through me. I will give you all the possible means you need, but it is up to you to dig deep and be the athlete you want to become. You must have the drive and the passion to go places. I am just here to guide you down that path and show you your capability." He paused. "This, Adrianna, is your chance to leave. I can rip up these papers and you all can go home."

I looked at Konstantin and realized two things: I was about to get my ass handed to me, and he didn't use contractions.

CHAPTER 4

O kay, so I was still a little obsessed with what came out of his mouth.

I couldn't help it. That accent was sexy as hell.

I stared at Konstantin with confidence. He met my gaze. With all the passion and drive that breathed through my veins for my love of gymnastics, I poured it into my next sentence.

"I'm not leaving."

The wicked smile that slid across his face nearly knocked the wind out of me.

"Well, that wraps up all the necessary formalities. If you would like, I can show you around the gym now."

Konstantin opened the door leading into the impressive gym.

We followed close behind, taking in every square inch around us. I couldn't stop the unsteady leaps in my stomach from the adrenaline pumping through my blood.

It reminded me of walking into home period on the first day of school. I hadn't had this feeling in quite some time since I'd been homeschooled for the past year, but I remembered it like it was yesterday. Everyone hated the first day.

Gymnasts on the nearby apparatus glanced up, surveying us from head to toe. Mom didn't miss a beat in her three-inch Christian Louboutin heels while my dad strutted around like he owned the place. And here I was in dark denim shorts, a baby doll shirt and sandals, feeling every bit as relaxed as I was.

Konstantin showed us all the parts of the gym, including the rooms in the back that I was curious about. I assumed they were for strength training, but they were actually used for various dance classes and stretching techniques.

"Holly, watch yourself on that dismount. Remember, even the smallest step is a tenth of a deduction. Girls, I would like you to meet Adrianna. She is a level ten, but plans to test for elite. She will be your new teammate here."

He made his way over to the uneven bars and introduced the girls. "This is Reagan." He nodded his head at her, arms crossed firmly against his chest. "She is a senior gymnast and has trained in the elite program for a couple of years. If you have any questions about what goes on here, I am sure she will be more than happy to help." Motioning to another girl, he said, "This is Holly. She has been with World Cup since she was a child, and her twin brother is also training here."

"She'll be training with us?" Reagan scoffed.

"That is what I said," he said sternly.

The ugly glower on Reagan's pinched face fueled a fire inside me. It was hard not to stare at her. Her features bunched together, giving her an overly dramatic expression. Just because I wasn't in the elite program yet didn't mean I couldn't train with them. Gyms all over the world had mixed classes, and most gymnasts benefited by watching the technique of their teammates while on an apparatus.

I could see her being a problem. Living amongst the wealthy had shown me how to view the true colors of people quickly, no one could pull off bitchy better than blue bloods, and I had been conditioned by some of the best.

"Coach, why isn't she training with her level then?"

Coach? Coach!

"You're the coach! *My* coach?"

"Adrianna!" my mother gasped, mortified over my outburst.

"Last time I checked. Who did you think I was?"

The girls on the team snickered. Warmth climbed my chest and hit my cheeks and ears over my outburst.

"You mean you didn't know, Adrianna," Mom said, adding fuel to the fire. How convenient of her to pay attention now.

Lifting one shoulder, I said candidly, "He's dressed for a business meeting, not prepared to be covered full of chalk for the next eight hours. How's he going to spot in those clothes and dress shoes? I assumed..." I trailed off, biting my bottom lip. My shoulders dropped. "I don't know what I assumed, honestly. I just thought he owned the gym and didn't coach. A lot of owners don't coach."

My cheeks blossomed with heat when I glanced at my *new* coach. The veiled smirk he donned matched the glimmer in his eyes. I'd never had a young coach before, much less someone as attractive as Kova. Intimidating was an understatement. How the hell was I supposed to concentrate when he was the *coach* for fuck's sake?

"As for the rest of you, I decide who you all train with, and as of right now, she is with us." Kova turned toward me and gave a pointed look. "Is this going to be a problem for you?"

"Not at all," I lied.

Yeah…This was definitely going to be a big problem. Like when your gynecologist is hot kind of problem.

"Good, let us continue and finish the tour so your parents can settle you. I expect you here early Monday morning."

I nodded and we walked over to the men's team, where they were sharpening their skills to perfection. Just when I thought gymnastics couldn't get any tougher, I observed the brute strength it took for a male gymnast to balance himself on the rings while keeping them steady with very little movement. It was quite impressive to watch their arms slowly extend out to the sides, perpendicular to their bodies while their legs were straight and together to perform an Iron Cross. The control along with the upper body muscle it took was utterly astounding and probably why females were unable to do it.

"Gentlemen, this is Adrianna Rossi. She is a level ten but will be joining the senior girls to train."

There were three senior gymnasts Coach introduced. Solid bodies with flawlessly sculpted, vascular arms. Their shoulders were carved and contoured, the silky smooth skin curved around the tissue and hugged the muscle underneath beautifully. And the best part was it was all natural muscle from years of training, not the steroid-induced kind of shit.

Something about a male gymnast's body just did it for me. They yielded so much power and control. It was beauty hiding in plain sight.

I waved. "Hi," I said shyly, and they gave a few polite smiles.

Basketball shorts hung low with form fitted shirts that stuck to their bodies from exertion. One guy, I think his name was Hayden, was shirtless and had that boy-next-door charm written all over him. Washboard abs, dimples on both cheeks, and perfectly straight, white teeth. He had it all. This guy could cut steel on his abs, which were covered in powdery white chalk. And the V all girls went crazy for—sharp as a knife and pointed right down to his groin. I couldn't help but admire it. But the best part of him, by far, were his arms. From his broad shoulders to his wrists, his honey colored skin glowed with vitality.

I knew my main focus was to train with the best, but they were going to make focusing more difficult. They were not bred like this back home. At least not at my old gym that was for sure. That whole no boyfriend thing no longer sounded as easy as I'd thought initially.

"I usually have the men's and women's senior teams train at the same time in the early morning," *Coach* said.

My coach. I still couldn't get over the fact he was the coach. Or that my mouth got me into trouble once again. I never knew when to keep it shut.

"They will take a lunch break or go to school, and then the younger ones come around mid-afternoon for practice. After that, the seniors return and train for another couple of hours."

Konstantin led us down the hallway and back to the lobby. His shoulders were broad, the dress shirt he wore stretched across his back. He was rolled tight, and it was apparent now he was once a gymnast. At first glance, he looked like any regular guy in casual business attire.

I kid. That was such a lie. He definitely didn't look like *any other guy*—other guys weren't built like him. No gymnast's body could ever be considered *regular*.

Turning around, Konstantin's chin slowly dipped, giving us a solid stare. "Now that we have cleared everything up, I will let you guys go. My gymnasts need me," he said to my parents before turning to me. "Adrianna, it has been a pleasure. I look forward to our first workout where you will be evaluated to see what you are suitable for."

My jaw dropped for the thousandth time since entering World Cup. I hoped this wasn't a precursor for what was to come. My heart pounded, prickly heat coated my arms, and I was sure my blood pressure was steadily rising. This had to be a fucking joke.

"What do you mean evaluate me? I am suitable for elite. With my age alone, you have to train me for senior elite. I can't be in any other level. I'm supposed to start the program so I can test this season. That's why I'm here." I had to be with elite by the rules set forth by USA Gymnastics. Not what he wanted.

He raised a brow, his green eyes scolding me once again. With the amount of staring he had done since I stepped through the door, I felt like I needed to decipher his thoughts through his eyes as if he was too lazy to open his mouth to speak his mind.

"I am well aware what the guidelines are. However, I am your coach now, so I will be making the decision to see which level *I* think you are fit for, which skills you will learn and master," he stated. "You will train with the seniors and do your previous routines until I do my assessment, along with the other coaches. We will decide if, and when, you can practice for senior elite."

"Ana," my father said, demanding my attention. Dad read the expression on my face and knew I was ready to contest his comment.

Pursing my lips together, I grinded my teeth. I wasn't sure what he thought he could do. It wasn't as if he could just change the rules everyone who trained in the United States had to follow just to suit him. The sole reason I came to World Cup was to be in the elite program, and I'd make damn sure I did.

I hadn't even officially started training and I was already frustrated with my new coach.

CHAPTER 5

Like most nights, dinner was stiff and uncomfortable.

Mother eyed my plate as she shifted her food, trying to appear like she was eating, which she hardly did. She had an image to maintain, which meant I did as well. I had to be careful with consumption when she was around. I was cautious in general due to gymnastics, but she just made it much more stressful.

"So you have everything you need, Ana?" Dad stated more than asked the question. He washed his steak down with a glass of bourbon. They were getting ready to drive back home.

My parents had been doing better with letting a little rope go the past few years with less and less restrictions. I had three rules I had to follow: don't get arrested, don't do drugs, and be home by curfew. I was still a teenager, but living the Palm Bay lifestyle was like growing up in Hollywood—you matured much faster and fended for yourself. So those rules were not always easy to abide by for my brother. You were thirteen going on eighteen. Parents were hardly present and money was thrown around left and right for anything their kids wanted. Old money, new money. The upper crust with Gucci squad kids. To the outside youth, it was what every teenager dreamed of having—money, fame, and fortune. But it all came with a price.

"I do."

"Use your Centurion Card for anything you need."

Confused, I asked, "My what?"

"The black American Express Card. I gave it to you last week."

Oh. I didn't know it had a special name. "I will."

"Come on, Frank, our driver is waiting." Mom's distant eyes looked around the unknown.

Leaning down, my father kissed the top of my head and said, "Keep me updated with everything, okay?"

I nodded, squeezing him in a hug as tight as I could. "Thanks, Dad."

"Of course, sweetheart."

"Behave, Ana. Focus," Mom added. I tightened my jaw. I wanted to snapback, *I've always focused and behaved.* But I didn't. "I will, Mom."

"You'll let us know when your first meet is?"

Bewilderment with slivers of hope wedged through me. "You want to know?"

Joy jutted out her hip and propped her hand. "Of course I do."

This was news to me. Mom hadn't been to one of my meets in years, and not for lack of trying on my part, either.

"Ana, we're paying a lot of money for your ridiculous hobby. Don't make us regret it."

My shoulders dropped. I should've known. "I'll let you know once I find out."

Her patronizing tone over my "ridiculous hobby" was heartbreaking. For a split second, I thought she actually wanted to watch me do what I love. How foolish of me to think otherwise.

Then she did something surprising. "Please, be safe. I know you're self-sufficient, but I—we—still worry." She leaned down and kissed my cheek. I wasn't sure how to react. I forced a smooth smile and took joy in it.

Mom pulled back, and I saw the love she so rarely showed in her eyes. I had yet to figure out why she rode me the way she did. I hated it, but I'd take what little bits of affection I could from her. She was still my mother after all, and I loved her.

⩗⩕⩒⩙⩔⩘

WHEN SUNDAY ROLLED AROUND, I tried to get settled as quickly as I could. I didn't have many things to unpack since my condo was fully furnished before we arrived, but I did want everything to be just right. Dealing with the chaos of unpacked boxes and shuffling through them to find things was not something I wanted to deal with. I was used to structure and needed it in all aspects of my life. Monday was the first day of my new workout schedule and I knew I wouldn't have much time for anything once it started. I woke up early and began emptying boxes, finding places for framed pictures of Avery and me, my family, and of good times back home. I even hung some of my most prized medals.

My nerves steadily climbed as the day went on, anxious for to-morrow to come. I was eager to rub my hands through the chalk bowl, feel the springboard beneath my feet as I flipped backwards onto the vault. I couldn't wait to learn more about my teammates, and bond with them.

Into the afternoon, I took a break and pulled out a meal from my mom's favorite fresh food delivery company. My cell phone rang and I smiled at the name on the screen.

"Hey, girl!"

"Hey!" Avery responded. "How's it going? I miss you already."

"Ave—I haven't even been gone a week."

"I know," she whined. "But you're my bestie and you moved thou-sands of miles away!"

I chuckled at her exaggeration. "You act like I moved to China. It's not thousands of miles away. I didn't move across the world, I'm literally three hours away...max."

"True, but who am I going to people-watch and gossip with now on Ocean Boulevard? I need my girl."

A smile spread across my face, reminiscing about fun times with Avery. Ocean Boulevard was equivalent to New York's 5th Avenue, it had all the top designer stores and restaurants. Tall palm trees lined the streets, flower bushes with the most vibrant colors I've ever seen bloomed beneath the high sun climbing the buildings. Ocean Boulevard was a picturesque little spot.

Avery and I had been best friends since we were infants. Our parents were extremely close—her dad was a partner at Rossi Enterprises, so we were inseparable. Leaving her was more difficult than I expected. I knew it wouldn't be anything for us to drive to see each other for a quick visit, our parents wouldn't bat an eye, but that wasn't the point. I left behind my one true best friend. She was the closest thing I had to a sister—my confidante and my lifeline.

"Stop being so dramatic. We can still do that on the phone. Plus, I'll be home for holidays and stuff."

"Whatever, so what are you doing now?"

"Taking out all the meals my lovely mother ordered for me," I said sarcastically. After all these years, Avery knew how my mom loved to micromanage certain aspects of my life. "I don't even know what half this stuff is."

"You've got to be kidding me. She's still controlling you from three hours away?"

"Sure is. She had that delivery diet food service set up for me—the same one your mom uses. It's all naturally prepared meals. Though, I've never taken the time to actually look at the food, have you?"

"Nope, never ate the crap either."

"Ugh. Lucky." I picked up one tray and inspected it. "This one looks like..." I trailed off, looking at the name, unable to determine what it was. "You have got to be kidding me. Tofu? She's making me eat tofu? With gluten free croutons?" I scrambled around to look at the rest of the meals in the vibrant green mesh bag. "Oh, my God, they're all gluten free meals! Why the fuck is she ordering me gluten free? I'm not allergic to anything!" My stomach churned as I sorted through the rest of the contents. This stuff would taste horrible.

Chuckling, Avery said, "Gluten causes belly fat and she wants you fit and trim, dumbass."

"Thanks, Captain Obvious. I know that, but I have no belly fat left to lose. She acts like I'm fucking overweight."

"I can only imagine what she thinks of me."

"I'm not eating this shit," I said, dumping one of the trays into the garbage.

"Last time I checked, there's a lot of salt and sugar in gluten free diets. Sugar turns to fat and salt is going to bloat you. What else is in there?"

"Let me see...There's a whole week of terrible looking meals and snacks." I grimaced at the appalling food choices. "Lamb meatballs? How do people eat this stuff? This looks like mystery meat patted together. I can't believe she's expecting me to eat this shit. It doesn't look appetizing at all, it looks disgusting."

"Take a picture and send it to me right now. I have to see this."

I pulled another tray out and mumbled to myself, "What the hell did she order me?" I turned it to the side to examine it. "Well, this doesn't look too bad. It's turkey and green beans in a gluten free wrap." I opened the plastic container and took a bite. "The wrap tastes like cardboard, but I'll take it over the tofu," I said with a full mouth. Before I knew it, the small snack size wrap was gone and I was still hungry.

Avery moved to another topic and began chatting about the sport she loved, talking a hundred miles a minute about her tryouts.

"You'll make the cheer team for sure. I'd be shocked if you didn't."

"I hope so! I mean, I want to make the All-Star competition team. I should be able to after all the private lessons I've had."

"I have no doubt you will. I've seen those girls, and you're so much better. Oh shit, you're never going to believe this. I met my coach."

"Yeah?" she said, unimpressed. "And?"

I sipped my water and told her how I made a fool of myself. "He's young, a former Olympian, but I just can't picture him training us. It's weird."

"How young?"

"I have no clue, I didn't ask, but I would say around twenty-five? Thirty? I have no idea." I puckered my lips, my forehead bunching together. "That seems kind of young for my dad to be friends with."

"I didn't know you had to be a certain age to be friends with someone."

"You don't, obviously. I just wasn't expecting it."

"Is he hot?"

My cheeks flushed. "Avery! He's my coach!"

"And?"

"And what?"

"Is he hot?"

Hot was an understatement. His jet black hair complemented his stunning green eyes perfectly. A square jaw with hollow cheeks but profound cheek bones. I loved that he was tall and had broad shoulders. All my other coaches had been short and stumpy.

"Well...I mean, he's hot, but I can't think of him like that. I'm going to be working closely with him for like forty hours a week."

"Send me a picture."

I burst out laughing. "Avery! And how the hell am I supposed to do that? I can't just bring my phone in there and be all 'Hey, Coach, let me take a picture of you.'"

"Fine. I'll Google him. He's an Olympian so there's bound to be a picture of him. Hang tight, what's his name?"

I paused for a moment, my brows pinching together. "Well, he addressed himself as Konstantin, but search Konstantin Kournakov. I mean, Kournakova. Or Kova. My dad called him Kova. I think he changed his last name, though."

"Okay. Let's do one name at a time because you just threw like thirty at me. Core...ne—"

"Konstantin Kournakova," I said in a terribly fake Russian accent.

"How do you spell that? There are too many vowels and corn in it."

Rolling my eyes, I laughed under my breath from her exaggeration then spelled it out. Dead silence for a good ten seconds, then...

"Fuuuuccckkk, Adrianna, seriously."

I chuckled into the phone. "What?" I said blandly. I knew what she was getting at.

"Fish lips and all, he's smoking hot!"

"Fish lips? You did not just say that. He most definitely does not have fish lips."

"So you admit to checking him out," she replied swiftly.

"No!"

"Admit it!"

"So what? I already said he's hot."

Avery laughed again. "Okay—I won't call them fish lips, but they are nice and full. Kissable." She paused, then shouted, "Oh, my God! Coach Kissable!"

I groaned loudly. The last thing I wanted to think about was my coach's *full, kissable* lips.

"And it appears he is...actually thirty-two years old."

"Wow. If you saw him in person, you'd never guess."

"Seriously, though. He's fucking gorgeous. Have fun with that. I wouldn't mind having a cheerleading coach who looked like him. Shit, I wouldn't mind having a damn co-ed team in general. All those strong guys to lift me and then cradle me to their chests with their huge ass arms? And have you noticed how hot the guys are? What the hell are they eating to bulk up the way they do?"

"You're crazy, Ave," I laughed, cutting her off. Avery lusted after every boy who crossed her path. She took boy crazy to a whole new level.

Sighing, I looked around at the boxes that still needed to be unpacked.

"I need to finish getting things unpacked and hit the sack early. I have practice at 6:30 a.m., which means I need to be awake by 5:30 to get ready and be there on time."

"Oy. Why so early?"

"Practice, lunch, school, practice again. I won't end until close to six-ish, I think? I'm not sure."

"Wow. Well, try and call me tomorrow if you can."

"Will do."

"Have fun! And remember—snap a picture for me."

"I'll do my best."

"Later, girl."

The smile I heard in her voice made me miss my best friend dearly. Moving to Georgia's South Coast was my choice and something I desperately wanted. I'd prepared for it, and was ready the day it finally came, but I hadn't anticipated missing my friend so much so soon.

I needed to stay focused on my goal, all these sacrifices would be worth it in the end.

CHAPTER 6

The sun hadn't even begun to peek above the horizon as gray clouds drifted across the charcoal sky when we pulled up to World Cup.

Thomas, my driver, knew exactly where to go.

My eyes were swollen and puffy from the restless night of sleep I had. I'd been so anxious for the following morning, I tossed and turned all night in bed, thinking about how my first day would go. I was finally going to begin the next phase in my gymnastics career, and it was all I could think about. Just as I was about to fall back asleep, my alarm clock went off, jolting me upright. If I had to guess, I'd say I had about three hours total of sleep.

Stepping outside with my duffle bag, the humidity in the air smacked my face. "Bye, Alfred. I'm not sure how many hours I'll be here, so I'll text you when I get out." Alfred was a personal nickname I used for Thomas. He wasn't crazy about it, judging by his expression every time it rolled off my tongue. In fact, I think he loathed it, but went along to appease me.

"I'll be on standby, Miss Rossi."

An exasperated sigh escaped my throat. "Alfred. How many times do I have to tell you to call me Adrianna?" I had been reminding him more lately. I hated the Miss crap.

"How many times have I told you my name is Thomas?" he retorted.

My eyes narrowed, trying to appear mean, but I knew it was a piss poor job.

"Old habits."

"I'll try harder," he said with a wink.

Shutting the door, the sound of fallen leaves fluttering in the wind caught my attention. I glanced over my shoulder but couldn't see anything in the dark and continued on.

Stepping onto the sidewalk, I walked in front of the SUV. Thanks to the headlights shining through the window, I got a glimpse inside World Cup. When we arrived the first day, I hadn't been able to see through the tinted glass, but the early morning hours and bright lights illuminated a large portion of the gym.

My eyes zoomed in on a gymnast throwing a tumbling pass. She must've been warming up since all she did was a round-off, back handspring, one and a half twist, and then walked off like it was nothing. It really wasn't much on our level, but she made it look effortless. Like a ribbon floating in the wind. Beautiful, really. I could only pray I had that kind of grace. Coach Kova clapped his hands, his lips moving and head nodding in approval. I took in his attire and noticed he wasn't wearing dress pants.

I shuffled my duffle bag around and opened the door. As I did, another hand reached above me and pushed back the metal frame. I looked over my shoulder and came face to face with muscular arms. Stepping inside, I locked eyes with the cutest boy next door smile I'd ever seen. He hardly had any clothes on – shorts, flip flops, and a loose tank top with huge arm holes. Typical southern beach attire.

"I got it."

I gripped my strap tighter. "Thank you."

"I'm Hayden," he said, walking in closely behind.

"Adrianna."

He smiled, and a dimple appeared in the center of his chin. "I know, we met the other day. I'm Holly's twin."

"Huh." I stared at him. "I wouldn't have guessed."

His smile grew larger. "That's good to know. The last thing I want is to hear I look like a chick."

Chuckling at his comment, I followed him down the hall into a small room that had two walls of lockers, one each for the boys' and girls' teams. He stuffed his bag into a metal cage. His movements were comfortable and natural as if he'd been doing this for ages, and maybe he had.

Hayden looked over his shoulder. "Are you nervous about today?"

I bit my lip and shuffled my feet. "Yeah, is it obvious?"

"Not really—but I just remember my first day being able to train at a new level. It's exciting but more nerve-racking than anything."

Hayden reached behind his head and pulled off his shirt. He rolled it into a ball and chucked it with the rest of his stuff. It took everything in me to keep my jaw from dropping to the floor, but that didn't mean I didn't give him a good once over, openly gawking at his body.

"I'll be honest...I'm petrified."

"That's totally normal. You'll get past it in a couple of weeks once you're comfortable." He slapped his door shut. "Want a tip?"

"Of course."

"Don't talk back. Do what your coaches tell you. Don't show them you're scared. Don't hesitate. They don't want to hear excuses. Show them you're confident and want to be here, that you can handle what they give you and have what it takes. Basically, just agree and nod and that will take you far. They know what they're talking about. I've been through a handful of coaches at this gym, and these are the best." He paused, then said something I needed to remember. "And most importantly, there will be days when you'll want to quit because you can't take any more. Those days will come and they'll come often. Just don't give up, because the reward will be worth it in the end."

I took in Hayden's words with a serious nod. He cupped my shoulder with compassion and said, "Good luck," then pulled the door to the gym open and stepped inside.

Looking through the window, there was only one girl out there, and I thought it was Reagan, but I wasn't sure since I met her for only a split second the other day. I watched as she landed a front handspring double twisting front layout into a punch front tuck, her arms out in a T landing to balance herself, but she pulled to the right and took a large step.

"What are you waiting for?"

A deep, baritone voice startled me from behind. I jumped, looking over my shoulder as my heart raced. My hand flew to my neck. Where had he come from?

"What?" I stammered.

Konstantin tilted his head to the side, his face expressionless. "I thought you were a gymnast, not a spectator. My time is valuable. Get in the gym now or leave."

I pulled back, my mind reeling from his unexpected nasty tone. My jaw hung open, silently moving up and down. I struggled with words, trying to find the right response. The way his eyes bore into mine made him unapproachable...And intimidating.

"Where...Where do I put my things?"

He gave me a look that said I should know where my stuff went. He hadn't assigned me a locker, but I had a feeling mentioning that wouldn't be good, so I didn't bring it up.

"Okay," I responded quietly. "Where to after that?"

"This is just like any other gym, Adrianna," he said with a bite, rolling the R in my name. "Let this be a lesson learned after today. After you come in, you place your things in a locker, and you get your ass into the gym quickly. I do not care where you start, as long as your feet are on the blue floor every morning by six thirty and you are coming to me. Yeah?"

With wide eyes and parted lips, I nodded at his dick attitude. Coach marched off and I quickly did as he said as my knees shook. Jesus. He acted as if I was late, which I wasn't, he just hadn't explained what to do once I arrived.

I stripped out of my hot pink, Juicy Couture two-piece zip-up and pants set and rolled it up, shoving it into a metal locker. I'd stick it in my bag later, the last thing I wanted to do was make him wait any longer. I threw my long burgundy hair into a messy ponytail and made my way toward the gym.

Swallowing back the lump in my throat, I pushed my shoulders back, stepped into the gym and walked over to where the women's team was. Coach stared me down, tracking my every footstep. His gaze made me feel two inches tall and insecure.

I chewed the inside of my lip as our eyes locked. His black short-sleeved shirt hugged his muscular biceps. His arms were firmly crossed in front of his chest, muscles perfectly rounded, and his stance spoke of authority. He tracked me across the gym. Heads turned my way in the middle of their stretching, so I quickly tiptoed to the floor. I'd have to let Alfred know we needed to get here a little earlier tomorrow to avoid these uncomfortable stares, just in case. No one liked being the center of attention, so I needed to make sure I'd slip in quieter and unseen.

Legs spread out, I leaned forward and lay on the floor, my arms and legs parallel to each other. I expelled a breath and closed my eyes, rejoicing in what my body was doing. I loved the way my muscles pulled tight and then loosened like they were just waking up. It hurt and felt good all at the same time. Flexing and pointing helped my shins, and I pushed my legs as wide as they could go by scooting up to stretch out my groin.

I was lost in the feeling when I felt the spring floor dip as someone came up next to me and grabbed my ankle, lifting my leg.

"What the..." I mumbled under my breath. I sat up and looked over my shoulder. I almost said fuck, but I caught myself. Coach knelt so close to my face that I noticed how incredible his eyes were. A brilliant green, the color of fresh basil and lime interwoven with each other pulled me in. Mesmerizingly beautiful, and when his hand moved to the crease of my hip and thigh, I drew in a breath.

His fingers dug into my skin where my leotard met my bikini line and he carefully rotated my leg so my knee faced up.

"Back down," Coach ordered. I had no idea what he planned, so I listened and laid my chest flat on the floor, which ended up being a good thing. I didn't want to get caught staring into his eyes.

Or think about where his hand currently was.

Slowly, he lifted my leg and pressed down on my back so I couldn't move. A little grunt left my lips as he stretched out my hips.

"Toes pointed, knees up, Adrianna," he said, like I was an idiot. Maybe the arrogance in his tone was a Russian thing.

Coach slowly pulled my foot up so it was slightly higher than my back. I felt the burning stretch in my groin grow as he raised it. Unwillingly, my body tried to sit up at this tense position to ease the strain, but Coach just pressed harder on my back, not allowing me to move. I held my breath, my fingers spreading wide on the carpet and my stomach flexed. His forearm dug into my back as he leaned over and pressed me down. This shit hurt. I thought my groin was about to be ripped to shreds, and even my butt felt like the muscles were being pulled to their max.

"Breathe," he whispered.

I groaned in the back of my throat as he lowered my foot to the floor, where I began to melt and release the tension in my muscles. It felt so good, but not for long because he switched to my other side and applied the same amount of force. This took stretching and flexibility to a whole new level for me.

"Girls, sit across from the low beam, put your toes on it, and wait for me."

Opening my eyes, I was faced with two large knees just inches from my nose. He may have been wearing workout shorts, but I could see the width of his thighs and the muscles surrounding his knees. They were huge and his legs were free of hair.

Not to mention, he smelled really good. *Too good.*

Twenty years later, Konstantin lowered my leg but I was stuck and stiff. Slowly, I sat up by walking my hands toward me.

"Partner up and take turns stretching out your knees. Bounce lightly, girls. We don't need any broken knee caps."

That accent...I was quickly realizing I liked his accent a helluva lot. It demanded attention every time he opened his mouth. Maybe it was an American thing to like someone else's enunciation, but then I wondered if foreigners liked American accents too. Probably not. There was nothing exotic about an American dialect. We didn't roll our R's the way Russians did. It would come off as a speech impediment if anything.

Moving behind me, Coach's fingers grazed delicately down my forearm. He grasped my wrist, then reached for the other one. He carefully extended both wrists back, stretching my arms out behind me.

"Do not drop your chest. Shoulders back, back straight."

CHAPTER 7

What are they doing?" I found myself asking as my eyes drifted over to the girls on the low balance beam just a couple of feet away.

"It is a stretching technique that overextends your knees. It helps with jumps so your legs are bowed. You have never done them before?"

"No." I watched the girls lightly bounce on their teammates' kneecaps. This had to be something he picked up in Russia. I could actually see their knees bending backwards as they sat like soldiers taking it. Never in my life had I seen this. I began to worry my knees would pop out.

"What happened to using two mats and putting our feet on them in splits?"

"We do that too, but I change things up and like to use my background. It is things a lot of other coaches do not do. It is a little intense, but it gets the job done."

He let go of my arms and said, "Shake your legs out." I bounced them lightly to a closed position so I could stand. My legs were stiff and now I had to overextend my knees even more?

A hand appeared in my vision and I reached for it. Coach helped me up, and I automatically fixed my leotard from the slight reposition.

Gymnasts picked wedgies out left and right without a second thought and kept walking, me included. Hey—it came with the territory. Sometimes it got stuck up in there, so it was either fix it or let your ass hang out.

"Reagan, please work with Adrianna, yeah?"

Reagan glared at me for some bizarre reason as I got into the same position as the other girls, my toes elevated on the low beam. I ignored her. When she sat down, she didn't hold back and bounced on my kneecaps like she was bouncing on a giant yoga ball.

It took everything in me not to scream at her and call her a bitch. I didn't see the other girls jumping this hard, but I knew better than to complain. So I rolled both my lips between my teeth and took the newfound pain being delivered to my body.

We switched places, but I didn't go as hard as she did. Honestly, I didn't want to injure her.

"Harder," Reagan demanded. "You won't hurt me."

I stopped and looked at her, because I was really worried I would. "You sure?"

"Yup. Just do it." I followed her command, all the while smiling internally and taking way too much delight in inflicting a fraction of the pain she just handed me.

After group stretching, we split up amongst the different apparatuses: vault, balance beam, floor, and the uneven bars. Coach walked over to the bars.

"Do a few warm-ups and when you are ready, let me know so I can see your routine."

"Okay," I said, tightening my grips. Then he walked to another part of the gym.

Taking a deep breath, I watched as one of the girls warmed up on bars, doing light release moves where she flowed freely from bar to bar, giant after giant, an overshoot that involved a half-twist mid-air to the low bar, clear hip circles, where the gymnast circles backward without touching the bar to her hips, and then an easy dismount, like a back tuck. The other two girls went and then I was up. We all pretty much did the same warm ups, some adding pirouettes and other elements, but the real fun was about to begin.

A straddle back was one of my favorite skills to do on bars. It wasn't used as often since most did the half twist mid-air to the low bar, but I loved it. There was something powerful in releasing the high bar to straddle the low bar mid-air into a handstand. It took me a while to master this move. My ankles kept hitting the bar, not to mention, initially it scared the shit out of me. Until I figured out the trick to tackling this skill was getting your hips to rise as high as you could manage by flicking them up and back, *not* your feet. Lifting your feet in a straddle back was a hard habit to break, but it didn't actually pull you in the air the way your hips did like you'd think it would. Basically, I lifted my ass, stuck it up and out, and I was golden.

My bars routine wasn't as intense as the other three girls who went before me. I guess it wasn't supposed to be since I was a lower level, however, I became consciously aware I was behind. I didn't have an early start in the sport like most did who were elite. Although I was young when I began recreational gymnastics, I was almost ten when I joined the girls' team and officially began rigorous training.

There was a difference between recreational classes and team classes. Both were taught the same skills, but team trained more hours a week and focused on the smallest of details. In the end, those details could make or break you. There was commitment and motivation involved, too. Not just from the gymnasts, but from the parents as well. The financing, traveling, and attitude were brutal. Team was much more grueling but also very rewarding.

I performed my routine a handful of times more before I mustered the nerve to ask Coach to watch. It wasn't my best practice—I could tell by my jittery movements and racing heart, that had nothing to do with my actual routine and everything to do with the intimidating Russian and three hours of sleep. I felt like I was competing for a spot on the US World team and everything relied heavily on this moment.

This was my chance to prove I was ready for elite.

Konstantin stood near the side of the bars, his eyes trained solely on me, and showing no emotion. I thought for sure I was about to be sick. It was a blank stare, and honestly, I wasn't sure if I'd rather that or to see his face fall. My heart was in my throat and all the noise faded away.

Shit. I was so nervous.

A bars routine can last anywhere from thirty to forty-five seconds, mine was thirty-six, and that was simply because of my level and what I was capable of doing. A great deal of training and conditioning went into a bar routine. Most people never realized how short they actually were. After being captivated by jaw dropping release skills and eye-popping combination sequences, it was easy to forget it wasn't even one-minute long.

As I performed my routine, it felt like an eternity of wishing and praying I'd catch the bar, hit my handstands, legs together, and didn't wobble or bend my arms. I mentally chanted to myself, *I got this*, repeatedly with every little element before the dismount happened.

"Once more," he ordered before I could catch my breath. After I chalked up my grips and did my routine again, he dipped his chin and said, "When you get to vault, follow the same instructions," and then walked off. I had no idea if I did well, and there was no gauging his thoughts either. He was like a slab of concrete.

"Don't stress—he's always like that." I looked over at the voice beside me. "You'll never know what he's thinking no matter how hard you try. I swear, it's his goal to make you feel like you suck at life." I breathed a sigh of relief knowing it wasn't just me. "I'm Holly, by the way."

I smiled politely at Hayden's twin. "Adrianna. And thanks for the heads up. It doesn't help that I'm nervous as it is, but the way he acts puts me on edge."

"Oh, that's how he normally is. You'll get used to it. We all have."

Note to self: His default personality is dick. Got it.

"Hopefully it doesn't take long. He made me feel like it was the sloppiest routine ever."

Holly laughed. "We all went through it and had the same sentiments. Kova has a keen eye, so while there were probably things you did mess up on, he can spot talent through it."

"Why do you call him Kova? I thought his name was Konstantin."

She shrugged. "It's just what he goes by. None of us call him by his real name."

Interesting.

"Are you from here?" I asked curiously.

She nodded. "I've been with World Cup for years. My family used to live here, but my dad was offered a job in Ohio he couldn't refuse. He moved there while my mom, Hayden, and I stayed back so we could train with Kova. My mom left once we hit sixteen though, because she missed him a lot. She was nervous to leave us, but luckily we have friends and family nearby if we need anything."

I knew in the general public it was absurd for parents to allow their children to train alone at such a young age. It wasn't uncommon for us to go to summer training camp in Texas for three months alone, or to train long hours in the gym without any parental supervision.

The gym became our second home. The coaches were extremely close to the parents, which put them at ease when it came time to leave their kids. Plus, we were never completely alone, there was always an adult around, a friend or a mom to help out. While we thought nothing of it, I was sure it looked like neglect to the outside world.

"How old are you?"

She tightened her wristband, her eyes focused on the movement of her fingers. "Almost seventeen."

"Oh—" My voice heightened. "Wow. So you've been here for almost a year on your own?"

An innocent smile spread across her baby face as she looked back up at me. "I know it's crazy being away from family, and hard at times, but you get used to it. Luckily, they understand our love of the sport and allowed us to stay. But it doesn't come easy. My parents took out a second mortgage so we can continue to train and compete here.

"Last year we had a girl here—Sage. She was incredible, better than all of us and had future Olympian written all over her. Her form was impeccable and she was only nine years old. We used to watch her in awe, but unfortunately, her parents couldn't afford to live in two different places anymore. She has an older brother and it wasn't fair to him, so they packed up and went home to Washington. She cried, we all did. Seeing that made me realize how fortunate I am to be here. I don't know if she's training anymore though...hopefully she is. She was too good not to."

"Holly. You are up," Coach announced.

Holly smiled brightly. "See you later...and good luck."

While Holly geared up, I stripped the grips from my wrists and made my way to vault where a pair of brown eyes stood watching.

"Hey, Reagan," I said, being friendly. I was looking forward to making team friends.

She turned to me, paused, then said, "Hey."

I wasn't sure why, but I got the impression that she wasn't a fan of me being here, which bothered me. Team girls were just that—a unified team. We worked together, were like sisters, and usually had an unbreakable bond. I had a good team of girls back home who supported each other to the end, so I expected to have the same here.

"How long have you been on the team?"

"I've been with World Cup since I could walk," she responded hastily without picking her head up from the chalk bowl. "My family is actually from Cape Coral. I'm not a transfer."

CHAPTER 8

She gave me her back and geared up to take her vault.

I watched Reagan perform an Amanar, landing almost perfectly without the slightest movement, not even a balance check. My eyebrows hit my hairline over her nearly perfect vault. Knowing I was next, I looked around for Kova to see where he was and noticed his eyes trained on her. Holy hell...there was a smile on his face. I mean, there should've been with that vault, but he didn't seem like the type to ever crack a grin. Reagan beamed at him and walked to the end of the vault runway with confidence in her stride.

I'd been practicing a double-twisting Yurchenko. Unfortunately, I almost always took a step once I landed, which earned me deductions. Most gymnasts took a step or a hop. It was hard not to with all the power and momentum forcefully flying out of us.

My best bet would be to work on my alternate vault, but I wasn't crazy about anything requiring front flipping, so I avoided them as much as possible. I wasn't a lazy gymnast, they just made me uneasy turning in the air in that direction. Not to mention, a blind landing was risky because I didn't want to hyperextend my knees.

But with that bizarre conditioning of bouncing on your knees Coach had us doing earlier, I was almost positive I was training my knees for hyperextension anyway.

"That was incredible!" I said to her excitedly. While it was becoming more popular, an Amanar was one of the hardest vaults in the world for women to get right. It required blocking really hard by pushing off the vault table with your shoulders and keeping your arms straight.

"I know."

My mom would've slapped my face if that had been my response.

"How long have you been practicing it?" Even with her nasty attitude, I was genuinely curious.

She shrugged, not making eye contact. "Not very long. It was easy for me, actually. None of the other girls can stick it like I can," she said smugly. "Kova said my vault will help my all-around and boost my score."

Wow. I didn't want to know if she was capable of becoming any more pretentious.

"Well, that's fabulous for the team. I'm sure the girls are grateful for your capability, seeing as you think they're lacking." I couldn't help it, I had to get in a little jab. Growing up on an island with some of the richest people in the world, I really disliked snotty girls, and I could tell Reagan was just that. So I knew how to get in and get out with a plastic smile.

I made my way to the runway and performed a one and a half Yurchenko, instead of a double. I wanted to impress and went with a clean landing, so I played it safe. The key was to start with a high-tall hurdle with my chest up, then round-off, and drive my arms back into the vault to execute a big, powerful block. Then kick my legs together and scoop my toes, squeezing my butt and using my abs to drive momentum to follow with a tight twist. Spotting my landing, I drove my heels into the ground.

Once I landed with a hop, Kova swirled his finger around for me to do it again. This time, I landed with a huge hop from too much power and grimaced, squeezing my eyes shut. I knew I screwed up and he caught it.

Opening my eyes, I looked at Kova who stared me down without any emotion on his face. He said nothing, so I opted to speak.

"Shall I do it again?"

"Can you do any other vault?"

I bit the inside of my lip. "I can do a double Yurchenko. It needs a little work, but I can try it."

"Are you going to injure yourself trying it?"

"No." I could do a double, but I was too nervous to so I did the one and a half.

"It is something you have done before?"

"Yes."

"Then do it. Reagan!" he yelled. "Let Adrianna go again real quick."

Reagan made an audible grunting sound, so I apologized to her. The quickest way to make friends was not having the coach ordering me to cut in rotation.

I chalked up my feet and then took a deep breath, shaking out my hands.

I could do this...I could do this...

I snuck a glance at Kova, who stood with his arms crossed in front of his wide chest across from the vault. Rising up on my tiptoes, I leaned in and took off running, pumping my legs as fast and as hard as I could to gain speed.

Just before I reached the vault, I did a round off onto the springboard, flipping backward so my hands would land on the leather vault to complete my Yurchenko. Blocking as hard as I could by pushing off with my shoulders, I pulled my twist around and spotted the ground. I landed it perfectly—with a smile—and no hop. Not too much power or rotation.

Finishing, I looked for the same smile Kova gave Reagan. My stomach dropped when I saw the disdain in his eyes.

He cocked his head to the side and said more than asked, "You can do a double? Yes?"

I swallowed hard. "Yes."

"What about a two and a half?"

"Yes, well, not really. I'm working on it."

"So, why didn't you do it?"

"Do what? The two and a half? It's not great." I shrugged helplessly. It wasn't the best way to start, but I was nervous.

I could feel another set of eyes glued to me, but I couldn't break his gaze to see who they belonged to. And truthfully, I was embarrassed and didn't want to see the stares. Luckily, I was slightly hot so the flush on my cheeks would be brushed off as nothing more than exertion.

One brow arched to a point. Fury radiated off him. "Did you really think I would not know? That landing was too perfect—the whole vault was too good for it to be your alternate. If you want to succeed, you have to try harder elements. Take a risk, trust your body, drop the fear.

"Now get over there and do it with the two and a half so I can see where you need work. I do not have time for games. I need to know what you are capable of right now, today, not next month. What good will that do if I am training you for a two and a half and you have already been working on it?"

I wanted to correct his stiff pronunciation, but I refrained. He sounded like a robot talking at times. So instead I nodded vehemently, and took a stand behind the line. Reagan wore a smirk that deserved to be slapped off her face.

A low groan escaped my throat, irritated by both Kova and Reagan's faces. But more importantly, I was angry with myself for not giving my all in the one moment I truly needed to.

I didn't waste any time before I got behind the line and started running toward the stationary object. Gymnasts had to be a little crazy in the head to come up with the idea of doing back flips over objects such as this one.

Once I hit the vault, I blocked hard, taking flight, and pulled a double twist—adding a half turn. I cranked as hard as possible on my rotation but knew it wasn't enough. It was risky and I was sloppy in the air. Gymnasts instinctively knew their bodies, but I took the chance and threw it anyway.

Landing, I stumbled to the side, but I caught myself before my knees went down, which was huge. Knees were never to touch the floor on a landing.

Standing, I finished and looked at Kova.

"Same thing with the floor and beam. Do *not* hold back," he stated before turning his back to me and continuing.

It was going to be a long day.

IT WAS NEARLY NIGHTFALL, AND I was exhausted. Without looking in the mirror, I knew I was a hot mess. Chalk coated my body and leotard, strands of hair fell from my ponytail and surrounded my face, and my eyes were puffy and swollen, heavy with fatigue. I sat with my legs spread in my little shorts in the middle of the gymnastics lobby while scrolling on my phone. It was unladylike and my mom would've killed me for it, but I didn't give a shit. I got my ass handed to me today, and I was damn tired.

All I wanted to do was go home, shower, pop some Motrin, and go to bed. Motrin, the breakfast, lunch, and dinner of champions. Screw eating a fresh cooked meal.

Unfortunately, I couldn't do that just yet. I had to wait for Coach to finish up before I could leave. Judging by the first actual training session I had today, I could tell the next couple of weeks were going to be rough in more ways than one.

After I had done the other two events earlier like Coach had asked, I met with my private tutors. They reviewed my syllabus for each class, what would be expected of me, and my gym hours. Mr. Landry would teach Chemistry and American History, and Mrs. Taylor would teach Pre-Cal and English. I tried to focus on everything they both said, but my mind kept reverting to the routines I performed and wondering how I did. If my wobbly turn on beam impacted my ability, if the step out of bounds on the floor hurt me, or if the fact I held back on vault in the beginning made a difference.

I sighed loudly. I didn't know who I was kidding.

After school, Alfred took me home for lunch, which was small and short since my stomach was in knots. I couldn't eat, my nerves were shot. Plus, I hated training on a full stomach. Once I returned to the gym, Kova had me repeat the same things as this morning so other coaches could judge my routines, which I was sure were shit by that point.

Maybe I was being hard on myself.

The door slammed shut, taking my attention away from my friends' fun updates on social media. Kova snapped his fingers as he brusquely walked past me. "Let us go."

Dick mode—activated!

Following him into his office, he waited for me to walk in then shut the door. He took a seat behind his desk and I sat in front. I tightened my ponytail and braced myself.

Looking me directly in the eyes, he got right to the point. "Today was a test, an evaluation to see where you currently are." He sighed tiredly. "I am going to be blunt. You do not come close to my standards, Adrianna, and that worries me. You are not ready for the senior team. Not even close. Nowhere near prepared to test this season. You are setting yourself up for failure if you do."

My mouth dropped open, and tears formed in the back of my eyes. I would not cry. I wouldn't allow it. Shit, I'd been schooled not to cry. But fuck, that hurt.

Being told you're not good enough in gymnastics was like being kicked while you're down. It was heartbreakingly devastating. Aside from sustaining an injury that forces you to rest, it's probably the worst thing you could possibly hear. You're already hard on yourself as it is trying to be the best. You give your all, and you silently deal with the pain and aches, the gnawing hunger, the exhaustion, when you know there will always be someone who will come along that is better than you. It's a double-edged sword. And this shit runs through your head on replay.

"I spoke with Madeline, the other elite coach who evaluated you, and she agreed that you need work. You have a lot of bad habits we need to break, which is going to be a tedious task. Little details matter in this sport. Had I evaluated you before you came, without a doubt, I would have turned you away from the elite program. But your father made a generous donation to have our café funded, which allows you to be here." He folded his hands in front of him, looking jaded. "So here you are."

"I'm not even a level ten in your eyes, am I?"

He shook his head, his lips a thin flat line. No Coach Kissable here.

"My standards are high, but that is what wins. Doing safe, mediocre gymnastics is going to take you off the podium. I think you will agree with me. You were scared today and held back. That concerns me."

I tried hard not to cry, but I couldn't stop the tears from resting on my eyelids. I looked up at the ceiling, willing them to disappear so they wouldn't fall my cheeks. I was mad at myself for letting my emotions get to me. I wanted to appear strong, but this was equally as frustrating as it was hurtful. A larger beast was tackling the clawing inside my gut to be better.

"The worst part is," he continued, "I agreed to train you. Once you test and you do qualify, you must train at the senior level because of your age. You are too old for any other level."

Konstantin Kournakova was a cold man. I wondered if he had kids and prayed that if he didn't, he was sterile.

I knew he wouldn't go easy on me, but Jesus Christ. His words were as upsetting as a career-ending injury.

CHAPTER 9

Seeing how it is March and you arrived in the middle of elite season, did you plan on competing for the rest of the regular meet season as practice and then test next season?"

"Since we have until June, I thought I could test elite since a lot of the skills are the same."

His eyes were empathetic. "I do not think that is a wise decision. You are just not ready."

The last thing my heart wanted was to sit a season out, but if it furthered my career, then so be it. I lowered my voice and said, "I'd rather hold off on competing and use this time as practice so I could be prepared next season to test."

Kova sat back in his leather chair. His head tilted to the side and his eyes narrowed to thin slits. He cupped his jaw and ran a hand over his mouth. "Do you want this, Adrianna? Really want this deep down? Because it will take many more hours of gym time for you to be where I need you. I am talking private lessons after practice and possibly longer hours. Pushing your body past the brink of sanity to master the elite level skills but master them perfectly. And even with that, I do not know if you will get to where you need to be by the time you want. This is going to be complex to manage. A challenge. I am not sure I am capable of moving mountains."

My jaw moved, but I was utterly speechless, trying desperately to form words but nothing came out. Kova's green eyes stared harder, waiting for me to respond.

"I am not getting any younger, Adrianna."

Sucking up my stupid emotions, I needed to be positive, because despite his hurtful words, I was a strong, confident person.

"I want it more than anything. Gymnastics is my life. My dream. Let me prove it, please. Give me one chance to show you. I won't give up and I'll work harder than everyone else in the gym, and you'll never hear me complain."

He stayed quiet, assessing my answer and said, "Bring me your schedule tomorrow, I will see where I can fit extra time in for you. You may have to come in on your day off, maybe do a half-day just for conditioning. I will go over it with Madeline, then call your father and tell him the joyous news."

Ignoring his jab, I responded eagerly. "I'll do whatever it takes."

I quickly learned Kova was a difficult man to read with his prolonged silence, but agreeing to whatever he said got me the approval I sought in his eyes.

"What is it that you are going for?"

Confused, I asked, "What do you mean?"

"Do you plan to compete in college? Retire before or after college...I need to know what I am working with."

I had one goal, and that was my only focus.

"I want to go to the Olympics."

Kova was a deer in headlights. It was the only reference that came to mind as he stared at me, unblinking. He didn't think I could do it. It was obvious.

Snapping his head to the side sharply, Kova cracked his neck. The sound echoed throughout the room, and I cringed. "You do realize how many young girls have the same ambition, right? How difficult it is to achieve?"

"I do."

"And you are aware only five girls in the entire country will make the women's team? That alternates hardly ever get called up?"

"Of course."

"And they are normally making the U.S. Team around fifteen years old?"

I knew where Kova was going with this, and truthfully, I didn't want to hear it. I'd had enough kicks to the gut for the night.

"I'm well aware I'm older than normal to begin the elite path and that my chances are low because of my age, but I have the fight and drive to make it happen. I have passion and determination. I don't care what anyone else thinks. If I don't push for it, I'll regret it. Everything I need is at my fingertips. I can do it...I know I can. I will practice until I can't get it wrong, until my hands are bleeding and my feet are raw. I'll go to the Olympics, and *nothing* is going to stop me. Especially not my age."

Seemingly impressed, Kova nodded slowly, taking in my words. "Go home. I will see you tomorrow, Adrianna."

ᛕ ㅊ ㅌ ㅋ ᒧ ᕯ

THE MOMENT I STEPPED OUT of the shower and dressed in my pajamas, I called Avery to vent.

The entire meeting with Coach Kova replayed in my head, making me sick to my stomach. Even though I should've been heading to bed for tomorrow's early practice, I knew my best friend would still be up. I gave her a play-by-play of my day and the results of my shitty evaluation, feeling bad for myself the entire time.

"Give up, that's basically what he told me," I complained. "I'm shit, Avery. A joke. I can't believe it. And here I thought I was good enough to be on a senior team. He clearly doesn't want me testing for elite, doesn't think I'm good enough, yet he has no choice to."

"What do you mean he has no choice? So he gave you all that shit for nothing, but at the end of the day, he has to train you?"

"Yes. There are junior elite and senior elite gymnasts. It's all based on age and you have to qualify by testing elite through national competitions with a minimum score. I need an elite coach who knows how to train higher level gymnasts and create routines that work with the elite scoring system. There's a certain level of difficulty, artistry, and execution where by combining skills, it gives me a higher start value. I continued training the way I did back home because a lot of the senior and junior elite skills are similar, but I couldn't advance, so technically I can't be deemed elite just yet."

"Just shut up and stop with the pity party. If he has no choice, which it sounds like he doesn't, it's obvious he's saying that shit on purpose to motivate you. You know you don't suck."

"Motivate me? Telling your new athlete they aren't up to your ridiculous standards and may never be is motivation to you? And seriously, Avery, if you'd seen these girls and what they're capable of doing, you'd feel worthless too."

"He's purposely messing with your head and you're allowing it to happen. Brush that shit off and go in tomorrow and act like he never said any of it. Hold your head high and show him what you're made of. I bet Fish Lips tells all the new girls that."

I giggled at her fish lips comment with her. "Why do you keep calling him Fish Lips?"

"Excuse me, Coach Kissable." She chuckled. "He reminds me of Tom Hardy, and Tommy has Fish Lips."

Oh, my God. "You know, when you put it that way it's hot. Now I won't think of a blow fish every time you say fish lips, I'll think of Tom."

"See?" She laughed. "I told you."

I sighed, bringing me back to the moment. "I really hope I can prove him wrong."

"You can and you will. It's just like when your mom talks down to you."

I paused, thinking about what she just said. "You're right, but I really don't want to hate my coach. Not that I hate my mom, but you know what I mean."

"How can you hate a face like that? He reminds me of a brooding, mysterious guy with a dark side to him. I bet his body is even better."

I rolled my eyes, smiling at her comment. I wondered where the hell she came up with this stuff. "I can say with all honesty that I haven't even given his body a thought. I was too stressed about performing today to look." I lied. Of course I had.

"Yeah, okay," she responded sarcastically. "Whatever you say, but maybe you should take a Xanax before you go in tomorrow, you clearly need it."

"No way. That'll only make me tired and I can't have that. I need to be on my A game, remember? Speaking of pills, I need to take some Motrin before I forget. I'm going to be sore as shit tomorrow." I reached under the bathroom sink and grabbed the white bottle that housed my favorite little orange pills.

"I was only joking with you."

"Ha." I shook two orange pills into my hand and filled the glass I kept by my bathroom sink with water. Swallowing back the pills, I said, "Thanks, Avery, for talking to me. This wasn't how I expected today to go at all. Not even close. I feel like a fool for thinking it would go any other way."

"You mean, listening to you bitch? Anytime!" Her smile seeped into her words, making me grin in return. I wasn't sure what I'd do without this girl.

Shaking my head, I said, "I'm gonna go. I have to be up at 5:30."

"Ugh. Good luck with that. Later, babe."

"Later."

⟡ ⟡ ⟡ ⟡ ⟡ ⟡

FIVE MINUTES. THAT WAS HOW long I slept before my obnoxious alarm clock went off. I had to do a double take to make sure I read the clock correctly.

Dear God, save me.

Sitting up, my legs dangled over my bed as I rubbed my blurry eyes. My back was tight, as were my shoulders and thighs. It wasn't too bad though, but maybe that was due to the Motrin I had taken before bed. Only time would tell.

Alfred would be here in forty-five minutes to pick me up, so I quickly brewed a cup of coffee from my Keurig and began to get ready.

About a year ago, my mother started giving me coffee to drink to replace meals. To shut her up, I told her it helped curb my appetite, but it never really did. Maybe an hour at most. I worked out hard, and I was hungry often.

In the end, I just developed a taste for Starbucks.

I packed my bag quickly, making sure I had two of those tasteless meals my mom loved so much, along with some protein bars and water bottles. And just in case, I grabbed the bottle of Motrin. Today would be another long day and I was curious to know how I would fare.

Like clockwork, Alfred texted me saying he was outside. That man was perpetually on time, something I appreciated. Locking up my condo, I took the elevator down and jumped into the SUV.

"Miss—"

I gave him the look. "Thomas." I only used Thomas when I was serious.

He smirked. "How are you this morning?"

"Eh. A little sore, but not as bad as I thought I'd be," I said, fastening my seatbelt.

He dipped his chin. "That's good to hear. Do you know what time you'll be done today?"

"Not really, and after what I learned yesterday, who knows. I don't have school today, so I guess whenever Coach says I'm done. I'll text you when I get out and just wait for you to get there."

How about you send me a text during lunch and give me a roundabout idea?

"I can do that."

Changing the subject, he said, "I hope you're paying attention to where we're going. From what your father says, when you get your license, you're on your own."

"Do you really think my parents will let you leave me alone in this city all by myself? It's one thing being alone on the Island, it's another thing in a town they aren't familiar with. I just don't see it happening anytime soon, especially when the media gets a hold of the fact I'm not there anymore."

Rossi Enterprises was a well-known real estate developer. They were responsible for many residential and commercial buildings in Atlanta. The company had been in my family for many years, beginning with my grandfather Angelo, who founded it. He started small with money he was given by his father, who had been a successful real estate agent at the time. Angelo took a chance against his father's advice and built a hotel with the money, then bought land from that income and built more commercial real estate and eventually residential properties. He did very well, but it was my dad who partnered with Avery's father, Michael Heron, years before either of us were born and created an empire, building high-end properties in major cities around the world. The name grew quickly, as did fame and fortune, and with that came unwanted press. Rossi Enterprises was now responsible for more than twenty-five hundred properties worldwide, coming in as one of the top developers in the world.

But leave it to my brother and his wild friends to attract bad publicity from their drunken crusades at the nightclubs and private parties, not to mention public arrests. It didn't help that Avery had twin brothers around the same age as Xavier. It was an ongoing joke between both families that both pregnancies were planned. My brother and Avery's were thick as thieves and only fueled the press. I lost track of the amount of times Dad had to bail them out of jail for things like drugs, crazy parties, and reckless driving. The band of brothers, as the media called them, were a force that couldn't be stopped. They flaunted whatever they could and took advantage of everything at their disposal. If outsiders only knew what went on behind closed doors.

The Rossi name was soon on everyone's lips. Anything we or the Herons did spread like wildfire, therefore making the boys a magnet for the paparazzi. My parents paid a lot of money to keep things out of the media, but some still made the front page.

Pursing his lips, Alfred snuck a glance at me. "Honey, when it comes to your parents, I have no idea what they'll do. I want you to be prepared. Personally, I'd like it if you got used to your surroundings and the street names before I leave."

I nodded, agreeing with him as we pulled into World Cup. My stomach was immediately in knots, anxious for what was to come. I was running on five minutes of sleep, Starbucks, and a prayer.

"You're right...I'll pay attention starting tomorrow."

"Have a good training sesh," Alfred said as I stepped out of the Escalade, causing me to pause and look over my shoulder.

"Did you just say sesh? Tell me you did not just say that." Sesh was the slang everyone was using for session back home.

"What? Isn't that what everyone is saying these days? I'm just trying to keep up with the times."

"Alfred," I said, shaking my head with a big smile. "See you later."

CHAPTER 10

Lugging my duffle bag over my shoulder, I walked into the gym, feeling slightly more comfortable than yesterday.

Even though I'd been on time the day before, I was much earlier this morning and had time to put my belongings away, therefore preventing any awkward stares from my teammates...or reprimands from Coach Kova. After last night, I planned to prove I was worthy of being here. I'd shut up and do everything he said I needed to. I wanted this, and I refused to let a few unconstructive comments bring me down.

I undressed down to my leo and was in the middle of sipping water when Kova emerged at my side, scaring the shit out of me. He was like a fucking ninja, always appearing out of thin air without a sound.

I sputtered and water dripped down my chin. I wiped it away with the back of my hand and looked at him, capping the container.

Kova eyed me with anything but concern. "Are you okay?"

"Fine." I coughed.

"Good. Let us go into my office."

I threw my hair into a messy bun, worried about what he wanted to talk about. He shut the door behind me and I took a seat, waiting for him to kill my hopes and dreams once again. It seemed to be his main goal every time I stepped foot into his office. My stomach twisted as our eyes locked, nervousness rippled through my veins as he stared at me for a long, hard moment. This couldn't be good.

"I spoke with Madeline and we devised a new schedule for you. Until you can reach the level where we need you to be, you will be here six days a week with lunch and tutoring in between. Of those six days, two of the days will be dedicated to your favorite ballet class in the morning." A sardonic half-grin tipped his lips. My belly fluttered at the way his eyes flickered when he said that. "Since you do not do tutoring every day, you will be here. Those will be about ten-hour days, coming in at just under fifty hours a week. You will get only one day to yourself for now to do whatever you need."

He had to have been out of his ever loving mind. But knowing better than to argue, I curtly responded. "Okay."

Looking down at his notes, his eyes scanned a few sentences before looking back at me. "You are going also to take some strengthening classes. We need you to improve your flexibility, and I think a couple of private sessions with me before practice will do it. So long as you continue with the drills."

My last coach used to say my hips were tight, but I didn't understand what that meant. I guess I'd find out when the private session begun.

"There will be lots of conditioning in between, and every day before you start and when you finish, you will run two miles on the track outside."

"There's a track outside?" I hadn't seen one.

"Yes, just a few blocks over there is a high school. You will use their track. Four laps equal one mile, so you will run eight in the morning and eight in the evening."

I fucking hated running. "Whatever you say."

"This schedule is extreme and not something we do for everyone. If you cannot handle it or even think you are incapable of it for a minute, you should tell us. My time, as well as all the coaches in this gym, is precious. I do not want you wasting it."

That pissed me off. Since I had no one to speak for me, I had to stand up for myself. "You haven't even given me a chance. Not even twenty-four hours have passed. What makes you think I can't do it? Yesterday I made mistakes, I know I did and will own up to it, but I was nervous. Give me another chance."

"There are no second chances in gymnastics. You should know this."

"I'm well aware."

"So no excuses."

"I won't make any." He remained silent, so I continued. "World Cup produces champions. I came here to be coached by the best to be the best. I'm not leaving."

"It is not about being the best, it is about how hard you work and how much you give without expecting anything in return. How much you train, how much you push when no one is looking. It is about how deep you dig within, knowing you did all you could do and have no regrets at all. Even then, there is a chance it is still not enough." Kova exhaled a heavy breath. "I cannot make you the best, only you can do that. Your body can endure just about anything—it is your mind you have to convince."

Determined, I looked directly in his eyes. "I'll prove I can handle it."

Kova nodded slowly, a devious smile gracing his handsome face. I swallowed hard.

"What doesn't kill you only makes you stronger. Right, Coach?"

"In your case, only time will tell."

⚹⚹⚹⚹⚹⚹⚹

"LET US GET STARTED."

Following behind Kova, he led the way down the hall to one of the rooms in the back. He walked like he was on a mission. His shoulders were rigid and I found the way he marched when he walked intimidating. It was like he had a one track mind—an assignment needed to be tackled and dealt with. I guess I shouldn't complain since he'd taken time out to help me personally, but he reminded me of a drill sergeant. He was all listen, look, and don't talk.

The "don't talk" part was my biggest weakness.

World Cup was much larger than I ever imagined when we first showed up. Aside from the remarkable gym and dance rooms, there was a muscle therapy room, showers—which I would never use—and a cafe equipped with a kitchen and tables scattered throughout. Thanks to my dad, the cafe was built as part of the agreement for me to train here.

Pushing the door open, Kova flipped on the lights. He didn't waste time starting the private sessions. It'd been three weeks since we had our little chat and he implemented the new schedule.

The room held two exam style tables with navy blue, cushioned tops. There was a tall storage cabinet on the other side of the wall and various exercise equipment. Black folded mats, large yoga balls that were fun to bounce on, and elastic ropes used for restraint training hung from the walls. I knew he was concerned about my lack of flexibility—or so he said—but I was pretty sure he was delusional.

"Get undressed."

My leo was already on, so I took off my shoes, pants, and shirt, and stuffed them into my bag. I always wore loose fitted comfy pants and a regular tee to practice. Easy on, easy off. I took out a pair of black spandex mini shorts and slipped those on and waited.

"So, what are we going to do?" I asked curiously.

"*We*, are not going to do anything—you are." I fought the urge to roll my eyes.

I tracked Kova as he moved around the room. "You are going to stretch without stretching. A lot of athletes believe the more you do will help with flexibility. That is not always the case. Sometimes stretching aggressively backfires. It is short lived and can cause injuries." He paused. "Every athlete is different, so what works for one may not work for the other. It is all trial and error, but I have found this helps with flexibility the best. "

I nodded, listening to him. I'd never heard this, but then again, I'd never seen anyone bounce on kneecaps either.

"Your former coach was concerned about your range of motion." Kova patted one of the tables, motioning me over. I closed the distance and jumped up. "I have been watching you the past few weeks, your shoulders and hips are tight. I have noticed you cannot go straight into a split, how it takes time for your hips to loosen until you hit the floor. Your leaps could use work and so could your angles. You are careful and it is obvious. Being cautious is not a bad thing, but it will hold you back. It is almost like your brain is subconsciously protecting you from over doing it, which will hinder your advancement in this sport."

I eased into conversation. "Yes, it does take me a little time to loosen up, but I thought that was normal before a workout for anyone."

He shook his head. "Lie back. Scoot forward so your legs are dangling off the table." I did as he instructed. "Good. Now lift your knee and bring it to your chest. It should be flat to your chest without your other leg coming up."

It wasn't flat, and my knee did come up. Kova gave me a knowing look. "See?"

"Don't you think it's because I just walked in and haven't stretched at all?"

"No, this is a simple thing that you should be able to do. Do it again."

This time when I did it, Kova laid a hand high up on my thigh to hold my leg down. When I couldn't bring my knee to my chest, he stepped in closer and helped widen my range of motion by pressing my knee to my chest, pushing on my shin, and holding down my other leg. His hands were large and capable of covering a vast amount of my skin. I grimaced inwardly so he wouldn't hear me complain about the strain on my muscles.

"You feel it, yes?" he asked, looking into my eyes.

I didn't want to give him the satisfaction, but I also had a feeling he'd be able to tell I was lying. "I do," I grunted when he pressed harder, "but I also think it's because I haven't warmed up yet."

Kova let go and stepped back. "Now, scoot up, bend your knees, and put both feet at the end of the table. Place your hands flat by your sides and then lift your hips."

I wasn't sure where he was going with this, but I did as he asked.

"How does that feel?"

I shrugged my shoulders. "I don't know. Good?"

Kova's eyes slowly grazed the length of my torso to my thighs and a shiver ran through me. "Can you not feel that your hips are not elevated all the way?" My brows cinched together and he stepped closer again. "Lift higher," he ordered, placing his hand to my butt and holding it there. Warmth surged through me from his searing touch. I finally felt it and I couldn't hide the tight pinch in my hips as he lifted me higher.

"I still think this is just because I haven't done any warm ups this morning yet, Coach," I grumbled. Apparently, I needed to remind him the sun was still rising, too.

Ignoring me, he said, "We are going to do various stretching techniques and breathing drills to help you. It is really all a mental thing, so we will train your brain to accept it."

"Train my brain to accept it?" I paused, trying to find the right words because this was the most ridiculous thing I'd ever heard. "I'm sorry, Coach, but I don't understand how basically manipulating myself is going to help with tight hips and shoulders."

He stared at me for a long moment before he said, "It is like relearning a skill you already know how to do and learning it correctly. Like breaking a bad habit. But in order to break a bad habit, you have to think differently. In your mind, if you keep stretching and over stretching, it will help, yeah? It will give you the range of motion you need?"

"Well, yes."

"So you are over doing it, and pushing and straining harder because you *think* it will make a difference when it clearly has not. Over stretching does not necessarily work. It is bad for your muscles. The stretching techniques I am about to teach you do in fact help. There will not be any strain on your body and they are safer for you. At your level, you should have a wide range of motion, but you do not. We can correct that. It is not uncommon, and this is not the first time I have seen this happen, but typically it comes with injury."

This was, by far, the most idiotic thing I'd ever heard. Somehow lying to myself would fix my tightness. Oh, how about I just lie to myself and *think* I could do a triple front tuck on the floor when, in reality, I couldn't. Training myself to think I could do it would only give me a broken neck and a wheel chair for the rest of my life, not the actual ability.

CHAPTER 11

Kova propped his hands on his hips. "You are skeptical."

Sometimes, just sometimes, I wished he'd use contractions. "I am," I said honestly.

"So we will do a little test. Today, we warm up my way and then you start your workout. Tomorrow, and the next couple of weeks, you do it your way and see how it goes."

I smiled. "I like the sound of that."

Kova ushered me up and took me to the floor, where I did a split that didn't quite reach the ground, and a squat where my hips were parallel to my knees, but I couldn't go any farther. It actually hurt to squat this low without stretching the way I normally did.

"Now, remember where you started this morning, yeah?"

I nodded and he took me back to the table. I decided not to question him. Regardless of his unusual training habits, I knew I was limited with my range.

Kova had me lie down, face up, and place my foot on my thigh. My back bowed just a bit and my knee didn't fall to the side, which meant my hips weren't open just yet. I did this with both legs. Then brought my knee to my chest again, and this time he stepped up to my side to help, catching me off guard. Kova placed his hand on the back of my bare thigh and my heart did a little somersault in response. He pressed my knee to my chest and used his other hand to hold down the opposite thigh.

The silence was odd. Really, really odd. Kova fixated his gaze on the white wall behind my head. I was curious to know what went through his mind since his eyes hardly moved. He was focused and in the zone. His body was so close I could see a hint of his facial hair growing in, but he smelled amazing. So good I inhaled a little too loud to get a better sniff.

He looked down and instructed, "No. Breathe with your stomach, not your chest and shoulders. Your stomach should come out when you inhale and your ribs will expand. We will work on breathing too, just not today."

With my eyes locked with Kova's, I drew in a measured breath. My heartbeat picked up in the silence and I took note of where he placed his hand—way up on my leg near my mini shorts. Okay, maybe it wasn't way, way up. It wasn't like I had these long super model legs or anything, he just had large hands that took up a lot of space on my thigh.

I exhaled leisurely and he gave a slight nod of approval. Kova let go and walked around to the other side of the table where he applied the same technique to my opposite leg. He watched me, as I did him, and I wasn't sure what to think of the dense silence between us. I couldn't tell if his focus was on making sure I breathed correctly, or to count the freckles on the bridge of my nose.

His hand moved to the back of my thigh and pressed inwardly, deeply massaging my hamstring with his fingers. My stomach clenched, the sensation shot straight to my core, causing a burst of heat to strike through me. I had a notion it wasn't supposed to feel this good.

"Your hamstrings feel a little too tight. Even with muscle, you should feel soft here, not hard like a rock. Loose and pliable," he said, voice low, and continued to feel around. "This is probably due to over stretching and overuse. Stiff muscles are not healthy and can cause lack of flexibility in both your hips and legs, which then could result in an injury. Stretching your hips consistently is key and should be done daily."

The pull inside my leg was tight and the urge to bend my knee was strong. Kova sensed the lift in my leg and firmly said, "No."

His callused hand leisurely drifted down my leg and gripped my knee. "Breathe. Feel what your body is doing, what position you are in, what it will help you accomplish. Focus on the movement and what it will do for you." His hand continued to my calf and he clucked his tongue in disapproval when he prodded the toned muscle.

I closed my eyes and followed his instructions. My body began to relax as I imagined the position I was in, the new way of stretching that would help me in the future. Opening my hips, I counted to ten and then reopened my eyes, only to find Kova immersed in me.

He was close, so close his breath hit my cheek. I knew his eyes were a pretty shade of green, similar to mine, but where I had wide, doe eyes, Kova's were more prominent and forward. Demanding. The lime green encased by the black circle was remarkable.

"Your eyes…" I whispered, "they're beautiful."

The corners of his mouth curled up, his full lips twisting into a grin. My cheeks glowed with warmth and I became innately aware of my surroundings, Kova's close proximity, and where his hands were, how his fingers pressed into my skin. A flush of heat surged through me and I wondered if he could feel my skin warming. He leaned in just a bit more to press on my leg. The strain was more acute and I fought against a grimace.

Just before backing away, Kova's mouth opened as if he was going to say something. Only, his eyes hardened and a crease formed between his wide brows. Nothing came out.

Me and my stupid mouth.

The weighty silence was too much for me to handle. "You guys should get a radio," I suggested, anything to bridge the weirdness between us. Kova looked perplexed, at a loss for words over my idea. As if a radio was such an appalling suggestion.

"We do not need a radio in this room, only in the gym for floor routines and the dance room. You will lose focus with music. Do eight counts in your head."

This had to be his idea of a joke. A really lame joke. He wanted me to do eight counts, counting to eight over and over to myself…a million times!

My eyes scanned around the room. "I don't see how that's possible with you nearly lying on my leg."

Fuck. Avery would have a field day with me once I told her the stupid shit that came out of my mouth.

"I am not going to acknowledge that sarcastic little comment of yours." Kova stepped back and took my ankle into his hand. "Put your leg down," he said. I did, and he placed my ankle over my thigh to lie flat, in a half butterfly position. Standing in front of me with one hand on my knee and the other on my ankle, he applied pressure.

Jesus Lord, did I ever feel the strain in my hips now. This was a different pull compared to the times I stretched, and I was beginning to see what he meant earlier. My chest pushed out and my head angled back. I squeezed my eyes shut to deal with the burn. "Uh-uh." He lightly slapped my thigh, bringing my attention to him. "Lie flat and breathe correctly. I will let up a little bit."

Focusing on his eyes, I did as he instructed. He kept his word and eased up, but not as much as I would've liked.

"Inhale, exhale, Adrianna. Stop breathing like you are running for the first time in your life. You are not a fish out of water. It is not that bad."

A burst of laughter came out of me. My eyes widened and I flattened my lips between my teeth so I wouldn't laugh again, or smile, which only made it worse. Between his odd comments and heavy Russian accent, I couldn't help but want to imitate him. Not to be mean, but because it sounded funny.

"I'm sorry for laughing," I said, covering my mouth. "I don't know why I found that funny."

Just when I thought he was going to scold me for my outburst, Kova's face relaxed and a flash of humor settled in his eyes. Shaking his head, there was a faint grin on his face.

"If you keep that kind of breathing up, it will only work against you in the future."

"How do you feel now?"

Standing, I lifted my knee and pulled my leg up in a half circle in front of my hips. "I don't know, I think I can tell my range is broader. My hips feel more open, if that makes sense." And they did feel a bit looser, which was nice.

He nodded. "Good. That is what I want you to feel. Now go get ready for practice, I will see you over there."

Kova patted my shoulder and then left. I quickly gathered my things and made my way to the locker room, where I found Hayden.

"How'd it go?" he asked from the other side of the room.

"As good as it could possibly go, I guess. His methods are a little strange. "

"What do you mean?"

"With his drills and stretches. He does things I've never seen or heard of in my life."

Hayden smiled, his dimples showing as he looked in his duffle bag. "But he knows his shit." Shutting his locker, he walked over to my side. "You want to go to Starbucks after practice? Grab a coffee?"

I pursed my lips together. "My, Hayden Moore, I hardly know you. Are you asking me on a date?" I said in a heightened, sarcastic, southern belle voice. "'Cause you know Mr. World Cup himself says that's not allowed."

Hayden cracked his knuckles as a smile slid across his face. He was pretty cute. "How about you buy your own coffee. That way it won't come off as a date, because believe me, it's not."

I shut my locker door and turned toward him. "Sounds like a plan."

⁂

"IS WORLD CUP EVERYTHING YOU thought it'd be?" Hayden asked. It was early, only five in the afternoon, and we were finished with practice.

We grabbed our coffees, plus a sandwich for him, and made our way outside to one of the tables. I'd called Alfred and let him know I was going to get coffee with my new friend and that he would give me a ride home.

I chuckled, unsure how to answer his question. "Hard to say, it's only been a few weeks. Ask me again in six months."

Sitting down, he unwrapped his food and I could smell the delectable scent. My stomach grumbled. I was starving, but I also needed to watch my weight.

"Want half?" he asked.

I gave him a droll stare. "You know I can't have that."

"Sucks to be you," he said playfully, popping a piece into his mouth.

Cupping my venti coffee, I took a sip of the dark roast I'd come to love. With just a splash of coconut milk, I was good to go.

"I'm curious," he said swallowing. "How did you find out about World Cup?"

My eyes shot to the table. "My dad's friends with Coach and gave him a call. They do business together sometimes."

"Ah, that makes sense. So, honestly, what'd you think of Kova?"

I was glad he didn't prod. "He's...interesting. And different than any other coach I've ever had. I'm open to anything that's going to help me, but at the same time, I don't know what to think. You know what he told me this morning? That I have to basically manipulate myself. He didn't say manipulate, he said train my brain, but I'm ninety-nine percent positive it's what he meant. Train my brain to do what exactly? Things I know I'm not ready for so I can break a bone and be out for the season? Who encourages that?"

Hayden laughed and I felt myself loosening up. "I don't think he means it in that sense. I think he just wants you to change your way of thinking to a safer route that will have a lasting effect. Think outside the box. He said similar things to Reagan from what I'm told. And I only know this because my sister told me one night. I've seen what he's capable of, and it's big things."

I nodded, taking in what he said. Interesting that he worked with Reagan. A light breeze blew the unruly strands of hair that had fallen loose from my ponytail across my face and I pushed them aside.

Hayden grew serious. "Don't be afraid to question things, but also trust your coach would never do anything to put you at risk. He can be Captain Dickhead when he wants to be, but have a little faith in what he's capable of doing. You wouldn't be here if he didn't think you could do it."

I sighed and took another sip of my coffee. His encouraging words helped. So much was up in the air, I wasn't sure what to think. I wanted so much in so little time. "You're right."

He ate the last bite of his sandwich and rubbed his hands together. "When do you work with him again?"

I shrugged, looking around. "I have no idea. I guess when he has time. But God, Hayden. The silence was so strange. He was up close and stretching me and shit." Hayden smiled, his blue eyes twinkling, and I found myself smiling in return. Oddly, his presence unruffled my feathers. "I didn't know what to do, what to say. Do I say anything? What did Holly do when she did this?"

"Holly didn't have to do any extra conditioning." My shoulders dropped, along with my self-confidence. Hayden sat up taller. "She didn't have to do what you're doing because we've been at this gym for many years, since we were kids, so she's already accustomed to its ways."

I pursed my lips together. He had a point.

"Why don't you ask Reagan how her sessions went? She worked with him for a while."

"I have a sinking suspicion she doesn't like me, so no."

Hayden looked toward the sky as if he was lost in thought. "Listen," he said, leaning forward and looking me square in the eyes. "Don't stress about the small shit. It won't mean anything in the end. Focus on what's important, the big picture. Your love of gymnastics. Just do you and you'll be okay."

Taking a deep breath, I expelled it and smiled. "I think that's exactly what I need to do."

CHAPTER 12

Kova sighed, dragging a tired hand down his face. Doubling my hours and adapting to a new coach proved to be much more daunting than I expected. I'd been to hell since starting this new journey.

And stayed there.

No matter how much I tried, no matter how much effort I put into training, it was never enough for Kova. He could at least give me a little credit so I knew he saw my effort.

"Adrianna," he said, curling the R again. "Why are you holding the bar like that? What the hell did they teach you at that damn gym?" He mumbled to himself in what sounded almost like disgust. My brows bunched together. Every day he had something negative to say. At first I tried to ignore his little comments, but the more he said them, the more aggravated I became. My old gym wasn't shit. It was good, I just outgrew it.

Kova jumped off the blue spotting box and grabbed my wrist, pulling me to the lower bar. "Hang on here."

Confused, I looked at him. "I don't understand."

One brow arched perfectly. I hated when he did that. "What do you not get? Hang on to the bar and pick your feet up. Now."

Shaking my head, I obliged, as always, and looked past my arm up at him. My knees were bent, scraping the mat while I waited for him to speak. Coach shook his head, looking dumbfounded at my hands.

I was beyond puzzled.

"Are you not gripping the bar correctly?" he questioned.

"What?"

Kova touched my fingers to answer my question. "You are resting your fingers on your grips, not gripping the actual bar correctly. It is incredible you can even hang on. Do your wrists hurt?"

I stood and let go of the bar, rubbing my wrists. I learned to block out the pain long ago.

"All the time." In fact, I could use some Motrin right now.

"You are barely holding the bar."

Mystified, he took my wrist into his hands and began removing my dowel grip by unwinding the Velcro. The grips helped execute high velocity maneuvers during swings that were followed by releasing and catching the bar.

Kova held the slightly tattered grip in front of his face. "This is dangerous. You need new grips. I trust you have more?"

"Yes." Of course I had more grips. I just liked this pair because they were worn in.

"Good. You should know better than to use this." He dropped it to the floor, along with the worn out wrist guards before moving onto the tape.

"There is no need for so much tape," he said, more to himself than to me. "No one even does this anymore. Then again, if you were doing it right, you would not need this."

As much I loved removing the tape after a long, rigorous bar training, I wasn't very happy about it coming off since I still had practice time left on this apparatus. It took time to cut the holes and place my fingers through them properly. There were layers upon layers of athletic tape to protect my hands from rips and tears. He pulled off each strand until my hand was bare.

Turning my wrist over to inspect it, Kova hissed at the sight before him. His fingers gently ran over my tender flesh, like feathers dancing erotically over me. Even though I used pre-wrap to prevent the adhesive from sticking to me, my skin was still as bright as a tomato with indentations and outlines. I wrapped it tightly every time, and once my wristbands were on, I wrapped more around them. I used an insane amount, but it got the job done. It helped to keep my wrists straight and locked to give me support. It's what I'd always done in the past and no one had ever said anything.

Kova held my wrist in his hand while he laced his long fingers through mine with his other hand. His palm kissed mine, his long fingers draping over my knuckles. Our hands locked together for a moment before he tenderly pulled on my knuckles, squeezing them as he did. He repeated the gesture and my heart skipped a beat at his skilled touch. *God, it felt good.* Incredibly good. My hands were overworked and dried out, they ached on a daily basis, but the feel of him massaging my fingers was heavenly and I almost sighed out loud. My entire body relaxed and I almost prayed he wouldn't stop.

There wasn't a part on my body that wasn't sore on a continual basis since I started at World Cup. I ached in places I didn't even know possible. A full body massage was something I needed to consider after this.

Glancing up from our entwined fingers, I found Kova observing me. I couldn't decipher what he was thinking as he stared down through thick lashes, his eyes unwavering. I focused on his lips, the fullness that begged me to wonder how soft they would feel pressed to mine. Heat rose to my cheeks and I flushed before him. His hand was much larger than mine, his fingers showing dexterity. He knew exactly how to manipulate my wrist and how to stretch my hand out gently, but with force, pulling on my fingers and then rotating my wrist, making it feel damn near euphoric.

Carefully, he bent my palm back, working it out in circles, flexing it. I stepped closer to him and my fingers curled around his fisted knuckles, lightly holding on to him. His presence dominated the air surrounding us. Why that made my heart race faster, I wasn't sure. Taking a chance, I naturally added a little more weight to my fingers so I could feel him move under my touch.

There was a slight pop and I swallowed, hiding the twinge of pain.

"Did that hurt?" he asked.

"A little bit, but it's nothing I'm not used to."

"Pushing through the pain is a sure fire way to sustain an injury."

Kova moved my hand to the side, but this time, he held my elbow so I couldn't bend my arm. His fingers pressed into my skin. I dipped to ease some of the pressure, but he shook his head.

"You are straining your wrists hanging the way you do. Since you are not gripping the bar properly, all your weight is balancing here." He shook my wrist with his thumb and forefinger. "It makes complete sense now why you use so much tape, you are trying to avoid excess movement. If we do not train you the correct way to hold the bar, you will retire much sooner than you want. Just another bad habit I need to break you of."

"Of course I'm gripping the bar properly. How else would I hold on?"

He shook his head. "You do not understand. You are holding on, but not completely. It is like a lazy hold, you are resting your fingers on the dowel instead of gripping it. When you swing and pivot around the bar, you are pulling and tugging on the ligaments inside your wrists, and the bones are under a lot more stress than needed. We need to rectify this fast."

Coach removed my other grip and tape and worked out my left wrist just as he did with my right. He was gentle with me, his face softening to concern as he worked.

After a few more minutes of tending to my sore muscles, Coach said, "Get back up there."

I reached down for my grips but he stepped on them.

"I need my grips."

"You will do it without them."

My mouth popped open in shock. "But, I'll get rips."

He shrugged like it was nothing. "Then you will learn real fast how to grip the bar correctly. Trust me, you will perform better in the long run."

"You've got to be kidding me."

Never, had I ever, heard of a coach training like this. No one took away a gymnast's protective gear.

No one except Coach Kova.

His mesmerizing eyes bore into mine, his features turning hard, showing me just how little he was kidding. I got the impression he was going to enjoy the pain he knew I was about to endure. The only thing I could figure was he learned it from his previous coaches in Russia.

I was starting to understand just how unconventional Russian coaching could be.

"Look at my face, Adrianna. Does it look like I am kidding? I do not care if it takes you hours and your hands are bleeding. You will grip that bar the *right* way," he emphasized the word with a sneer.

In that moment, I'd come to the conclusion Coach Kova was a closet lunatic. It was the only plausible explanation for his ridiculous training techniques. My hands were about to take a serious beating.

I shook my head in utter disbelief and walked to the chalk bowl. "Am I allowed to use chalk, Coach?" I asked in a heightened voice. He was being such a dick.

When he dipped his chin, I picked up a bottle of honey laying at my feet and squeezed a pile onto my palm, then smashed my hands together to help spread the sticky substance. Honey would create friction and a rough grip on the bars. Since Kova was already under my skin and I was sweating, I applied a hefty amount of powdered chalk next. A sweaty bar could cause me to slip and seeing as I wasn't allowed to use my grips, I didn't want to take a chance. I even used a chunky broken piece of chalk and ran it roughly across the back of my knuckles where the honey clumped together and then said a little prayer.

Clenching my jaw, I stood in front of the bar locking eyes with Kova. I stared hard, letting him see my irritation, not giving two fucks whether he liked it or not.

He pointed to me. "That look in your eyes? That is what I want to see. That is the kind of digging deep and pulling from within I was talking about when you first came here," he added, building a fire within me. "That is what I want to see!" As much as I hated him at the moment, I knew he was right. He was only trying to show me the correct way.

I swung into a kip then used my feet to stand on the low bar, jumping to the high bar. Chalk dust floated in the air, and I closed my eyes for a brief second and held my breath. The amount of chalk I inhaled on a daily basis couldn't be good for my health.

"Legs together!" he yelled as I did a pike kip and moved into a handstand. They fucking were together!

Of course, I didn't actually say that.

A free hip circle into a handstand, I took a deep breath and swung down to do a Gienger, a release with a half twist flying over the bar in a slight pike position, my legs bent at my hips so I was in an L position. Coming back to a handstand, I swung again, this time into a blind change right before moving into a straddle back. I grasped the bar harder than I normally did out of fear of falling, the burn began to resonate through my skin with all the twisting and releasing I'd already done. Kind of like when you wore a pair of high heels for the first time and the back of your feet weren't used to the friction. It was that kind of burn.

The tips of my fingers weren't used to holding and sliding against the bar this way. I'd have blisters by the end of this ludicrous form of training for sure.

A toe shoot to high bar, to a handstand pirouette. Giant to another pirouette and I reversed my grip. My Jaeger was coming up next, and from the corner of my eye, I saw Coach move to spot me. Even though it was normal for coaches to step in, fear streamed through my belly for a split second because there was always a chance any-thing could happen. My heart jumped into my throat as I mentally prepared for the fast paced bar release. It was now or never. And as much as I loved doing it, it terrified me each time.

Releasing the bar, it ricocheted loudly as I flipped up and forward into a pike position, the muscles in my hamstrings pulled tight while I reached for the high bar. This move would've been easier if I did it in a straddle position, but I liked the challenge of the pike.

You know, to make my life harder than it already was.

At least I'd get a bonus point for added difficulty.

Coming down, I gripped the bar as tight as possible, my palms began to really burn. I clutched it so forcefully the chalk had worn off and I wished for my grips, cursing Kova to hell at the same time. My bare skin rolled and pulled against the bar, but it hadn't ripped yet. It'd blister first before it actually tore open. The pain was like road rash, your hands grinding down on asphalt as you slid across the ground. All I had left were a few more releases and then the dismount. I was good to go.

Once I landed, I looked back at Coach, unable to stop the smug grin on my face. Bars was all about hitting handstands and perfect lines, and it felt like mine were on point. Surprisingly, the routine was actually really good. I had more control than usual. I did my release moves well and landed my full-in dismount, a full-twisting double back tuck.

My smile faltered after mood-killer Coach looked at me. He stood there stone-faced and expressionless.

"I think I actually perform better without my grips," I said confidently, and rubbed my hands roughly together, trying to ease the sting.

He shrugged, unimpressed. "We will see how you feel about that after you do it ten, fifteen more times."

I was stunned into silence.

He pointed with his head. "Back up. And Adrianna?"

I looked up in the middle of coating my hands with more chalk. "Yes?"

"Straighten your knees in your Jaeger. They were slightly bent when you reached for the bar. That is a deduction. You need to extend yourself, elongate your torso, and do not bend your arms." He stepped to me and pressed my shoulders back, and used his hand as an example to lengthen my torso. "Everything you need is already inside here." He tapped his temple. "Prove to me you want it."

Tight lipped, I nodded. I had dug deep, and really did try. I'd worked my ass off to prove myself worthy.

"And point your toes. Flexed feet are ugly."

I have ugly feet. Got it.

"Your elbows were bent in numerous places, it was sloppy looking. Tighten it up."

There went my confidence. And here I thought I did well. Nevertheless, I sucked it up and didn't say a word. Not like I could do or say much else anyway.

"Did you even spot?"

Of course I did.

"Hit your handstands in your cast."

I swallowed back the climbing tears.

"You need to hold that handstand perfectly straight before swinging down in the overshoot. I have some drills you can do to get those lines. You want to test elite..." He muttered to himself before switching over to Russian.

I seriously hated the sight of Coach Kova right now.

CHAPTER 13

With chalk covering my thighs and hands, I performed my routine more than a dozen times before practicing the skills individually.

I asked for my grips—only for Kova to deny me. My eyes widened and my jaw dropped when he said no. I couldn't believe he wouldn't let me use them. He was beyond delusional. Surely he realized inflicting this kind of torture on my hands would render them useless tomorrow.

Unless he just didn't care and expected me to train just as much.

Dear God, I prayed he wouldn't.

I moved onto my dismount with Kova spotting to give me a tad bit more height.

"Tighten up."

"Wrong!"

"Do it again."

"No, no, no, stop doing that."

"Just go for it! What are you waiting for?"

And when he was really fired up, he spat in Russian.

There was always something for him to gripe about. Kova was hardly satisfied, but today he acted like he was the one who slammed his shins on the bars. I was pretty sure there'd be a handful of black and blues blooming beneath my skin by morning. His entire focus had been on me at one point, perfecting my every move. He'd shown me numerous ways to correct my positions, his hands lingering a little longer each time, which I couldn't help but notice. He had the rest of the team do conditioning in between working with Madeline. While I appreciated his keen eye and wouldn't change a thing since he was making me better, in this moment, I despised it.

My hands hurt to make a fist. My skin was searing hot and tight, and I knew if I did any more practicing there was a good chance they'd bleed next.

When you held onto a bar for dear life, like I did, the skin on your palms bunched up and created either a blister or a pocket of blood. Of course I didn't get lucky with just a blister. And now little red bubbles of blood were ready to pop any minute.

Bloody bars were just nasty.

"Take a five minute break and get some water. We will start again." Coach turned to walk away before I could say anything.

"He's really doing a number on you." Hayden appeared by my side.

"Tell me about it. He's refusing to let me wear grips since I apparently hold the bar incorrectly."

I turned my hands over and Hayden inhaled a sharp breath. "Is that all from today?"

"No, my wrists are usually beaten up pretty badly, but the blisters are new." There was never a time when a gymnast didn't have some type of rough or beaten palms.

"Do you have any Prep H with you?"

I looked at him in confusion. "Prep H? Like the stuff for hemorrhoids?"

"Yeah, it's supposed to help with rips. It will help reduce swelling and numb the rip."

I smiled shyly. "I've never heard of that."

"I bet you never heard of using Bag Balm either, then."

"Can't say I have."

"It's used on cow udders since they tend to crack and split often."

I stood with my mouth agape. I pictured the poor cows with the metal clamps, hyped up on steroids and growth hormones, forced to produce more milk than naturally occurring. Hayden chuckled at my expression. "That's disgusting."

I knew of all kinds of treatments, like using Vitamin E Gel, or a Band-Aid. Some believed in using warm tea bags on the rips with a sock to hold it in place overnight. A gymnast would do just about anything to heal a rip as swiftly as possible so they didn't tear their skin any further. Some even went as far as using a pumice stone to scrub around a rip, removing any calluses and dead skin. Just the thought made me cringe. Hopefully I wouldn't reach that stage. But hemorrhoid cream and the cow balm were new ones for me.

"My mom came up with a secret trick...I don't share it with anyone, but I can stop by your place sometime with it and show you if that's okay. I have a feeling you're going to need it. But you have to promise not to laugh. Or tell anyone."

I met his gaze. We hadn't known each other very long, but I was willing to take my chances. "Thanks, Hayden. I promise not to say a word."

"Social hour is over, girls." Kova's sarcastic tone did not go unnoticed. He clapped his hands and said, "Get back to work."

Hayden nodded, his lips flattened to a thin line. "Make sure to give me your number before you leave."

Back on the bars and my hands were raw, I'd never been in such pain before in my life. They were on fire, like burning flames of heat rolling across my palms.

Coach became relentless, forcing me to keep moving without a second to catch my breath or give my hands a break. He just kept yelling out orders until he was blue in the face and I mastered them to his imaginary level of perfection. My arms ached, the muscles strained and I was exhausted. But at least I had conquered the skills for the day. I was seriously contemplating calling in sick tomorrow.

But I couldn't. There was no excuse to miss a practice. Ever.

With another two release moves and dismount coming up before I was done for the night, Kova moved in to spot me. I was capable of doing them alone, but having a spotter was always comforting. It was a built-in trust that came with the territory, one I knew he'd never break. He'd catch me before he'd ever let me fall.

After I landed my full-twisting double back tuck dismount, Kova patted the side of my ass the way coaches do with football players. I glanced up and he gave me a deep nod. We stood inches apart with our eyes on each other, but I couldn't get a beat on his thoughts. I'd say he was pleased with me, but then again I just wasn't sure.

The team parted ways and prepared to leave. I said goodbye to the girls and gathered my things from the locker room. Food was the only thing on my mind and it wasn't one of those plastic prepared meals either. I was famished. Maybe I would have Alfred hit up a drive-thru on our way home for once.

As I was leaving the locker room, I pulled the door closed behind me and stepped into the narrow hallway as Kova came out of his office. He strode down the hall, eyes on me.

My skin prickled in awareness and I raked my gaze down the length of his body. Navy blue basketball shorts displayed the power and muscle in his legs, and a seemingly tight heather gray T-shirt clung to his chest, showing off his pecs. He was a man who took charge and one you didn't argue with. How someone could be so incredibly good looking and a complete jerk at the same time was beyond me. I bet he knew it too.

Tilting my head to the side, I noticed a look on his face I hadn't seen since arriving here. Contentment.

He stopped in front of me and peered down. "You did well today, Adrianna. Very well. You are coming along just fine, surprisingly." He took a swig of his bottled water.

It was almost too good to be true. I looked into his darkening eyes bound by thick eyelashes and saw he truly meant his words. I wasn't sure how to handle his appraisal without grinning like a fool. He caught me by surprise. Every day I wished he'd say something positive, and not once had he until now.

"Thank you, Coach."

"I will see you tomorrow," he said before continuing his walk down the hall.

"Ah, Coach?"

Kova paused, looking over his shoulder.

"Will I be able to use my grips next practice?"

"Not a chance. I know there is no way *you* learned after one day how to hold the bar correctly."

My jaw dropped in disbelief. *You.* As if I was an idiot. "But my hands are raw, it hurts to even wash them with soap. I'll bleed tomorrow and be completely useless."

Kova turned around to face me, his broad shoulders pulled back, one hand clenched around his water bottle. "Do you think you are the first gymnast to show wear and tear on their hands from bars, *malysh*"

Kova visibly tensed, stopping short from his last word. Since I didn't speak a word of Russian, I had no idea what he said. But judging by the alarmed look on his face and the thick air between us, whatever he said couldn't have been good.

Snapping his head to the side, he cracked his neck. "I am not going to go light on you. Get used to it. Nobody said it was going to be easy, it only gets harder from here on out. You need to learn to toughen up and take it. Remember what I said earlier? Prove it to me. Every time you step foot into that gym—make it count. I do not care if your hands hurt, or your back is sore or you are running on an hour of sleep. Prove it. Champions are not made by complaining. They are made by the endless pursuit of their dream despite the obstacles they are faced with. Push through it and do it."

I took a minute to let the weight of his words sink in. While an outsider would think they were laced with malice, I knew they weren't. That was the furthest thing from the truth. I knew he was pushing me to be better. Not only to prove it to him, but myself as well. Without a doubt, Konstantin Kournakova was a hundred percent right.

Slowly nodding, I looked into his eyes and said, "You're completely right, but I never expected you to go light on me. That's not what I wanted. That's not why I came here. I want the challenge. I want to be better. It's why I pour every ounce of blood and sweat into a sport that gives me so little in return. The truth is, I've never been challenged by a coach the way I have by you, so I'm learning to adjust to it." I held up my hands and showed him the bloody blisters threatening to pop under my palms. "You won't hear a complaint come from me again."

Kova's shoulders loosened and he blew out a ragged breath. His gaze openly traveled the length of my body, taking in every inch. The way his eyes pierced mine, like he was pleased with my response, made my heart rush against my chest with satisfaction.

I took more verbal beatings than any of the girls on the team. Constructive criticism at its finest. The only explanation I could think of was he was frustrated over having to break a seasoned athlete of old habits. He was always on me for something I was doing—grilling me, yelling at me.

"Good. That is what I want to hear." He gave me a lengthy gaze. Stepping closer, he gently brushed his thumb across my cheek. "Chalk," he said in a softer tone, and walked away.

I couldn't explain why, but my gut said there was more than meets the eye with him, I always trusted my gut. And him calling me whatever he just said in Russian, and the speech that followed, cemented it.

That being said, he was out of his ever-loving mind if he thought I was going through another day without using my grips.

CHAPTER 14

Stepping into World Cup this morning, I felt fresh and ready for practice.

Dropping my duffle bag to the floor, the fabric of the strap scrapped along my sore palms and I sucked in a pain filled breath. Looking down, my hands were tattered, the skin pulled tight, aching from working bars. Pressing down on one of the blood blisters with my thumb, I watched the fluid shift under the skin in morbid fascination.

Grimacing, I shook my head and removed my pants and top, shoving them into my bag along with my flip flops. Today, I went with a faded, light blue sports bra and black mini shorts instead of the leo. This wasn't something I typically wore, but I'd seen the other girls do it and decided to. I pulled my hair into a messy bun and then placed my things into my locker and made my way into the therapy room.

Of course Kova was already there. His back was to me and I took the time to study him for a long moment before I made myself known. There were so many things I was curious to know about him. Like how he got started in gymnastics, what drove him toward the sport. How long he'd been a gymnast, how he ended up in the States. How he and my dad became friends. I was oddly intrigued by him. I tried to picture what he'd look like competing at the Olympics. Large, muscular arms. Broad shoulders and a fit waist. Overworked hands and tight buns. Focus pouring out of his eyes. For male gymnasts, their workout consisted mostly of bodybuilding exercises, unlike ours. They couldn't get too big and hefty, strength and balance went hand in hand for them. The rings were commonly used for straight arm work. They'd hold an Iron Cross position with weights tacked on to their feet or waist. This built an incredibly large and tight top half.

Not to mention, high levels of strength. I sure as hell couldn't hold a T position, even without the weights dangling on me.

Kova wasn't ripped anymore like I'm sure he once was, but he was still quite built and trim. Sinuous was the perfect way to describe his body. He was definitely easy on the eyes. The muscles in his forearms rippled with strength, and if you watched closely, like I was doing at the moment, you'd see his back flex under his white shirt, along with two round mounds of steel that shifted with each step he took. I could stare at him all day long.

"Ah, Adrianna, you are here," he said pleasantly, taking me out of my daze. I stepped into the room, the cold tile zipping through my bare feet and I shivered.

"I'm here." I walked up to him. "What's on the menu for today?"

Kova turned toward me. "We will work on proper breathing and more of the same stretching we did the last time." He motioned toward the large square blue mat on the floor. "Go lie on your back, legs straight and together."

Walking over, I got into position as Kova followed closely behind. He kneeled on my left side and looked down at me. He spread his hand out and placed it on my stomach just below my ribs.

"Along with brain manipulation, as you so lovingly called it during our last session, you have to breathe correctly, or this extra work will all be a complete waste. It works much like a jigsaw puzzle. One wrong piece and nothing will connect how it is meant to. Proper breathing gives you back and core control. You will have more stamina and won't get tired so fast." He tapped on his temple. "It is all a mental game of tug-of-war. You want more belly breathing, more of using your diaphragm. It will lessen your chance of spinal injury as well. Remember, no fish out of water gasping like last time either. Now, take a deep breath."

I nodded and inhaled. He pinched my sides. "No, wrong. See how your stomach went toward your head and your chest popped up? We do not want that. We want your ribs to expand and your shoulders relaxed, not in your neck. Do it again."

I did it again. "No, keep your hips down," he ordered, and placed his other hand flat on my pelvis. "Again."

I focused on his words as Kova focused on my stomach. His brows furrowed. Breathing shouldn't be this complicated.

His hands stayed in place and pressed into me. "Good. Perfect," he said. "Let us do a set of ten."

I wanted to ask Kova how he knew to breathe like this, who taught him, but thought better of it and decided to wait until stretching came. I didn't think he'd like me to talk while I was learning to breathe properly anyway. So instead I focused on his hand resting on my lower belly. Wondered at the warmth surging through me from the feel of his fingertips on my skin.

"Beautiful," he said softly. "Yes, just like that." He looked into my eyes, almost as if trying to make me believe his words. "It is all about training yourself and remembering it. Doing it a thousand times until it actually sticks. Like muscle memory. Think of it like this—when you flex your abs and breathe at the same time, you are using your diaphragm. It is what gives you a strong core, which is key in so many aspects of gymnastics. The last thing you want is to overexert yourself."

Twenty minutes or so of instructional breathing skills passed, when I said, "I didn't know how important this was. How it can hinder me in this sport. It's very interesting."

He clucked his tongue on the side of his cheek and winked. "Stick with me."

Kova stood up and placed his hand out. I grabbed it and he helped me up. My belly fluttered in response and I averted my gaze. He pointed to the exam like table and said, "Go lie on your back."

I did as he ordered and pulled my knee to my chest and winced, feeling a slight tightness in my hips at first.

"Now, when you do these stretching techniques, remember to breathe properly. It all goes hand in hand, Adrianna."

Kova placed one hand on my leg and the other hand on my hip to steady me, pressing my knee deeper to my chest. I grunted. "All you need to do is hold this position, along with the others, for twenty to thirty seconds every time you stretch. I promise you it will make all the difference."

"Kova? How did you learn all of this?" I asked.

He peered down at me like it was common sense. "I learned most from my coach back in Russia. He was an extraordinary man and taught me well. I also took classes on it to further my comprehension. I wanted the upper hand when it came to coaching, and by applying both methods, I feel like I have that extra something the majority of coaches do not."

A small smile tugged at my lips. He was cocky and I liked that. I liked how he wanted to be a step above other coaches. It's what set them apart. We shifted to my other leg in the quiet room. The heat from Kova's hand danced across my pelvis and my belly dipped in return when he clutched my leg.

"Did you always want to go to the Olympics?" I asked curiously.

He gave a blasé shrug. "That is a tough question. Gymnastics for me was an escape from the life I was born into." A shadow formed in his eyes but it quickly disappeared before I could ask what he meant. "I looked forward to practice every day, but I never saw it as anything other than a hobby that would soon come to an end. My love for the sport definitely ran deeper compared to my teammates that is for sure. I was always trying to do more and I never cut on conditioning. I showed up early and I did not play around. I was devoted. My coach saw something in me and he spoke with my mother. He devised a plan, much like how Madeline and I did for you, and we stuck to it." He took a deep breath and angled my leg to the other side. "It was not until we changed my training and I had a new goal, that I realized just how much gymnastics meant to me, what security it brought me each exhausting day. It is why I went straight into coaching."

Something shifted inside of me and my heart constricted. His fingers dug into my skin as he focused on what he was doing. I felt his words, felt his love for the sport filter the air around us. He spoke from his heart. It was overwhelmingly obvious and I relished it. I didn't have friends who felt this way about sports the way I did, it was just fun and games to them. But watching Kova's eye color change, and hearing his heartfelt words really struck a chord with me. Gymnastics wasn't just a job for him, it was his lifeline. His salvation. And I respected him so much for it. I wanted to know more, like how it brought him security. I suddenly was very interested in my coach.

"In a way, you sound like me."

His brows furrowed as he moved me into another position. I winched when I felt the pinch in my hips and the heat of my hamstrings stretch.

"What do you mean?" he asked.

"Like you, I used gymnastics as an escapism from my life, from my family. I don't have a hard life, and I'm aware of how fortunate I am, but people don't see what goes on behind closed doors that shape us. This may sound terrible of me to say, but I don't look up to my mom as a role model. My dad, a little bit because of his drive, but not my mom. She wants me to be so much like her, but she's everything I don't aspire to be. I don't want to be anything other than me. I'm a gymnast with a craving to take it to the next level. So I decided the only way I could make that happen was to put every waking minute I could into the sport. When I think of gymnastics, I have peace of mind. I see me, and I think that's the most important thing as a person. To be who you want, not how others want you to be. It was how I decided I wanted to go all the way." I paused at the strained look in his eyes. "I'm sorry for rambling."

Kova's eyes tightened at the corners and his forehead scrunched together. He lessened the pressure on my legs but his hands stayed in place. I exhaled lightly. His voice dropped low, but the sincerity in his eyes showed strong when he said, "Even at a young age, taking the road I was offered was eventually a choice my mom left up to me. She did not push me, but coming from someone who has been down that path, listen to me when I say it is not easy at all. It is extremely hard. It was so much more than what I expected. Adrianna, I do not think you have any idea what training for the Olympics entails, or what you have to give up. I lost out on school dances, parties, hanging out with friends, everything a young adult is supposed to do and have a memory of. I missed out on my adolescent years. Maybe your mother does not want you to miss out on that. Yes, it was my choice, and I would not change a thing, but you really have to decide if it is something you want."

I didn't hesitate. "I want it more than anything."

"But why?" he asked, curiously. "What is the driving force?"

"Isn't it obvious? I just told you I love gymnastics and what it means to me."

He scoffed and it annoyed me. "A lot of people love the sport, it does not mean they give up everything and make a career out of it. So few make it that far. You can compete in college and still have a life. Collegiate gymnasts are only allowed to practice half the hours of what you are doing now."

My brows furrowed and my heart began to speed up. I didn't like the direction this conversation was going in.

"I feel like you're against me."

Kova pulled back, his nose flared. "I am not against you, I just want you to be aware of what is required of you. What you stand to lose. I am telling you what your other options are."

"I'm not going to lose anything, Kova, I'm going to gain. I don't need dances or parties, I need to be in the gym. If I don't take a shot at my dream, I'll live with regret, what-if questions that will plague me for the rest of my life. I need to try and see if I can do it. I have all the means to succeed at my fingertips to accomplish what I want." My voice rose and I became heated. I sat up and pulled my shoulders back, his palm rested high on my thigh. "I don't know what kind of life you were born into, but others would kill for mine. I'm going to use it to my advantage," I said firmly. "I want this. I want to be elite. I want to make the National Team, and one day, I want to go to the Olympics. I thought by coming here and telling you my aspirations you'd understand."

Kova's posture became rigid, his fingers pressed into my skin.

I was pushing his buttons.

CHAPTER 15

understand more so than any coach here," he retorted.

"Then what's the problem? Isn't this what every coach wants to hear?"

We faced off in a battle of wills, both of us determined to make the other one understand. Thing was, I was stubborn and hardheaded. There was no way I was going to back down. Then again, I didn't think he would either.

I placed my hand on his forearm, hoping he'd understand how strongly I felt about this. He flexed under my touch and his grip tightened, but his eyes didn't waver and he didn't pull away. His palm warmed my skin and my cheeks flushed from the reaction.

"You're either with me or you're against me, Kova," I nearly pleaded, just inches from his face.

Silence thickened between us. Kova's jaw flexed and he looked straight at me. "I will be completely honest, no other gymnast I have trained has wanted it as badly as you do. It is rare. You have no idea how refreshing this is to hear." He sighed heavily, his green eyes burned with newfound desire, and I liked it. Being this close to him and having this conversation caused my heart to patter against my ribs.

"If this is what you want, what you truly want, I will do my best to help get you there. But you need to have a good understanding there is a chance you still will not make it all the way. There will be many obstacles in your quest that could eventually halt you instead of finding ways to overcome them. Are you ready for that?"

I absorbed his words deep into my soul and took in the compassion in his eyes. My pulse was racing. A small smile tipped my lips, one I had to refrain from splitting across my face.

"Do you mean that?"

He nodded slowly. The side of his mouth tugged up in challenge. "If that is what you want, but there is no going back once you decide. It is not fair to me, or you."

"This is my dream, and I'm going to show you. I'll prove it. Actions speak louder than words."

He was silent for a moment, then I saw a flash of hunger enter his eyes. I loved it. "I am going to hold you to that."

"I hope you do." I raised a brow. "It wouldn't be in your nature not to."

The room stilled as Kova tilted his head to the side. Pensive eyes stared down at me, and I felt myself falling into a bottomless pit. He had my full attention, I couldn't look away. He was sucking me dry, feeding off my emotion. And truthfully, I didn't want to look any other way but his. I wanted him to see I wasn't kidding about my future.

"You are not what I expected you to be."

That caused me to grin and I laid back down on the table. "Good...Exactly what I wanted." I grew quiet, then asked, "What did you expect?"

"Not someone as determined as you that is for sure. You are strong-minded."

A little laugh rolled off my lips. "I'll take that as a compliment."

Kova ran his tongue along his bottom lip and I tracked the movement. Something clicked between us, an understanding only someone as ambitious as us could identify with. It was there. I felt it, and the look his emerald eyes penetrated me with told me he did too. I hadn't realized it, and I didn't think he did either, but at some point in time during our conversation, Kova had stopped stretching me. One hand was now half on my waist, half on the table. His other hand cupped the back of my leg, nearly holding onto the crease of my ass. I didn't remember him moving them, but I liked it. The tips of his fingers pressed into my inner thigh and caused a rush of heat to sear me. They were dangerously close to my sex and I swallowed as a throb resonated in my core.

I breathed in deeply, the way Kova taught me. One small move and he'd touch me where no one had ever touched me before. I didn't know which was worse, wanting to feel his fingers there or the fact that I didn't find the action repulsive.

I parted my leg slightly and looked in the direction of his hand. Kova followed my gaze, and swiftly pulled away, clenching his eyes shut.

He cleared his throat. "All right. Where were we," he said more to himself than me. He guided me to my stomach and into position. He placed a flat hand on my hamstring, prodding the muscle for tightness and grabbed my knee, pulling it backward.

"Ah, not as hard as last time I see," he said. "This is good."

I watched his movements from the side, my right cheek to the cushioned mat. A tightness developed in my pelvis and a little grunt escaped my throat. I grabbed the edge of the table. Kova glanced at me when I winced and gave a knowing look to breathe. He tapped the side of my butt twice with the back of his knuckles, and I exhaled slowly, then drew in a breath with my stomach. He nodded in approval.

"You know, I was a scrawny thing when I started gymnastics. I could barely hold the bar for more than a couple of seconds."

My eyes widened playfully and I bit down on my lip. I eyed his strong arms. "You're kidding me."

He shook his head. "I wish I was." Then he went into a story about when he first started gymnastics and it lightened the private session, leaving me with a slight smile and a blooming heart, wanting to know everything I could about my coach.

AFTER A FULL DAY OF training, I was exhausted, and the blisters on my palms were getting progressively worse.

Kova didn't go any easier on me today, if anything, since agreeing to help me with my goal, his dick factor increased. The blisters were tender to the touch and filled with fluid that needed draining. I tried not to pick at them so they could be treated properly at home, but something had to give. My hands were on fire and throbbed from irritation.

As much as I wanted Hayden to help me heal my impending rips, I didn't want him to go out of his way and make him stay up later than usual. It was almost ten o'clock at night, and I imagined he was just as tired as I was.

Before I could give it any more thought, my doorbell rang. I quickly got up from the couch and peeped through the hole.

After unbolting the lock, I opened the door to Hayden standing on the other side in gray sweatpants and hoodie, a pharmacy bag hanging from his hand.

"Hey, come in."

With perfectly white, straight teeth, Hayden smiled and walked in.

"Are you sure it's not too late for you? I kind of feel bad."

I decided the lightning in my kitchen would be best for him to doctor my hands. With the condo's open floor plan, it was parallel to the living room, and the pathway to the two bedrooms was in view. Hayden's nose scrunched up as he took in the view, a grin working across his face. "It's like 9, Aid."

I shot a glance at the clock. "It's 10:15...and I know you have to get up early."

He dropped the plastic bag on the countertop. "I'm a big boy, I think I can handle it. But since you're so concerned about my bedtime," he chuckled playfully, "let's see what you got here so I can get home for my beauty sleep. Show me your hands."

I jumped up and planted my ass on the cold granite countertop, sending goose bumps down my body from the contact. I wore a loose fitting white T-shirt and a pair of cutoff denim shorts. Holding my hands out for him to view, I placed them face up on my thighs and waited while Hayden unzipped his hoodie, revealing nothing underneath except for extremely low sitting sweats.

My jaw went slack and my eyes widened. Hayden draped his jacket over the back of one of the high back chairs I used to have breakfast and began rummaging through his bag. I swallowed hard at the sight of him so close, wanting to reach out and run my fingers down his solid chest. Every inch of his body was honed to perfection, every muscle ripped, curled, and dipped.

This wasn't the first time I'd seen Hayden shirtless, but it also wasn't something I paid attention to at the gym very often. He was just a guy doing the same sport I loved. In fact, I rarely noticed. I had a tendency to get tunnel vision, and lately, it had been nothing but Kova and gymnastics, shutting out everything else around me.

Maybe I should have taken notice though, because his body was a work of art.

"Ah, do you always go out dressed like that?" I asked hoarsely.

Hayden paused, then looked down at his body before meeting my gaze. He cleared his throat and said, "I didn't even realize it. I came from practice and didn't feel like slipping on a shirt since I was hot and sticky. I can put my jacket—"

"No!" I yelled, blinking rapidly. "You're fine, I just wasn't expecting...it."

A half smile tugged on the side of his mouth. "You see me like this every day."

I shrugged, trying to avoid his impish gaze. "Guess I never noticed before." He was right. I did see him like that all the time, just never secluded like we were in my condo. Or so close...

"You guess you never noticed," he deadpanned.

I tried not to smile by flattening my lips, but my cheeks gave me away. They were flaming hot. "What! What do you want me to say?"

He smiled and my gaze drifted to his hair. It was chalky and messy, and I had the sudden desire to know what it felt like against my skin. Feel the softness.

I shook my head, erasing the thoughts.

"All right," he said, stopping to look in my eyes. "Promise not to laugh?"

"Promise."

"My mom is a labor and delivery nurse. When my rips were getting bad and nothing was working," he said, shuffling through the bag and pulling out a purple box but keeping it out of view, "she came home with this stuff."

"What is it?"

Hayden opened his palm and showed me what was laying in it. "It's, ah, ointment," he said sheepishly.

"Let me see," I said, taking the purple box. Flipping it over, I read it out loud. "Lanolin. Soothes and protects cracked..." I trailed off. "Nipples?" Nipples came out high pitched and I looked up at him, bemused.

A rosy hue filled his cheeks and I couldn't help but grin.

"Yeah, it's nipple cream. My mom says mothers who breastfeed use it on their boobs to, ah," he avoided my gaze, "help with cracking and bleeding."

"Bleeding?" A frown formed on my face. "Bleeding nipples? And cracked?" My nipples ached at the thought.

"Yeah, well it works. Take my word for it. At least I didn't bring over nipple cream for cows."

"You mean to tell me you use nipple cream? Hayden Moore uses nipple cream on his hands."

I tried hard to hold it in, but a fit of hysterical laughter over the situation escaped.

"Oh, my God! Do you bring this to practice? Do you share it with your teammates? Do you buy this, or does your mom?"

Hayden didn't seem impressed with my questions, or the fact I that couldn't stop laughing. He leaned over, coming close to my face, and placed his hands on the counter next to each side of my legs, effectively putting his body directly between my thighs. He lifted a brow and waited for me to calm down. I tried to stop humiliating him by pursing my lips together, but I burst out again the moment I looked at his face.

"I'm sorry! I don't know why I find this so funny, I just do!" My head rolled back, tears coated my eyes as I imagined Hayden buying nipple cream and trying to hide it. He pressed a hand to my bare thigh in an effort to gain my attention.

"Laugh it up. By the end of the week you'll be kissing my feet and thanking me."

I grimaced. I hated feet. No way in hell would that happen, no matter how thankful I was.

"Done?" he asked, trying to hide his smirk. I flattened my lips and gave a hasty nod. It was the only way I wouldn't laugh.

Hayden's thumb grazed my skin in circles and it was then I realized he hadn't moved his hand from my thigh.

Our gazes grew deeper.

My breathing slowed as his head tilted just slightly to the side to take me in. I hadn't noticed before, but up close Hayden had the most stunning cobalt blue eyes.

Dark and elusive with shadows of slate gray hidden in between, he was pulling me into him, and he didn't even know it.

CHAPTER 16

y breathing deepened.

Hayden stood to his full height, stepping in closer between my legs so his waist was pressed to the countertop. My lips parted, a breath rolling off as he stared deeply into my eyes. His hand carefully cupped my cheek, his fingers holding my jaw steady. I swallowed when his eyes traveled to my mouth, his head dipping down just inches away from closing the distance.

"You're so pretty when you laugh, Aid," he whispered, his nose rubbing mine. Goose bumps broke out across my skin. "Your whole face lights up," he added, this time against my lips as his hand slipped into the back of my hair, kneading my head. "You can make fun of me all you want if it makes you laugh the way you just did."

He closed the short distance and pressed his lips to mine, soft and gentle. My heart pounded, unsure what to think of this moment.

Tenderly, he pulled my bottom lip into his mouth and nibbled on it. I gave in with only a slight hesitation. A simmering heat washed over me when his warm tongue slipped inside and met mine.

I moaned, liking Hayden's kiss. It was completely unexpected and I wasn't sure what to think. Not that I could—or wanted to. Leaning into him, I pressed my chest to his, my back arched and my hands came up to his firm shoulders before sliding into his chalky hair. Even with the fabric of my shirt between us, the heat of his bare skin against mine was heavenly.

Hayden deepened the kiss as I tugged on his hair, and my thighs squeezed his hips, feeling pleasure streaming through my body. Our mouths mimicked each other's, our tongues dancing perfectly as a sweet bliss hit both of us.

Hayden was a damn fine kisser.

And I had a pretty good idea he knew when he pulled me closer. He took control and set the pace, and I allowed it. There was no space between us, my legs wrapped around his back, and my heels pressed into him, wanting to feel him closer to me.

Hayden's mouth became aggressive. Pleasure flowed through my body, starting from my head down to the tips of my toes. A blaze of warmth steadily grew between us and we both drew from it. I'd kissed a couple boys before, but Hayden's kiss belonged in another league.

My hands moved from his hair down his neck and onto his firm pecks, skimming over his honey colored skin. He exuded strength beneath my touch, and I wanted to feel every inch of his body. Moving to his hips, the back of my knuckles danced over the V that dipped into his sweatpants. His stomach twitched, and he squeezed me just a little tighter. Sliding around to his back, I cupped his round ass. This time it was his turn to groan into my mouth, and I liked the sound of it. I gave his ass a little squeeze and he tensed.

"Hayden," I whispered against his lips, but he didn't process my words. His hands didn't stop caressing and kneading my waist, my back, or my thighs. He was everywhere.

"Aid," he mumbled on my lips, palming my cheeks.

"Hmm?"

"I want to feel you all over me." Then he slammed his mouth to mine. His hands roamed my body, as if he couldn't touch me fast enough. My panties dampened at his touch. Hayden moved my hand to the front of his pants to cup his hardness. I held back a grimace, my palms pulsated from my rips, but I sucked it up because curiosity got the best of me. The urge to dip my hand inside his pants was strong. I wasn't a prude, but I didn't have a ton of experience either. I'd had a boyfriend back home who I'd fooled around with, but nothing serious. When he realized gymnastics was more important to me than having sex with him, he dropped me like a bad habit. I was fine with that.

My chest rose and fell, my breathing deepened at the contemplation of my hand exploring him.

The heat of his breath tickled my cheek. "What are you thinking?" he asked roughly.

I had a feeling the look in his eyes mimicked mine. Heavy and glossy, drowning in the intense air enveloping us.

Unable to find the right words, I showed him. My nails grazed the lip of his low sitting sweatpants ever so slowly. Hayden drew in a shaky breath and his hands tightened on my nape, my head tilted back. His jaw flexed as the tips of my fingers dipped inside and brushed his pubic hair. I swallowed hard.

"I think we should stop," he said gutturally.

I paused, insecurity consuming me. "Oh, okay. Am I doing something wrong?" Maybe this was another reason my ex-boyfriend dropped me.

"No," he murmured. "You're not doing anything wrong, it feels good, but if you keep touching me like—"

He cut himself off, clutching my wrist tightly. My fingers were about to slide deeper when he stopped them.

"Adrianna. Do you know how good this feels?"

"No," I answered quietly when he released my wrist.

A brow lifted and he placed his hand on my hip. "Have you ever had a boyfriend?"

"Yes."

His other hand stayed in my hair. "And?"

"We didn't do much, just played around."

"You're a virgin," he stated more than asked. I nodded, inhaling. "I don't think this is such a good idea," he said.

Just as I thought he was about to pull away, Hayden dove in for another kiss, claiming my mouth. For me, that was the green light to dive into him.

Hayden held my face between his hands as he devoured my kiss, my hands slid around his hips. His hands quickly shifted to my chest and I released a little sigh. My stomach tightened and my heart jumped into my throat at the thought of what he—we—would do next. His fingers ran over the sides of my breasts, and my fingertips plunged into the waistband of his sweats and pushed them down just a bit so I could feel how low the V dipped.

He broke the kiss and stepped back.

"No, no more," he panted. My lips were swollen and my breath heavy when he pulled away. "I don't know what I was thinking. This is a big no for our gym. If any coach found out, we could get in a whole lot of trouble. We don't need that."

Overwhelmed with lust, I didn't take a moment to stop and think about how this could affect us down the line. Looking at the ground, I apologized.

"Hey, there's nothing to be sorry about, okay? I liked kissing you and, under different circumstances, maybe we would've kissed longer, but we have bigger things to focus on." He ran a hand through his hair and blew out a ragged breath. "Let's get those hands fixed for you."

Turning my hands over, I chuckled remorsefully at the blisters. "You know, I forgot my hands hurt. You took the pain away for a bit."

The dimples in his cheeks appeared and his eyes glistened. My stomach was full of butterflies and my heart pounded in my chest.

Hayden was so damn cute.

Opening the package, he took out the ointment and uncapped it. He squeezed a small amount on his fingers. "I'm just going to apply this to your wrists right now. Before bed, you'll need to apply a generous amount to your palms and put socks over your hands. Otherwise, it'll get everywhere."

Hayden clutched my wrist and turned my hand over. "Luckily you don't have rips on your wrists too from grips and tape, so this will help heal them nicely."

He began applying the balm, rubbing it into my skin and making sure it got absorbed. "You know we're going to need to pull those off, right?"

I groaned. "Do we have to?"

"I think you know the answer to that."

I did.

His skillful fingers did wonders to my aching muscles and I almost groaned from the sheer delight of the massage. Maybe I needed to hire a masseuse. "You have no idea how good this feels. My wrists are always in pain."

"I overheard what Kova said, how you hang on the bar and all. To be honest, it's amazing you've lasted this long. Between the grip on bars and the bizarre way you wrap your wrists, I'm surprised you haven't quit."

Never. There wasn't a chance in hell I'd ever quit gymnastics.

He grabbed my other wrist and changed his tone. "I'll be honest. I like you, Adrianna. I have since the moment I met you." He shook his head and then met my eyes. "There's a light in your eyes, a will I don't see often from the other girls at World Cup. I see the way Coach grates on you, pushes you down, picks at every little thing, but you never give up. Sometimes I wonder if he has it out for you. You don't cry, you don't want empathy, you don't walk around with a chip on your shoulder—"

"Like Reagan."

He smiled softly, and my heart melted. "Like Reagan. You're determined."

I bit the inside of my lip. "I feel like that's how all the girls are though."

"Yeah, but I don't know." He shrugged. "You're just different."

Reaching into his bag, Hayden pulled out a package of needles and a lighter.

"No," I whined, knowing what those were used for.

He paused. "You have to, Aid. You know this."

I did know this. It didn't mean I wanted to do it.

"This can't be worse than straddling the beam."

I pursed my lips together. "You may have a point, but this is going to make tomorrow even more painful and you know it."

"No, *not* popping them will make it worse. You have to drain them. At least get the fluid to release a little. I won't do to you what I do to my hands, I'll just pop at the corners."

Curious, I asked, "What do you do for your hands?"

"I pop the blisters and then cut the skin off all in one shot. I don't wait for the skin to tear back and die."

I grimaced. I wasn't going that far tonight. Hayden began lighting the needle to sterilize it and prevent an infection, after which he planned to use it to pop my blisters. I'd had rips and blisters before, but never to this extent. I was always given time to heal my hands, so I never really had to treat my skin to this degree before.

"Do you have any other ointment in your bag of tricks? Like some antibacterial kind? I can use that." My heart began to pound. I really didn't want to do this.

"Yeah, but you know none of that will help."

Hayden stepped back and I jumped down off the counter and reached for the filmy, plastic bag and began rummaging through it. Chap Stick, tape, scissors, socks, honey, a pumice stone, antibacterial ointment, all things used for rips.

No...

I pulled the stone out of the bag, but Hayden yanked it out of my hand and held it above his head.

"Give it back to me."

"No."

I jumped, trying to reach it, but it was useless. I was too short.

"Hayden, it's one thing to pop my blisters and cut off the dead skin. It's another thing entirely to scrub my hand. Just please give that to me. You're not doing it." I knew what would happen after.

The dreaded pumice stone. Fuck that. I'd never had to go that far with the stone, mainly because I never had a psychotic coach before like Kova, or gym hours like I did now, but I'd heard war stories, and it wasn't something I wanted to test out.

Plus, they didn't look terribly bad. I may have overreacted with how they looked.

"You know I'll just be back here tomorrow, right?"

"Please," I begged, my forehead bunching together. "Please, Hayden, I'll take my chances. You can drain the blisters, but no stone."

Hayden's eyes softened, pitying me. "Are you sure that's what you want to do? I'm obviously not going to scrub the blisters, just around them to get the calluses off, but you need to start using it every night in the shower to toughen the skin."

I shrugged helplessly, sighing. "I know, and I will after these heal."

"Fine." He cocked his head to the side with a know-it-all look. "Are you a religious person?" he asked out of the blue.

Puzzled, I said, "I mean, we go to church on major holidays, but we're not devout Catholics or anything. Why?"

"Because you're going to need the grace of God on your side tomorrow. I'll be praying for mercy and that Kova will go light on you. Now give me your hand and let's work on those rips."

CHAPTER 17

Yesterday morning when my alarm went off, the first thing I did was remove the socks.

The swelling on my hands had gone down tremendously, and the redness on my wrists looked almost healed. The nipple cream was like a magic potion. After practice, I had Alfred take me to the nearest pharmacy to buy every tube I could get my abused hands on.

Much to my surprise, Kova took mercy on me and gave me a day off from bars. It didn't follow into the next day though, because when I walked into the gym this morning, he insisted we work on bars again first thing. He wasn't confident I had learned my lesson.

"You should have popped those," he said arrogantly in a thick Russian accent, eyeing my blistered hands. I swear, because I hadn't popped them entirely, he'd do anything he possible could to make me suffer.

I was certain Kova was a sadist.

Reaching inside my bag, I pulled out a string of tape Hayden had prepared for me. He cut some pieces and showed me how I should apply them to cover my blisters since I wouldn't be allowed to use my grips. "Can I at least use this?"

Kova stepped over the cables and looked down. "Go ahead, it won't help though."

I ignored his flippant tone. Anything would help at this point. I looked at the rest of the team girls, envying the grips they had covering their hands. Placing the strip over the blisters, I ripped a piece of tape from the roll with my teeth and layered it. I was tempted to tape my entire hand, but I wasn't that ballsy to take the chance of getting yelled at and being forced to remove all of it and go bare skinned. I repeated the same method on my other hand and then applied chalk. Lots and lots of chalk.

"Did you stretch out this morning?"

I nodded.

"My way or yours?"

"My way."

He gave me a pointed look. "I did not see you stretch."

"Uh, when...when you were in the back," I stammered. "I warmed up with the girls."

"Did you run?"

Shit. "No, I didn't."

He glowered. "Before you break for lunch, you will run, and you will do three miles." Fuck my life. I hated cardio. "Have you been using any of the drills I showed you?"

Jesus Christ. This felt an awful lot like an interrogation. Like I was under the spotlight. The urge to lie was stronger than ever, but for some reason, I just couldn't. Call it intuition, but I had a feeling he'd know I was being dishonest. "No, I haven't. I mean I have, just not every time."

"You are not proving anything to me this morning, Ria. When I am not around, you must still use these exercises on your own. You are only hurting yourself in the long run." He clucked his tongue in disappointment. "Tonight, after practice, we will work together again before you leave."

Ria? The way he said it gave me butterflies. That was a new one, and I liked it a million times more than Ana.

"All right, let us go." He clapped his hands enthusiastically and stood near the low bar, watching me closely. That was it. No yelling, scowling, or glaring at me? His cheerful mood caught me off guard, and I wasn't sure what to think of it.

Swinging into a kip, I cast to a handstand, free hip circle cast to another handstand, then I piked down and used my core and hips to release and fly to the high bar. Coach watched my posture closely, probably analyzing every little thing I did wrong so he could berate me later. All I wanted to do was please him and prove I was trying, but it never came off that way.

Kova was hard and honest to a fault, which is what I'd wanted when I transitioned to World Cup. It was something every coach should be, regardless of our feelings, but some days we needed a break. Some days it was too much. Some days it could break our spirit.

I found myself making more mistakes than normal when his eyes were trained this closely on me, or when his hands touched me when he spotted. He didn't miss a beat and if I messed up, he caught it and corrected me immediately. He had eagle eyes, and that was both a blessing and a curse for a gymnast.

When my hands gripped the high bar, chalk dust sprinkled in my eyes and I winced. There was a slight burn but I ignored it and continued. I'd use that mind over matter logic and push through the pain.

I could do it. I knew I could.

A simple back tuck for my dismount and I felt more confident with my feet on the soft, blue landing mat. The pain in my hands wasn't nearly as bad as I anticipated, however, I felt a pull in the back of my calf I wasn't used to. Bending down, I rubbed the twinge of heat and walked away wiggling my leg with each step.

Chalking up, Kova moved the spring board to the front of the low bar. "We are going to start with your mount," he said, his eyes raking over my body from head to toe. "We are going to change it up."

"What? Why?"

He expelled an annoyed sigh. "Adrianna, it is too early for your questions this morning. Just do as I ask and do not question everything I say. It is exhausting. Think you can handle that and just keep quiet?" When I didn't move, he voiced, "It will help with your score. Now please just do as I say."

Well *excuse* the fuck out of me. "Sure."

"You are going to do a hecht mount. I will adjust the low bar so you can get used to it. We are going to do this until we nail it. The key to this mount is to pop off with your shoulders without bending your elbows. Arch your back just a tad once you release the low bar and keep those legs tight and together."

Tight lipped, I nodded. I actually knew how to do this, but I wasn't going to tell him. He told me to keep quiet, after all. I grinned to myself when I turned around and walked to the end of the mat, gearing up.

"The bar is low enough that you should have no issue getting over it. I will spot just in case," he said, and I nodded.

Call me crazy, but I wanted to fuck with his head. It seemed he had little faith in me as it was, so why not?

Wiping the excess chalk from my hands onto my legs, I shook my hands out. Sprinting toward the apparatus, I jumped off the springboard, pushed off the low bar and reached for the high bar. In doing so, Coach wasn't prepared for me to actually reach the bar the first time, so when he stepped in to spot and catch me, I plowed right into him. He stumbled, tripping over his feet and fell to the ground, his eyes going wide. I missed the bar and landed partially on his hard body, trying not to laugh. My cheeks burned and I rolled my lips into my mouth when we locked eyes.

Coach moved me off him and stood slowly, towering over me. "I am glad you find humor in this. Why did you not tell me you knew how to do the hecht mount?" he said gravely.

"You told me to just keep quiet." I stifled a laugh, returning his words once I stood.

Rubbing a hand down his face, his jaw flexed. He looked like he was struggling between the pros and cons of strangling me.

"I have never, in all my years of training, had a smart-mouthed one like you. You think this is all fun and games." Lowering his voice, he steadily said, "Get back over there and do it again."

"Yes, sir!" I joked, trying to lighten the mood. Holly snickered from the side, while Reagan gave me a death stare.

I wasn't sure why, but I was in a playful mood this morning. However, when I turned to Coach right before going again, he most definitely was not.

Just another prime example of my mouth getting me in trouble, even when it was closed.

⚡︎

IT WAS THE END OF the day, and I was dead exhausted. After a long session on bars, I worked beam, which was a blessing in disguise considering how much I hated it. Hardly any abuse was done to my hands. It was a nice little break until I got to vault. The pain had subsided since this morning, but I wasn't stupid. I'd have to take care of the rips properly.

Everyone had gone home for the evening and here I was, stuck in the gym after hours, waiting on Coach for one of his "not stretching, but stretching" drills. I rolled my eyes hearing his voice inside my head saying it.

"I hope that eye roll was not for me," Kova stated, swiftly walking past me. I had no idea where the hell he came from. The man loved to appear out of thin air.

Keeping up with his long stride, I nearly had to power walk to keep up with him. "Uh, nope. I just have some chalk in my eye."

"Right," he responded, drawing out the word. He knew I was lying.

When we made it into the therapy room, he flipped on the lights and got right to it.

"I think an hour in here will do, but Adrianna, I do not teach you these drills for fun. I expect to see and hear that you have been doing them. You have to trust it will help down the line."

Hayden's voice drifted through my mind about trusting my coach. I nodded and decided to go with the truth. "To be honest with you, I don't feel I get the same effect doing it myself. You applied a lot of pressure and held me in the position. I can't do that myself in the same manner you can."

Folding his arms across his chest, Coach studied me. I hoped he saw the conviction in my eyes. While I could do the drills, what I confessed was the truth. I didn't get the same result from doing them myself.

Kova strode over to where I was standing. He captured my gaze and stood inches from me, placing his hands on my biceps.

Affection laced his voice as he said, "If you need me, all you have to do is say something. That is what I am here for, Ria."

Heat rose to my cheeks as the intensity of his gaze thickened. Truth was, I did need him, and he clearly knew it.

His hands slowly slid down my arms to just above my elbows. My heartbeat quickened and I inhaled through my nose to steady my breathing. He gave me a gentle squeeze before releasing me, and ushered me over to the therapy table.

Even after hours of training gymnasts, I could still smell the faint scent of his spicy cologne.

"You will only set yourself back if you do not use what is readily available to you. *Me.*"

Him?

"That is what I am here for." He cleared his throat. "What Madeline is here for. Use us, ask questions."

I bit the inside of my lip. He was right. "I just try not to ask too many questions, you know? I like to show I can do things on my own."

He raised a brow and countered me. "You?" A sexy grin slowly appeared on his face and my cheeks grew hot. "You love to talk back. Is it not almost the same thing as asking questions?"

I lowered my face, trying to hide my growing smile. I bobbed my head, agreeing with him. Kova slipped two fingers under my chin and raised my head so our eyes met again. His touch was thrilling and caused a rush of heat to stream through my body. My heartbeat picked up and the energy in the room grew thicker.

My lips parted as we stared into each other's eyes, unsure what to think. This man was beyond confusing, and his touch left me with questions. Questions I had about myself and my reaction to him. Thing was, I began to like the attention he showed me, liked the touch of his hands and the way they seemed to linger on me.

"Remember to use your resources, Ria. I am sure your dad would agree with me on that."

Yeah, I was pretty sure he didn't want me to use my resources in the way my body wanted to at the moment. Especially not with the way I stared at my coach's mouth.

"Why do you call me Ria and not Ana like my parents?"

He paused. "It suits you better. Ana sounds like a child's name, *Ria.*" His thumb caressed the side of my face. "And you are no child, not to me at least."

Kova dropped his hand and walked to the side of the table, murmuring under his breath in Russian. My heart was nearly in my throat and my eyes were huge. Never once had Kova touched me so...so...I wasn't even sure what to call it. Adoringly. Affectionately.

"Okay, we are going to do the same drills as last time, but add in a few more that will be helpful to you. Get on your back and bring one leg to your chest. Hold it for me."

"Yes, sir!" I replied sarcastically, which earned me a smile from him. "I'm sorry, sometimes I can't help it."

Kova shook his head and laughed lightly. "Never had a gymnast quite like you before," he said. "Never a dull moment."

My face lit up. "Why, thank you!" My reply came out in more of a grunt when he leaned in with his body. Kova used one hand to press my knee to my chest, the other on my thigh to hold me down. While I'd been joking only seconds before, the fun was over and I had to focus. Only, it was difficult to focus when all I could think about was how his fingers had been on me and the reason why he called me Ria. Not to mention, where his hands were at the present moment. Well, one hand.

On the crease of my hip and covering most of the mini shorts I had on. His large hand dug into my skin, his fingers pressing down. I wasn't sure why, but I liked his hold on me more than I knew I should.

His touch was hot and my body responded to it.

My hips began to slowly open up as Kova got close to my face.

"You feel that? How your body is relaxing and releasing?"

I think he meant opening up, but I didn't correct his English. Instead, I nodded with my lips pressed together.

"I actually feel it this time."

"Good." He pushed a little more. "This is what we want." Kova held the position a few more seconds and then moved over to my right side. I switched legs and got into position.

"My left side is more flexible than my right." Just about every gymnast had one side that was more flexible than the other.

He dismissed it. "Not a problem for me."

When he pressed into my right leg, even after hours of training, my hip was still so tight I grunted.

"Let me guess, you forgot to breathe how I taught you," he stated more than asked, just inches from my face.

I pursed my lips. "Maybe..."

Kova shook his head, closing his eyes. "What am I going to do with you?" he asked jokingly.

I liked this side of him. He was playful and easy to be around. Not edgy and tense like he was in the mornings. Maybe our time should be restricted to the evening, but I doubted I could make that happen.

Just when I thought we were going to move into another position, Kova applied a heavy amount of pressure that caused my back to bow and my knee to lift in response. My knee was nearly past my shoulder now.

A grumble escaped me and I grabbed Kova for support. My small hand couldn't wrap around his wrist and he twitched under my touch.

"Adrianna, focus on breathing." When I didn't answer, he said, "Look into my eyes and focus. It does not hurt, I am not hurting you. Your muscles are just tight." His Russian accent was strong.

I nodded fast, locking eyes with him. "Breathe in through your nose and release it slowly," he guided me.

Kova's thumb drew small, little circles on my inner thigh, making my stomach flutter. The touch was light, but enough for me to notice. I didn't speak up in spite of knowing he probably shouldn't be doing this, especially considering how close he was to my sex. He was inches, literally just inches away, and I was okay with it.

I liked it.

I wanted to push myself closer to make him touch me.

He created a perfect storm of tension and heat around us. I held my breath as his hand skimmed higher up my thigh, slowly, almost seductively, and held it there. My stomach fluttered and I didn't know what to do other than to allow it.

I couldn't imagine my former coach being this close and touching me. The thought of it repulsed me, but with Kova, it was the complete opposite.

The small therapy room began to feel like a furnace, and I knew I needed to switch the focus to something else or else I was going to do something we both wanted.

CHAPTER 18

Kova?"

"Hmmm?"

"How come there's an A in your name now? Why not Kov?" I wasn't sure why I asked all of a sudden.

Kova stiffened, taking a moment to answer. "My mother always called me Kova since I was a young boy, even though it was not my given name. I never questioned why she did, but now I wish I had. She used to say it like it was an endearment and I loved it. In Russia, female last names end in—"

"Ova."

He tilted his head to the side, interested. "You know Russian?"

"No, but I know about the language through my family's friends."

He nodded. "So then you know males end with Ov."

"I do."

Kova leaned back, his hand dancing down to my knee and gave me a very tender squeeze. "Turn onto your stomach and scoot over."

Without questioning him, I did as he asked. He brought my hands to the side of my head and flattened them, then he climbed onto the table.

Grabbing my ankle, he made a fist and pushed it into my glute. When he lifted my ankle and pressed down, I grunted. My fingers pressed into the table and my nails turned white from the tightness in my hip. I peeked over my shoulder, trying to see his face.

"So my mother had me out of wedlock. I took her last name, but was given the male version. It is why you see my awards and titles with Kournakov instead of Kournakova. I added an A in honor of her the first chance I got."

"Out of wedlock? Kova, no one says that." I laughed lightly, trying to lighten the mood. "Where is your father?"

Embarrassment clouded his eyes. "I do not know. I have never met him." Shame laced his quiet tone and I felt bad for asking.

"Oh," was all I could say. I wasn't sure how to respond to his admission, but I was curious to know more about the story now. I wanted to know if he was the result of a one-night stand or a boyfriend who took off after he was born, not wanting to be a dad. Or maybe he passed away when Kova was younger. My brows furrowed, my mind playing out so many alternatives as I wondered about all the different ways this story could go, but I never expected his next words.

"She was raped," he confessed quietly, completely avoiding eye contact now.

"What?" I gasped, trying to sit up, only he pressed down harder and lifted my leg higher.

"She was raped," he repeated, and my heart broke at his forlorn voice. I wish I could see his face. I couldn't imagine any child would want to know they were born from such a vicious crime, but he knew.

"Your mom told you she was raped?" I asked, astonished.

"Not at first. Only when I pressed her enough about my father did she open up. When I got older, she finally told me the truth."

I'd never known anyone who was raped, or had been the product of one. "What did you think when she told you?"

He snarled, jumping down and moving to the other side of the table. "That I wanted to kill him. You see, my mother was my hero. Unlike for you, my mom was my role model. She did anything and everything she could for me, to give me what I needed to succeed because she did not have the support she needed when she was growing up. She was alone. It was not her fault she got pregnant with me, and she did not have to keep me. It was a brave choice she made. So when I found out about the rape, pure hatred ran through me."

He applied the same method to my other leg. "So you have no idea who he is then." I couldn't imagine what that would feel like. While my dad wasn't around a lot due to his business, he was still there.

"Oh, I have an idea who he is."

"What? How? I don't understand."

"He is my cousin."

What. In. The. Ever. Loving. Fuck.

"How can that be? That's...but that's incest..." I tried to turn around again, but he put a stop to it. Now I wish I had waited to change the subject so I could read his facial expressions.

"She said growing up he had always touched her in places no one ever had. But she was scared to go to her parents because she was not sure if it was really wrong. It was her family."

"How come your mom didn't go to the police after it happened? Tell her parents? What do they think now?"

Kova tapped the back of my thigh and I turned back over. He guided me to the yoga mat on the floor near the wall.

"Kneel with your back to the wall, about two feet away. Arms up." I did as he asked, and looked up at him expectantly for him to answer my questions.

He got on his knees to the left of me and looked at me sadly, shaking his head. "She did, but no one believed her. Shortly after she found out about the pregnancy, she was thrown out with nowhere to go. She went to some church that housed pregnant teenagers but then moved out after I was born. Soon after she left, she realized she could not afford to live on her own and ran into an old friend from the church she had met. She was working in a gentleman's club and offered my mom quick cash and a babysitter on hand. So she took it. It was the only way she could support us."

I looked into Kova's tortured eyes and my heart bled for him, but my ears were eager for more. He placed a flat hand to my shoulder blade and angled me back so my arms were straight and my hands were flat on the wall. I grunted at this odd position of a half back bend.

"Why didn't she leave once she had enough money saved up?"

"Because she could never make the money she did while working behind the counter as a cashier. When I asked her, she said she did not want to struggle and wanted me to have everything she did not have."

He moved to the front of my body and placed both hands low on my hips. Gently and carefully, he pulled them forward with a squeeze. His thumbs pressed daringly into my hip bones and a shot of heat jolted through me. My chest burned and my heart raced. Even after all the hours of practice today, I felt the burn from the stretch, but more outrageously, I could feel heat radiating off him.

The cloth of his shorts danced against my bare legs. I took a deep breath and exhaled. He relaxed his hold, allowing me to breathe. My hips shifted back for a moment, but he never removed his hands.

"Once I got into gymnastics at a competitive level, I am sure you can understand how expensive it was for her, there was no way she was stopping. She said she saw potential in me," he huffed sadly as he drew my hips toward him again. Breathe, I told myself. *Breathe.* But it was more difficult than I deemed possible with my hips pinned to his. I wondered if he realized our position. My body tightened and I nearly fell over, but I kept my composure as he continued.

"She made sure she was at every practice, at every meet, and paid for it all on her own."

His mother sacrificed anything and everything to give the son, who was a product of rape, a life she never had, and Joy, my mom, the socialite who threw money at her problems, was the ice queen extraordinaire and more concerned about what I ate than what actually went on with me.

Kova's eyes grew distant, filling with longing and grief, his mouth a firm, grim line. "I did not need anything, though. I would give up everything, give it all back, to have her here." The warmth of his hands heated my hips. He breathed his pain into me through his touch. Sorrow coursed through his tone and I believed every word that left his mouth.

My heart ached, feeling so incredibly empty for Kova and the life his mother was dealt. Life wasn't fair sometimes.

"So after she died, I added an A to my last name for her. I did not want to ever forget her or what she gave up for me."

I couldn't take anymore, from both his words and this new skill. Tears brimmed the back of my eyes while I listened to him talk about his mother and her struggles. I placed my hands at the crook of his arms to comfort him, his hands still clutching my hips, tenderly now. Warmth spread throughout my body being face-to-face and just inches apart. Kova peered down at me through hooded eyes as I said in a cracked whisper, "That is the most incredible thing I have ever heard."

He continued softly. "She came to my first two Olympics with me. She was so happy, happier than I was I think. It meant so much to me she was there, too. However, when my third Games came around for me, she was too ill to travel. In fact, her doctors were highly against it, so I gave it up to be with her. She was upset I did, but I had no choice. She was always there for me. How could I not be there for her? The alternate gymnast on the team stepped in and ended up taking home some medals of his own, then went on to compete in the Games four years later." He grew quiet, seemingly lost in his thoughts. "I do not regret it at all. I got to be with my mom and take care of her as she did for me, and someone else got their chance at the Olympics. Is it not crazy how things happen?"

I knew what he meant. Being an alternate on the Olympic team pretty much meant you were a bench warmer—that was it.

I wanted to turn away from his anguished filled gaze, but I couldn't. He'd expose himself in ways I never anticipated. Raw emotion came from him in waves, and it was felt deep inside my gut. I didn't know what to do or what to say next. I had hardly experienced life the way Kova had, let alone death. I grew up with a silver spoon in my mouth and had everything I could ever want. Kova had not.

So all I stupidly said was, "Yeah, it is."

Kova leaned in and tightened his hold. One hand slid around to the small of my back as my hands moved to flatten on his firm chest. His fingers splayed out dangerously down my ass, one digit pressed between the center. I held my breath. The heat of his hands seared through my leo and I fought back a tremor. He was just an inch away from my lips when his eyes traveled down to my mouth.

"Thanks for listening to me, Ria."

Ria. I smiled, liking the nickname an awful lot.

Slowly, he inched closer, and my heart beat rapidly against my chest at his nearness. I had no idea what he was about to do, and I briefly wondered if he'd kiss me. He was my coach. No way would he do that.

Unease swept through me without an inkling of how to proceed. Never mind I knew what I was supposed to do, should've moved away, not silently wished he'd press his lips to mine.

The stillness between us was thicker than humidity, and it took all of me not to lean in to kiss him. I knew I should've been repulsed by him, but oddly enough, I wasn't. I was intrigued if anything. Every fiber in my body told me to lean in, not run in the other direction.

"A couple of weeks ago you said something in Russian...it started with an M. May-lash-a? What did it mean?"

A smiled curled his full lips. "Maa-lish. Malysh." My sight trained on his mouth, his tongue tapped his top teeth as he said again, "Ma-lysh." The word washed over me in a wave of rapture.

"How do you spell it?"

"M-A-L-Y-S-H." His accent was stronger than ever.

Our breaths mingled, and one of Kova's hands carefully slid up my waist and rested on my ribs. His thumb ran in circles, his body creating heat between us as he caressed me. He slid his hand onto my back and up to my nape where he cupped my neck. My breathing deepened and I thought I was going to hyperventilate if I didn't calm my racing heart. His dark brows formed a deep V and his shrewd eyes didn't waver.

"What does it mean?" I asked softly, my back arching and my chest nearly pressed to his.

He shook his head as if he didn't want to say. "It was an accident. I did not mean to say it."

I frowned at him. "Please? I want to know."

His deep stare caused my stomach to flutter. One hand brazenly moved up to rest on his firm pectoral. My fingers spread out and he flexed under my touch, his fingers pressing deeper into me in response.

"Baby," he said gutturally. "It means baby."

Baby. He had accidently called me baby just weeks ago. I had to wonder why the word would have been on his mind to begin with if it was an accident like he declared.

My gaze traveled down his straight nose to his mouth, where it stayed. My head tilted to the side as my eyes traced his full, *kissable* lips, wondering what they'd feel like pressed to mine. His Adam's apple bobbed slowly, like he took a long, hard swallow.

This wasn't me. I didn't kiss my coach, teacher, or really anyone older than the legal age, or someone who was off limits. Not that I'd ever had the desire as I did now. I'd heard countless stories over the years of gymnast and coach relationships, some consensual, some not. Though, not nearly as many as the married moms having affairs with coaches.

With that being said, in this moment, I could fully understand why some of those forbidden relationships were acted upon. This was completely and utterly enthralling. Nothing was forced. It was a craving woven with lust, a newfound hunger clawing inside.

"You are done for the day," he abruptly said in a broken whisper. As Kova stood, something hard dragged up the inside of my thigh. He placed a hand out to help me up and I hissed as my skin made contact with his. I'd forgotten I had rips the entire time I was with him. He turned my hand over and inspected them, his thumb delicately running in circles on my palm.

"Sorry about these." Then he turned his back to me and left, leaving me speechless.

It was then I realized Kova had a thick and hard erection

CHAPTER 19

Two things I was sure about.

One: Hayden was right about treating my hands properly.

Two: There was something mentally wrong with my coach.

I paced my condo, wearing out my carpet while I waited for Hayden to show up again. He'd be here any minute to help me out.

Today had been awful, the pain, unbearable at one point. So crippling, it nearly brought me to tears, but I sucked it up and refused to give them to him. I guess Kova thought I was in dire need of training because we spent hours together. Him screaming at all the little things I did wrong had me wanting to throw a block of chalk at his head. The tutoring between gym sessions that gave my hands a little break, but it wasn't enough. They needed days to heal.

After changing a few things up in my routine, Kova made me repeat it until I couldn't get it wrong. Every single skill, he had a conditioning technique for. Don't get me wrong, it was a good thing, but it can also become tedious, and quite frankly, fucking annoying at times. He was on top of everything I did, breathing down my neck, ready to attack. More so than usual. He reminded me of a gnat that just wouldn't go away. Always in my ear, always making sounds. I'd banged my shins, jammed my toes on the bars, and even lost my grip due to exhaustion and fell on my hips. The bar had caught me, not the floor. There was only so much one could handle after hours of relentless coaching.

It wasn't long after the change in my routine that my rips got caught and the skin tore back. Sometimes when the pain is so severe, you don't feel the injury, and that's exactly what happened to me. I was chalking up, too focused on Coach explaining something, when he paused and pointed it out. I looked down at my bloody hands covered in chalk and shrugged. There wasn't much else I could do at that point. I couldn't very well beg for mercy and ask to move to beam where my hands could get a little break. Although, I'm sure he would've loved that.

And as much as I hated to admit it, the outcome had been rewarding. I knew I had nailed my routine near the end, and the slight smile on his face confirmed it. He was proud of me, though he struggled with the words. Like every man in the world did.

My hands had gone through the stages of hell, from feeling like I had dipped them into a fiery red ant pile, to being completely numb. I had managed to block the pain and push through it and not complain, and I think that bought me some points in his book. At least I hoped it had.

I was sure Coach Kova thrived on the tears of young hopefuls, it was the only thing I could come up with at this point. He was a raging lunatic when he wanted to be.

But surprisingly, he could be rather tender too...

I could still feel his hands on me, the whisper of breath that rolled across my cheek, the way his erection glided up my thigh. I couldn't get the image out of my head. He'd been on my mind since our private session, and astonishingly for the first time, I actually looked forward to another one. Kova opened up and showed me a different side of him, one I was curious to learn more about. A side that made him human, one that had a heart.

A knock at the door shook me from my thoughts, and I ran toward it. Hayden stood on the threshold with another pharmacy bag.

"You know, I'm gonna have to start charging an in-house doctor fee."

I laughed, welcoming him in. "Bill me."

"So are you regretting not listening to me?"

"Do you think it would have made a difference in the end?" I held up my palms to him. Hayden grimaced, shaking his head.

"Honestly, I'm not so sure."

He placed the plastic bag on the counter and then walked over to me. Taking one of my hands into his, he used his thumb to feel around my palms. Aside from the actual blisters, my skin had rolled up and peeled in various places. Those weren't too bad, they were manageable. It was tender behind my knuckles, so that always tore first and caused the most pain.

"We should probably do this in the bathroom, or over the kitchen sink. It's going to get messy."

My heart dropped, fear exploded through me of what was soon going to take place. Before he began, Hayden pulled out a small steel container from his duffle bag.

"But first, you're going to need this."

"What is it?"

"A flask of vodka."

I frowned. "I can't drink all that. I'll get sick."

He was amused. "Not all of it, of course you'll get sick. Only a shot or two to help take the edge off. Have you ever had vodka before?"

A tremor worked through me at the memory. "Yeah, once with my best friend, Avery. Let's just say it didn't go over well."

Hayden walked through my kitchen and looked through my cabinets as if it was a completely natural thing for him to do.

"You look good," I admitted, slamming my mouth shut.

Hayden glanced over his shoulder with a saccharine smile I'd come to really like seeing. He wore a dark pair of distressed jeans, molded to his butt and thighs, and a solid white shirt that accentuated his biceps. He was jacked and looked better than any other guy his age.

"Not too bad yourself." I glanced down at my rolled up shorts and flannel, button-down shirt. My long auburn hair was braided loosely to the side with little pieces sticking out and I was makeup free. I looked ready for a hayride.

I walked over to Hayden and watched as he poured two small drinks. "This shouldn't really hit you hard, but it should help."

"Where did you get it from?"

"Snatched it before my mom packed up. She won't even notice it's missing".

"Why are you having it, too?"

"To help with what I'm going to do to you."

"Oh..." I frowned.

He handed me a glass and asked, "Ready?"

I took a deep breath. "Ready as I'll ever be." Then we clinked glasses and tipped them back quickly. I wasn't a fan of vodka, or any other liquor, so I swallowed fast and cringed, shivering hard.

"Gross." I made a disgusted face and Hayden laughed. "Do you drink often?"

He looked at me like I was dense. "No, Aid, how could I with training?"

I shrugged. "Well, I don't know! I'm just asking."

"No, hardly ever. Only when the time calls for it. Go ahead and wash your hands so we can get started." I did as Hayden requested while he rummaged through his stuff.

"You think Coach is going to go easy on you tomorrow?"

I turned my battered hands over and said, "I don't think he has a choice, you know? We worked on bars all day—"

"I know. He doesn't normally do that. You'd think he was purposely torturing you."

I paused. "What do you mean?"

Hayden turned around and leaned against the countertop right next to the sink, while I rinsed my hands. He crossed his arms in front of his chest. "I've been training there for years and I've never seen him work an entire day on one event, or push someone the way he does you. Don't get me wrong, he's a hard-ass coach and can be a real dick when he wants to be, but he grates on you. You'd think since your dad is friends with him he'd go a little easier, you know?"

I thought about what Hayden said and asked, "Do you think it's because I need a lot of work, more than what he's used to training?"

He shook his head, unsure. "You're really not that bad off, so I'm not certain what his issue is. Kova wants perfection, to be the best, better than anyone else. We can all appreciate it because it's what we want ourselves, but sometimes I think he pushes too much...I don't know. He can easily make people hate him, that's for sure. He only coaches the rings for my team, so I'm just analyzing from that, I don't spend as much time with him as you do."

I stood there, stunned. The only thing I could come up with was, "He must really hate me."

Hayden chuckled. "He doesn't hate you. Has he put you on a special diet yet?"

I eyed him wearily. "No? Do I need to be on one?"

"No, but his diets are ridiculous and we all swear when he reaches the diet level, it means he secretly despise you. Or so we all think.

Don't reach that level. He's only been that way with a few and let me tell you, it wasn't pretty."

Hayden was giving me anxiety. "What do you mean?"

"He follows this insane paleo related diet that only lets you consume under a thousand calories a day. With our workouts and the calories and fat we burn, you know we need more than that, or else it isn't healthy."

No, it's not. "Well, it can't be much worse than the diet my mom has imposed on me, so I'm sure I'd be fine." I paused. "Who has he been like that with?"

"Reagan and a few others who aren't here anymore."

My jaw dropped. "You're kidding."

He shook his head. "I wish I was."

"But Reagan's so good."

"Now she's his golden gymnast. He only had to build her to his level of perfection." He looked at me with raised brows. "And so were the others. Some went on to compete at Division One colleges, some even went to the nationals training camp in Texas. I'm telling you, he's a mean bastard, but he gets results. Don't give up or take it to heart."

I exhaled, releasing an envious breath over this news of Reagan. He knew my mom had me on a diet where my meals were delivered, so maybe I was already at that level since there was nothing left for him to do.

Feeling the vodka course through my veins just a little bit, I said, "Let's get this over with."

Hayden and I walked to my bathroom. He flipped on the lights and placed everything on the counter, pulling out the pumice stone, needles, a lighter, and hydrogen peroxide. I groaned when he sterilized the needle and wanted to cry at the sight of the brown bottle.

He filled the sink up with warm water and I soaked my hands for a few minutes to soften them up. Aside from the rips, I also had calluses on the backs of my fingers and middle of my palms, which were now raised and white, easy to find due to soaking.

Hayden took one of my hands into his and looked into my eyes before snipping the dead skin away. Then he took a dull butter knife, placed it at a ninety degree angle, and very gently shaved off the calluses. Little white flakes pooled in my palms. This part hadn't hurt, but my heart began to throb and panic battered through me. I didn't want to do the next step. My knees trembled and I thought I'd be sick. With the fear so high, maybe another shot of vodka would've helped.

"I don't want to hurt you, Adrianna."

I nodded and stepped closer to him. With the pumice stone in one hand, he held it above my palm and gripped my wrist tight so I couldn't pull away.

"I'm just going to file down the calluses and scrub around the rips." Tight lipped, I nodded. "Close your eyes."

The moment the stone hit my hand, my fingers retracted and curled up. Hayden forcefully held my hand open. He scrubbed each finger, filing down the calluses and then feeling for smoothness. It didn't hurt, but it didn't feel good either. Moving on to my palm, he used the stone for the rough skin around my rips. He accidently nicked a corner, apologizing profusely. I gripped Hayden's arm with my other hand, my nails dug into him as I gasped loudly, and my eyes squeezed shut as he began to scrub.

The pain.

The throbbing, pulsing, pain.

Heat seared my palm and went straight through my skin, hitting muscles and nerves as it radiated out the back of my hand, only to repeat, continuing on an endless loop. He was cautious not to hit an open rip, he knew better, but he did a few times.

Hayden scrubbed back and forth, pressing down so roughly I thought he would hit my bones. I instantly became nauseous and worried I'd throw up. I tried to focus on the scent of Hayden's cologne. The beach. Avery. Nothing helped. It hurt so much!

"Oh, my God! Please stop for a minute!" I shouted and he jumped. Opening my eyes, my stark white bathroom sink had crimson water running toward the drain and blood splatter that speckled the sides. With Hayden pressing down, blood automatically pushed through my rips. I couldn't see my palm, blood completely coated my hand.

"I'm sorry, I didn't mean to scream in your ear," I panted.

"It's okay. I'm just sorry I have to do this to you."

I swallowed hard, shaking with a pain so unbearable I couldn't find words. This was agony. Teardrops rested on my eyelids, but I refused to let them fall. After this, I'd make damn sure to never grip the bar wrong again.

"Here," Hayden said, seeing my eyes. "Try this. Stand behind me, wrap your other arm around my waist and squeeze me when it gets bad."

I nodded and did as he suggested. If I wasn't so consumed by pain, I would've noticed how nice it was to be pressed against his backside, or how well our bodies fit together.

My arm went around his stomach and I held him lightly, leaning my head against his back. Taking a deep breath, I exhaled. Maybe if I focused on his body, it wouldn't be as bad.

Who was I kidding? When he picked back up, I pressed into Hayden so hard, I felt his feet shift from my weight. I squeezed, holding him to me while I dug my head between his shoulder blades. I used every ounce of strength I had and held on for dear life. I didn't care that my boobs smashed into his back, or how my hips rolled against his ass and molded to him in a bit of a sexual way. The shots of pain were so awful, I bit him. I rose up on my toes and sank my teeth into his bicep. In some odd way, it helped.

"Almost done with this hand," he said over the running water, ignoring my bite. I leaned into him when he placed my hand under the warm water, removing the blood and feeling for the dead skin. Unconsciously, I squeezed him tighter, ringing his shirt in my fist, using him for strength because I knew what came next.

Hydrogen peroxide.

When I heard the cap flip, I gripped Hayden's stomach so hard I felt him flinch under me. I didn't mean to hurt him, but I didn't think I'd make it much longer before I passed out.

"How's it going with your private sessions with Kova?"

"Wh...What?"

More scrubbing. "Think about the question, Aid, not the pain."

"The question...What was the question?"

His back vibrated with a chuckle. "How are your private sessions going?"

"Ah, going well I guess..." I struggled for breath. "Not as bad or as weird as I expected."

"I take it you found something to talk about?"

I gripped his shirt tighter as he rinsed my hand. "We did…" I didn't want to go into detail about the conversation I'd had with Kova. It was private and I had a notion he didn't tell very many people, so I said, "As much as I appreciate what you're trying to do, Hayden, I can't think straight right now."

"Take a deep breath."

The cool liquid poured over my hand and I inhaled loudly, throwing my head back. White-hot pain shot through me and I almost blacked out. Tears coated my eyelashes but they didn't stream down my cheeks, and I clenched my teeth so hard I was sure I was seconds away from chipping one.

"Hayden, please," I begged. My hand shook violently under his hold. My fingers tried to curl up again, but Hayden held them open as he rubbed around the rips.

"Shhh…It's all right. We're almost done," he said apologetically. Hayden rinsed my hand again and plucked off any dead skin he missed with the nail clippers.

"I think I need another shot…Or an entire bottle. Make that two bottles before you do the other hand."

He laughed, his back vibrating against my cheek. "I'm pretty sure you'd die if you drank two bottles of vodka."

"I'll take my chances. It can't be worse than this."

Shutting the water off, Hayden turned around and I stepped away from him. My jaw dropped when I looked at my trembling hand. It looked like raw meat.

"We need to let it air dry before we put anything over it for the night," Hayden instructed.

"Do you think that's a good idea? To put stuff over it? Shouldn't I cover it during the day and let it breathe at night?" He looked at me like I should know the answer. "I've never done this before, Hayden, so I have no idea what to do."

Hayden's eyes softened. Using the pad of his thumb, he wiped away one lone tear. "Don't cry," he said sympathetically. The gesture was sweet and for some reason made me tear up even more. My jaw quivered and my chin dropped to my chest. I hated this, this pain, these emotions, this sport. I hated it all and wished it would go away. There was no way I could go through something like this again. If

Kova made me do any kind of bar work tomorrow or in the next few days, I would straight up murder him.

Hayden pulled me into a hug. Cradling my hand to my chest, I leaned into him and let the tears fall. Screw fighting it. This kind of torture would bring a grown man to his knees.

Exhaustion suddenly consumed me and I let out a loud sigh. "I'm sorry for crying."

He rubbed my back in circles and his hips dropped to the counter to sit. "Want to know a secret?"

"You seem to have a lot of secrets, Hayden."

He laughed. "The first time I had rips this bad, my mom had to take care of them the way I just did for you. I cried. Like a little, fucking baby, I cried and sobbed into her hard and she had to hold me afterward. It was embarrassing and I never forgot it. Since then, I've made sure to do everything humanly possible to avoid rips to this capacity ever again. I know it's inevitable, but I do try and I know you will too from here on out. I'll help you and show you what to do to toughen your skin up a bit more. Once your palms heal and new skin grows over, you'll need to pumice them every day. I feel your pain, Adrianna. I do, babe. And I'm sorry I had to cause you more."

I let his words sink in and relaxed a little into his body. For someone who was built with as much muscle as he was, Hayden was unexpectedly soft.

He dropped a friendly kiss to the top of my head and then said, "Let's take care of your other hand. Lucky for you, it isn't that bad off, so it shouldn't be as painful."

Shouldn't, being the key word.

CHAPTER 20

When I first moved to Cape Coral in March, I worried I'd be a little lonely, even though I was ready for more freedom. But with the training and long hours, and getting accustomed to my new life, I hadn't had time to actually feel alone. I guess it was a good thing. Weeks flew by, and before I knew it, summer training arrived. With no more school, it was train, train, train every minute of every day.

From what I'd heard, the members of World Cup and the coaches got together each year and had a Fourth of July barbecue. It was their way of bringing the team and coaches together and blow off a little steam. This year it was held at Kova's impressive two-story home that overlooked the intercoastal. Considering he was from Russia, I found it amusing he would host a holiday that celebrated America's Independence.

With the help of GPS, Alfred drove me to his house. Reagan arrived at the same time as me and we walked in together, without saying a word except to exchange pleasantries before going on our separate ways. They walked toward the grand windows that overlooked the river to where other people were outside, but I knew the first thing I needed to do was greet the host. Manners went a long way, and my mom always made sure we were courteous.

Kova's house was much bigger than I anticipated. He had a large, open floor plan and I wasn't sure which way to go first. From the amount of parties we had back home, it was a given the host would be in the kitchen prepping, so that's where I headed off to. I followed the sound of voices and water running and found the kitchen. As I drew closer, a pan clattered to the tile floor and I jumped. Faint, hushed voices filtered the air and I scrunched my brows trying to figure out who they belonged to. Rounding the corner, I knew for sure one was Kova, the other, I did not. My chest drew tight when

I realized I walked in on Kova and a stunning brunette having an obvious argument. Kova's jaw dropped then snapped back together, his arms flexed at his sides. The woman's face faltered when the bitter bite of low words were exchanged from Kova. The tension was so thick between them it was suffocating. I couldn't make out what was said since it was in Russian, but whatever it was couldn't have been good because she looked on the verge of tears. Kova turned and forcefully threw something into the sink, and it rebounded around the stainless steel. He placed his hands on the ledge and leaned over, his eyes clenched shut. The woman placed a comforting hand to his shoulder only for him to shrug it off. Her face dropped and she threw her hands in the air, muttering under her breath and sauntered away.

I receded quickly before they saw me, but stood near the wall wondering what happened between them. I'd never seen Kova so worked up before. Sure, he was a dick at practice, but seeing it outside of the gym was not something I expected. I just figured he was that way because he was trying to bring out the victor in us. Maybe it really was just his personality.

I needed to find some friends to talk to quickly only to realize I didn't have many here.

I heaved a sigh. I still felt a bit like an outcast among the rest of the team. They were nice, but mostly reserved and kept to themselves. Very cliquey. I probably should've made more of an effort to be friends with someone other than Hayden and Holly, but it wasn't something I was pushing for. I came here to train, to be the absolute best I could be and gain the title of elite. Not to win Miss Congeniality.

Trying to befriend Reagan had been a challenge. I wasn't any competition to her, she was an amazing athlete and much better than me. She knew it, and I knew it. So I wasn't sure what the issue was. There was just no friendship with her, I was on my own. Sometimes I liked it, but most of the time it was frustrating when you wanted a friend to vent to who understood what you were going through. Maybe if I had pushed for it, I wouldn't have been standing by myself, staring at...I had no idea what the hell I was staring at. A shrine?

Before me hung medals upon medals, framed photos, trophies, articles galore. You name it, it was here. And it was all about Kova. This was something only a proud mother would do, so I found it oddly bizarre a man of his stature would have his own hall of fame in his home.

Then again, I hadn't accomplished what Kova had, not even remotely close, so I guess I shouldn't really say anything. I could only hope. I'd probably have the same thing in my house. Hell, I had medals from competitions displayed in my condo right now.

Moving closer, my fingers grazed one of the gold medals, my heart yearning for one. Just one. God, what I wouldn't do to have a beauty like this of my own one day. I'd probably never take it off. Well, maybe to sleep and shower, but that was it.

Kova had three gold medals and a handful of silver from two Olympics, the rings being his top event. I chuckled to myself. He probably hated the silver ones.

"What is so funny?"

I jumped, my hand flying to my racing heart. I looked behind me and saw Kova holding a glass of beer.

"Jesus!"

A sensual grin pulled his full lips to the side. His eyes softened and I swallowed. Totally different side of him from what I'd seen earlier when I walked in on the spat he was having. He seemed relaxed now, not tense. This man's beauty was in a league of its own. He was charismatic when he smiled, and I could feel his goodness. A rare occurrence, and it was times like these I forgot he was my coach.

Kova looked incredibly amazing in his navy blue dress pants and crisp white button-down shirt. His sleeves were rolled up to his elbows, a silver watch with a large face adorned his wrist. His hair, although messy, looked as though he ran his fingers through it so it matched the two-day dusting coating his jaw. This was the first time I'd seen Kova wear something other than shorts in a long time. Amber skin, perfectly straight nose, and emerald eyes complimented him. He could've passed as an Armani model with flying colors.

"I did not mean to frighten you."

"It's okay. But I'm going to need you to put a bell around your neck as much as you sneak up on me."

Kova looked down at his glass and swirled the amber liquid. He stepped up next to me and looked at his wall. He smelled like cinnamon and tobacco with a hint of citrus. I knew he wasn't a smoker, yet the scent on him was seductive and sophisticated. I drew a silent breath into my lungs and felt it all the way to my core.

"What did you find so amusing?"

"Ah..." I turned back to the wall, heat rising to my cheeks. I seemed to blush a lot when Kova was around. I snuck a glance and he nodded his head, waiting for me. "I was just admiring your medals and wondered what you thought about your silver ones."

He squinted with discerning eyes and looked at his wall, pursing his lips together in thought. I zoned in and noticed he had a deep cupid's bow, where as I had full, ample lips.

Maybe Avery was right. He was Coach Kissable.

"I think I am very fortunate to have them, but also that I worked very hard and that I deserve them. Going to the Olympics is an accomplishment very few can achieve. Not even luck can get you there. It is pure determination, unwavering commitment to the sport, and a love that runs so deep for it that you would give up anything to achieve it. Sometimes even your life and childhood." Kova took a sip of his beer. "Though, the truly dedicated would say gymnastics is their life, it is the air they breathe, so you are not really giving up your life at all if you are living it through gymnastics, are you?"

I read the underlining meaning in his eyes and felt the tone in his voice. He gave up everything in his childhood to achieve his dream. His devotion was contagious. My heart soared and a lazy smile spread across my face.

I looked back at his wall of medals and agreed. He was right in every sense. Luck had very little to do with it, but he forgot something else.

"You forgot timing," I said, looking directly into his eyes. "Timing is everything, especially in gymnastics."

"You know what else I did not mention? Selfishness."

My brows cinched together, not fully agreeing with him. "Selfishness? I wouldn't necessarily say that."

"Sure it is," he countered, stepping closer to me.

"There is nothing wrong with being selfish," he continued. "Gymnastics, once you reach a certain level, becomes your entire life and everyone is just revolving around you. It is all about *you* meeting *your* goals, *you* competing, *you* spending hours upon hours in a gym fighting to be the best. It is climbing a rope and everyone is just sitting back watching *you*. You have to give one hundred and fifty percent with this sport. Gymnastics, in a sense, is all about you."

Rope. I smiled to myself at his gymnastics analogy. Most people said climb mountains, but he used rope since part of conditioning for many athletes was rope climbing.

"I hadn't really thought of it like that before. I mean, in a sense, you're right, but isn't everyone selfish in some form then? Why a gymnast more so than others?"

He shook his head, disagreeing. "It is not the same."

I knew what he meant, and he was right. It wasn't the same. Most people were selfish to an extent. This was a personal drive trapped inside no one could help with, except one thing. A coach who understood. Gymnastics was like a drug. No matter how many times we got knocked down, no matter how many injuries we sustained, no matter how many times we're told we're not good enough, not the best, we always came back for more. It was a need that ignored all those around until it was filled, no matter the length of time it took. A gymnast's drive outweighed everyone else's and it never died.

"You know, I would almost rather have a bronze medal than have a silver," he said, changing the subject.

"Why's that?"

Kova shrugged one shoulder, as if the answer was obvious. "Silver is the first place loser."

My eyes widened. I'd never thought of it like that when I'd won silver at meets.

"Coming in second place is the worst feeling after you just gave your all. There are winners and there are losers. You play a sport to win—that is it. Nothing else. You have one chance to prove yourself. One." He shook his head, his eyes distant as he reminisced about the past. "I remember feeling completely and utterly gutted, like I was just given a consolation prize for all my hard work. I was up on the podium, thinking about what I could have done differently. Did I wobble? Did I take a step on a dismount? Did I bend my legs? Did I not have enough control in flight? Did I not train enough? I knew I should have been happy I secured silver, but it was not enough to win gold, and that was heart wrenching." He looked at me as if trying to remember what he did wrong. "You can lose it all by a tenth of a deduction. So small, yet so powerful it can bring you to your knees in a mere second. It all happens so fast, you know? Once the flame is lit, the Games begin. You are there, in the moment, living it, breathing it, fighting for your dream. You are at each event for such a short period of time until you rotate to the next one. Once you get home and you finally have the chance to think about your experience, you have to ask yourself if it was real because it does not feel like it. It is like a blurry movie you want to tune and focus, but cannot..."

Kova's words trailed off. He gave me a questionable look, as if he wanted an answer I didn't have. His words stung my chest. I could hear the vulnerability in his voice, felt each word as he relived his past and tried to cope with it. The sincerity written on his face was full of meaning and emotion, and what he said packed a punch.

He spoke from his heart, and I felt every bit of it.

CHAPTER 21

This was a pivotal moment between us.

He stood so close his words trailed over my skin, igniting a flame under me. He'd exposed deeply personal parts of his life again and it unknowingly opened a connection between us. I felt it, saw it. His eyes bore into mine and his lips slightly parted, a little opening in the center of them. The silence in the air caused a stirring. Without saying another word and with his eyes trained on mine, he lifted a hand and moved a lock of hair from my shoulder, tucking it behind my ear. A shiver ran down my arms as the back of his hand delayed, his finger peppering my jaw with the lightest touch possible. He stepped closer to me and I held my breath as his eyes took in every inch of me. His knuckles danced down my neck to my clavicle, his callused index finger gliding over me like a soft breeze.

"I bet your mom was proud of your silver medals," I said softly.

Kova's face dropped, his smile vanishing along with his hand. His eyes took on a blank stare and I suddenly regretted my comment.

"She was. She was proud of everything I did. She was my biggest supporter."

I swallowed hard. "How long ago did she pass away?"

Kova took a deep breath and exhaled. "Eight years ago," he said delicately.

My heart sank even more at the sadness in his tone. Instinctively, my hand reached out to comfort him.

"I'm so sorry."

I rubbed his arm, my thumb going in circles. It wasn't a wise decision, but I think I did it mostly because I felt his loss so strongly I wanted to soothe him. He flexed under my touch and his eyes shot to mine. I dropped my hand and cleared my throat awkwardly.

Kova shook it off.

"Was it cancer?" I asked curiously.

"I wish it could have been that."

He wished it could have been that? "What do you mean?"

Him being vague wasn't working for me, but that was Kova. Always so elusive. I wasn't sure I should use the opening to ask more questions, so I stayed silent and waited for him to collect his thoughts.

"Since we have been upfront and truthful with each other...She was HIV positive," he whispered quietly.

My jaw dropped, along with my gut. HIV. I was glad we hadn't eaten yet, otherwise with all this tumbling between my heart and stomach, I'd probably vomit right now. That was extremely personal and not at all what I expected. Not one bit.

Wait a minute. If she was HIV positive, then that would mean...

My eyes popped, my head snapped to look at him. "I do not have HIV," he answered my questioning stare. "She contracted it many years after I was born." Kova sighed sadly, looking into his beer mug. "I would not be in this profession if that were the case."

I was about to ask how she contracted HIV when a woman walked in, looking radiant as ever with a perfect sway to her hips.

"I was looking for you."

I looked over at the singsong voice. It was the woman from earlier. Whoever she was, she was the definition of flawless. A perfect, glossy shine to her pin straight chestnut hair. Ivory skin, bright hazel eyes and a megawatt smile complemented her supermodel body. There wasn't a thing wrong with her on the outside. Truly perfect from her French manicured toes to the top of her deep brown head.

Kova cleared his throat. "I apologize, *malysh,* I was just explaining my medals to Adrianna and how it was not done by having luck." Kova looked at me, strained. "Adrianna, this is my girlfriend, Katja."

Malysh. He called her *malysh* like he'd once called me. Blood drained from my face, a knot formed in the pit of my stomach at the endearment he used on both of us. I knew he said it was by mistake when he said it to me, but it bothered me, and I wasn't sure why. Maybe because she was perfection and I was not. Maybe it was because I secretly liked that he used it on me more than I wanted to admit, and now knowing he used it on her made me slightly envious.

My insecurities I worked so hard to overcome, thanks to my mom, were making an appearance and I didn't like it one bit.

She smiled and placed her hand out.

Katja looked back to Kova with a pointed brow. The tension was thick between them once again. "The grill is almost ready. Would you like me to get you another drink?"

"No, thank you."

"What is that?" she asked, brows angled together.

"Beer."

She pulled back like he spoke another language. "Beer? No vodka for you?"

His sheepish eyes shot back to me. "I was thinking it would not be such a good idea to put my Russian half on display tonight." He chuckled, his hand reaching out to cup Katja's cheek, his thumb circling her immaculate skin. Her face tilted to the side, a honey smile on her lips. I got the feeling they were putting on a show after what I'd seen.

"Ah, I see. Well, we need you on the grill soon and more guests just showed up." Katja placed a kiss to his lips, turned, and walked out.

Quietly, I admitted with a sliver amount of jealousy, "Katja is very pretty."

He flattened his lips, his face faltering and I was curious to know why. "Yes, she is a very beautiful woman."

Woman. Whereas I was a teenager.

Wanting to change the focus, I asked, "What other nationality are you?"

"I think I have spilled enough today...again. You heard Katja, I need to go." And there was the stone-faced Kova I knew.

Coach Kova was back, ignoring my question. All I did was ask about his heritage and he shut down. It was by far the least intrusive of everything he exposed.

Kova left and walked back in the direction of the dining room and I followed behind, but the vibrant colors of a Georgia sunset caught my eye and pulled me into a room just off from where the awards were.

Looking out the window, deep pinks and an array of blues swathed the darkening sky behind a body of water. I smiled to myself at the warmth filling my heart. I seriously loved living in Georgia.

Glancing around, I realized I'd stepped into an office. It was similar to my dad's but smaller. The desk was placed in front of the window and a bookshelf adorned one wall. My eyes locked on a framed picture of Katja on a shelf.

Walking over, I picked it up. She wore a white button-down men's shirt. The sleeves were rolled up, but the front was left opened so it showcased an outline of her plump breasts and toned stomach. She looked like she just woke up. Her messy hair was flipped to the side while giving a wide, playful smile as she sat upon an unmade bed. She appeared to be the happiest woman on the planet, and there was no doubt in my mind she wasn't. I could only hope to be as naturally stunning as her one day.

Placing it down, I looked around and noticed another framed photo, this time on his desk. Curious, I brazenly walked over and picked it up. Katja was sensually sliding off a rumpled sheet, wearing black stilettos and black thigh high lace trimmed stockings in a matching bra and panty set. Her dainty fingers just grazing her fair cleavage while her hair was curled loosely around her. She was every man's fantasy in this picture. Her back was partially against the side of the bed, her breasts perfectly round and plump as they pushed up. And the look she gave the camera screamed sex as she twirled a lock of hair around her finger.

The photo was breathtaking, striking.

I bet Kova took these photos of her. Why that stung, I had no idea. It shouldn't have. After all, he was my coach, but something in my belly tightened at the thought of Kova framing provocative images of her in his office. In that moment, I envied Katja. She oozed confidence and power. This was tasteful, artistic...and it made me realize this was something I'd want my future husband to do one day.

"Adrianna?"

Startled, I gasped, nearly dropping the frame.

"What the hell are you doing in here?" Kova spat each word, a hand propped on his hips.

"I, ah," I was rendered speechless. Completely speechless. My jaw bobbed and my eyes were huge as I tried to find words.

Kill me now.

Kova slowly stepped toward me, eyeing my fingers that gripped his frame. "I caught a view of the sunset as I was walking back and stopped to look at it."

He lifted a brow and waited for more. "And?"

"And...And I saw a picture of Katja." Fuck. I was scared.

"Keep going?" His voice was low. "Were you snooping around my office? This is a very private picture of her for my eyes only. Who said you could just waltz right in here?"

He was goading me, but with every right. I was in his personal space. "I wasn't snooping, I swear. I just happened to see the photo on the bookshelf. Then I saw this one on your desk and wanted to see it."

I glanced down at the frame clutched to my chest and pulled it back. Handing it to him, I apologized.

"I didn't mean to be nosey. I've just never seen photos like these before."

"They were a gift."

Confused, I asked, "What was?"

"The photos, they are boudoir photos taken by a local photographer. Katja gave them to me on our second anniversary. At first I fumed she would let someone photograph her in hardly anything, but once I cooled down, I found the photos alluring."

This was getting strange, and I wasn't sure how to respond. It was one thing to talk about his life and his mom, but not about Katja and how *alluring* her photos were. Kova stared lovingly at the frame while I stood awkwardly next to him. I felt like I was invading on his moment. "She really is beautiful," was all I could think of to say.

Hard eyes snapped to mine. Kova loomed over me and stared down. His eyes traveled down my face, pausing on my lips. His jaw flexed as he exhaled. The throbbing vein in his neck caught my attention, it was beating as fast as my heart.

Tension swirled and the air thickened as his gaze landed on my chest. Only the tension wasn't like it was with him and Katja. Sensuality was woven around us and it changed the whole dynamic. I wore a white, low scoop neck shirt with a push-up bra that gave me heavy, supple cleavage. It wasn't often I wore clothes other than a leotard, so I took extra time getting dressed, carefully picking out my outfit. I wanted to look better than all the other girls combined.

The room grew hot as the weight of his stare was felt on every inch of my skin. This wasn't the first time an older man had stared at me, I'd met some men who were acquaintances of my dad's, but this was different.

Everything a woman could want in a man, Kova had it in spades. The perfect body, the perfect face, a successful business, goal driven. And no matter what I did, I couldn't get him out of my mind. He was tall, dark, and handsome. And the more he stared at me, the more I found myself liking it...wanting more of his attention.

Kova took one small step toward me and my lips parted. I could hear my heart thumping loudly in my ears as my chest rose faster with each breath I took.

"Kova," I whispered. "What are you thinking about?"

He swallowed and said hoarsely, "Things I should not be."

My stomach tightened, my panties suddenly wet from the raspy sound of his voice, it rumbled in a deep baritone. Rolling my lip between my teeth, I tucked a lock of hair behind my ear. "What do you mean?"

He groaned low under his breath. "Do not do that."

"Do what?"

"Look at me the same way I am looking at you."

My heart was pounding so loud I wondered if he could hear it.

"You are blushing."

"You know, that only makes me blush more," I whispered.

One more step closer, and we were almost touching. "I like the way it tints your skin." The back of his hand grazed my flushed cheek. "You know, you are just as beautiful. If not, more. Gorgeous."

A little gasp escaped my lips. My heart raced a mile a minute, my fingers trembled. Kova called me gorgeous.

Dropping his hand, he looked down at the picture frame and then back to me with remorse in his eyes. "I am sorry I made you rip so badly on bars that day...I have felt terrible ever since." And then he turned, and walked out of his office, leaving me speechless.

What in the ever loving fuck just happened?

CHAPTER 22

nce I caught my breath, I left Kova's office and walked toward
the formal dining room.

My head was spinning and I needed some fresh air.

Long, elegant crimson drapes held back by a gold sash gave
a spectacular view of the intercoastal. I stopped to take in the breathtaking sight before meeting up with everyone outside. After what
just happened only moments before, I needed to get my head on
straight and taking in the view did the trick. There was something
about the water that washed away any stress and helped me focus.
Growing up, I'd had a stunning view of the Atlantic Ocean from
my bedroom. Anytime I needed to get away, needed to think, the
ocean was where I went. Nothing could compare, but this was just
as spectacular. The sun was setting over the winding canal that was
wrapped between heavy trees. A warm cascade of colors illuminated
the sky, the most evanescent sunset worthy of being framed. It was
all so grand, and not at all what I expected from the man I saw every
day in the gym to have.

Freaking Coach Kova. Confusing. Contradicting. Exhausting...
And maybe a little sinful. I expelled a heavy breath and decided I'd
deal with that moment later.

Stepping outside, people were gathered around chatting with
one another. It was late afternoon, and with all the foliage in the
backyard, thankfully it wasn't too hot. Despite making the effort to
avoid him, I glanced around and my traitorous eyes automatically
found Kova. His back was to me as I watched through intrigued
eyes. My head tilted to the side. I could hear the lilt in his voice
drift through the air. He appeared deep in conversation, his hands
moving fluidly as he spoke.

With my shoulders back, I took a deep breath and confidently
made my way to a group of girls to make it appear like I wanted to

be involved in their conversation. Though, if I was being honest, I didn't feel like talking to anyone here. My mind was everywhere at the moment and I needed Avery to talk to. I smiled politely, but I couldn't take my eyes off Kova as he turned and began grilling. His girlfriend was at his side, dutifully helping him. He did a quick flip of the meat and shut the grill lid. He placed the cooking utensil to the side and wrapped a loving arm around Katja's lower back. Kova pulled her in, their hips meeting and he dropped a kiss to her cheek. With all the one-on-one time I spent working with him, it was obvious to me his jaw was set tight, but she smiled timidly in response and my heart gave a little pang. After what I witnessed when I arrived earlier, coupled with what happened in his office, I was more baffled than ever. I began wondering if this meant I had deeper feelings for my coach. I knew it wasn't right, but this feeling inside, this feeling of being unsure, the way my stomach tightened, and my heart fluttered, the longing said more than I wanted to acknowledge.

Kova must've felt my confused stare. He looked over his shoulder and his emerald eyes traveled up to mine. Something in my gut said to hold his gaze. His hand tightened his hold on Katja's hip and he tugged her closer to him. I swallowed hard at the sight and realized how I stupidly wanted that to be me. With a small nod of his head, Kova gave me a tight lipped smile, clearly only meant for me, then turned around.

Thankfully, thirty minutes later the food was placed on the table and chairs were quickly filled. I looked around and saw an empty seat beside Reagan. I'd rather eat my mom's bark flavored, pre-packaged meals than sit next to her.

To my left, Holly took a seat next to someone I wasn't familiar with. I moved to walk toward her when Hayden called my name.

"Adrianna! Come sit here." I groaned through a faux smile. There were chairs opened on both sides of Kova's. One of them obviously reserved for Katja. From the corner of my eye, I caught a glimpse of Reagan's scowl. I ignored her and made my way over to Hayden. He pulled a chair out and whispered in my ear, "I know how much you'd rather sit next to Reagan, but sit with me."

"You know me so well," I chuckled. Hayden thankfully sat in the seat next to Kova's. There was no way I could sit that close to him. This was enough. "The view is stunning." He followed my gaze.

"Growing up here, the view doesn't do anything for me anymore." He shrugged carelessly. "It's just a bunch of canals and rivers on this side, but people love them and pay good money to live on the water. I bet you feel the same way about back home."

I thought about what he said. "Yeah, I guess so. People from all over come to our beaches, but it's nothing to me either. Now that I'm here, I do kind of miss waking up to the sound of the ocean, the smell of the salt water, sand between my toes. I never thought I would."

I drifted off thinking about Palm Bay and how I was a bit homesick and I didn't even realize it until now. With gymnastics constantly on my mind, I didn't have time to think about anything else. I hadn't spoken to Avery in over a week, except for a few texts here and there.

"So, aside from this fabulous view, people mainly come here to apple bob."

I looked at Hayden with an arched brow. "Apple bob?"

"Yeah, haven't you gone apple bobbing? We're famous for that. There's a fall festival every year and a big apple bobbing competition. People from all over come to watch and partake in the festivities. We're a very homey town."

I stared at Hayden's straight face, gaping at him. "Tell me you're joking." Surely no one would travel for apple bobbing. Finally, he burst out laughing, a contagious smile spreading across his face. I found myself giggling and I playfully backhanded his arm. The empty chairs rustled next to Hayden. I looked up as Kova and Katja pulled out their chairs and took their seats. Katja was all smiles, not a worry on her serene face, while Kova stared intensely at me. His eyes darkened and shifted over to Hayden. My smile faltered the way he was watching him.

"I'm joking with you," Hayden said, grabbing my attention. I looked at Kova once more before giving my full interest to Hayden, but he was no longer looking my way. "You should see your face right now! Priceless!"

"You jerk. I thought you were serious!" I punched his arm but felt the weight of someone's gaze on me. My skin prickled in awareness but I refused to look up. I knew who it was. And call me crazy, but I had a sinking suspicion he wasn't keen on the idea of Hayden being by my side.

"I know you did." He paused. "For real though, no one comes here to apple bob. I don't even know if that's a thing here. Cape Coral is a great place for an outdoor enthusiast. Boating, fishing, lots of water shit to do. Much like what you're used to, I'm sure. There's no apple bobbing competition. Not that I know of, at least," he finished with a grin."

Before I could respond, Katja exclaimed, "Let's eat!"

Dinner was served and it was probably the best I'd had in a long time. It felt good not to hold back for once and eat what I wanted. I could now, since I was on my own, but I was so used to my mother either watching me or making sure my meals were proportioned that it was an unconscious habit of mine to be careful.

Plus, I didn't want to be one of those "extra cardio" girls.

Dessert was being brought out when Katja asked, "Adrianna, so your parents allow you to be here alone? Kova mentioned to me that you are here by yourself."

I glanced at him before I answered. "Yes."

"I must be honest, I cannot imagine allowing my teen daughter to live on her own even though I know others do it and cohabit with each other. How do you get around since you do not live with the other girls?" She had asked each one of us a few questions, so I knew my time was coming.

I sipped my water then responded. "Well, my parents hired a driver for whenever I need to get around. Where I come from, it's not uncommon for teens to be on their own at my age, or with a chaperon other than the parents. Plus, it helps that Coach is friends with my dad."

"Coach is friends with your dad?" Reagan repeated, with a look of disgust.

"You have a driver? Like a personal one? How did I not know this?" Holly asked.

"I do. He's been with my family since I was a kid."

"Your family?" Reagan asked.

I swallowed back, trying to figure out how to answer her statement without giving away too much. Thankfully Kova jumped in.

"Her family...is an affluent one," was all he said. He used his hands when he said affluent, as if it described the word. Everyone's heads turned my way. Heat rushed up my chest, to my cheeks. My ears burned from the stares.

"My dad's a real estate developer. Think the Hiltons, only smaller," was my explanation.

"That's pretty damn cool. So he can build me a house one day?" Hayden asked.

I smiled, silently thanking him. "Possibly."

"So what's your driver's name?" asked Holly.

"His name is Thomas, but I call him Alfred."

She grinned. "Like Batman."

"Yeah," I smiled. That lightened the subject. "Once I start driving he won't be here. So I'm not really alone per se, since he's always around...somewhere."

"It must be really lonely to have no one," Reagan said, feigning sympathy. "That's the one plus of living in a shared apartment, nothing like having a mom around to lean on. It's really the best feeling."

I nodded slowly, pretending to take in her words like they meant something. If she only knew how happy I was to not have my mom around.

"My dad is a bit of a control freak. There's no way I'd be allowed to stay in an apartment with someone he doesn't know, so I live in the penthouse in one of his condos. It's really safe and private. I love it. The view is incredible and I have a ton of space. If I need anything, Thomas will get it for me, or he'll take me. And since my dad and Kova are friends, if there's some sort of emergency, he's always here for me too. I'm really very fortunate to have what I have and the people around me."

My eyes locked with Kova. He deepened the stare before agreeing with my statement. That shut her up.

CHAPTER 23

Fear was a bitch, and in this sport, it could cripple you.

Literally.

Fear challenged courage. It challenged the mind. Once we found courage, it meant never looking back. It persevered and defied. It gave strength to conquer the obstacles that rendered one weak.

Successful people fought for what they wanted, what they desired in life no matter what they were up against. Willpower was key, and maybe if I turned my fear into desire, it would override my anxiety. It was the only way to escape the emotion.

I knew I needed to practice what I preached, but it was easier said than done. As was everything. I'd rather train for a new tumbling sequence with front flips, or Level E release moves and bar changes before jumping on beam.

I hated beam. Dreaded it. It was the one event I needed the most work on. I feared the four-inch piece of wood like it had the ability to incapacitate me. But only I could do that.

When I was a child, my dad surprised me with a small, low balance beam for Christmas one year. My fear of the beam started early and I hardly used it. This fear I created in the front of my mind was hard to break. Balancing on a piece of wood that was four feet off the ground didn't sound like much, but when you factor in leaps or turns while balancing on the tips of your toes—let's not forget the back-flips and full-twists with blind landings on a four-inch width—yeah, good luck.

Then try sticking it without straddling the beam and slamming down on your crotch and getting beam burn. That's what I called it, beam burn. It was like rug burn, but from the balance beam. It looked and felt the same. Hurt like a bitch from my inner thighs to my crotch. I'd fallen so hard in the past I actually bled.

It was literally like getting smacked with a piece of wood between your legs. Talk about excruciating pain.

"Come on, Adrianna," Kova groaned, while I wobbled on the beam after landing a double switch leap.

He almost sounded defeated. Again, I jumped off one foot, split my legs as far apart as possible, then switched them quickly so that the leg that was in the front ended up in the back. Once I landed, I took one step, and did it again. After landing quickly—wobble free—it required a full twist.

"Your hips are leaning forward which is why you are taking the extra step at the end! Do it again but without the turn!" Kova ordered, and my heart started to race. "*Relevé* your foot so you are up on your toes and bring your shoulders back before you leap!" He slapped the back of his hand into his palm to get his point across.

It was my stupid fear, even after years of practicing, that I was going to fall.

Stepping into the jump, Kova yelled, "Square your hips so they are centered over the beam!" I dropped my arms and looked at him. He was livid, past the point of angry and ready to move into seething with fury. The team girls stared at me and I was embarrassed. I chewed my bottom lip as I watched his expression turn darker while the fire in his eyes seared my skin.

"I told you to *relevé* into it first! My accent may be strong, but I know you understand what I am saying. Or did you forget that in dance already? Slowly lift your back heel before stepping into the leap. Do it again. And with some damn grace. You look like you are jumping on a trampoline."

He may be hot as hell, and I may have wanted to lick and slap him at the same time, but he could be a complete asshole. Kova muttered something in Russian. He was in rare form today. I had no idea what his deal was. I wish I had some knowledge of the language so then I'd know what he was saying.

I leaped again, but was shaky on the landing. I think I bent my legs too. I was second guessing myself and could feel how off-kilter I was. Kova made me nervous, and his constant yelling was affecting my performance. I hated today. I hated beam. And damn it, this was one of those moments where I wanted to quit altogether.

If I didn't get my nerves under control, I could critically injure myself.

"Tuck in your hips and tighten your stomach. Your chest will stay up and therefore your split will be wider. What part of that do you not get?"

"I'm trying, Coach."

He cracked his neck, sharply twisting it from side to side. The sound made me cringe. "If you were trying, you would do it the correct way. You are not trying hard enough."

Gritting my teeth, I said, "Yes. I. Am," enunciating each word. "You think I like messing up and having you yell at me?" I said out loud. I *was* trying, I was just doing a shitty job.

Another gymnast paused on the beam next to me, her arms slowly fell to her sides as Kova stood stock still. His eyes were wild, huge, and the vein in his neck noticeably pulsed. Fear streamed through me, which was only felt tenfold because I could feel my teammates' as well. I was legitimately frightened of my coach.

And I was quite sure he was about to strangle me.

"I am going to pretend I did not just hear that," he said, his voice low and controlled.

Flexibility has never been my strong suit, or keeping my mouth shut apparently, which was why I had difficulty with jumps sometimes. My legs did not split like they should. Lots of gymnasts suffered from inflexibility—it didn't come with the nature of the sport. Gymnastics builds muscle, which in turn hinders flexibility. It was a vicious cycle to find a balance. Typically, gymnasts who are good on vault and floor, often times find beam isn't their strongest suit.

People automatically assumed being a gymnast meant being able to flip into a pretzel at any given moment. It was quite the opposite. Long hours of manipulating your body at odd angles did it. Bending, flipping, and twisting, I could do. But my legs and my back did not curve the way some of these girls did. It was unnatural, but still, I strived for it.

"Jump down," he sighed, running a hand through his unruly hair. "Adrianna, you have to lift that leg up higher. And stop shaking up there, you look like a leaf blowing on a tree," he spit angrily. "Here, do it on the low beam first."

A leaf blowing on a tree...I let that one pass. He's Russian after all.

I leaped again, splitting my legs wider, but this time when I looked back at him, he looked puzzled.

"I do not think you are squaring your hips." He placed his jaw in his hand. "No, that cannot be right..."

This had to be some sort of joke. I knew how to square my hips.

"It is either that, or you lack more flexibility than I thought, which would explain why your jumps look like shit," he muttered to himself. He went from veins-in-his-neck screaming to quiet and pondering. "But you are still not hitting that one hundred and eighty degree split." He stared at me intently, his brows angled deep toward each other while rubbing his jaw. "Go into the dance room and do split jumps in front of the mirror. I will be there shortly."

I swallowed back the lump in my throat and nodded, making my way into the dance room. There was a piece of long white tape per-pendicular to the mirror. I stood on it and began doing split jumps, making sure to land on the make shift balance beam. I watched my body closely. My hips looked squared, but Kova was right. It didn't look like I was hitting the split all the way.

I wasn't sure how long I was in the dance room for or how many split jumps I completed by the time Kova walked in. He studied my jumps through critical eyes. I didn't ask questions and I didn't stop until my legs felt like rubber. Kova strutted over to me. He placed his hands on my shoulders and looked into my eyes, radiating con-fidence into me.

"Focus. Take a deep breath and exhale," he paused. "A quiet and controlled breath, Ria. Like I taught you." His palms warmed my shoulders as he massaged them to loosen me up.

"Shoulders back," he pushed my shoulders back which brought my chest forward. "Chest out," he dipped his chin in approval. "Like that." He grasped the sides of my jaw and said, "Chin up." I nodded. Before I could turn back to face the mirror, his knuckles slid beneath my jaw and danced across my throat seductively. A shiver broke out on my arms and his eyes darkened. "Perfect." He dropped his hands and I turned around to prepare for another jump. Kova came up behind me and repeated the movements, his eyes never leaving mine. He stood so close his clothes brushed against my tepid skin. Once

I was standing how he wanted me, he placed his hands on my hips, the tips of his fingers searing my bikini line as he pressed deeper to make sure my hips were square. His nearness caused my heart to thump wildly against my chest. He'd never been this daring before, this forward, and truth be told, I welcomed it.

"You see how you are standing? This is how you prepare before you leap." His breath accelerated. The tips of his fingers curved down and brushed my ass, dangerously low. Goose bumps immediately broke out across my skin and I was sure he felt them as his hands lingered evocatively, causing a rush of wetness to surge through me. A low, deep groan reverberated in the back of his throat, but I'd heard it before he stepped back. Kova gave me a slight nod and I forced my racing heart to get under control. I executed a split jump, which ended up looking much better this time.

"Beautiful," he said quietly, looking into my eyes through the mirror. It was so hard for me not to smile over his approval. "Again." With a nod of his head, he ordered me to perform the skill multiple times. My legs split higher, more gracefully, but more importantly, correctly.

At this point I was out of breath from doing them repeatedly. I waited for his next order with burning thighs while balancing on the balls of my feet. His incredibly handsome poker face was hard to read.

"Back to the beam."

Once we were back, I chalked up my feet and headed to the beam. I gripped it between my hands and jumped, feeling my thighs rub against the suede before I stood tall. I performed about a dozen split jumps perfectly before I moved on. Kova seemed pleased with me. I tapped the beam with a pointed toe and then stepped into the leap. I landed, slightly shaky and saved it, but I knew Coach saw it. He never missed a beat. His eyes narrowed to slits and I felt them inching up my body until they met my eyes. I exhaled a low and steady breath and waited for what he had to say.

"Adrianna, you should be able to land your leap on the beam if you can do it on the white tape. Get it right."

I blinked my eyes, abruptly feeling light headed. It'd been hours since I'd eaten. My lunch had been light, not wanting to work out on a full belly. And since I was at the gym for hours, half the time I was starving. After I finished on beam though, I planned to eat my protein bar to hold me over until practice was over.

I wanted to impress my coach and show him I was worthy of being here, but with him riding my back over a stupid leap, along with my gnawing hunger, I was stressing out big time.

"While I am young, Adrianna." He clapped twice. We were back to Adrianna. "Get moving. Ten more."

I gulped, then completed the leap eleven more times instead of ten. My legs were rubbery and I began to feel nauseous. I was training on an empty stomach with a barking coach in my ear.

On one of the jumps, I came down with shaky legs. My arms and legs went out to the sides just a little to balance myself. I tried to make it flow into a pose to cover it up, but any coach with a sharp eye would spot it immediately.

I wasn't sure why I even tried to hide it from Kova.

"Lock your leg, Adrianna," he gritted, his eyes were drilling holes into my head.

Coach dropped his head. Running a hand through his hair, he pulled at his scalp. Snapping his head up, he turned to the bars and yelled, "Reagan! Over here! Now!"

Great. My biggest fan was coming over to show me up.

"Yes, Coach," she said with a syrupy voice. It made me want to dry heave.

"Get up there and show Adrianna how a switch leap is done."

She smiled and said, "No problem, Coach."

I hoped she fell.

On her face.

CHAPTER 24

Turning toward me with her back to Kova, a conniving, small grin tugged at her knowing face. I couldn't help but want to smack her for it. I wasn't an aggressive kind of person, but she really knew how to get under my skin like no other.

Reagan jumped up on the beam and naturally landed a perfect leap. Of course she did. Balance beam was her favorite event, one she excelled at. Even though I couldn't stand to look at her at times, she really had skill.

Kova dipped his chin in approval before saying, "Do it again, but this time make sure you are watching, Adrianna."

Reagan landed a beautiful leap, as if she was born to do it. "Thank you, Reagan. You can go back to bars."

"Yes, sir." She hopped down and looked over her shoulder at me, grinning.

My patience was wearing thin. I was starving, tired, and I had a bitch on my team I shouldn't even care about who would love to see me fail.

"Don't fall, Ana," she whispered as she glided past, patting me on the shoulder.

The urge to stick my foot out and trip her, then kick her in her pinched face was stronger than ever.

Coach looked at me expectantly. I jumped on the beam and focused on the end of it, but I could feel someone's burning gaze on me. I refused to look up. I chewed the inside of my lip. I couldn't mess this one up, I just couldn't.

I got this, I got this, I got this, I chanted to myself. I had it.

Shaking out my fingers, I exhaled into the jump. Just as I was about to land, I could tell my body was off balance. I just knew—like a gut instinct, sixth sense sort of thing—I was off-kilter.

Peeking down to spot the beam, I froze mid-air, the worst thing a gymnast could do. I should've never looked down. I should've believed in myself more, trusted myself. Landing, my foot nicked the edge of the balance beam. I desperately tried to curl my toes around the edge, but I slipped and fell fast.

My stomach sunk with my body and I held my breath as I plummeted to the balance beam.

I quickly dropped my arms in an attempt to grab the beam to lessen the impact of my crotch slamming into the wood, but it was futile. My body tightened, slanting to the side; and my leg rubbed down the suede fabric, feeling the fiery burn immediately. My ribs crashed into the wooden slab and a gush of air left my lungs.

The sound of a gymnast straddling the beam was always a noticeable one. The impact was loud, and in my peripheral vision, I could see heads turning, but I didn't look. I couldn't. My eyes clenched shut and I was pretty sure a bone broke inside my crotch from the snapping sound the fall made. I reached blindly for the beam with my other hand, but my body rotated and I flipped over, falling onto the cushioned mat and into a fetal position.

Eighty-seventh time of straddling the beam. And moments like this made me hate gymnastics with every fiber in my body.

Fuck, I wanted to cry.

Oh, God, it hurt so bad. I was curled up into a ball on the floor, my feet cushioned under my ass with my arms wrapped around my waist. My forehead pressed into the mat as I took a deep breath preparing to stand. Tears formed in the back of my eyes, but I refused to cry and further my embarrassment.

As I knelt trying to summon the strength to get up, a large hand came to rest on my back. The weight of his body created a slight indentation on the mat. *Kova.* As if I wasn't in enough pain already.

Of course.

"Are you okay, Adrianna?"

I nodded silently.

"Let me help you up," he offered as his hand cupped my bicep and pulled me up.

"I'm fine." I choked out behind false bravado.

But I wasn't. My inner thighs were raw, my crotch was aching and on fire. It felt strange, like something moved inside and broke. I knew that wasn't possible, but something didn't feel right.

"Shake it off," Coach said. "Do you need a break?"

"No," I responded, then reached for the beam. I climbed up, feeling the heat race from inside my crotch area out and down through my thighs. Pushing back the tears, I bit my lip so hard I tasted blood. *I got this.* I knew I could do it. I just needed to refocus on the move and not what people were thinking—and staring at.

With my shoulders back and arms positioned, my knees trembled. The pain from the fall had my nerves all over the place. *Maybe this wasn't a good idea,* I thought as my heart beat frantically in my chest. I felt sick, and I knew I looked pale. I was truly scared.

Kova's deep voice eased into the next sentence, almost as if he was worried for me. "Lock your legs, Adrianna."

I exhaled, then stepped into the leap, but fear took hold of my heart before I could complete the sequence.

I slipped and fell. Again.

"Jesus Christ," Kova mumbled, his voice drawing closer to me.

Only this time it wasn't as bad because my ribs didn't hit the beam. However, my crotch suffered severely from the impact and I needed to check on it in the bathroom immediately.

My jaw trembled as tears burst from my eyes. I covered my face and cried silently into the blue mat that smelled like feet. I couldn't do this anymore. I was done, I wanted to go home. It hurt too much.

"Let me see," Coach said, squatting in front of me as I sat holding my stomach. The girls stared at me. Fresh tears dripped from my eyes and he used his thumb to wipe them away.

Kova's eyes met mine. He pushed my knee open to get a better look. From the tops of my knees to my inner thighs, they were both bright red and had scrape marks. Kova hissed. "Go get some ice and sit on it."

I kept my eyes trained on the floor as I made my way out, worried I'd see their gawking faces over my poor performance. I sighed inwardly. Today was the worst day of my life and I wanted to be done with it.

I looked like an amateur. No one fell the way I had today. Twice.

Before going to the cafe for some ice, I stopped in the bathroom and tore my leo off. Damn thing stuck to me. The stabbing pain inside my vagina was like a knife slowly slicing into me and I had to check. Something wasn't right.

Looking down, there were small, red droplets of blood. *Shit.* And I wore a violet leotard, so I'd need to change into another one before I went back out. Or just throw on some shorts.

With two fingers, I gently moved myself around and winced in pain. I was already the color of a cherry and swollen, and I knew by looking, it was going to take a good week to heal. And probably hurt to pee.

Redressing, I washed my hands then made my way into the kitchen. Thankfully no one was around to talk to or question me. I gathered two bags of ice and wrapped both loosely in a paper towel. Placing the bags on a chair, I carefully sat down so one bag hit my center and the other was on my inner thighs. As much as it burned from the chill, it actually felt good at the same time. I leaned over to find a comfortable position on the table and held my weight up with my elbows and dropped my head into my arms. I was trembling inside and sulking at how terrible I performed this afternoon.

As I sat alone icing myself, I visualized the switch leap over and over, landing it perfectly each time with elegance. How I could mess up something as simple as a leap but land a double back handspring back layout sequence perfectly made no sense. I pictured Kova nodding in approval, his striking face looking up proudly at me. Even when he was livid he was gorgeous. Anyone with eyes would agree with me.

Kova was attractively annoying. He put more pressure on me than anyone else and I couldn't decide if that was a good thing or not. I wondered if there was a motive behind pushing me the way he had aside from helping me achieve my dream of going to the Olympics one day. I wasn't that bad off, there had to be more. Couldn't he see I tried my hardest to prove to him I wanted to be here? My stomach was in knots and I clenched my eyes shut, fighting the climbing tears. I couldn't think of anything else to prove any of this to him.

Maybe he hated the ground I walked on. Maybe he saw potential. Maybe I got under his skin. Maybe in some obscure way he liked me. Maybe not...I thought of his stunning girlfriend and knew I was just making stuff up in my head. Katja was the complete opposite of me. Her eyes were a kaleidoscope of amber and peridot. She had a flawless ivory complexion. Not to mention a super model body girls would kill for. There wasn't a thing wrong with her. She was beautiful and smart, and to top it off, she was genuinely nice. The perfect package. Any man would die to be with her.

Since the Fourth of July barbecue, Katja had been to the gym a few times. Watching him embrace her made my heart throb. He'd lace his fingers through her perfectly styled waves, look deeply into her eyes, and pull her mouth to his with passion. As if he needed her to get through the rest of his day. When he pulled away, her mouth would be swollen and red, her eyes glazed over with bliss. But it wasn't just me who watched, the entire girls' team watched in awe, too. They were the perfect couple and we all wished we were her.

Then I remembered when Kova had said I was just as pretty. Gorgeous, even.

The vivid images of his hands roaming my body and not Katja's hit me with force. Wishing I was her was wickedly wrong. I groaned, both in pain from the fall and frustration over my deviant thoughts. There had to be something wrong with me to think of my coach this way, but I couldn't stop. I wanted him to look at me with the same intensity he did her.

His lips grazing my supple ones, his fingers digging into my backside, crushing me to him. His penis pushed against my stomach, not letting me move, hard and hot. His tongue sliding into my mouth and taking control, but with passion and heat like in the movies. He was much bigger than me. Brute strength and compelling eyes.

He ripped my clothes off, I yanked at his shirt and his buttons went flying. He couldn't take his wild eyes off of me.

"How are you doing, Ria?"

My head snapped up in surprise and my lips parted. Coach stood beside me and stared down with inquisitive eyes while he waited for a response. Shit, my breathing deepened while my cheeks flushed from the tainted thoughts I had. I was beginning to notice he only used that nickname when it was just us.

His eyes grew heavy, pupils dilating. As if he knew what I'd been thinking. I blushed again, remembering how he said he liked the pinkish color in my cheeks.

I swallowed and said nothing, averting my gaze to his crotch for some reason. Eyes widened, I looked back at his brooding face.

God, what was wrong with me to picture myself as Katja?

CHAPTER 25

I knew two things.

I was going straight to hell. And I was as red as a fire hydrant.

"Adrianna."

"I, ah...I'm okay," I responded, finding my voice.

He shoved his hands into his pockets. "How bad is it?"

I swallowed, wondering how much to tell him. I went for the truth.

"Pretty bad. I was bleeding a little from the fall. I'm not anymore though." After twenty minutes of icing it, the pain was numb.

Coach's jaw flexed. "Bleeding, huh. And your thighs," his voice was smoky.

Unsure at this point, I pushed the chair out and removed both ice bags. Looking down, I said, "They're pretty red. Scratched up. I'll have a nice burn for a few days."

Squatting, Kova got to my level. He placed a hand at the back of my chair to steady himself, the other on my thigh. I flinched, my legs automatically trying to close, but he stopped me.

"Let me see."

I gulped. While I was uncertain of what he wanted to see, I was positively certain the stain would show through. Talk about embarrassing.

My brows creased together as a shadow cast across his eyes. His thumb began rubbing small, slow circles on the inside of my knee. His touch was exhilarating and soothing, and I couldn't help but wonder if this was his way of apologizing for how he treated me earlier.

"Your thighs, where you hit the beam...let me see." With that, he placed his other hand on my opposite knee and slowly pushed my legs open.

The rise and fall of his chest matched mine. Our breathing grew heavy as the air thickened. Kova's large hands moved slowly toward my hips, pushing against me and opening my legs wider. My hips rolled up and my back arched, pushing my chest out.

He paused before he reached the apex of my thighs, and I mean *right* before. I held my breath and my heart froze. The room grew significantly smaller. He wouldn't dare go any further, would he? Desire coursed through my body and the thought of stopping him never once occurred. I actually wanted him to touch me where he never should go. The forbidden facet was possibly the calculating equation. His palms and fingers dug into my flesh, scooting me closer to him.

I began to tremble under his hold and he slowly licked his bottom lip. His eyes never left mine as I let him know it was okay. I arched my back, leaving only my shoulders to rest against the chair.

Gone was the cold shock of the bags of ice I had been sitting on moments earlier, and in its place was scorching, hot heat. Need. Want. Something, I just wasn't sure what. Kova paused, then resumed his glide up my thighs.

"It is a pretty bad burn." His eyelids lowered and he groaned in the back of his throat. "You are going to be sore for days, make sure to put some balm on it..." he trailed off, his focus at the center of my legs. His thumb soothed the burn that marred my tender skin. He was so close to my sex, I began to throb for his touch.

I nodded instinctively, and without thinking, I reached out. My nails digging into the curve of his bicep when his thumb stopped. He created an ache that needed to be released, a buildup was flowing inside of me.

He knew what he was doing. What he was creating within me.

If I breathed, he'd touch me in a place no one had ever touched me before.

And maybe I wanted that.

My hips undulated when the back of his knuckles swept over my thigh, the tips of his fingers brushing the side of my sex, close to the seam of my lips. A little gasp escaped my mouth, my chest burned from holding in my breath. The touch was so light, so faint, but I felt it, and I think he knew too.

Kova held stock still, frozen in place, as a throbbing pulse resonated from deep within me.

Oh God, it felt like I was ready to come apart and I wanted him to do it again. Imagine my shock when his eyes lowered and his thumb cautiously reached out and deliberately stroked the side of my pussy.

I didn't say stop. Or not to touch me. I'd always been taught to say no to bad touches, but this wasn't bad, it felt good. He made me feel good. It wasn't like he was a stranger. This was my coach, a friend of my dad's.

And deep down, I wanted it.

"Kova." His jaw flexed at the sound of my cracked voice. He fought to lift his head, his eyes trained in one spot. My legs widened further, signaling I wanted him to do it again, ready to feel whatever was brewing inside. I was so close, I could feel it. Seconds went by and the pleasure receded.

And then, just when I thought he was going to pull back, his thumb moved a fraction and slid between my lips, over my leo, from bottom to top in a swirling motion on my pussy.

Sweet Jesus!

Instinctively, my nails dug deep in his golden skin as I pushed my chest out. My nipples tightened, hardening to little points. I gave Kova full access as my hips unwound in the chair, reveling in his touch. He growled low as I moved myself against his hand. I needed more, I wanted it. A million tiny explosions were climbing inside me, building up higher and higher. I wanted to reach that pinnacle of bliss.

Kova pressed his thumb hard against my clit and pushed in circles, his fingertips seeking entrance, but my leo was too tight. A rush of wetness coated through the fabric, directly beneath his thumb. Kova rumbled deep in the back of his throat as he rubbed the wet stain. My legs shook and it took everything in me not to yell out from the intensity of the pleasure.

"Oh," I breathed ever so quietly. "Oh...God. It feels so good." I was right there. My entire body came apart, tingling with the euphoric bliss he brought me as I blew up. His thumb circled faster, my hips rolled in a wave as I exploded in front of him. I gripped the side of the chair, and released a heavy breath. My shoulders relaxed back.

Kova was breathing low and heavy when I finally found my voice. "What...what was that?"

His shocked gaze snapped to mine and held still. When he didn't say anything, I asked again, "What was that?"

Removing his hand from my sex, he squeezed my knee painfully hard. His hand shook and the skin on his knuckles tightened. The vein in his arm twirled down in a spiral as he stared at the ground, lost in thought.

"An orgasm, I presume," he choked out.

I shook my head vehemently. "No way. I've had orgasms before and they never once felt that incredible."

Kova's knees cracked as he stood, his pelvis directly in front of my face...along with an obvious erection. I swallowed back and looked up at him, his intoxicating eyes were already trained hard on me. He cupped himself, stroking his hard length. I glanced down, mesmerized as I watched him wrap his hand around his thickness, moving it around almost as if he was trying to push it down.

I licked my dry lips and glanced up. Kova had never taken his eyes off me. He dragged a hand through his hair and expelled a loud breath. His eyes finally left mine and scattered around the cafe.

"Do you think you will be able to go back out and train again?" he asked.

Wait—What? He wanted me to train after that mind-blowing orgasm I just had—he was certifiably insane.

I cleared my throat. "Yeah, I need to change my leo first."

That got his attention. "Actually go home, Ria." His face was void of any emotion and my stomach tightened. "You had enough for today." He coughed. "That, ah, fall was a bad one."

I frowned. I didn't want him to send me home.

"But I still have a half day of training left."

"I am giving you the rest of the day off."

I stood to get my point across. "But I need these extra hours, you know I need all the help I can get. I don't want to go home."

"Adrianna, at this point I do not care what you want. I said go home, so go. For once, can you not fucking argue with me and just go?"

I flinched and forced back my rising tears. He'd never used such a menacing tone with me since I began training, or cursed. At least not that I could remember. His sudden, hurtful glare got to me. "No, I won't."

Muttering in Russian, he glared at me.

"I'll suck it up and deal. It's my problem, not yours. It was only a little fall anyway."

Slowly, he looked in my direction, as if he was ready to body slam me to the floor. My heart pounded painfully against my ribs. I wasn't sure what I'd done that was so wrong.

"I do not want to see your face until tomorrow. Am I making myself clear?"

Breathing deeper and pulling from within, I pushed back. I was ready to blow, and not in a good way. The Sicilian in me was coming out.

"You can't make me go home for this. It was a stupid fall, and no one else has been sent home for falling!"

His eyes softened. "You misunderstand. If you do not go home and recover, tomorrow is going to be painful for you."

This man confused me. One minute he was growling and ready to strangle me, the next, like right this instance, he was concerned and caring.

I nodded. Actually, he was right. "I don't understand you."

"You are not supposed to."

Then he stalked off and left the room as if nothing happened.

CHAPTER 26

Sometimes when the day ended and everyone went home, I liked to come into the gym late at night just to lie on the floor and stare up at the ceiling, visualizing my routines over and over. My body would flinch and jerk as I pictured myself nail each skill and dismount, pleasing my coaches.

Every gymnast had access to the gym with just a swipe of their card, yet I'd never seen any here the few times I came.

In the hushed silence of the night, being surrounded by the equipment was freeing, and it brought a sense of security that filled my soul. No one to yell at me or stare down and tell me how wrong I was. No cold shoulders from my teammates. No side-looks or smirks to shake my confidence. It was just me and the gym as I breathed in the chalky air.

Switching on one light, it illuminated over the parallel bars, leaving the rest of the gym cased in darkness, which was just what I wanted. I liked the obscurity. It was serene and comforting.

A nice little bruise had formed on my pubic bone. I'd had falls on beam before, but this one was probably one of the worst since I'd fallen back-to-back. I iced myself religiously three times, soaked in a bath, and took four Motrin to alleviate the swelling. And nearly a week later, I was good to go.

Walking toward the blue-carpeted spring floor, I zipped up my sweater. The chill hit my bones, a tremble waked through me. Without the heated bodies to fill the gym, it was actually quite cold in here. Once I was in the dead center, I laid down and a shiver crept up my spine.

Meet season would soon be here and I needed to mentally prepare. I wasn't sure which meets Kova would put me in, but since this year was an Olympic year, elite season dates changed. I had roughly four months to go, then December to June would be nonstop. The competitions were much larger than what I was used to, competing outside the state, and competing against new athletes, mostly younger than me and with harder skills. The younger part worried me the most, though I would never in a million years admit it to anyone. The last few months had been pure hell, both emotionally and physically, and divulging it would make me appear like the weakling I felt I was at times. So I bottled it up and kept my mouth shut.

Just like I did back home.

Expelling a deep sigh, I had to find trust and belief from within to gain the confidence I needed. I had experience and maturity due to my age and upbringing. Hopefully that would work in my favor.

I slipped my ear buds in and began playing *The End* by Kings of Leon. His deep, baritone voice along with the beats drowned out the negative voices in my head and allowed me to think freely. I was able to forget the weight of my life for a little while without the added pressure of anyone. The music spoke to me and I listened.

I wasn't sure how long I'd been there when something caught the corner of my eye. Craning my neck to the side, I looked toward the light from the door and my stomach dropped.

Coach Kova.

I had no idea what he was doing here. Surely, he got enough of the gym being here all day.

He looked to be on a mission as he strode toward the now illuminated rings, determined and completely oblivious I was present.

Thank God. He probably figured he berated the gymnasts enough they wouldn't be here after hours.

Wait, I take that back. He only berated me to that extent. I was his punching bag on a bad day.

Reaching behind his neck, he fisted his gray shirt and pulled it over his head. It slid off his back smoothly, like a piece of silk, and dropped it to the ground. I sucked in a breath as he undressed under the muted light. I'd never seen him without a shirt before. Other than an occasional tumbling pass where his shirt would rise up and show a hint of his stomach, it was all the skin of his I'd ever seen.

He toed off his sneakers, leaving only a pair of black basketball shorts on, then cracked his neck, rolling it around in circles. He threw his arms out to the sides, swinging them around wildly to stretch them out. From behind, his golden back was lean, honed to absolute perfection, the muscles flexing as he stretched out his upper half. I couldn't help but lie still and stare at him in awe. His back was a work of art. Just like him.

He was fucking gorgeous.

I whimpered internally. Only I would see having a hot coach as a curse.

Kova jumped and grasped the rings. The corded muscles in his shoulders tightened and I watched as he began whipping his pointed toes back and forth while he held steady. Arching his back, then hollowing his chest, he had great form.

He went straight into full swings, handstands, and flips, warming up his body. My jaw went slack. He maneuvered the rings with precision, like a champ. I'd never seen him use any apparatus at practice before. He was focused, completely unaware anyone was watching. And I was happy he was oblivious. I was mesmerized by the sight before me. He had such grace and beauty coiled in his toned body that I think if he knew anyone was watching he'd stop. His control was remarkable at his age. Thirty-two wasn't old by any means, but for a gymnast it was ancient. Christ, eighteen was over the hill for a gymnast.

Most gymnasts retired around the age of eighteen, very few made it to their mid-twenties. Not by choice, but because their bodies could no longer handle the physical strain and demand of the sport. Almost always, there was an injury we sustained.

We defied gravity on the floor with insane jaw dropping tumbling passes, ran toward stationary objects to flip over, and balanced on a four-inch piece of wood with turns, tucks, and fulls. All the while killing our backs and feet from landings and dismounts. The impact shocked our ankles and zoomed up our spines, making us wince in pain. But we grinned and dealt with it and did what we were born to do, because we couldn't imagine life without it. Just as Kova was doing now. He couldn't let go.

Kova pulled up into a handstand then slowly extended his arms out to the sides so now he was in an upside down T, his back facing me. His body was pulled tight and locked solid. Roped muscles in his shoulders jutted out, and cut sharp as he began to slowly lower his body into a plank position. I held my breath as I watched. The skill was not an easy one to master. I'd seen teammates shake from the brute strength it took to hold this form. But Kova didn't move, he didn't shake. His arms were as steady as the rest of his body. There was no blowing like a leaf, as he once said I had on beam. It was beyond remarkable my coach could still do a skill of this capacity.

With incredible accuracy and control, he rotated his arms just a fraction so they were turned out. From his sculpted shoulders to the veins that snaked around his arms, he didn't waver in his hold. It was utterly fascinating. His body exuded raw power and strength, and it was beautifully captivating. Remarkable. I've tried so hard not to associate Kova with anything other than him being my gymnastics coach. But seeing his determination and fight to make me a better gymnast on a daily basis compelled me to think of him in more ways than I should. And now, with how he was conveying control without anyone around, it was hard to see him as just my coach.

Once in a forward facing T, he pulled his legs up into a pike position. My gaze traveled down his solid chest, taking in his lean abdomen.

And my mouth gaped open, a gush of hot air rolling off my lips. *Mother of all hell.*

There was a fairly large Olympic ring tattoo on the left side of his ribs. Unlike the colorful rings the symbol was known for, Kova's five ring tattoo was in solid black. And with each breath he took, the tattoo moved as if it were floating on his skin.

Sweet Jesus, Mary, and Joseph. I was gawking at his body, and it was hard to tear my gaze away. The tattoo and placement was unbelievably sexy. It upped his hot factor by ten million, not that he needed it.

Suddenly, he began swinging hard in circles and then landed a back tuck dismount. His feet pounded the ground, the chalk lifting in the air from impact. He rose to his full height, eyes closed and shoulders rolled back as his chest expanded from deep breaths. The tattoo grew then shrunk with each breath he took. It was almost impossible to tear my eyes from his ribs. My gaze traveled down his waist to where his shorts sat extremely low. He had those indents on his hips that formed a V, and my God, my mouth started to water.

For a split moment, I forgot he was my coach. I pictured myself running my hands slowly up his stomach, massaging his worn muscles, before tracing his tattoo and exploring his body. My fingers gliding over his arms, roaming over his shoulders in the dark where no one could see us.

Ten more minutes passed while I secretly watched Kova as just him, a man on the rings, and nothing more. I didn't move a muscle, just watched in awe...until my phone started ringing.

Fuck. Fuck. Fuck.

Grabbing my cell, I silenced my mom then looked back over to the rings to see him glaring at me from under the apparatus. Standing up, I had no choice but to walk over to him.

Kova let go of the rings, whipped his hands back and forth, and firmly crossed his arms in front of his bare chest, his stance intimidating as he stood under the rings. His biceps grabbed my attention and I could feel his searing, pissed gaze focused on my face.

"Adrianna," he stated more than called my name.

"Coach."

"What are you doing here?" He asked, dropping his arms to rub his wrists then crossed his hands behind him, his pecs flexing. I openly raked my eyes down the length of his gorgeous body. There was no way not to, and honestly, I didn't care that he saw me do it.

I shrugged, closing the distance between us. "I needed to think. Sometimes I like coming here when it's empty."

"So you come to the gym to just lie on the floor?"

He was skeptical. It was obvious, but I told him the truth. He could decide what to do with it.

"I do...I feel free in the dark, no one here to judge me," I said, pinning him with honest eyes.

"But you are lying on the floor?"

I let it all out. "Exactly. No one can say I'm doing anything wrong, that my form is incorrect, or how my legs aren't locked. Stupid things I already know. I'm not fearful I'll slip on the beam, or I'm not blocking hard enough on vault. No one to make me feel like I'm not good enough, that I'm not graceful enough. There's no one to hate the ground I walk on in here when I'm alone. No one can see me in the dark to point out my imperfections. It's just me and the gym, all by myself to do as I please."

He almost looked remorseful at my admission. "And you cannot do this at home?"

I looked away to conceal my emotions. "No, it's too quiet there. Usually the loneliness doesn't bother me and I embrace it. Some nights it gets to be too much, so I run away and come here," I finished quietly. "The oddness of it all, I feel more at home here than anywhere else. Tonight, the silence in my condo was deafening and I needed to get out. The gym speaks to me."

He took a step toward me so he was only inches away.

"It is okay. I understand why you are here alone."

His eyes locked with mine, and through the muted lights a shadow covered half his face as something stirred between us. My heart stammered, feeling it, and I knew he felt it too by the look of his dilating pupils that took up most of his bright eyes. His jaw locked, shifting back and forth.

Kova continued, as though talking to himself. "Why do you think I am here?"

CHAPTER 27

Time stood still.

"How do you do it," I whispered. He took a small step toward me and I held my breath. I watched as his eyes skated across my face, my eyes, nose, to my cheeks...where they locked on my mouth. We were balancing on a fine line and we both knew it.

My heart raced, the blood in my veins heating as his gaze struck me to the core. My lips parted, a soft breath expelling. I didn't know what to do, what to say. Kova was so close as we stood alone in the darkened gym. I thought about how he touched me the other day in the cafe and the way he looked at me. It was nothing compared to the way his eyes were boring into mine in this moment where no one could see us. It rendered me speechless. Anything could happen now—and that intrigued me.

Tension crackled and I knew he felt it. There was no denying the invisible pull or the gleaming look in his eyes. Lifting his hand, the back of his chalk covered knuckles brushed across the edge of my jaw. I knew he shouldn't be doing it, he sure as hell knew he shouldn't be, but I tilted my head into his hand, asking for more.

Leaning down, he whispered, "Do what?"

"How do you hold steady on the rings the way you do? I was in awe watching you. You move so quietly, I can't tear my eyes away."

"Control."

The heat of his body radiated on to mine and I felt his response on my lips. My heart pounded painfully against my ribs. Kova was as exhilarating as his touch. I wanted so badly to reach out and grab him.

"Control. Power. Muscle memory," he responded huskily, the look in his eyes piercing me. "You have to know your body inside and out. When to let go. When to hold on. You have to feel it, visualize it...want it."

"How do you know when to let go?"

"Your body will tell you. Listen to your body, Ria. Trust it. What is it telling you?" he asked in a smoky voice, sending goose bumps down my arms. I loved when he called me Ria when no one else was around.

Biting my bottom lip, my eyes slowly met his as I gripped his thick wrist that cupped my face. My other hand reached for his waist and latched on. I couldn't stop myself, I wanted to feel him...I *needed* to. If he was touching me, I could touch him. It was only fair. At least now I had an excuse—a justification. But what I really wanted to do was trace the tattoo on his ribs.

My fingers caressed his taut hips, the back of my knuckles dragged along the waistband of his shorts ever so delicately. Kova's eyes widened and he drew in a shaky breath as his stomach flexed. He wasn't expecting it, and truthfully, I didn't know where I got the courage to do it. I stepped closer to continue my exploration.

I couldn't keep my hands to myself, I didn't want to. I wanted to know what it was like to be pressed against him, my heart to his, beating at the same time.

Our chests nearly closed the distance, our gazes locked, and I could feel the heat of his skin under my hand. A million thoughts were running through my mind. Every second passed was like torture. His body was solid as stone but soft to the touch. I slid my hand up his ribs, my thumb finally circling the tattoo.

"I like your tattoo," I admitted. "A lot." A slow breath rolled off his lips and into my face. A faint hint of cranberry and vodka.

"I want to learn control like you," I whispered.

"All in good time."

"Teach me."

"Control?"

I nodded, taking in every inch of his chest.

"You ask for too much."

I stared up through my eyelashes, trying to conceal my emotions. He was right. I was asking for more than gymnastics and he knew it, but at the same time I didn't know exactly what I was asking for. I had no idea what I wanted and more importantly, I had no idea what the hell we were doing.

We'd been dancing around each other for weeks now. The lingering touches, the long stares. It was building, simmering between us.

With both trembling hands now resting on his firm chest, one of his hardened nipples grazed the bottom of my palm and he contracted. His head angled down, his eyes boring into mine. If only I was a little taller.

"Is this what control is?" My gaze traveled to his mouth as I slightly tilted my head and lifted up to the balls of my feet. I wanted to kiss him desperately, to feel his lips pressed to mine. "Wanting to try a new skill without preparing for it first? That I could be risking everything?"

I was purely infatuated with him.

Kova reached out and gripped my arm from my temptation laced words. His fingers dug into my bicep. I watched his control waver, and for a selfish moment, I hoped it snapped.

"That is exactly what it is," he said quietly. "Wanting to try something so badly but knowing it is not the right step. At least not yet. Knowing when to spring forward and knowing when not to. You perfect your craft to the best of your ability when you are ready. It is also about control and trust. Trust more than anything in yourself."

"When will I know?" I whispered.

"Practice. Practice. Practice. It is all about being able to execute a flawless routine. A feeling that streams through your body. You will know when the time is right."

"What if I don't?"

He paused, his cool breath hitting my face. "Gymnastics is very similar to everyday life. It is trial and error, Ria. It is about taking chances, is it not? It is about power. A mental war. It is about not being afraid to try something new even if it scares you. If you do not jump, you will never know how high you can soar. It is about controlling your leap once you let go, but not being afraid of switching your directions. It is a chance you are willing to take."

"And what if I take the leap and slip?"

My heart was racing. His hands cupped my jaw, tilting my head back. "Then you get back up and try again."

For a moment, time stood still. Everything was forgotten except the two of us standing in the empty gym. We were inches apart, an intake of breath away from doing something that would go against the rules, and the law. The code of ethics. Morals.

And for whatever reason, none of that mattered to me.

Kova's thumb circled my jaw so softly that it took everything in me not to shiver. It was as if he was touching me beneath my flesh, purposely heating my body and tugging on every fiber. His caress was powerful.

The look in his beautiful, deep green irises stripped me bare. I couldn't seem to tear my focus from his. And truthfully, I didn't want to. His eyes were hypnotic. Spellbinding. Alluringly tantalizing, and I felt him down to the bone.

My hold tightened on his bare skin. The palm of his hand grazed my cheek and slid down to my jaw, leaving a trail of heat in its wake where his warm hand cupped my nape. My heart pounded and my breathing grew shallow. I wanted him to lean in and kiss me, to press his lips to mine and kiss me hard. I just wanted to feel his flesh on me.

My body ached from standing on my tiptoes, but I didn't dare back down. Instead, I tilted my head, giving him access to my mouth, the same way I gave him access to my hips. His stare shifted down to my parted lips...then to my chest.

I waited to see if he would take it or not.

Kova inhaled deeply and I curled into him like I was the air he was breathing in. His fingers found the zipper to my jacket. Carefully, he pulled the zipper down. His gaze met mine again as he reached the bottom. Kova's callused fingers slid under the material and pushed it down my shoulders until it fell silently to the floor. He hissed, his eyes crinkled. Looking down, I wore a solid white cami, sans bra. And there was no mistaking the outline of my breasts or the hard-ening of my nipples. Attentively, his hand came up and his knuckles grazed the outside of my plump breast ever so slowly. Our breathing mingled together and my body reached for his touch.

His arm circled my lower back and tenderly pulled me to him. *Yes.* He was so big, so strong and dominating in the way he held me. A long, hard length lay angled against my pelvis and my body melted into him. His erection tapped my pussy and my eyes rolled shut. I placed my hand on the curve of his neck, feeling his raw power contract beneath my fingertips. The man was a walking sin. I kept telling myself I couldn't help it, that I needed to feel more of him, to make something happen. Sometimes a little self-convincing helped.

His stubble grazed my cheek, and his breath tingled my neck. I gasped, my stomach tightened.

He made his move, and I mimicked it.

Something shifted deep inside me, an awakening of an emotion heated my blood. A dark desire inside my belly was aching to come out. I tilted my jaw seeking his mouth. No words were needed, just a single touch and a sigh would be enough to get what I—we—wanted. We were so close to closing the gap fully, our lips pressed to one another, but neither one moved. Probably because whoever took the first step knew better than to.

I wanted to kiss my coach...And I was positively certain he wanted to kiss me.

It was that simple. Only it really wasn't. A gymnast and a coach? That was anything but simple.

What it was, was morally wrong.

But who was asking?

"What are you doing, *malysh*?" His breath tickled my neck. *Malysh*. He called me *malysh* again and I almost melted.

"Maybe I'm..." I paused to lick my lips. "I think...I don't know."

I had no idea what the hell I was doing. The only thing I knew was I was in way over my head and there was no going back. Nothing was going to stop me from moving forward. I wanted his mouth on mine. I wanted to taste his lips and feel his tongue tangled with mine. I was just too nervous to take the plunge.

"You should be practicing control," he whispered, angling only a breath away from my lips. His Russian accent was stronger than usual, and I liked it a lot. His erection grew harder and I loved it, loved that I caused it. The tension was stifling and my chest burned from the rapid beats of my heart. I wished he'd just kiss me already.

"But you are not practicing at all."

"I asked for your guidance. Show me control and I'll practice it."

"You should step away."

"I should? Or I need to."

"Both."

"And if I don't? You told me to use you, remember? So here I am, asking."

He paused, his lips curling in satisfaction.

"After a workout, my body is weak, and my control sucks, Ria. I have no control now," and then he slammed his mouth to mine.

CHAPTER 28

A*-fucking-men!*

I whimpered into him. His lips were firm and bruising, much like his personality. My hands slid up his chest and I squeezed his shoulders, my nails scoring his skin. A flood of heat pulsed through my body, my hips rolled into his, feeling the hardness between them. Finally, we were touching the way we both secretly envisioned it.

At least how I have.

The tight grip on my arm moved to my waist, pulling me flush against him. His fingers threaded my hair, holding my loose ponytail in his hand. We didn't stop moving our mouths back and forth. His plump lips were soft, pliable, coercing me to bend to his will. They were exactly what I imagined they'd feel like.

I wanted more. My body craved more, to see how far we could take this.

With a flick of my chin, I reached up and grabbed the back of his head and pressed him further into me. His hair was damp with sweat from working on the rings. He groaned, biting my bottom lip and pressed his hardness into my stomach. It was sexy as hell to hear him moan and I was desperate for the sweet sound again.

Sweet Jesus. Yes... Screw the embarrassment over the sounds I was holding in. I moaned in the back of my throat, letting Kova know how much I liked this. I was hot, achy, and reached blindly for something I wasn't sure of.

With a tilt of my head, I opened my mouth and gently pulled his bottom lip with my teeth. He clutched me to him hard, his fingers dug into me and he exhaled into my mouth. Hesitantly, tracing the seam of his lips, I slipped my tongue inside. A soft whimper escaped me. The taste of him was as sweet as candy, and cool with the hint of vodka I'd smelled earlier.

Just as I was getting comfortable with him, Kova stiffened. Shockingly, he pushed me away and covered his mouth, uttering a string of Russian curse words hidden behind the back of his hand.

The hurt in my eyes could not be contained from the sudden ache he just caused in my heart. Glancing down, I eyed the mat.

"Shit," he muttered, followed by something in Russian again. "Adrianna, I am sorry."

I was confused. "It's okay."

"No, it is not okay. I should not have let this happen, let anything happen for that matter. Like the other day after you straddled the beam. It was wrong of me." His stomach hardened to granite with each hard breath he drew in. "Do you know how wrong this is?"

My head snapped to his. "Wrong? How is it wrong? I don't understand. It was just a kiss."

Appalled, he looked at me sharply and I flinched. "Do not look at me like that."

"Like what?"

"Like you are hurting, upset. It..." he stammered, "affects me more than I care to admit."

Rolling my lip between my teeth and releasing it, I said, "I am upset. It isn't like you're hurting me, or forcing me to do anything I don't want. I don't see how this could be so wrong when it feels so right." I sighed dejectedly. "I didn't want to stop."

"You are not making this any easier." Then he strode toward me and crushed his lips to mine.

Kova wrapped an arm around my back and hauled me to him, his fingers trembled beneath his touch. It was obvious he struggled with what he shouldn't be doing. But there was no denying the way he held me, the way his passion and emotion oozed into me. He wanted me. The hard length pressing against my stomach was evidence.

Our tongues collided, heat flared between us. They wrapped around each other, grabbing and fighting, twisting with desire. My God, the man was a skilled kisser and knew exactly how to tangle his tongue with mine and tug, stroking it simultaneously. My body tingled in his hold. This kiss was unlike any other I'd experience in the past. He was untamed and wild and it made me want to feel every inch of him.

"Adrianna..." He growled against my mouth before he kissed me again.

"Shhh, I'm practicing control."

"This is control?" He chuckled between kisses and I realized how much I loved his laugh.

I replied by searching for his tongue again and sucked on it. Kova's fingers dug into my back before skimming down to my ass. Cupping me, he hiked me up and my legs automatically locked behind his back. "You're so light," he said when I nearly slammed into him. I gripped his shoulders for support. His body shook as he held me, fighting to hold back, and I loved it. I loved how strong he was, how he could do anything to me, and I'd let him.

Slowly, Kova turned around with me in his arms. He walked a couple of feet and pressed me up against a tall spotting block that shielded us from the front window of the gym. Darkness surrounded us and gave way to the illicit act. He leaned against me and the softness of the block pressed into my back. His erection strained between us, long and hard, the back of it rubbing against my clit. I sighed, and his eyes lowered at the wispy sound that escaped me.

"Adrianna..." he said, his voice thick and husky. He placed his hands on my hips and gripped me with power. There was a real struggle to resist around his eyes that made me almost break contact with him. I wanted so badly to ask him what he was thinking as he searched my face, his breathing deepening by the second. But the fear of being rejected was high, so I didn't.

Instead, I pulled him closer. "It's okay, no one can see us."

My body was simmering with rapture, and he began to move my hips ridiculously slow, up and down. I skipped the panties, so the only barriers between us were my paper thin yoga capris and Kova's usual basketball shorts. The thought of too much clothing passed through my mind, but the friction was just perfect as he stroked his dick against me. I rotated my hips up to feel the pressure against my sex. As he glided against me even more, a breathless whimper escaped.

"Kova..." I whispered when his lips touched my neck, the dusty shadow of his beard scraped along my skin. His hips moved against mine.

"You are missing the point. I am your coach, and a man. You should be repulsed by me." The ache in his voice hurt my chest. "Girls your age do not look at men like me. You are supposed to like guys from boy bands or something."

A smile caressed my lips. I shrugged. "Quite the opposite actually."

Placing my hands on the back of his neck, my fingers threaded his hair and a rumble sounded in the back of his throat. I was getting hotter by the minute. Kova didn't break his stance and kept on rolling his hips into me. My orgasm was climbing higher and I wondered if he was close to having one too.

"God, that feels amazing," I cried out. Even in the dim lighting I could see every rigid plank of muscle from this angle. My fingers timidly trailed over his chest, skating down his arms. My back bowed and Kova hissed.

"Adrianna." His tone disagreed with himself and his body contradicted his words.

I could tell his conscience was weighing heavily on him as his nails dug into my skin and his breathing became ragged. As selfish as it was, I didn't care or really give it much thought to how he felt. I didn't even try to bring this to an end. Instead, I opened up the gates and gave him free access to do as he pleased.

Kova tilted his head down and slammed his mouth to mine. He kissed me hard and inhaled like he was trying to breathe me in. My arms wrapped around his back, my hands kneading him roughly. He continued like he was a starved man in need of vitality. My heart bloomed inside my chest and I loved it. I loved that he wanted me.

I broke the kiss. "I want to touch you."

He swallowed so hard his jaw flexed. "I guess we are both learning control tonight," he quipped, shaking his head. His tongue slipped out to lick his lips. I wanted to look and feel every inch of him, to watch him respond to my fingers, to see the rise and fall of his muscles.

"I cannot stop kissing you," he admitted. Kova leaned down and took my mouth with a growl, nipping and biting. This time though, much slower. Like he was savoring me.

I never dreamed a kiss could be so sensual.

Kova's tongue was dangerous. No, he was dangerous. I was shocked by how slow he could kiss. He was precise and seductive. And it was erotic—torture. He knew how to bring a girl to her knees with just the touch of his lips.

With a kiss like this, he could have anything he wanted.

He groaned into my mouth, much louder this time, a vibration rumbling against my chest and I scratched his back. It made me feel more like a woman knowing I could draw this sound from him. His length hit the spot between my thighs and I melted into him, rubbing myself on him. *Heaven help me now.* A million sparks went off inside of me, goose bumps coated my skin as an orgasm shimmered through my body.

Unlocking my legs, they slid down his hips so I could stand on tiptoe. He bit my lip and tugged it into his mouth when I stepped to close my legs, trapping his penis securely between my thighs. The waistband of his shorts angled down and my eyes fought to get a better look. There was no denying that Kova was hard and *really* big. His hands trailed up to my nape, my stomach clenched at how rough he fisted my hair and tilted my head back. I moaned loud enough for him to hear, letting him know how incredible the sensation was. The tight hold he had on me coupled with his thickness felt unbelievable. It was doing things to my head. My hips rolled into his, needing more. We were at the right height when he started rubbing my swollen flesh with his. I gasped, clutching him to me, pleading for him not to stop.

"Oh, fuck. You like that. Tell me you do not like it." He begged against my mouth.

"Yes, just like that." And I did. I loved it.

Another orgasm was brewing, soaring from the growing friction. My hands were everywhere on him, drowning in the sensations surrounding us. A fiery concoction of heat and craving swept through me. He kept hitting that one tender spot, and if I arched my pelvis into his, I'd get a better angle.

Sweet Jesus, I was ready to combust.

Inhaling his sultry blend of cinnamon and citrus scent, Kova's hand cupped the back of my head and guided me to his chest. I took note in how his hands stayed above my shoulders the whole time, like he was afraid to touch me anywhere else. I dropped little kisses to his heated flesh, tempted to run my tongue over his nipple.

Glancing down his stomach, the waistband of his shorts pulled forward even more and I was able to get a peek at his black curls.

I couldn't resist. I delicately traced his tattoo with my middle finger, circling the rings. He inhaled and watched my fingers. I pressed my hands to his abs, feeling every rigid abdominal muscle until I reached his hips. Kova held still as he allowed me to explore his body. My nails grazed the indentation toward his groin, dipping lower until a softness touched my knuckles. His stomach flexed in response.

Kova swiftly gripped my wrist and pulled my hand away.

"No, Ria."

CHAPTER 29

I pursed my lips together, unhappy with his decision.

"Adrianna, we need to stop." I ignored him since I didn't agree, but he pressed on. "It is hard for me to control myself when your hands are on my body like this..." His eyes darkened and he licked his lips.

"Don't stop just yet. I want...I want to..." I trailed off.

"To what?"

My teeth dug into my bottom lip and I looked at him coyly. "To have an orgasm like this."

A low growl escaped him. "What I would give to feel the real thing, to feel you on my cock."

SWEET JESUS! MOTHER OF ALL GODS!

He just said that.

To me.

And I didn't know how to respond.

My heart pounded against my ribs, and despite how scorching hot I was, I shivered from the searing heat that zipped down my spine when he looked deep into my eyes.

Kova whispered in Russian and clenched his eyes shut. I loved when he did that. It was so sexy. "Imagine the pressure building between your hips, the tightness," he groaned. "Your small, wet little pussy wrapped around my cock. So tight..."

"Kova," I breathed, almost gasping for air. I was about to combust. Who knew dirty talking could be so hot. Never, had I ever, had anyone talk to me like that before.

"I...want...yes..." I couldn't find the words, so I let my actions do the talking. I dug my nails into him again, scoring his skin as I struggled with temptation. Poor guy was going to have nail marks all over him.

I was so close, and I think he knew. Kova began stroking me with himself, bringing me higher and higher. His hands clenched around my hips, pulling me forward and then back. I had a sudden image in my head of throwing him to the floor and jumping on him. I gripped the back of his biceps and shook with need. My head dropped to his chest and I released a heated breath against him.

"Look at me," he demanded. "Tell me how you feel, I need to know you want this."

I looked up and met his gaze. "Good. Too good," I panted.

"You want this? You like how you feel?"

I nodded rapidly.

"Do you want me?" he asked, pressing against my center so hard I whimpered.

I nodded again, reaching for his mouth with mine.

"Good. I like that you want me," he said with a wicked grin that matched his eyes.

Once again, my hands went everywhere when our mouths locked together. They moved to his backside where my fingertips dipped into the waistband of his shorts, feeling his warmed flesh. I wanted to push in more, but I was nervous. Another groan left his mouth, my thumb skimming his pelvis near his groin again.

"Do it," he ordered.

Do what, I wasn't sure. And I think he could read my mind when he grabbed one of my wrists and moved it to the front of his pants.

"Do it," he ordered again, his voice husky. "Touch me."

There was no way I could resist his command. I was high on Kova. I couldn't think straight, only that I would do anything he told me to do at that point. Swallowing hard, I teasingly traced my nails along his shorts.

"Inside. Put your hand inside my pants, *malysh,* and touch my cock. Feel what you do to me." He finished the last sentence with pride in his voice.

I slipped my hand inside and felt fine, little hairs thread through my fingers as I shyly reached for him.

"That is it, keep going," he said in a guttural voice. "A little farther. Do you want to come?"

I nodded eagerly, because, hello, there was no other possible response.

"Then put your little fingers around my cock. Stroke it hard. You know you want to."

Truthfully, I was kind of afraid to keep going. Not afraid of Kova, but because for the simple fact I had no idea what to do when I reached him. I mean, my friends talked about it, I knew, but I'd never done any of it myself.

"Go ahead," he encouraged.

Desire to please Kova took over. I didn't want to show my inexperience, so I did as he commanded and wrapped my hand around his erection. His skin was soft as silk yet his dick was as hard as granite, not at all what I expected. I kind of liked the velvety soft smoothness. My fingers curved around his meaty tip and a sticky moisture slipped through my fingers.

"Like that...just like that. Keep going," his voice cracked, hips moving. His hands reached above my head and gripped the edge of the spotting mat. "I am about to come in my pants," he openly admitted. Interestingly enough, so was I. "Right there," he whispered. Reaching down, he clutched my ass and hitched my knee around his hip.

I imagined what I thought would feel good for him; I stroked him from tip to base, twisting my wrist. Inaudible sounds laced with pleasure were coming from him. He was...thick. Heavy. Large. Kova devoured my mouth, kissing me so hard I was sure I tasted blood. His body was a rolling wave crashing into me and I couldn't help but wonder if it was how he had sex. Because if it was, well, fucking sign me up. He could have my virginity any day.

"Use your other hand," his hot breath tickled my neck. "Cup my balls and play with them."

Wanting to please him, I reached inside and the elastic of his shorts stretched open. His balls were heavy and firm, similar to his shaft. I couldn't stop staring at his body from this angle, the defined lines of his muscles, and the movement of my hand. The brute strength he yielded. The sensuality of it caught me off guard, a flush of ecstasy hitting me hard. My hands caused his shorts to push down and I became needy. I wanted to sneak a quick look at his dick, but the overwhelming desire to have an orgasm hit me hard. I moved to angle myself so I could rub up on his length, but his hand landed on my pussy, hitting the tiny bundle of nerves.

"Oh, my God," I cried out when he began rubbing me vigorously, my hand pausing for a second. "Yes…" I purred, my head rolling back.

He growled. "Christ. You are soaking wet. Fuck my hand," he rubbed me in rough circles. My leg supporting me became weak as my orgasm climbed. I strained on my toes, thrusting my hips back and forth all while jacking him off.

"That is a good girl," he said when I used the moisture that seeped from his tip to coat his penis. He twitched in my fingers. I'd given myself plenty of orgasms in the past, so I figured he would like this. "Come on my hand."

I didn't think anyone could come on demand, but I was sure as hell going to try. He rubbed faster, harder, hitting my clit. My breathing labored and I felt a flame ignite within.

Just as I was about to reach that pinnacle of ecstasy and combust, a sound echoed in the distance and I froze. It was delicate and far away, but I'd heard it.

"Kova?" a honeyed voice called out.

Oh, my God. We both paused instantaneously. My heart dropped into my stomach, my throat closing up. Kova had gone ghostly white himself.

"Katja," he whispered, wide eyes looking down at me. Heels click-clacked against tile while Kova looked around, his eyes landing on the foam pit next to us.

"Jump in there and hide. Wait a bit and then sneak out." I nodded frantically. Kova looked disoriented. He kissed my forehead then pushed his dick down and quickly regained control. He thrust me toward the pit where I jumped in and hid. I shimmied myself lower to conceal every part of my body. I hated the pit. It was great for practicing new release skills or landings on a high bar, but it smelled terrible, probably due to all the sweaty bodies that fell in here daily. Plus, it wasn't so easy to pull yourself out of ten feet of blue foam squares.

Nestling down, I panicked when I heard Kova's voice. "Katja?"

"What are you doing here so late?"

"It is my job to be here, Kat," he snapped angrily, picking up his shirt from the ground. He looked to the left and our eyes connected. I shimmied down more. "Have you not figured that out yet? After all these years that I need to be here?"

I pulled back at the sound of his insensitive voice.

"You never spend time with me anymore," she whined. "I miss you."

Kova sighed and began walking away from me. "What do you want from me? I am doing the best I can."

"I want you to spend time with me, but you are always here. You know I have no family. I am lonely." She paused and said, "I thought we were going to talk about our future tonight? You said we were. I cooked dinner and waited for you, but you never showed. You did not even call."

His voice grew more distant and he scoffed. "I wish you would understand there are going to be days when I need to work late, days when I need to work out to relieve the stress and pressure of everyday life. I work so you do not have to, therefore no stress for you," his voice boomed furiously. "I have not heard you complain about your days lounging around by the pool or going shopping whenever you feel like it."

My heart hammered in my chest. I thought back to the argument they had at his house. I would've never guessed there was still any strain between them, and now I was more curious than ever to find out why.

"Why am I even here? I came to this country for you, but all you want to do is spend every second in the gym. This is not what we agreed to!" she yelled back. "My time is running out."

Kova began sounding off in Russian, his voice heated and muffled as they moved farther away. I couldn't make out the low rumbling between them before a door slammed shut and I flinched. Probably from Kova. It echoed throughout the gym and I was left alone.

Once again he left my mind confused, and now my body ached for the orgasm he failed to give me. I waited a good five minutes before I climbed out, found my hoodie, and left.

CHAPTER 30

Nearly an hour after my first kiss with Kova, I was home.

And I was still aching, swollen, and aroused.

Between the material of my pants and throbbing wet lips, I was heightening by the second. The urge to finish myself off was strong. I'd been so close to release until Katja showed up, and judging by how heavy Kova was breathing, I'd say he'd been close too.

Once inside my condo, I couldn't get to my bedroom fast enough, stripping off what little I wore along the way. I climbed into the center of my bed and brought my knees up and spread my legs wide. My hand immediately went to my sex. I sighed as I slowly circled my clit. I couldn't remember a time when I'd been so desperate to come. As visions of Kova entered my mind, I knew it wouldn't be long.

My hand glided against my bare pussy, the same hand I touched him with. It had been a first for me. I thought of his soft skin beneath my touch. His hard cock. His dirty words. "What I would give to feel the real thing, to feel you on my cock." Little moans vibrated in my throat as the friction from my fingers took me higher. God, I needed to come. I shivered as I remembered the feel of his mouth devouring mine. Our tongues tangling and teeth nipping at lips. Beads of sweat broke out across my skin as my orgasm climbed, reaching that point of no return.

Rolling over, I pressed my stomach to the bed and began riding my hand. I thought about how he told me to fuck his hand as I was fucking mine right now. My hips lifted in the air and I rubbed faster, remembering the way his penis stroked me through my clothes. The comforter felt cool against my hardened nipples. The weight and pressure, divine on my clit, and I moaned into my sheets. Slipping a small finger inside my pussy, I went in just enough and rocked back and forth, creating a firestorm of pleasure that was just seconds from erupting from me. "Your small, wet little pussy wrapped around my cock. So tight..." Sweet Jesus, I wanted to come all night, as many times as I could, to the beat of Kova's hand and erotic words. I'd do anything for it to happen with him.

Shit. This was wrong on so many levels. I shouldn't be thinking of him in this manner. But I couldn't stop. An orgasm ripped through me so violently I shook from the gratification zipping down my body. My eyes squeezed shut and I felt Kova's touch in place of mine and pretended I was riding his hand instead, coming harder than ever. A loud rush of euphoria escaped me and I cried out, sighing breathlessly while the orgasm carried on.

Turning over, I swept my hair away from my face and caught my breath. My breathing evened out. I was completely sated and didn't want to move. I couldn't believe how something that felt so deliciously good could be so morally wrong.

Clearly, we both weren't thinking straight to let something like this happen. It was beyond dumb and careless, not to mention we could've gotten caught. My heart nearly stopped when I'd heard Katja's voice. I couldn't even begin to imagine what the repercussions would be.

I debated calling Avery. I wanted to tell her everything that happened but was hesitant, given the nature of the situation. It probably wasn't the wisest idea, even if she was my best friend and we told each other everything. This was a totally different scenario. Totally different. I needed to talk to someone though, and she was dating an older guy at the moment, which her parents had no idea about, so she really was perfect. I needed to get my thoughts together first and the lies I would need to tell her. Because let's be real, there was no way in hell I could admit it was my coach.

After I took a quick shower and got dressed, I grabbed my cell and dialed Avery's number, but after one ring it went straight to her voicemail.

Holy hell, she just hit the fuck you button on me.

I called her again. It was nearly eleven at night, so I knew she was home. Bringing the phone to my ear, it rang twice then went to voicemail. She did it again, and then I decided to text her.

Pick up your phone, b. I need to talk to you. I know you did not just hit the fuck you button on me.

The fuck you button was just the decline button on the phone. When I caught my boyfriend cheating on me last year with a mutual friend of ours, I dumped him immediately. He was devastated and regretted it, or so he said, and wouldn't stop calling me. One day, Avery grabbed my phone and yelled, "FUCK YOU!" and clicked decline. We laughed so hard and it stayed with us ever since.

I'm w/bf! Shhh...give me 5

Her older boyfriend, the one I knew nothing about. Finally, forty minutes of stewing later, my phone flashed with a picture of Avery and me.

"I hate you." I skipped the pleasantries.

"Fuck you, no you don't. You love me."

I grimaced. Avery was right. I could never really hate her.

"Now what's going on that you had to blow my phone up while I was blowing my man?"

"Ugh, Ave! I did not need to hear that!" She began laughing. "Wait, you stopped to text me in the middle of it?"

"You didn't get the hint when I sent you to voicemail—twice!"

"Ah, yeah. You're not allowed to hit the fuck you button on me, just like I never would with you. Next time you don't answer for me, I'll know why."

She chuckled. "All right, what's going on that you're making me call you at midnight?"

I had to be careful with my words. "Let me ask you something, this mystery guy of yours you refuse to tell me about, which I secretly hate you for by the way, is nineteen. Isn't that, like, illegal since he's over eighteen?"

Avery sighed into the phone as if she couldn't believe I asked her that. "You have so much to learn, bestie..."

Now it was my turn to laugh. "Seriously?"

"Of course I looked it up. Google is my second best friend and my father would murder me if he found out. I did my homework and it's not actually illegal. The law is different in each state. Regardless, my mom is the one who introduced us, so she only has herself to blame. Plus, we're just having some fun."

"She didn't introduce you for the sole purpose of having sex!" I laughed.

"Well…" She trailed off. "She didn't deliberately introduce us. We met at an event my family put on. Our family met his…you know how it goes."

"Yeah, I do. So he lives on the island?" The island was fairly small. I'd figure out who it was eventually.

"His family does. He goes to college but was in town to see me. Enough about my amazingly wonderful love life. So why do you want to know about the ages and what's legal?"

I laughed at her sarcastic response. Avery was hardly ever serious. "Sooooooo, I have something to tell you. And before I do, you have to swear on our friendship that you won't tell a soul. No one, Avery. Not even if your life depended on it."

"Oh, this has to be juicy! Let me grab my cup so you can fill it right up."

I rolled my eyes and stifled a laugh. "I'm serious, Ave. You can't tell anyone."

Avery scoffed. "I can't believe you would ask me this. You know I'd never betray you," she said dejectedly. "You can trust me."

"I know, but this is a big deal. You know we say it to be sure."

"True. Now, spill."

I swallowed hard. "How would I know if I had an orgasm? I think I did…but I don't know."

"Whoa. Hold. The. Phone. I was not expecting that! With whom?"

I had a feeling she'd perk up. "Just answer my question."

"You answer my question," she retorted in a high pitch.

"Ave, I can't say," I said regrettably. "I can't."

"Really? You're not going to tell your best friend?" Avery was hurt, and I immediately felt bad. We told each other everything, we never held back. The fact that I was for the first time didn't sit well with me. But this was different.

So I lied. Again. "I didn't want to say, but have I told you about my library friend?"

She clucked her tongue. "It seems you're holding out on me."

"I'm not holding out on you. It's just, he's older and I don't want to get into any trouble."

"How old?"

I bit my lip nervously. "I don't know, I haven't asked."

"Can you at least gauge it? Ten, fifteen, twenty?"

I grimaced. "Years? Twenty years older? Ave, that's gross."

"That's why I said give me an idea."

"Okay...so he's about twenty-ish years old?"

"Keep going."

"So library guy...We kind of hooked up."

"Define kind of."

"I just need to know if it's legal."

"Define kind of," she repeated stubbornly.

I gave Avery all the details, but instead of Kova, I used the name Ethan, and instead of the gym, I said the library. I told her how he'd been there when I was studying, how our eyes locked and we couldn't stop looking at each other. Real mushy shit.

"But how did it happen?" she asked, perplexed.

"I needed help reaching for a book. There was no one at the desk and when I turned around, he was behind me. He saw the annoyed look on my face and asked me what was wrong. I told him I was studying and couldn't do my work without this book. He said he'd help me."

"Can you just speed up and get to the orgasm? This part is boring me to death."

I laughed. "No, I can't. You have to listen. When we got to the aisle, he pressed up against me and reached for the book. I looked over my shoulder and his face was right there."

She groaned, unimpressed. "Keep going..."

My eyes scattered around my room as I thought of how I could continue this lie. "He leaned down and kissed me. One thing led to another, and his hands were all over me and it happened quickly. It was completely unexpected. He touched me, I touched him...he said some really hot, dirty things to me...someone almost caught us..."

"He did not! Who? Where? You have to tell me everything!" Now Avery was too eager for her own good.

"That's all really irrelevant. I told you what you needed to know."

"Adrianna Francesca Rossi! I'm your best friend, practically your sister! You have to tell me! I demand that you do. How often do you see him?"

"You are such a pain in my ass." Quickly, I conjured a lie and kept my voice steady. "It's just on and off when we see each other, I guess a little while after I started tutoring."

"So this has been going on for a couple months and I hardly know a thing," she stated.

"I've been busy trying to be an elite gymnast, you know."

"A quick text would've been sufficient."

"I could say the same about this mystery beau of yours. You barely tell me anything."

She became quiet. "I'm just not ready yet...please don't be mad at me. I want to know more about what happened between you guys."

My voice softened. "He calls me Ria. No one has ever called me anything other than Adrianna or Ana. You know how much I hate Ana, so I kind of love this."

"Awe, that's nauseatingly sweet. Let me grab my detective cap while my computer is starting up. I need his real age, *Ria.*" She mocked. "And don't guess. I know you know." I laughed and decided I needed to write all my lies down so I could keep track.

"He's in his late twenties. He took a long time off before going to law school."

"How old, Ria," she insisted. "You're hiding something, I know it."

"Ave, haven't you ever heard someone say, the less you know, the better?"

"Psh. That doesn't apply to your bestie. Like, ever."

I heaved a loud sigh at her response. She had a point. "Thirty-two."

"Thirty-two."

"Thirty-two."

"That is *not* late twenties. That's not ten, fifteen, or twenty. That's old! You sneaky thing, you. I'll be right back, I need to alert *Fox News* over this Breaking News before I can comprehend anything further."

"Avery, please do not tell a soul—I'm begging you." My heart was in my throat at my own admission, regret soaring through me. I was beginning to sweat. Maybe this was a mistake.

"I'm just playing with you. I swear on my trust fund I won't ever say a word."

Avery loved money, so I believed her. "Promise?"

"You can't see it, but I'm crossing my heart."

I smiled to myself. I knew she would never open her mouth, but I still had to ask it. It was a girl thing. She'd do the same to me.

"Okay, back to your original question," she said. "I'm not sure how to describe it other than you'll just know when it happens. Like, you'll know. An orgasm is an indescribable feeling, one that rocks through your whole being, and once it starts, it only builds higher and higher until an explosion goes off inside of you, and you see stars. It's the best feeling ever." She paused. "Wait. Was this your first time having one?"

"No, but it just never felt this good before. It was incredible."

"When were the other times it happened?"

"With my stupid ex...and myself."

I didn't want to tell her I just used my hand, and thankfully she didn't probe.

"Some orgasms just feel different. That's all. Your hand isn't going to feel as good as the hand of the guy you like. It's just how it is."

I felt bad for lying and like a total jackass for not realizing the difference. It was just so much more intense. If I was being honest with myself, I wanted it to happen again.

I could hear Avery typing away on her computer. "All right...It looks like the legal age of consent in Georgia is sixteen so long as it isn't with an old man and saggy balls—"

She was back to this. "Ave—he's not old and his balls are not saggy. Be serious for a second. I don't know why—" I paused. The line went silent. "Avery?"

"Wait. Wait. Wait. Back the fuck up. "Did you say his balls aren't saggy? How would you know that?"

I groaned inwardly and clenched my eyes shut. "Fuck."

CHAPTER 31

O h, my God!" she yelled, and I had to pull the phone away from my ear. "You saw his balls! Did you touch them! What else happened, you lying sack of shit!"

I chuckled at her odd enthusiasm and said, "I didn't see or touch anything. I'm just saying they're not saggy because he's not old. They're firm, I assume."

"Lies, all lies!"

I couldn't stop laughing at her playful tone. "I'm not lying. Just get back to what you were saying."

"Yeah, okay. Whatever. If I find out you lied to me, there's going to be hell to pay." Avery cleared her throat. "So what you did is not illegal, and since he's in law school, I'm pretty sure he knew he was skating the line. Just don't have sex with him. Oh wait—"

"What is it?"

"Hang on. I'm still reading."

I sat still, biting my lip until she finally spoke.

"Oh, never mind. Good thing we're not in Florida. They got some fucked up laws, probably because people are on flakka there and do some crazy shit. I would just be really careful if I were you."

I frowned. "Why's that? If I didn't do anything wrong, what does it matter?"

I felt like I needed to write down what she was saying next to my list of lies.

"Call me crazy, but I just think there shouldn't be any penetration with the old man. I mean, if you consent, you're fine since you're of age. Consent is consent once you're deemed legal by the state. But that doesn't mean it won't bring a whole new shit show to the table if you bang him." She paused, then her voice rose. "Could be fun though."

"Did you just say penetration?" I couldn't help laugh. It sounded so comical coming from her.

"Yes, because that's what old people say when they're having sexual relations, Ria." Sarcasm laced her tone and it caused me to smile. Avery was hysterically funny tonight. She didn't judge, only teased me. "They don't say fuck."

"I didn't know you were an expert."

"Wait—you don't think your tutor is hot, do you? What about Alfred? Because that would be breaking the law since he's like eighty years old. Not to mention, really fucking gross, Ria. I would have to reconsider this friendship based on your horrid taste."

"Now those would be some saggy balls," I laughed into the phone. "No, I'm not attracted to any of them."

"Oh, good. And yes, penetration is sex, and no sex is allowed," she stated.

I was pretty sure I was never going to have sex with my coach, so I was good to go.

"Speaking of penetration, we should give the balance beam a name," Avery suggested flippantly.

Closing my eyes, I shook my head. "What do you mean a name, Ave?"

"Well, you know how my mom named her car, Bradley Cooper?"

I chuckled, thinking back to the day Avery's mom came waltzing through the front door, saying she fell madly in love with Bradley Cooper because he gave her a ride like no other. Her mom was a riot.

"And you know how she named her Kindle?"

"I do. Isn't it like Mikko or something?"

"Mikko? What the fuck kind of name is that? Not even close. His name is Cole, and Cole brings her more pleasure than any other man ever could. He's up all night with her and never talks back. She can cry ugly tears and he never makes fun of her."

I groaned. "Avery, your mom is crazy. I can't believe she tells you those things. Mine would never say something like that to me."

She laughed.

"So, I'm thinking we should name your beam, so every time you fall we can say..." She trailed off. "Johnny! Johnny Depp! We can say Johnny Depp fucked you again today."

I knew Avery was happy with herself from the other end by the high pitch of her voice. Her and her wicked sense of humor. "Because every time you fall it's like you're getting fucked."

This time we were both in full on belly laughs. She had a point.

"No way! You're insane!"

"Oh, come on," Avery said. "If you don't like the name Johnny, we can pick another. What are the names of the other guys on the team?"

"Well, Johnny's pretty hot, but there's a Hayden on the men's team I've become friends with. But Ave, I just can't call the beam, Johnny. I would die if anyone heard me say, Johnny fucked me good again today. No, just no," I snickered.

"Let's use Hayden. It would be more fun that way!"

"You're sick, you know that? You have an evil sense of humor."

"I'll take that as a compliment, thank you very much."

I paused, thinking about what she suggested. "The girls on my team would think I was talking about Hayden. I can't do it. They hate me as it is."

"Oh, my God. We have to use Hayden! Because fuck them."

I shook my head from the other side of the phone. Avery. She was my polar opposite, yet I loved her so much. She knew how to make me laugh when I needed it the most.

"Say it."

"Ave...I feel weird saying it."

"Don't be a little bitch."

I laughed again, shaking my head. "Fine! Johnny fucked me pretty hard today...I'm all red and sore. It even hurts to walk." I bit my lip, waiting for her response.

"OH MY GOD!" Avery shouted, laughing again. "Look at you! I wasn't thinking of adding to it!"

"Well, it's what happens when you straddle it." Looking between my thighs, I thought about the day I straddled the beam and what transpired after. I told Avery everything, minus the Kova touching me part.

"My thighs were all roughed up, too. God, Avery. I even bled from it."

"That bad?"

"Yeah. And it looked like a contusion was forming. I had to ice myself three times a day."

"A contusion? You mean a black and blue? Can't you just say bruise?"

I laughed and she heaved an exaggerated sigh. "Just think, by the time you're actually ready to have sex, the impact won't be as bad."

I paused. "Where do you come up with this stuff?" Shaking my head, I stifled another laugh. "There's no filter with you."

"Nope," she said proudly.

"Can I break a bone in there? Because that's what it felt like when I fell. I swear something shifted."

"Well, I'm no doctor, but I don't think there's a bone in your vagina."

I grinned. "You had a bone-r in yours tonight."

"Oh! She's got comebacks," Avery yelled sarcastically. "I sure did. But seriously, why don't you see an OB and find out. Or maybe head over to Planned Parenthood so you can get birth control while you're at it. Rather be safe than sorry."

"What do I need birth control for?"

"Do you plan to stay a virgin forever?"

"Well, no, but I only have time for one piece of wood in my life right now, and his name is Johnny."

Avery burst out laughing. I was pretty proud of myself for that one.

"That being said, it wouldn't be such a bad idea if I planned on having sex soon, not that I am. I'd have to withdraw money before I went. I can't imagine my dad would be happy seeing a visit to Planned Parenthood on his credit card statement."

"I doubt he even looks."

Avery had a point. "Still, I can't take the chance."

"How's practice going anyway?"

I huffed into the phone.

"That bad?" she responded to my sulk.

"Some days are harder than others, but I refuse to give up. I'm not where I should be so I took on extra training, but I feel like I'm progressing. I'm pushing my body to the brink of exhaustion. The team girls have like a *Mean Girls* type club, so the only friends I really have are Hayden and Holly. Some days I wonder if I would be here if it wasn't for my dad's money. And to top it off, my mom wants me to send her pictures of the scale while I'm on it."

"I really hate your mom."

I puckered my lips together. Some days I hated her too.

"Still, I won't quit. I love gymnastics too much to do that. It's my life, and with this sport, I only have so much time left. I really have to get my ass in gear. Meet season is coming up and I need to be in top shape."

"You know what else is coming up?"

I paused, scrunching my brows together. "What?"

"Your birthday!"

"Ave. It's not like I can plan anything, I have to train."

Her excitement vanished. "Can't you take one night off?"

"To do what? Sit by myself?" I laughed bitterly, thinking about how my mom forgot my birthday a few times in the past. What a joke. "Unless I'm on my death bed, there's no taking an extra day off. It's really not a big deal to skip my birthday, I'll have more."

"God. You're such a bore. I can always come up for your birthday, so you're not alone," Avery said, taking me away from my thoughts. "And if my parents don't want me to drive for some reason, maybe I can convince our brothers to ride with me." I paused, at a loss for words, as she continued. "You know, they're older, and our parents would trust them for some bizarre reason. Plus, if they know there are hot girls, I'm sure they'd be quick to come."

Her parents were pretty lenient. I couldn't imagine them saying no to her driving two hours away.

"I guess. While we hang out, they can go off, but you'll be bored during the day since I can't take off from practice."

"That's no biggie. I'll come for a weekend and watch."

That could be worked out.

I yawned and looked at the clock. "I'm gonna go. I'm so tired and luckily I don't have gym tomorrow. I plan to sleep in and catch up on my homework."

"Let me know if you need me to do any more research for you. If you need to talk about it, I'm here for you, Ria."

I smiled into the phone. "Thanks, girl. You're the best. Are you going to call me Ria from now on?"

"Every minute I can," she retorted. "And remember, no penetration, Ria." Then she hung up.

After grabbing a bottle of water, I jumped into bed, thanking my lucky stars I didn't have to face Kova tomorrow. I had the following day off to panic about what had happened. It was going to be awkward once I went back to practice, but I knew how to train my emotions and conceal my thoughts. Only thing I needed to do was not make it obvious and ignore Coach as much as possible. That wouldn't be a hard feat. He tended to be an asshole at the gym anyway. An angry Russian dick.

Just before I was about to doze off, my phone beeped.

COACH

Did you make it home okay?

My heart dropped. I responded with a quick yes, clutching my phone to see if he would say anything else. But after ten minutes of silence, I ended up passing out.

CHAPTER 32

gnoring Coach was an issue I expected to hurdle after what had happened between us, but fortunately I didn't have to work through it the next day.

Or the next.

He'd been absent from the gym for three days now and I wasn't sure whether I was happy about it or not. Madeline took over and I worked closely with her. While she was my vault coach, Kova was my main coach and he oversaw my schedule—which skills I'd learn and when. It was a completely different type of training with her. I wasn't stressed to the max, I didn't make mistakes, and I felt a bit more confident. I was actually able to eat something, too. I didn't feel the need to impress her the way I did with Kova. She didn't ridicule every little breath I took, she encouraged me and gave me hope. Hope was what gymnasts thrived on, and mine had gone down the drain. There were moments of the day when I wished she was my coach. She was a great instructor, but Kova's attention to detail was exceptional, and that mattered in the world of gymnastics.

Kova's absence only built the impending awkwardness of having to see him when he did return, which was apparently today. No coach or gymnast ever missed gym time unless it was absolutely life altering. No one knew why he was out, only that he had business he needed to attend to.

But I had a feeling I knew what it was.

Alfred dropped me off early to practice. None of my teammates had shown up yet, so I shoved my stuff into my locker and did my usual morning run. My calf started acting up again, a twinge of heat encompassed it, but I shook it off and finished. I noticed it flaring up a little more lately. Nothing a little Motrin couldn't fix.

After I came inside and wiped myself down, I got ready to head inside the gym to start stretching. I loved being the only one here, breathing in the air and mentally preparing myself for training. I smiled. A new day, a new goal, a new ambition. My love for the sport was embedded deep in my bones and something I couldn't quite explain.

Rounding the corner and walking down the quiet hallway, I wasn't paying attention as I separated the wristbands that had gotten stuck together by the Velcro, and I walked straight into someone.

A whoosh escaped my throat. "Oh, I'm so—" I froze.

Kova.

My jaw dropped, all logical thoughts escaped me. "Hey," I said delicately.

Kova stood tall in front of me, his broad shoulders back, and his face unreadable. I wasn't terribly short, but he was over six feet, so he towered over me.

"You were gone."

He said nothing.

"Are you okay?"

Again, nothing.

"We should probably talk?"

He just stared right through me.

"Ummm…" I proceeded but stopped when his hands locked on my upper arms. He shuffled me to the side, walked past me and ignored all questions.

Oh, good. So we skipped dick and went straight into asshole mode—awesome!

Anger bubbled in my veins. Arrogance was written all over his saunter as he made his way back to his office. I had to grind my jaw to keep from lashing out.

"So you're just going to overlook…everything?"

He said nothing, so I took a risk.

"What does Katja mean to you?"

Kova paused, his stance rigid. Interestingly, that must have struck a nerve. After witnessing two arguments between them, one he didn't even know I knew about, I wanted to know if she was more than just a girlfriend to him, if he saw a future with her. I rested my hand on my hip, waiting for him to turn around. I was so positive he would respond that a smirk crept along my face.

I was shocked when his head twitched to the side, and he continued walking away from me, slamming the door shut to his office.

A GOOD PART OF MY morning workout had been fairly demanding. I had my ballet classes, which kept me busy for nearly two hours, then I moved on to conditioning. The two things I despised doing were the most strenuous and challenging. Challenging in the sense that it was easy to cut corners and do it half-assed and not get caught. Which I didn't. I'd only hurt myself in the long run.

When I moved on to vault with Madeline, I made a conscious effort to avoid Kova. I purposely didn't look in his direction and I acted like he didn't exist, but it was a difficult feat. He was on my mind every few seconds and the fight to not look for him was a struggle. I got the feeling I was being watched, but didn't want to make it obvious I was aware of his gaze. I could feel his eyes on me, crawling over my body. But I didn't acknowledge it. The fear of seeing disgust sat heavy in my gut, and not something I wanted to face.

This morning I'd been working on my vault. I was trying to perfect the Amanar, a two and a half twisting Yurchenko. It was the hardest vault for women to master because of its level of difficulty, but also gave the most scoring points in difficulty too. If I didn't pull through and only completed two twists instead of two and a half, I'd be downgraded for difficulty and not execution, surprisingly. The key to execution was a huge block. I had to push with all my might off the vault table using my shoulders and keeping my arms straight. If I bent my arms, it absorbed my power and I'd really mess up. But no matter what I did, I just couldn't stick it. I'd step forward, land on my butt, land off to the side, bend my legs. I either under rotated or over rotated. I was an utter disaster. All of those landings would earn me deductions I couldn't afford. The last thing I wanted was to lower my vault to two twists, but I knew if I didn't start making progress soon, I would be forced to scale it back. I wanted the Amanar so bad I could taste it.

Vault was mine. I normally excelled at it, I just needed to stick my landing. But since I had come to World Cup, I'd been doing terribly.

At least, it felt that way. I needed to be a little tighter, a little faster, a little higher, and I'd have it.

Easier said than done. Nerves and self-doubt got to me, I knew that was playing into my overall performance.

Madeline had mentioned we needed to start working on my alternate vault soon. Gymnasts always had two vaults, usually one that brought more points to the table. The new vault would be front flipping, I just wasn't sure which one yet. Doing a front vault showed diversity.

"Adrianna. Instead of starting at seventy-three feet, try seventy-five. Do a double and land it. You're getting there, but you may need more momentum."

I nodded.

Madeline pulled her arms up to her chest, her hands in fists, and jerked to the left—giving me an example of what she meant. "Pop off the table and pull up high, squaring your shoulders and then twist hard. Got it? You really need to block."

"Yes."

"Good. Go for it."

I walked back to the end of the runway, looking for seventy-five feet. Grabbing a piece of chalk, I drew a line where my toes needed to start and then chalked my hands up good. I raised an arm and then took off running. My arms stayed like sticks by my side until I gained speed, and they bent. I pumped my legs harder than ever about twelve feet away and did a round-off onto the spring board, then a back handspring onto the vault table to complete the Yurchenko, popping off with my shoulders with a loud huff and pulled my twist up and into a double. I had height, a tad more than usual, but ended up taking a huge step forward on the soft practice mat.

Looking over my shoulder with my arms still in the air, I raised a brow at Madeline. She chewed her lips, staring at me curiously.

"Try starting off a bit slower." I looked at her with a question in my eyes. I needed speed if anything. "Meaning, take a few larger, but slower steps at first, and then gun it around twenty-five feet away. And throw the Amanar instead. The double isn't helping."

I got to the end of the runway and chalked up again when Madeline yelled. "Practice a few slow starts first."

The slow starts had a funny look to them. The knees came up higher, slower, and the step was much wider. It looked like giant skips at first. I knew what she wanted me to do, I just had never done it, and honestly, I didn't think this was what I needed. But she was my coach so I listened.

I quickly practiced a few off to the side while Holly vaulted twice.

I took a handful of slower, wider steps and performed my vault, but I didn't stick my landing. When I stood straight, the back of my calf started to glow with heat again, but this time it traveled down to my ankle. Bending down, I rotated my ankle around and massaged the muscle to relieve the warmth.

Her brows angled toward each other. "Are you okay? What's wrong?"

I nodded. "It's nothing, I'm fine."

Her eyes narrowed. "Are you sure?" I nodded and she asked, "Okay, so how did that feel?"

"It makes sense to start off slower, I think, and I can feel the change in momentum. I have more power. Can I try it again?"

"Of course."

I got in line and waited for Holly to go. Once she finished a couple sets of vaults, it was my turn. I took off even slower by pulling my legs higher to the ceiling, but it wasn't easy. I could feel my stomach clench and the muscles I needed to build in order to run like this. My vault was better, and my height too, but it didn't feel perfect and I knew it.

"Okay—I know I'm throwing a lot at you right now, but what if we try to get your round-off closer to the ground, too."

"What do you mean?"

Madeline stood in front of the springboard. She raised her arms and demonstrated what she meant. "You see how my shoulders are up with my chest, but back? You're too open up here, there's too much space between you and the board. But if you lean toward the springboard, when you rebound out of your round-off, you'll get the power you need to get the perfect flight. Let's try it into the foam pit so you can see."

Madeline looked over at Holly. "Can you practice on your own for a bit? We'll be right back."

An innocent smiled splayed her lips. It amazed me she was friends with a bitch like Reagan. "No problem."

"Use a cushioned mat, okay? I don't want you getting hurt."

"Okay."

We walked over to the runway with the foam pit where Kova was with Reagan. It was the same foam pit I hid in days earlier. Our eyes locked for a split second and his jaw set tight before he looked the other way. My nerves climbed with each step that brought me closer to him. When he looked at me again, he visibly tensed. Reagan looked like she wanted to vomit at the sight of me.

"Mind if we share with you? I want Adrianna to try something new." Madeline asked.

Kova stepped aside and waved his hand in front of us. "By all means."

Madeline turned to me and went over what she wanted me to try while Kova watched intently. His presence was powerful, and standing this close, it was hard to ignore him like I had tried pitifully to do this morning. He made me extremely nervous and I started chewing on my bottom lip, a habit I needed to break.

"Remember, slow at first, and stay low near the end. Got it?"

I swallowed, my eyes sneaking a glance at Kova before I nodded at Madeline.

Standing at the end of the runway, I took a deep breath and exhaled. I focused solely on the vault and what she told me to try. One last breath and then I took off running. My heart raced, not from the coaches, but of my love for vault. Adrenaline pumped through me and my feet pounded into the floor as I neared the springboard. The pain in my calf was back and stronger than ever, but I pushed through it. My nerves were on edge, but with Kova and Reagan standing there, I knew my legs ended up looking sloppy in flight, and if it hadn't been for this pit, I would've eaten shit when I came down.

"What the hell was that?" Madeline asked with shock in her eyes. "Thank God you landed in that pit."

"Let me try again."

Kova reached down with an opened palm and without thinking twice, my hand slid into his strong, callused one. Heat shot up my arm and through my spine. Shit. This wasn't good. He gripped my palm and yanked me out. Before Madeline could say anything, Kova spoke up.

"May I?" he asked quietly, and she nodded.

"I see what Madeline is going for. Slower start and a deeper angle near the board, yeah?" he asked her but was staring directly at me.

I groaned inwardly. He should never use the word deeper in my presence. My mind traveled back to the night in the gym, and the things he said and did.

"Yes, more acute," Madeline responded. Acute sounded better than deeper. Kova and his stupid Russian accent.

Gripping my arm lightly, he guided me to the board. When he placed a flat hand to my stomach and one to my back, I tensed. His eyes narrowed at me knowingly, telling me to get my shit together.

He cleared his throat. "You need to use your core for what you are doing. Chest back." He patted my stomach, and continued. "We may need to focus on building more muscle here to help you carry though. Prepare for a cartwheel."

Using his hand on my lower back, he leaned me over so I was head first toward the board and my back leg was up.

"You want your hurdle long and low, but your chest and arms up tall. Push off your back leg hard." He tapped my leg, as if I didn't know which leg he meant. "It is quick and fast and it takes time to learn, but this is where you start, so when you rebound off the board, you will have the power you need to go back and off the table for a strong block. From there, you know what to do." He paused and then asked, "Does this make sense to you?"

"Yes."

"Good, now do it, but just do a layout." A layout was no problem. No twisting, just straight as a board, stretched out body, flipping back once.

I walked and stood behind the chalk line, mentally picturing myself doing it correctly. Looking at Kova, he gave me a small nod. Leaning forward, I lifted my knee and took a few of the longer running steps and then went full force and ran as fast as possible. There was that burning again in my calf that seemed to make an appearance when I ran. When it came time for my round-off, I got low, knees to chest like he said, and felt my pelvic muscles tighten.

Kova was right. I could tell I was going to need more muscle there from the strain inside.

He was also right about the exploding power I'd have if I got lower. I eyed the foam pit for my landing and saw how much extra height I had.

I came up, wide eyed and looked at him. "I wasn't ready for that kind of power!" I yelled enthusiastically.

He nodded, tight lipped and turned to Reagan and Madeline. "Would it be okay if we swapped gymnasts for a bit? I have a few things I want to work with her on."

"Of course. Come, Reagan."

Reagan scowled. I picked my wedgie and asked, "Where're they going?"

"We switched."My stomach churned, excitement falling from my face. "Oh, okay."

CHAPTER 33

e stared at each other for a moment, my cheeks beginning to heat.

Clearing his throat, Kova rubbed his jaw and said, "Instead of running slower in the beginning, I think you need to just take off at your normal speed. I do not think slowing down will help you. Let us get your round-off right and then we will work on squaring your shoulders and reaching for height."

I nodded. "I wasn't crazy about slowing in the beginning either, but I did it anyway."

"If you do not think it will work, you can always speak up."

I gave him a droll stare. "Really? You once told me not to question you." When he didn't respond to my dig, I said, "I wanted to try it at least, but I didn't like the feel."

"What is your starting point?"

"I'm at seventy-five feet."

Coach contemplated for a minute. "Try starting at seventy-nine feet. You need as much momentum as you can get. And just do the double again."

I nodded and walked to the seventy-nine feet mark. I did exactly what he said to do, and honestly, I couldn't tell if I did it right or not.

"Again," he said.

I did a handful more vaults before he finally said, "I see things I want to do to you—" Coach stopped himself when my eyebrows nearly reached my hairline. "What I meant was..." He trailed off anxiously. His voice cracked and he used his hands to talk. "I think I should be working with you more on this, not just Madeline. There are different techniques you would benefit from." He exhaled with an exhausted sigh, broken almost, and it made me feel bad. "Let us work on this vault and do some layout timers."

Coach took me to the other side of the gym where there were huge, thick mats stacked behind a vault. They towered high, just roughly under ten feet and they helped with gaining height. It's where layout timers came into play. It was a back flip, pin straight body and legs, and instead of landing on my feet, I'd land on my back, rotating with a hollow chest.

"Okay. I am going to spot you and give you a little pop. Just land on your back. Yes?"

"Yes."

I wasn't sure if I loved the idea Kova was ignoring our little indiscretion or not. I guess it was a good thing since I was here to train. But I couldn't help but wonder what was going through his head.

I did my vault with Kova's help and nearly panicked when my heart jumped from my chest and landed before I did. I had so much air my feet came up and I rotated into a back roll.

"That wasn't a little pop. You nearly threw me in the air. I could've hurt myself."

He gave me a blank stare. "See the height you got?" he retorted, his voice stern. He ignored my comment, because the truth was, I knew my coach wouldn't let anything happen to me and he knew it too.

"That is what you need in flight. Do it again and keep your legs tighter. This vault, more than others, must have straight, tight legs and body."

I was well aware how tight and straight my legs needed to be, not just in this vault, but in so many other skills in gym. Hearing it over and over was annoying. I wished he'd tell me something I didn't know.

I did the vault, feeling Kova's pop on my lower back. He wasn't as hard this time and I felt the difference, I barely landed on my back.

"Feel the difference?"

"Surprisingly, yes."

Kova paused, not expecting my response, then continued. "The key to the Amanar is height, drive, and power. That is where we start. We do this a thousand times if we have to, until I feel confident you can move on," Kova said enthusiastically.

A thousand times, like he did with me on bars. At least I wouldn't get rips on vault. But I could break an ankle if I landed wrong.

I vaulted again, ending with a layout timer. After at least an hour or so, I was worn out and in dire need of food. My calf throbbed fiercely, but there was no way I would speak up. Kova's help and push really made a difference, so I stored the pain away and focused on the conditioning.

Walking back over to the pit, he placed thick practice mats over the foam squares to practice my landing since I wasn't ready to land on the floor yet.

Standing at the end of the runway line, I looked for Coach.

"Do your double without my help. Let me see where you are at."

After I landed my vault, I looked at him. He wasn't pleased.

"Stronger hurdle. Power, we need power, Adrianna," he ordered, clapping his hands. Thing was, the bottom half of my leg was on fire.

I nodded and vaulted again with his help. Over the next hour, all I heard was:

"Adrianna, squeeze those legs and make them straight as a damn board. Do you want to tear your ACL?"

"Adrianna. Tighter body."

"Adrianna," he said slowly, with irritation. "Set higher. Do you really think you can pull a two and a half like that?"

"Adrianna, push harder!"

"Do you really want this?"

"Block, Adrianna!" He groaned. "Get that set higher."

"You got it... crank it tighter now!"

"Faster, higher, stronger. That is no good!"

"You are under rotating, that is why you are hopping back!"

Then he started in Russian. At that point, my body was sore and I'd reached the point of exhaustion. I had another hour or so before I had to break for class. And for the first time in my gymnastics career, I couldn't wait to be done with gym and for tutoring to start.

"You are a power tumbler, but we need more muscle, so for the next thirty minutes we will condition and then cool down. Okay? We need to do this after every workout."

Ugh. I groaned loudly, my head falling back. Every gymnast hated conditioning with a passion, but we also knew not to skimp on it. We'd only be holding ourselves back if we did.

Kova took me to a side of the gym meant only for stretching and weight training. We didn't lift weights like body builders, but we did use them for specific muscle building drills where we needed to target.

"Okay, get on your back and lie flat. Arms by your ears."

No problem.

Coach picked up one twenty pound dumbbell and walked over to me. Getting on his knees, he sat behind my head and instructed me to open my hands, placing the heavy weight in my palms. He was so close I could smell his citrusy, cinnamon scent, not that powdery chalk smell of the gym.

"You are going to keep your arms by your ears. Lift your legs and arms at the same time and come together, but only half way. This is going to build muscle here." Kova placed a flat hand to my pelvic region and my stupid body heated all over from it. I looked around to see if anyone could see us. Tingles broke out across my skin. His fingers were like a sparkler on the Fourth of July, and I wondered if Katja had the same reaction to him.

"Now, slowly lift," he said, his hand still on me.

I lifted, but too fast. "You are not in a race to finish, Adrianna. Take it slow."

Be still my heart. I loved how my name rolled off his tongue.

Kova continued to stare at my stomach like he was unable to make eye contact with me. "Lift slower," was all he said impassively.

"Tighten," he ordered when I began lifting slower, hollowing my body into a small boat look. He pressed his fingers into my stomach feeling for muscle. "This is what I want to feel. Right here...tighter." He nodded to himself in satisfaction. His hand burned my stomach.

I cleared my throat and our eyes locked. "Seriously? You couldn't think of any other word to use?"

The corner of his mouth lifted and his emerald eyes gleamed. I dropped to the floor. "English is not my first language. Forgive me."

I lifted again and this time he placed a hand under my calves and the other hand under my arms. I was shaking. Lifting a twenty pound dumbbell wasn't really all that heavy, but in the position I was in, and how I was doing it, wasn't so easy. Kova helped guide me slowly up and then down so many times my muscles were on fire.

"Remember to breathe."

After another set, my arms were trembling.

"Okay. Let us take a break," he reached for my arm and began massaging the muscle, shaking it out. His knuckles brushed against my ribs. His fingers kneaded the tissue deep and the sublime feeling took over.

With Kova still seated next to me, I was able to get a good look. I watched him, where his eyes were, the tick working in his jaw. I wanted so badly to ask about our kiss that night in the gym, and what it meant.

"Kova," I whispered just for him. I tried to get his attention, but he wouldn't look my way.

"Not now, Adrianna."

"When?" He continued to ignore me so I said, "I'm not going to tell anyone."

He shook his head incredulously. "There is more to it than that."

"Please, look at me." When he finally did, I said, "I swear."

He shook his head in disbelief again, and murmured, "Do you understand the rules I broke? The fact that I could go to jail?"

"You wouldn't go to jail, I looked it up. We only kissed," I whispered, and looked around. "We didn't do anything else. It was just a kiss."

He stared at me in horror. "You do not see the problem because you are too young." Then he stood, and by the look in his eyes, I instantly knew he regretted what happened.

"Grab my ankles and give me yours."

I looked at him, perplexed.

"Put your hands around my ankles," Kova said slowly, like I was hard of hearing. "And bring your legs up."

Well, well, well. From this view, there was a lot to see, meaning Kova's bulge. The outline from this angle made me picture what was inside his shorts and if he was wearing boxers or not. I could tell he wasn't fully erect, yet still pretty large. At least I assumed he wasn't erect and I knew he felt big, but I hadn't actually seen it. My grip tightened around his ankles as I thought about how he stroked my pussy with it, a river of sensations streamed through my center.

"I am going to push your legs down, but you are not to touch the floor," Coach said, breaking my forbidden thoughts. "I will push you side to side and straight out, but never let your legs hit the floor."

"Got it."

Kova threw my legs out and my back bent in desperation to keep my feet from touching the carpet. I gripped his ankles tighter, holding on in order to bring my legs back up.

"Snap them up," he ordered. "Faster. I am taking time out just for you here."

"I didn't ask you to help me," I gritted out.

"Adrianna, I am here to make sure each gymnast reaches their maximum potential, so if that means taking over for another coach, I do it. It is nothing personal."

Nothing personal.

Screw him. I didn't ask him for this. I could've stuck with Madeline but he wanted to step in.

When he pushed my legs to the side, my hips swiveled and I snapped them back, struggling a bit. It was harder than it sounded and my stomach flexed every time. And every time, I looked at his bulge and watched it bounce.

I was going to hell.

My stomach burned, like fire ants coating my flesh. My legs were beginning to bend as I pulled them up. I wanted so bad to ask for a break, but I knew better.

"I am tired of telling you to keep those legs together and locked straight." He threw my legs down so angrily and fast I struggled to bring them back up. But they didn't touch the ground and I was proud of myself for that. My nails dug into his flesh, I let out a gush of air when I pulled them up. He repeated the motion.

"It will only make me do this to you longer."

In that moment, I decided I was going to study witchcraft and put a spell on him for this kind of torture.

And have him use correct English words, and some fucking contractions.

Every time he pushed my legs down, I took a deep breath and held it, using it to throw my legs back to him. Sweat dripped down the sides of my temples, and I was pretty sure I was going to pop a blood vessel in my eye.

Who knew how much time had passed when I reached the point where I couldn't take anymore. My inner thighs trembled, they shook so hard that in conjunction with my burning stomach, I was queasy. He must have sensed it when he said, "One last time." And when he threw my legs again, I let them drop to the floor with a thud. One leg fell out to the side, the other coming up in an effort to bend, but I didn't have the strength to hold it up, so they both fell open. The position wasn't very ladylike, but I was too worn the hell out to care.

Panting heavily, I felt like I just ran a marathon. "I think I'm dying."

"Do not be so dramatic."

My grip loosened and my elbows flopped to the side. "I'm not. That was hard." But he ignored my comment and stood above me, his gaze between my opened legs.

I should've closed them, it would've been the logical thing to do, but I was rooted in place. Partly due to the fact that I just couldn't move, but I also liked the way his eyes licked across my body. His heady stare caused a throb between the crux of my thighs, and my pulse quickened.

God. What was wrong with me? I should've been repulsed. Hell, maybe I should've gotten up and walked away. Maybe I needed to speak to a therapist about my Kova addiction.

Actually, scratch that.

Opening up about having a crush on my much older coach could seriously backfire on me. Keeping my mouth shut was the only plan of action I had.

Mustering the strength, I brought my legs together slowly, adding pressure to my swollen center with my thighs. Coach cleared his throat and reached out his hand to help me up.

"I will see you later for floor."

"Coach?"

"Go."

"No, I feel like we should talk."

Stepping toward me, his eyes quickly scanned the gym. "There is nothing to talk about. It was a giant lapse in judgment. It should have never fucking happened," he sneered. "And now I have to live with the fact I took advantage of a minor, my gymnast no less. I am sick over it, I cannot sleep."

I reared back, feeling only a small dose of pity. "You didn't take advantage of me."

"It is even worse you think that way," he gritted out under his breath. "You should have been revolted with what I said and did."

"I'm not, I wasn't. I liked it, everything, and I didn't want it to stop. You felt better than when—"

"Adrianna," he said sharply, cutting me off. Running a hand through his hair, his eyes traveled to my chest and lingered for a moment.

"I do not have anything else to say to you. I am a man, you are a...teenager," he said with disgust, making me feel two inches tall. "Had Katja seen us, we could have lost everything. I am not willing to risk that for anything or anyone, no matter what."

I swallowed back the empathy I was suddenly feeling. His eyes softened, shame filling them. "You have worked too hard to just throw it away, and so have I. Keep your hands to yourself and I will do the same."

Then he turned and walked away, gutting me.

CHAPTER 34

Two hours of advanced chem, plus ten hours of gym time, and I was ready to crash.

It didn't matter that I turned another year older today, it felt like any other day to me. Avery was out of the country. She hadn't been able to visit me for my birthday like she wanted. Her parents scheduled a family vacation to Spain and dropped it on her and her brothers last minute, but she promised she'd come and see me when she got back. My dad was away on business, Xavier was off with his friends doing God knows what, and other than a text from my mom, I hadn't heard a single word from my family. The gym was the gym, same as any other day.

I'd learned to turn off emotions when the time called for it, so being alone on my birthday didn't affect me.

However, Alfred gave me a cupcake with a candle last night when he handed over the keys to the Escalade, my very own Tonka truck. I thanked him and actually called him Thomas.

Aside from being famished and probably capable of eating a cow right then, I just didn't have the strength after the long and draining day I had.

Stepping out of the private tutoring room housed in the back of the library, the lights were soft and the vacancy in the air left me feeling a little cold. My grades were good and I stayed on track, so I really didn't need to come, even though I skipped class that morning to take my driver's test. Where my mom peeved about my appearance, my dad focused on school and how important grades were. I knew he was right, because at the end of the day, I wasn't naive to think money could buy everything like it had in order for me to come to World Cup. One day this would all be over and I'd be living in the real world with real responsibilities.

We were a few weeks into August and the weather changed in Georgia. Although still stifling hot during the day, the humidity was thicker and stickier by nightfall. I began fidgeting with my zipper so I could remove my jacket before I walked outside, but it was stuck on the material. I placed my books on a nearby table to fix it.

I was oblivious to the world when a whisper of breath brushed across my skin. "Do you need help with that?"

My hand flew to my neck and I spun around at the voice in surprise.

Hayden.

"Shit! You scared the crap out of me!"

Hayden grinned, his dimples showing. My eyes shifted to his shoulders, and even through the light gray hoodie, I could see his well-defined muscles.

"Sorry, I just saw you were stuck and thought I'd help."

Simmer down, hormones.

"Aid, do you need help with that?" he asked, nodding toward my hands.

Shaking my head, I snapped out of it. "Ummm, yeah, thanks."

Hayden fiddled with my zipper and asked, "Are you okay?"

"I'm sorry...I'm just exhausted." He grinned and my stomach rumbled.

"And apparently hungry, too."

Heat crept up my neck and into my cheeks, embarrassed over how loudly my stomach grumbled.

"Yeah, that too, but I'm too tired to eat, and the last thing I want is one of the prepared meals I have waiting for me at home."

Hayden's brows angled toward each other, so I answered his perplexed look.

"My mom has fresh meals prepared and delivered to me weekly. The thought of putting that in my mouth right now doesn't sound as appealing as face planting into bed. Most of the time I can deal with them, but if I never had to look at another piece of fish or bark again, it would be too soon. So I'd rather not eat."

"Bark? Like from a tree?"

I chuckled, thinking how funny that sounded. "Not really bark, just food that has nothing in it, no spices, and tastes horrible. Not to mention, they're small servings."

He nodded, accepting my answer. "Why don't you just go food shopping?"

I shrugged. "Truthfully, my mom would have a conniption if I bought something she didn't approve of. Plus, I just don't have the energy."

"So you're just not going to eat?" He fumbled with my zipper and finally got it down my body.

"I have some fruit I can pick at."

"Adrianna, you have to eat," he said, grabbing hold of my hips. Since that kiss in my condo, Hayden hadn't been this forward with his touch. So naturally I noticed his hands on my body.

"Let's go. We're going to grab something to eat together."

"Where would we go?"

"There's a Gino's Pizza up the street. How about there?"

"My mother would kill me if I had pizza."

Squeezing me closer, Hayden looked around aimlessly. I followed his gaze, curious to see who he was looking for, but I didn't see anyone.

"Adrianna, do you see her anywhere? She won't find out about it and I promise not to tell her." The corner of his mouth perked up.

Hesitating, I bit my lip. I haven't had pizza in so long.

"Come on," he coaxed, and grabbed my books, then laced his fingers through mine. "My treat."

I must've stayed in the library longer than planned. A murky fog sat low in the parking lot as we walked hand-in-hand. I didn't typically hold hands with someone I wasn't dating, but Hayden was different. Much to my surprise, he'd become a really good friend. I expected to be close to my team girls more than anything, and I wasn't.

"Which car is yours?"

I pointed to the black SUV with the almost illegal tint and twenty-two inch rims. It was the SUV Alfred had driven when we first came to Cape Coral earlier this year.

"That's your ride?" His brows rose, skepticism in his tone.

God, I just wanted to crawl into a hole and hide. To say Hayden was flabbergasted over my top of the line Escalade was an understatement. It was the Platinum edition and aside from being slightly embarrassed, I really did love it. No one's first car was this nice unless the family had money. But back home, this kind of thing was normal, and the kids I grew up with had even nicer cars. Avery had a sleek BMW that I voiced to my dad wanting on numerous occasions.

"Yes."

"When did you get that car?"

"Umm, well, I've had this car for a while now actually. I just happened to get the keys to it last night."

"Last night?" he questioned me.

I bit my lip. "Today's my birthday."

Hayden stopped in his tracks, jaw dropped and his face lit up. "Today's your birthday and you didn't tell anyone?" He slammed into me and gave me the tightest bear hug possible. I laughed when he picked me up and spun me around, wishing me a happy birthday.

He put me down and said, "When did you get your license? I can't believe you didn't tell anyone."

"I skipped tutoring and Alfred took me this morning."

"Dude, your car is sick. I'm buying dinner, but you're driving."

Relieved over his opinion, my shoulders relaxed. "I'm okay with that."

Hopping into the car, I pushed the button to start the engine as Hayden looked over his shoulder at the two rows behind him.

"Why do you have such a big car? And how come I've never seen it at the gym?"

I sighed before diving into it.

"My dad insists a bigger car is safer to drive, but he's wrong. He just worries about a small car crushing me to death, so he got me a Tonka tank. He's not the type you argue with and usually what he says goes. End of story. Plus, Alfred used to drop me off, which is why you probably never saw it," my voice trailed off.

"Hey," Hayden said softly, pulling my chin up to meet his steady gaze. "Don't feel embarrassed or ashamed of anything you have. I think it's pretty cool. Gotta be honest, I'm a little shocked to see you drive something so big as small as you are. It's a badass truck, but I'd never make you feel uncomfortable over it. I swear."

His thumb gently grazed my jaw, and I felt his touch all the way to my stomach. I nodded, accepting his genuine words.

"So what does your dad do?"

"He's a real estate developer."

"Oh, that's right. You mentioned it at Kova's barbecue. I forgot." I turned onto a busy street and he asked, "Do you live in a gigantic house?"

"Well, it's average sized...for the island."

"What's averaged sized?"

I bit my lip. "It's a little over nine thousand square feet. There are seven bedrooms, all the boring formal rooms, two kitchens, a guesthouse, movie theater, wine cellar, gym, sauna room, and a game room. We have a three car garage and live off a private road, which I actually like."

His eyes grew wide. "And it's on the beach?"

"No, we live on a golf course. My dad is a big golfer."

"Wow," he was speechless.

"It's actually really beautiful and originally belonged to the Post cereal heiress. It's a Mediterranean style home with the original floors and same architecture from when it was first built. Nothing was touched. So for my dad, buying it was a no brainer. He appreciates that kind of stuff. My mom wanted to rip the floors up and redo everything, but he put a firm stop to that." Unexpectedly, a shot of homesickness hit me and I frowned.

"The beach isn't far, which was where I spent most of my free time. Nothing compares to a Georgia beach. Pale sand, crystal clear water, endless rays of sun, it was really beautiful. Especially when the sun sets and the sky turned orange and pink sometimes."

"Well, it's settled then."

"What's settled?"

"That I'm coming home with you over Thanksgiving break. You're going to take me to a beach and then show me around the island."

I couldn't stop the loud laugh that erupted from my throat. It felt good to relax and let go, and surprisingly I could with Hayden.

"You do realize you have the ocean over here, right? You can go any time you want?"

"I do, but after what you just told me, I want to see where you live."

"Well you're in for a surprise then. People are different over there." I flipped my blinker on and turned into the parking lot. "I'm not like them, I don't want you to get the wrong idea."

"What do you mean?"

I shrugged, unsure of what to say. "First, you have to understand I'm not trying to flaunt my family's money or anything. Okay? Because I don't typically talk about it. It's embarrassing how people do, honestly.

"People on the Island are snotty. Everyone has money, and lots of it. Like an obscene amount. It's all about what kind of car you drive, which designer you're wearing, where your money comes from and so forth. A who's who pretty much. The air is full of wealth and The Islanders turn their noses up quickly and talk so much shit. Their children are even worse because they're raised with that kind of mentality, so their egos are the size of a watermelon by the time they enter middle school. And don't get me started on the socialites."

Hayden grew silent while I looked for a parking spot and slowly tried to pull in.

"What?" I asked, glancing at him.

Brows cinched, he gave me a skeptical look. "Are you okay driving? You don't look so sure of yourself right now?"

I laughed. "I'm still not used to driving a real life Tonka truck, so I tend to pull into the parking spot the way eighty year old's typically drive—barely able to see over the steering wheel and slower than a damn turtle."

Hayden barked out a laugh and I continued.

"The elderly give me road rage."

I parked outside of Gino's, and Hayden hopped out, making his way around as I locked my car and dropped the keys into my purse. Stepping inside the pizzeria, Hayden wrapped an arm around my shoulders and drew me to him. He rested his chin on top of my head.

We stood together looking through the glass at the pizza we could order by the slice.

"She's staring at you," I whispered to him, hardly moving my mouth.

Hayden pretended we weren't talking about the counter girl. "She probably wants to see my abs," he said casually, near my ear.

"I see them every day. They're nothing special in my opinion," I said teasingly, turning away to hide my grin. I knew his golden stomach was flat and toned. And don't get me started on his obliques and that tightness. Damn gymnast. She'd be in for a surprise if she saw what was under his shirt.

He tugged me closer and leaned in to the side of my neck. His lips brushed the shell of my ear. "Adrianna. Remember, I know what your lips taste like."

My eyes widened as Hayden's mischievous ones flashed back at me. I was instantly red, my cheeks blazing hot. I glanced around and spotted a girl a little older than me behind the counter.

"Lucky girl," she said and smiled. "What can I get you guys?"

CHAPTER 35

So did you like the pizza last night?" Hayden asked while I chalked up my hands.

"Yeah, it was really good. Who knew there were so many different kinds? We don't have that kind of selection back home."

"Where is back home again?" Reagan chimed in. I was pretty sure I already mentioned this to her.

Glancing down at the chalk bowl, I grabbed the block of chalk and cracked it. Kind of the way I wanted to crack Reagan's head sometimes.

"Outside of Savannah."

She scowled. "I know that. Where?"

Squatting down, I looked inside my bag for my grips, but I didn't spot them anywhere. Shit. The last thing I wanted to do was answer her while I was frantically searching for my gear.

Pushing things around, I pulled out my extra leos and dropped them to the floor. I found the wristbands, but my grips were gone. I couldn't do bars without them, not again, and if I ripped my hands open it would take forever to heal at the rate I trained.

Gritting my teeth together, I responded. "Palm Bay. It's outside of Savannah. Amelia Island, to be exact. It's in—"

"I know where it is. I just don't understand why you would leave there and come here," she stated. "Your dad couldn't build a gym for you?"

Was she serious? The urge to roll my eyes was strong at her condescending comment. "I wanted a better gym and my dad happened to be friends with Kova, so it worked out perfectly."

I didn't like confrontation, but I also didn't cower away from it when the time called. She had absolutely no reason to feel the way she did about me. Plus, the last thing I needed was for Coach to think I had drama with any of his team girls.

"Seriously, Reagan?" I asked and waited for her to look at me. "What's your problem? You hardly speak to me, yet you clearly can't stand the sight of me. What did I do to you? Let's just clear the air now because your attitude is getting old."

She gnashed her teeth together and stepped to me. "You want to know what my problem is? My problem is Coach pays you more attention than anyone else and I just don't get it. It's like his sole focus is on you and it's not fair. You don't deserve it."

Cry me a fucking river. "What are you talking about? He trains with you and all the other girls everyday as usual."

She shook her head, huffing. "He took time away from working with us so he can work on you more. I mean, God knows you need the extra hours and all, but it's still not right. And believe me, we've all noticed how he looks at you."

I froze. No. No way could someone see anything at all between us. We were good at hiding the tension, at least I thought we were. Reagan's words hurt, but I needed to shield my emotions immediately. I pushed away her last comment and planned to deal with it later.

"So you want more attention, then? Is that what it is?"

"I don't need attention. I need a coach who puts in as much time with me as he does for every gymnast here. He used to be like that, but once you got here it's like he completely changed, which can only mean one reason. You." She lowered her voice and looked down at me. "I work harder than anyone here, and I refuse to have it all taken away. I have goals and dreams, too. Not just you, Adrianna."

As much as I tried not to let her words bother me, they did. The looks, the comments, they all grated on my nerves. I was tired of feeling like I wasn't good enough. I worked just as hard as any of these girls.

"You're wrong." Standing up, I decided to walk away. Tears were welling in my eyes and I didn't want her to see. I refused to listen to any more of her bitter bullshit. Rips were most likely happening, so I knew I needed to load up with as much chalk as I could now.

With my stomach in knots and tears burning the back of my eyes, I felt myself slipping. The toll my emotions were taking came close to the edge and I needed to get them under control before I broke.

Grabbing the honey, I squirted my hands, and patted on more chalk. Reagan's words replayed in my head as I repeated the process, over and over again.

Walking to the uneven bars, Hayden grabbed my arm midstride to stop me.

"Where are your grips?" he asked, glancing at my wrists then back to my eyes, knowing the kind of end result I could face.

I shrugged. "I have no idea, Hayden." I said, dejectedly. "I thought I had them—"

"Hey Reagan, let Adrianna borrow an extra pair of your grips, would ya?"

"What are you doing," I whispered at him, yanking my arm away. "You know she can't stand me and honestly, I don't want any favors from her."

I could swear I'd seen my grips in my bag this morning. The thought crossed my mind that maybe Reagan purposely took them out. I wouldn't put it past her. She seemed hell bent on wanting me to fall.

"If she's so rich, then why doesn't she have more?" Her squeaky voice was like nails on a chalkboard. I'd give anything to rub chalk on her vocal chords so she didn't sound like a mouse.

"Don't worry, Reagan. I like the bloody rips on my hands. It feels so good when the chalk hits my red, irritated skin, turning my hands raw. What doesn't kill you only makes you stronger, right?"

Tightening my ponytail, I gripped the low bar and swung into a glide kip. With my hips back, I extended my legs as far as they could go so I was in a perfect horizontal line, and felt the pull in my stomach. I brought my toes to the bar and piked to a kip, then cast to a handstand, holding it for three seconds, before doing a glide kip out so my arms were straight and my thighs rested very lightly on the bar.

I turned to Reagan. "Guess this means Coach will just be giving me more attention since I'm without my grips today."

Casting to a handstand on the low bar once again, I piked down and swung around in a straddle position and released the low bar. With my hips high in the air, I twisted my body completely around and reached for the high bar.

Chalk sprinkled down lightly when I grasped the bar, and I closed my eyes. Doing a few light release moves allowed me to warm up as I swung from bar to bar with ease, while it stretched out my sore muscles. It felt good, and I had to admit I loved the pull on my body. Everything just faded away. It was like a stress reliever and I embraced it every single time. Especially now.

I warmed up with a few handstands and pirouettes, making sure I hit them in vertical, then a Giant to a flyaway dismount. I warmed up once more and decided instead of doing a flyaway again, I would go for a double layout. It wasn't really common in a warm up, but it was something I mastered long ago and could do in my sleep.

Two Giants completed, I released. The bar ricocheted loudly, springs bouncing. I flew through the air, making sure I kept my body straight as a board and my hips opened while I flipped back two times before driving my heels into the ground. I landed with a slight wobble. A rolling flame of heat shot up my calf, but I forced it out of my head.

"Nice, Aid!" Hayden yelled excitedly as he walked over to the pommel horse.

All Reagan could manage was a glare. Before I could say anything, Coach Kova yelled across the gym, "Nice job, Adrianna. Tighten up a little more."

Naturally he saw my wobble, but nothing got past the man. "It was just a warm up, Coach." I responded back and he nodded in approval, his eyes gleaming with contentment.

That was the first real thing Kova had said to me in weeks. I needed it, I needed his backing after what Reagan said. I needed to know I was making progress in his eyes, that my hard work did not go unnoticed. Other than commands about gymnastics skills, we hardly spoke. I'd come to accept his stiff personality after what happened between us.

I turned and smiled brightly at a seething Reagan, who stepped around to mount the bar and begin her routine. But just before she did, she threw an extra set of grips at my feet.

"You know, Coach works with you the way he does because he feels bad. You're not good enough to be here, and it's obvious you never will be. Why do you think he puts in so much time with you?

It's the same way with Hayden. Holly told me Hayden said you have no friends and you're alone all the time, so he's friends with you out of pity. I'm not surprised, though. Hayden's a good guy. It's in his nature to go out of his way to help those in need."

The satisfaction I felt moments earlier was gone. Tears pooled in my eyes again at her heartless words. Months of hard work and emotional avoidance bubbled at the surface. I didn't want to cry, but her words stung and I felt them ready to spill over.

"No one here likes you, and the one friend you have isn't a real one. Your coach and your only friend have no faith in you whatsoever." She laughed, mockingly. "You should just leave now. You'll never amount to being an Olympic gymnast, Adrianna Rossi. You don't have what it takes and you never will."

With that, she smiled and turned to mount the bar. I walked back over to the chalk bowl, my heart pounding against my chest. I was sick to my stomach. Her words rang in my ears, getting louder and heavier. They couldn't be true.

A fat tear slipped down my cheek at the reality of my life and I quickly wiped it away. Embarrassment over forgetting my grips clogged my throat, and my chest tightened from the humiliation Reagan just dealt me. I was suffocating in a bowl of fucking chalk. Somehow I had been completely oblivious to my surroundings. I'd been used to snotty girls back home, but Reagan was a true mean girl, and I didn't know how to deal with it. I've been taught to handle things with poise and control, not act like a loose cannon, but her words were cruel and they struck deep. All I wanted to do was retaliate.

But I didn't. Instead, I took the higher road and began powdering my hands as another tear fell into the bowl, her words repeating in my head.

Taking a deep breath, I exhaled and let all the bullshit out. I looked up at the gym around me and locked eyes with Kova, who was staring at me intently.

I didn't want to appear weak, but there was no way to stop another warm tear from rolling down my cheek. Kova's eyes darkened, his jaw set tight. He glanced at Reagan for a long moment before giving me one more look. This time it was filled with concern that caused my belly to clench. His gaze said more than I think he wanted to give away.

Before turning toward the bars, I wiped the tears away so Reagan wouldn't see she got to me. I refused to show her she'd won this battle.

But she wouldn't win the war.

CHAPTER 36

Three long-assed weeks passed by where Kova and I skated around each other.

To be fair, I kept my focus primarily on gymnastics.

It wasn't as easy as I thought it would be. In fact, it was downright hard. Being in a gym and training for nearly fifty hours a week was a daunting task alone. I'd been taking extra dance classes and spending hours transforming my body just so I could reach Kova's standards. Sadly, I didn't know if I'd ever meet them, because he sure as hell wouldn't tell me.

Add in an illicit act between a coach and his athlete and see where that got you. Especially an athlete he has to personally train for a number of those hours.

I'd caught him sneaking glances, touching me more than needed during gym, practices lasting longer. In his defense, I'd been doing the same thing to him. The tension was mounting between us, but where was it going? There was no outlet for any of it. It was just brewing, the pressure building to an unhealthy level.

Worst of all, I started to worry if anyone else noticed. Especially after the comments Reagan made.

Things were getting to me. Not to mention, I was almost positive there was something wrong with my calf, which wasn't helping the situation—or my life. The pain would come and go in the beginning, so I tended not to focus on it. But now that it was starting to appear more often than not, I couldn't help but wonder if it was something serious. It was stressing me out more than ever. My mind was on edge with all the thoughts running through it, and the silence of my condo was eating at me.

Today was my one day off. I'd been restless, all alone and nothing to fill the void. I needed to get out. Avery was nowhere to be found, which was pissing me off. If I knew her, there was a good chance she was with her mystery guy. She'd given me the fuck you button a few times already. I cleaned every square inch I could and there was nothing on Netflix worth watching. I even tried to read a book in hopes it would help me escape the monotony of my life.

Nothing helped.

I was beginning to drive myself crazy over everything that had happened since arriving at World Cup. My head was pounding. I needed to zone out and forget about it all, and the one thing that would allow me any form of relief was gymnastics.

I wanted to train, I needed to. I needed the release it brought on.

Pulling open the door to the gym, I blew an unruly auburn strand of hair from my face. The gym was typically closed on Sunday, which meant I would be alone and without the constant observation from my team and coaches.

Just what I wanted.

Flipping on the lights in the dance room, I dropped my stuff on the wood floor and walked to the shelf that held the radio. Funny how Kova had radios in the actual gym, but he wouldn't put one in the therapy room. I needed music, otherwise the silence would ruin my train of thought.

I decided I'd work on the skills I learned in the stupid ballet classes I was forced to take. I wondered how much longer I'd have to take them. They weren't as bad as I thought they'd be, I just didn't care for them. Maybe this was what separated me from being a mediocre gymnast and an incredible gymnast in Kova's eyes. It was no secret I hated ballet, but I wasn't naive enough to think I didn't need it anymore. I hated admitting ballet played a large part in gymnastics. The components had not only increased my flexibility and balance, but the coordination and discipline required made a huge difference, especially on the floor.

Dance, primarily ballet, corrected my posture that was thrown off by the constant bending and twisting of gymnastics. Just like ballerinas, gymnasts needed to be tight with every movement—eliminating unwanted movement—control. Spotting a sloppy dancer was easy, even to an untrained eye. Gymnastics was the same way and it all started with building my core.

After pushing a few buttons, *Love Me Like You Do* by Ellie Goulding vibrated through the speakers, rejuvenating my spirit in its wake. I felt a hundred times better already and allowed her poetic voice to take me away.

"YOU ARE DROPPING YOUR CHEST."

I jumped, snapping my back leg down and spinning around in fear, my heart racing. Kova's unsympathetic voice startled me out of my concentration and I stared straight at him like a deer in headlights.

"What?" I asked breathlessly.

"Your chest. You are dropping your chest," he stated for the second time.

He casually leaned against the doorframe, his arms crossed. He took in the length of my body with a long gaze. Instead of a leotard, I went with black mini workout shorts and a green sports bra. Moisture dampened my skin as sweat trickled down the small of my back. I'd removed my oversized T-shirt earlier, throwing it to the ground. My long hair was thrown into a messy bun at the top of my head. Little hairs had slipped out I hadn't cared to fix.

I thought about what Kova said and I nearly growled. This man. I swear, he did everything he could to get under my skin. I most definitely was *not* dropping my chest.

"No, I'm not."

The corner of his mouth tugged up, as if to say, *Are you really going to challenge me?*

Dropping his arms, Kova prowled forward with determination. Each step made my heart beat a little faster. My skin prickled as he neared me, vibrations coursed through my body. I was suddenly hyperaware of his presence and how secluded we were in the dance room.

"Yes, you are," he countered. "Do it again."

Taking a few paces back, I inhaled deeply and visualized the Jeté before I moved again. With my shoulders relaxed back and my chest arched forward, I sashayed in two steps with my arms gracefully out to the side. Kicking one long leg forward, followed by a flick of my hip twisting in the air to bring my other leg around, I scissor kicked my legs quickly by tapping at the toes before I landed.

I looked at Kova who wore a lovely, sardonic glimmer in his eyes.

"Are you still going to tell me you did not drop your chest?"

"I didn't. I know I didn't."

Kova tilted his head to the side. "You have too much power in your back swing, so you cannot balance it out. Do it again, but do not try and force open your legs as wide. Watch yourself in the mirror."

I did as he said, only this time it felt less than perfect.

"That was a half-assed turn," I admitted.

Kova's lips curved upward, his eyebrows lowered, and I felt his agreement in my stomach.

"It was. It was terrible. But I told you why and you seem to think I am lying."

I did it again. And again. Four more tries and I became increasingly frustrated with each step I took, all while he watched closely with scrutinizing eyes. I wanted to prove him wrong, because surely I would know if I was dropping my chest or not.

After I finished the fifth turn, I ran my fingers through my sweaty hair and clenched it, groaning in irritation over the fact I couldn't master a move as basic as this.

"Show me how to do it correctly."

He raised an eyebrow.

"Please?"

He nodded silently. "Come with me."

Following Kova, he led me to the center of the floor. He stood in front of me and grabbed my forearms so my palms would rest in the crest of his elbows. He tugged me forward until both our arms were tightly bent at our sides, holding each other in place.

Looking directly in my eyes, he explained. "You are going to jump once for power, then jump again and do the same move as before, only this time you are holding my arms. It will give you momentum, but will also allow you to condition your back kick and keep your chest up. It is the same as you would do on the barre, but I am holding you. Your chest will not drop in my arms the way it would on the barre."

I nodded, took a deep breath and jumped into the kick, only to lean into his chest with a grunt, getting a hint of his cinnamon and citrus scent but with a trace of something more. Whatever it was, he smelled divine, and it assaulted my senses.

"Again. But this time stretch your legs as wide open as a kick split will allow you. Do it ten times, but on the last one stop with your leg in the air. Got it?"

My brows scrunched together. "But you told me not to open them as wide just before."

"This is different. You will not be able to lean in my arms. Just trust me."

I jumped and then kicked back ten times, just as he had instructed me to, stretching my legs as wide as possible with each kick. Kova was right. I couldn't drop my chest here and I felt the slight pinch in my back at this angle. I didn't move. My palms were sweating and I wish I'd chalked up my hands before I gripped his forearms to steady my balance. Our eyes stayed locked the whole time, never wavering. His persistence to see me complete this kick correctly shifted something inside of me.

Out of breath and leaning toward Kova's chest, I waited with my leg elongated in the air behind me for him to speak. The air circulated around us from the exercise and I could smell him even better at this angle, not that I should want to, but I also couldn't stop myself from drawing in a small breath.

God, he smelled so good.

Something felt different tonight while I waited in his arms to critique my form. I became more aware of the strength he exuded, the power in his hold, the way he stared down through his thick eyelashes. The complete domination. My stomach clenched at the sudden thought of what his strength could do to me...and the fact that we were alone in the gym...again.

Craning my head as far as my neck would allow from this odd angle, I peered through damp bangs that fell in my face.

The look from Kova's eyes seared heat into my skin. His fingers tightened under my forearms as if he was angry. Surely, I hadn't done it wrong again. A move that was normally so easy for me was giving me such problems tonight. Him staring at me like he wanted to wring my neck wasn't doing wonders for me either.

"What did I do wrong?" I asked breathlessly.

Kova's jaw locked back and forth at my question.

"Point your toe. Bring your chest higher."

Really? That was it? Point my toe?

He released the shell of my elbows and slowly slid his hands over to my ribcage, *my bare ribcage,* to rest right under my breastbone where the bottom of my sports bra sat. His hands held firm as my heart beat roughly against my chest.

"Steady your breathing. Remember what I taught you. Breathe with your stomach," he said, voice low.

I couldn't move.

I couldn't think.

And I tried not to take deep breaths as if I was gasping for air.

CHAPTER 37

His touch ignited a cluster of sparks throughout my body that went off simultaneously.

Never having this reaction to another person before, I didn't know how to respond to his presence. Heat pooled in my belly as my breath caught, not to mention, my calf and ankle started burning while my leg was still held high behind me.

"Your chest is too low and your hips are not squared," he stated, annoyed.

This fucking guy. He really knew how to push my buttons. He was irritating me, insinuating I didn't know what I was doing. My chest might have been at a little low, but my hips were most definitely squared.

My nose flared and I dropped my leg and stood defiantly. His warm hands slid to my waist then down to my hips.

"My hips are squared," I said through gritted teeth. "I learned that in beginner's gymnastics."

He challenged me.

"Either you had a shit for brains coach, or you just never comprehended the correct way to do it. Your hips are out and your chest is low. This is a very common mistake among gymnasts if they are not trained correctly from the beginning. I have seen you do this during practice many times and I thought we might have corrected it last time you were in here, but I guess I was wrong. Do not argue with me again over this, Ria. I have been doing this longer than you have been alive. I know what I am talking about, little girl. Now get over to the barre and I will show you how wrong you are."

"Little girl?" I mocked and pushed at him. "I didn't ask you to come in here to help me out. You just walked right in and interrupted my time. And if you did see me mess up during practice, I highly doubt that you'd keep your mouth shut. You love to pick at every little thing I do. 'Not enough. Faster. Higher. Why are you doing it this way? That is no good. Again,' is all that seems to come out of your mouth. If it's not that, you mumble in Russian under your breath."

My gut dropped. Oh God. Maybe I shouldn't have added in a faux Russian accent.

He stepped forward, and my heart skipped because I refused to step back. In a deathly quiet voice, he said, "If your obnoxious music was not blaring and echoing throughout *my* gym, I would not have had to come in here. Get your ass to the barre. There are so many things I need to correct where you are concerned. If I do not correct you now, you will just make more work for me down the line. There are not enough hours in the day for that, or patience."

Dropping my arms, I stepped back. "This wasn't why I came to the gym. I purposely came when no one was around so I wouldn't have to be ridiculed for every damn thing I did. I needed to not think about a gymnastics routine for once and let go for a few moments alone. I needed to be free, not having to practice."

"Needed to be free? Your life is gymnastics!" He roared. "It is all you are allowed to think about. Eat. Sleep. Flip. Repeat. Nothing more! I am not here to waste my time for fun. You are here because I get results and can take you to the next level, which is what you wanted. You want the Olympics. *You*. Not me. I have already been. You need me, not the other way around. I do not need you, do you understand? I took you in as a favor, a bargain for a bargain. If you are only here for fun, then we are done. I have spent a ton of time working on you, perfecting you, more so than I have ever done with another gymnast, God knows you need it. At least you can show a little respect in the process."

I hated him and his arrogant attitude and his deep green eyes and pompous tone. My chest was tight, his words struck hard. He brought me down and I didn't like it.

But he was right. And I despised admitting it.

Gymnastics was my life. It was everything I've ever worked for. I needed to shut up and take it, or take a hike.

Standing on my toes, I spun around and headed to a ballet barre that mounted to the wall.

"Teach me the correct way, Oh Master," I said sarcastically. I couldn't resist. I knew I was being bold tonight, more than usual. He probably didn't know what to do with my impulsive attitude, seeing as the only thing I did these days was take orders during practice. I'd reached my breaking point.

"Grab the barre and kick your leg back. Hold it there."

I didn't hear him move, but Kova was suddenly standing next to my shoulder. One of his hands gripped my inner thigh while the other was flat between my breasts to hold me in place. His fingers were splayed out, one fingertip accidently touching the plump mound of my breast. I gasped, sucking in the dense air and wondered if he realized it.

His warm fingers scorched my flesh. Kova squeezed my thigh hard, moisture pooled between my legs. I bit down on the inside of my lip, having to hide my reaction to him. I needed to control it, but I didn't know how.

"Look in the mirror," he spat out.

I looked.

"See? Your chest is angled too low for the height of your leg. Push off the barre with your arms to bring your chest up."

I raised my chest and a slight burn resonated in my back.

"More."

I did, but the burn crept higher up my back at the uncomfortable angle. "I can't go any more."

Kova shot daggers through his eyes at the word can't. Taking matters in his own hands, he ignored my resistance and pushed my chest up himself, never letting go of my leg, and bent my body in an unnatural position. I grunted as a gush of air burst from my lungs. I tried to lower my leg, but he wouldn't give.

"Your weakness is your lack of flexibility."

"I know," I gushed out. I was in serious pain and he wanted to have a conversation?

"You know and yet you do not condition yourself the way I taught you? Why did I spend time in those private sessions if you are not going to use the drills? That is not proving yourself to me."

He let up an inch so I could speak. "I've been conditioning, apparently not enough. I'll do more."

"Look at your hip now."

Son of a bitch.

"This is where you need to be with your form."

Christ, he was right. My hip was pivoted out and not squared at all with my shoulders.

"Hold your leg still and do not move," Kova ordered. Beads of sweat trickled down my neck as I fought to hold position.

Using the hand that was still tightly wrapped around my inner thigh, and dangerously near my sex, he leisurely slid it to the outer edge of my thigh, almost as if he was feeling for my flexed muscle. My breathing labored, and I struggled not to respond to the sensations of his touch as his hand glided up my leg almost provocatively. It was electrifying. And though I knew it was wrong, in this very moment, I wanted his touch more than I wanted to learn the correct stance.

"Do not move, Ria," he whispered.

His other hand drifted willfully over my waist, leaving a trail of heat dancing across my bare skin. I gripped the barre tighter, my knuckles turning white.

God, it felt so good. A purr resonated in my throat. I tried not to think of his touch in a sensual way, but it was pointless. I wanted his hands on me, I wanted them all over my body. I wanted him to show me the correct way to do more. I wanted the heat of his skin pressed against mine, to whisper in Russian across my neck. His fingers sat on my lower abdomen, and if I moved my hips just an inch more they would hit the throbbing spot begging for release. I needed his touch, yearned for his skilled hand to slide lower.

Kova's hand skimmed around my upper thigh, grazing my sex. His closeness made me wonder if he knew what he was doing, what he'd touched. I tried not to focus on the sensuality of his hand, but it wasn't easy when he was continually sliding past and dipping lower.

Leaning closer to me, he asked, "See how firm you are here?" Tight lipped, I nodded. "See how your hips are flat and down?" His hand slowly circled my pelvis. I nodded again. "This is what we want all the time. I know you can do it, Ria."

His belief in me, even over something as simple as squaring my hips, made my chest bloom with confidence.

Taking a deep breath, my hips moved just a fraction. I told myself I couldn't help it as I worked to breathe at this uncomfortable position, but I also couldn't stop the gnawing hunger of wanting his hand to move lower either.

The pressure of his fingers digging into my thigh, signified he was fighting not to move. Then finally, one long and unsteady finger hit the slit of my mound and I nearly groaned.

Swiftly, his hand slid to my hip and his fingers wrapped around and gripped me. Leaning in with his hip, he used it as leverage to steady, gluing himself to me. His pelvic bone dug into my side, showing just how close he really was. As he gripped my hip, he rotated it forward to square it correctly.

With a grunt, my leg involuntarily snapped down and my arms gave out. My knees buckled and I lost balance, crumbling against the barre with Kova crashing into me.

"Fuck," I muttered under my breath. All that touching so he could square my hips.

We were both leaning on the barre in a heap of heavy breathing when Kova's arm secured my waist and tugged me to stand. "Come on, try it again."

I didn't want to stand, I couldn't move. My body ached and I was exhausted after holding that position.

"Get up, Adrianna," his warm breath sent shivers across my damp neck. With my back pressed against his chest and my ass nestled between his hips, the hardness of his body was making it difficult to function.

Kova's hold tightened. A flush of heat coursed through my worn out body at his closeness, his breath on my neck, his fingers digging into me. My heart raced, and I knew he was the reason for it, not exertion. Strangely enough, I was okay with this reaction to Kova, this feeling streaming through my veins. Curiosity got the best of me and I embraced this moment.

Still glued to my backside, much closer than he truly needed to be, I decided to be daring. My lower belly was throbbing, an ache pooling inside for something more, so I leaned against him, slowly standing to my full height with a seductive arch of my back, hitting him in all the right places. Even going as far as to add pressure to the clearly obvious erection pressing into me.

Kova hissed. I was probably tempting him in ways he'd never been tempted before.

Ask me if I cared.

I didn't.

And the part that frightened me most—I wished he wouldn't hold back.

"What are you doing," he asked in a broken whisper.

I answered honestly. "I don't know."

"You are treading a fine line, Ria. You are testing me."

I answered by pressing into his groin again. His arm tightened around me, a rush of moisture coated my shorts as his fingers skated along my waist.

God, I wanted him to make me feel what I felt the night we were alone together.

"What is it about you that I cannot stay away from?" he whispered. His head dropped to my shoulder and his lips landed on my skin. My body melted in his hold. His breathing deepened against my back as he struggled. He didn't move, and I knew why.

I was his gymnast.

He was my coach.

There were many laws we would break if we took another step.

Not to mention, our careers would be in ruins if anyone saw the position we were in right now.

But in this moment, I forgot it all.

CHAPTER 38

Kova's grip was strong. I turned in his hold, twisting to face his body where he hadn't moved one inch. My back was to the barre with my elbows resting on it. Looking into his eyes, they were swirling with desire just as I was sure mine were. I may be a teenager, but I wasn't stupid. I could tell when someone wanted me. Lust, passion, want, need, it was all there. His mouth was only inches from mine, and if I stretched up on my toes I think I could touch his lips.

With lust overpowering the slight tremor in my nerves, I decided to push the envelope. I may never get the chance to be in this position again. *Carpe diem!*

The muscles in my calves strained as I stood on the tips of my toes. Hovering in front of his mouth, I whispered breathlessly, "If my flexibility is so terrible, show me ways to stretch."

Kova's jaw locked, the look in his green eyes penetrated me, and his hips pressed into me as if we were becoming one. I inhaled a strangled breath and gripped the barre, needing some type of leverage in this moment of insanity. I wished I could read the thoughts I saw running through his eyes.

One of his hands traveled down my ribcage to my hip. He squeezed hard and I groaned, my hips surging into his from the pleasure.

"You want ways to stretch out your hips? I can show you a few," he said in a deep, raspy voice, his eyes gleaming with words he couldn't speak. My lips parted with a sigh.

His hand curved around to my backside, rubbing in circles and heating my already tepid skin. He slid down the center of my ass and gave a good, hard tug, cupping me. A rush of wetness coated my shorts from his forceful pull. Kova pressed a finger between my cheeks while his large hand kneaded my small ass. My shorts rode up, the cool air hitting the crease as he continued to massage me into oblivion. If he asked me to give myself to him in every conceivable way and act out any fantasy he'd ever had, I wouldn't hesitate. He could have me. The thumping of my heartbeat echoed in my ears. My legs were already jelly, my hips curled into him, feeling his dick against my aching sex. A hum escaped my throat and my stomach clenched in eagerness.

I wanted him to go farther. I *needed* him to go farther. God, what the hell was wrong with me?

He gave a rough squeeze to my ass once again, his eyes never leaving mine. "Want me to keep going," he stated more than asked.

My eyes were heavy from just his touch and it wasn't easy for me to respond.

"Say it."

"Yes." Rolled off my tongue.

One side of his mouth tugged up, giving me a sexy as hell half-grin. His knees bent, pushing his hips into me deeper to get a better hold. My eyes rolled into the back of my head, a breathless moan escaped my throat, this time loud enough for him to hear. His hand rotated on the curve of my ass, turning and gliding up my inner thigh. I gulped hard, knowing my shorts were soaked and all he had to do was run his hand along the seam of my sex to know just how wet I was. His touch was electrifying and I prayed he wouldn't stop.

"I don't see how this will help me, Coach," I said sweetly. "I don't feel anything stretching out."

His paused for a moment and then moved with cat like reflexes.

His hand quickly slid all the way up the backside of my thigh so my leg was straight in the air and he was holding the back of my knee. There was a slight sharpness, a pulling on my hamstring, but it was nothing new for me. I was in an upright split after all.

"Square your hips."

I grinded down. "I am."

"No, you are not, Ria," he spat back, tightness laced in his voice. "Are you really going to try me again?"

I shrugged. I honestly thought my hips were squared.

He glared at my blasé attitude. "I am not here to play games with you."

"Who said I'm playing games?" I fought back with fire in my eyes.

Kova's jaw ticked. Eyes said so much when words couldn't. This position left me extremely exposed—and it didn't take much to know he was thinking about sex.

I mean, I was. He had to be, too.

Kova was able to let go of my leg and because of his height it rested easily on his shoulder. He slid both hands to my hips, and this time he squared them off, shifting my foot at the same time so it was positioned correctly. Little things like this, incorrectly squaring my hips, were what held me back. My leg moved on his shoulder and I could feel his erection through his thin gym shorts...and I wanted it. God, I wanted to feel more of it. All of it. See it.

My mouth began to water, blood rushed through me like a tidal wave. We held still in a seriously compromising position with his dick pressed into me, hard. It felt so good that I wanted to rub myself against him.

"Feel it now?" he asked.

"No, it feels like any other stretch I've done before," I lied.

He challenged me. "Oh yeah?"

"Yes," I rotated my hips just a fraction, feeling the hard tip of him. "Oh, God," I murmured.

Kova flattened his hand against the underside of my thigh and pressed my leg up higher, off his shoulder, and I grunted.

Then, I felt it.

Oh boy, did I ever feel it.

Not only the pull in my leg, but his dick straining into my wetness. Letting out a loud breath, my eyes rolled shut in pleasure. He pressed my thigh back harder to meet my shoulder. His power over me was incredible. It took so little for him to hold me in this position.

I was at his mercy.

"Is it too hard for you to handle?"

When I didn't answer, his other hand moved from the barre to my ass, gripping it. He shifted, settling deeper, locking me in as much as our clothes would allow. Kova didn't hold back this time as his hips pressed into mine without a worry he'd hurt me. I moaned loudly, and my head fell back.

Jesus...

Kova answered my sigh by pressing my thigh back even farther, past my shoulder where it began to quake. I couldn't take any more—I could hardly breathe. I wasn't fucking Gumby here. My body was being stretched to an unnatural angle, yet this is what I needed. The pull was tight, almost painful as the muscles ripped, but I said nothing for multiple reasons.

My breath caught in my throat as his hand ran seductively down my leg and his lips landed on my clavicle. He peppered my shoulder and neck with little kisses. The barre was bruising my back from the weight of both of us pressing into it, but I didn't complain. It's what I wanted, so I took it all.

"Tell me to stop," he croaked, breathing heavily. His hand crept down my back, shocking me as it slid into my shorts and touched my bare skin.

My lips were sealed, but if he looked into my eyes, he'd have his answer.

"Tell me to stop," he repeated, almost begged, against my heated flesh.

"Don't stop."

Kova lifted his head. His eyes narrowed, his fingers moving deeper, sliding toward my core and grazing my swollen lips for the very first time, from the back. He groaned loud, not holding back and his dick twitched against my center. Because of the tightness of the spandex shorts, I had gone without underwear.

His fingers rubbed along my slit, and I almost had an orgasm on the spot. Kova's tongue slipped out and ran across his bottom lip.

"You are supposed to tell me to stop."

"I can't help it. You make me want something more. Something I only feel when I'm around you."

Kova hesitated, my words rooting him in place. His hand stopped moving and he pulled away. I almost begged for him to pick up where he left off.

"You are too young to know what you want," he said gravely.

"Says who? You?" My leg slid down his shoulder and touched the ground. He stepped into me to close the remaining gap. His palms landed on my ass and he began rubbing in leisurely circles, warming my skin. I sighed, and rotated my hips into him, showing Kova just how much I knew what I wanted. I had a notion he was terrified to express what he craved, so I went out on a limb and did it for him. My chest constricted as I tried to interpret his gaze. If I was here and willingly giving myself to him, I wanted him to have me.

He grabbed my jaw, pulling it up to him in a savage hold and my stomach tightened. I looked him dead in the eyes while one of his hands slipped into my shorts. His fingers started up again and traced the outside of my lips, teasing my entrance.

"Please," I begged. "You didn't finish last time. I had to take care of it myself when I got home."

Kova's eyes darkened. "There is no need to beg, Ria," his voice cracked. "You can take what you want. In fact, I wish you would take from me. It would be easier that way."

Oh God. Why his words seized my heart, I didn't know. But one thing was for sure, I was right. He wanted the same things I did, he just couldn't actually verbalize it and needed me to take it. I wanted to take it, I just wasn't sure how to put everything into motion. Where to start, what to say. What to do. I was a bundle of nerves. How to make it uncomplicated for Kova while giving and receiving at the same time was a challenge, one I would gladly act on.

My body was on the verge of a powerful explosion, something so new I'd yet to fully embrace.

I decided to start with a kiss.

Straining on my toes, I cupped his face and pulled it to mine. "I want you," I whispered across his mouth. "So much," and planted my lips to his, shocking us both.

He grasped the back of my neck while his other hand sought entrance into my opening. I moaned, rotating my hips into his palm while his fingers caressed me gently. He kissed me hard, bruising almost, letting me know just how much he wanted me despite his hesitation.

Rolling my hips into his again so I could feel pressure on my clit, I groaned and silently asked for more. A skilled finger glided down my slit and nudged its way in. I pulled his tongue into my mouth as my hands drifted off his face, down his neck where he swallowed hard, to his taut shoulders. I gave a little squeeze, letting him know everything was okay. My hands roamed over every inch of his chest, his rock hard muscles that led to his beautifully strong arms I couldn't get enough of. Such curvature and sharpness at every arc. When my hands encircled his waist, I reached for the hem of his shirt.

The hand around my neck loosened its grip and his other hand gave one last caress over my opening before smoothly leaving the warmth of my shorts. He stepped back, separating our passionate lips, and I got what I wanted. Kova reached behind his neck and pulled his shirt off over his head and discarded it to the floor.

With a glint in his eyes and his arms spread wide, telling me to come to him, I tracked his every move as he backed away. *Take what you want.* Our eyes never wavered as he walked backward to the other side of the dance room. We both knew he wouldn't make the first move. He was going to make sure I really wanted this—and I did.

Once I reached him, I gripped the back of his neck and climbed up his body, wrapping my legs around his waist. I've fantasized doing this since the first time we were together. He was big and I was small and I wanted to be held in his arms just like this.

Kova hugged me tight, one hand behind my neck, the other under my ass as he turned me around and pushed my back to the wall.

Heat blazed in his eyes as he closed the distance and pressed his chest to mine. He was a breath away from my lips when he asked, "What are we doing?"

CHAPTER 39

I don't know." I locked my legs around his back, rolling my hips up. His shaft was long and heavy against my center, pressing into me. Kova's jaw flexed. Pulling his face down to mine, I licked my lips but he pulled back.

"Ria, think about what you are about to start." He breathed slow heavy breaths.

I nodded frantically. I already knew because I've imagined it numerous times. "What *we* are going to start." My fingers threaded his hair and warmth spread through me.

He ignored my last comment and asked, "You want this?"

I didn't hesitate. "Yes."

His eyes roamed my face, searching for an uncertainty he wasn't going to find. "Are you sure?"

I nodded.

"You realize the chances we are taking, right? What could happen to us?"

"I do."

His brows pinched together, his voice grim. "The repercussions we face?"

"I'm aware. I'm tired of fighting this, dancing around each other. I want you." I pressed my core against his erection.

"I am a man who can only be pushed so far." A tick worked in Kova's jaw. "You should not have told me that."

I bit my lip. "Why not?"

"Because then I will not feel as bad for doing this." He planted his mouth to mine with a fervor he'd held back until now, and I surrendered to his kiss.

Kova rested his weight on me, groaning loudly. The feel of his body on mine, the hardness of this man was euphoric. It made my head spin with bliss. He held me lovingly, his fingers caressing my face as if he was making love to my mouth. This kiss was much slower, methodic, showing me what he was capable of. His warm, thick tongue circled mine. My fingers tugged his hair, my hips undulated against him when his stubble brushed my face. He was suffocating me with his skilled mouth and I couldn't get enough.

Kova pulled back, panting against my lips. "We really should stop."

I ignored him. Licking my lips, I angled his head to the side and pressed my mouth to his neck. My tongue swept out, tasting his salty skin and pulled him into my mouth with a little bite.

Pushing off the wall, Kova spun around and brought our joined bodies to the floor. His lips found mine again and he quickly deepened the kiss. His arms planted on the sides of my head, caging me in. He was a beast over me, so big and large to my small frame. His raging erection settled between my legs. I wanted to feel his length, skin on skin, and maybe more. Sex would be scary the first time, no matter who I was with, but it wasn't like I was saving myself for anyone.

Not that I planned to sleep around, either.

"Is anyone else in the gym," I asked against his mouth.

He shook his head. "Just us. I looked around before I came in here and found you."

I wanted to get a better hold on him. My hands left his hair and made their way to his magnificently toned back, feeling every ridge and muscle as I skimmed down and slipped my hands beneath his elastic waistband to grab his ass.

Bare.

He was going commando and I wondered if he was always like this.

"Do you normally skip the boxers?"

Kova tensed when my hands touched his flesh, then relaxed. His grin was my answer, and I melted.

"I do not own a pair of boxers," he freely admitted.

His skin was so silky smooth, I wanted to touch him everywhere. If he didn't own a pair, that meant he didn't wear any to practice either. Why that enticed me more, I had no idea, but I loved the fact he was bare underneath. My hips widened as far as possible to accommodate his body, a light moan escaped my chest, allowing him to settle more deeply into my heat.

"God," I breathed. "This feels so good."

"More than I imagined it would."

His needy lips met mine again, his kiss was frantic, and his rotating hips never stopped. He slowly rocked his erection back and forth against me, eliciting another moan from my mouth. He hit my clit every time, pushing me higher. My body was on fire, my skin damp. I imagined this was how he made love.

"You're so hard, so big," I said between kisses and he chuckled. My thighs tightened around him, the pleasure almost unbearable.

Taking a chance, my hands gingerly moved outward to his hips. I hesitated, wondering if he'd let me or tell me to stop.

As my hand slid between our bodies, a thumb raked across my nipple and my hips bucked. I wasn't expecting him to touch me there and I surprised myself when I realized I wanted him to do it again. With parted lips and heated breath, I looked into his green eyes that had darkened while he ran his thumb in circles over my hardening nipple. Overwhelmed with sensations running through my body, I couldn't form words and just arched into him instead.

I pushed my hand between us, gauging his reaction as I did, but he gave nothing away. Little hairs tickled my fingers, his thumb picked up the pace, and his hips stopped moving. I threaded my fingers through the softness of his curls, circling his shaft before moving lower.

I was pretty sure he didn't expect me to cup his sack, his body tightened everywhere and his breathing became labored.

"Adrianna," he gritted, a vein jutted from his neck. His Russian accent was stronger than ever. I loved when he said my name like that.

"Don't tell me to stop," I begged, caressing him in my hand. "Oh, God. I'm..." I trailed off when he rubbed against me faster and faster. I needed to reach that high point so desperately.

Slowly, Kova leaned down to my neck. Not meaning to, I grasped his balls and held on. Kova cringed.

"Adrianna, lighten up. They are not stress balls. They are sensitive."

I chuckled into his neck and apologized, rubbing them softly. A throaty moan escaped him and I smiled inwardly. Lips pressed to my neck, he laid open mouthed kisses along my jaw as he said, "I have to go, I should leave." But he never got up. "You have to know," he said between kisses, "I have never done this with another gymnast before. Never looked at them the way—" he hesitated.

"The way what?"

"Nothing. Never mind."

He squeezed his eyes shut and ignored me. "Kova—" I lost all train of thought when his mouth suckled my neck so seductively. I relaxed my hold on him and moaned loudly, giving him more access.

"Ahhh...feels so good."

When I finally moved my hand, Kova pulled back and peered down at me. The back of my fingers gently scaled his erection from base to tip. Slowly, my thumb reached out and followed the same pattern, then circled the tip. Kova shuddered, his eyes tightly rolling shut. I wasn't sure if I was doing it right judging by the painful look on his face.

Moving to the top of his penis, moisture coated my fingers.

"Remove your hand," he demanded. But I ignored him. He was wet like me, only not as much. I had to be doing something right.

Opening my hand, hard, hot flesh scorched me while I wrapped my fingers around to stroke him. He was *really* big and thick. I couldn't fathom how anyone had sex with him. As I applied pressure, he pulsed against my hand and then pinched my nipple, forcing me to squeeze my thighs shut. My back bowed. The pain associated with the pleasure just about threw me over the edge. Kova dropped his lips to my chest. His fingers danced along my sports bra seeking permission but not entering.

"Remove your hand," he repeated.

"I don't want to."

"Adrianna, I can only hold on for so long before I snap. There is no going back once that happens. I will not be able to control myself."

I wasn't sure what that meant, but I acted like I did.

"That's okay."

"No, it is not. The things I am thinking right now," he said, and swallowed hard, "I should be appalled at myself."

"Tell me."

"Fuck, no."

"Please..."

"No."

"What if...what if I tell you what I'm thinking?" I whispered, squeezing the tip of his penis.

"Agh...Hell no. Please do not, I do not want to know." He dropped his forehead to mine, his eyes cinching shut as I stroked him. His hands moved and became fists on the sides of my head as he fought to maintain composure.

"I want..." I began, my voice shaking, "I want to know what this would feel like sliding in my pussy...deep inside of me."

"No. No. No. Not now, not ever." He grunted and groaned at the same time. His voice sounded like gravel. "Do not say those things to me. I am struggling to hold on here."

I whimpered. I was throbbing. "I need to come and I want to feel this here." I angled his penis toward my entrance, which ended up being a bad idea. My eyes rolled shut and we both strained against each other.

"Christ," he thumbed my clit.

"That feels so good," I whispered, my voice foreign. Even between the clothes it felt incredible.

Kova moaned so loudly I shivered. "No...We cannot..."

"We can go back to my place."

"Are you fucking crazy?"

I answered him with a stare and a slight tip of my brows. Kova made me want to discover more about my body, and his. "I would never say anything, I'm good at keeping secrets."

"Exactly. All the more reason for nothing more to happen. Your father would ruin me if we fucked, because you know if we go back there that is what is happening. I am two seconds from ripping your clothes off as it is."

My jaw dropped. I was rendered speechless.

He shook his head frantically. "I cannot be alone with you anymore. It is not safe for a number of reasons."

"Then let's do it here," I blurted out.

"Not a chance."

"Please, Kova, I'm begging you. I want to do it. You make me feel so good, I want more of that feeling."

"I do not do *it*, in the sense you are thinking, Ria. I would hurt you. Sex is not always gentle and sweet like you assume it is."

"I know, I'm not naive to think that." I paused, then said, "Please I...let's go to my place. It's discrete and we don't have to worry about someone showing up."

His head snapped up. "You think you have this all figured out."

"Honestly, not really. I'm just going with feeling, and right now I know what I want and what I want to experience." I took a chance and swallowed. "And I think you do too."

Kova pulled away and sat back on his knees between my opened legs. I should've kept my mouth shut, then maybe we wouldn't have stopped. Immediately, I missed the heat of his body, the weight of him on me, his thumb caressing my nipple.

He ran a hand through his hair as I looked down between us. He was sticking straight up like there was a pole in his pants. He followed my gaze, palmed his big erection, and began stroking himself over his shorts. His chest was as red as a cherry and his tattoo caught my attention. I was enthralled by the pure sexiness before me. I'd never seen another guy do this and found it extremely mesmerizing.

"You are soaking wet," he said in a throaty whisper. "I can see it." He licked his lips. Heat rose up my chest and burned my cheeks.

Releasing his dick, he placed both of his hands on my thighs, pressing my legs down. His hands cinched upward, his thumbs digging roughly into my skin. I clenched my thighs when he neared my sex, wanting desperately for his hand to be there again.

In what felt like an eternity, he placed a thumb to my clit, over my shorts. My back bowed and my head flew back, a loud sigh releasing from my throat.

CHAPTER 40

Put your arms above your head and do not move. Stay still, Ria."
I did as he ordered and kept my eyes trained on his. "I want to give you what you need. This is the only way we can do anything...I do not trust myself." I didn't question his sudden change of heart and allowed him to do what he pleased.

He began rubbing circles against my throbbing little bud, that exquisite feeling came back full force. My thighs flexed, and he stopped. "Still."

I nodded vehemently, then blurted out, "It's not easy to sit still when you're on the brink of an orgasm."

He paused and responded, "It will make it that much better for you if you listen. Trust me."

Kova continued his rubbing and as much as I loved it, I wished there wasn't a barrier between my pussy and his finger.

Another slow, but steady circle around me made me gasp. My heart climbed in my throat, sensations tingled throughout my body. My thighs quivered. A drop of wetness slipped out of me and I wondered if he could feel it. My chest rose and fell, my nipples were little pebbles as his breathing grew deeper with each stroke of his hand.

Kova applied pressure to his touch and I expelled a loud sigh, loving every minute of this intense feeling. Needing more, my hips started to roll but he stopped.

"What are you thinking about?" he asked.

"Nothing," I lied, and he pinched my clit though my thin shorts. My back arched, the pleasurable pain caused me to fade in and out. "Kova..." I whimpered.

"Tell me what you are thinking or I stop." He rubbed harder and faster. "Tell me," he demanded, and paused.

I whimpered, actually whimpered at the break, and then gave him the truth. "I was thinking about how I wish there was nothing between us, no clothes or anything, so I can feel your fingers…" I swallowed, "pushing into me."

He growled. "And?"

I eased into it, his thumbing sliding dangerously low to the opening of my shorts. "I…I wondered if you could feel me getting wetter… like, see it drip down my ass." Christ, my face was burning and I held in my breath.

"Ria, I do not know how to say this any other way but take your shorts off. Now."

I froze, my chest burning from lack of oxygen.

"Take them off, or else I will," he said.

Insecurity clouded my head at the thought of him seeing me naked. "But you told me not to move."

Kova's deep rumble in his chest caused my fingers to tremble at the waistband. With two hands blurring in front of my face, he swiftly ripped my shorts off, leaving me exposed and my bottom half completely bare to him. And I let him, without faltering. Even though I was slightly apprehensive going this far with a guy, the need for his touch, to be closer to him, overpowered everything, and I succumbed to his demand.

"Fuck," he hissed when his fingers immediately danced across my soft, plump flesh. My first impulse was to close my legs, but I found the inquisitiveness in his eyes to be appealing, so I fought against my own instinct. He was in awe while he stared down as a shaky breath left his chest, rushing from between his lips.

"I did not realize how bare you really are," his voice cracked, muttering something in Russian. "Not a hair to be found. So smooth…"

I wasn't expecting the change in touch to be so drastic, but Kova gripped my inner thighs and yanked me to him. He leaned down to my center, his nose grazed my buttery soft skin and inhaled. He tilted his head to the side, feeling me with his face before his tongue slipped out.

I held my breath again. *He wouldn't.*

Peering up through his thick eyelashes, he purposely locked eyes with me. His mouth was just centimeters from my pussy when his breath rolled against my hairless sex. My hips twitched against him and I let out a loud content moan. This was pure torture.

"I do not know what has gotten into me, I feel like a crazed man." I could feel his words drift across my pussy. "You are so beautiful like this, the things I want to do, what I am thinking," he admitted, his stubble tickling me. "You are glistening, soaking wet and dripping on to the floor for me. I love that I do this to you."

On the floor?

My chest flamed hot, the blood pushing to the surface. My clit was throbbing in pain, longing for release.

The tip of his nose touched the top of my slit. "Spread your legs more," he ordered, his words brushing against my center. He paused, his eyes taking on a new shade of green. "May I?"

My eyes were heavy with lust and they rolled shut. He was asking me? He didn't need to ask, he could just take and I'd allow it. All I could manage to do was nod and wait for him.

He flattened his tongue and swiped up my sex from bottom to top, kissing it gently. My head flew back, my hands slammed onto the wood floor as a gush of air exploded from my lungs. Never in my life had I ever felt something so incredibly delectable, so easily addictive. It was like being high on drugs, not that I knew what that was, but I imagined this was better.

His tongue was soft and careful, and his eyes closed shut as if he was savoring me. My entire body was tingling, my head a hazy mess. I was growing wetter against his mouth when an orgasm began rising. I burned for release, desire pooling in my belly when his teeth scraped my clit.

"Oh, God, Kova," I whimpered. The pleasure was so intense I could cry from it.

Kova pulled back and I immediately felt the loss. I sat up on my elbows and asked, "What...what are you doing? Where are you..." I trailed off.

He didn't answer me. Instead, he got on his stomach and sealed his mouth back over my pussy. I fell back to the floor and clenched my inner walls when his finger unexpectedly delved in and out, exploring every inch of me, massaging over my swollen lips teasingly, down and back up, like he was memorizing me.

"So good." I rocked into his mouth. I couldn't help the little moans that escaped my throat. Just when I thought it couldn't get any better, he inserted another finger. I wondered if he knew I was a virgin, but my nipples tightened in response and my thighs trembled before I could think any more of it. I wasn't sure how much longer I would last. I was on the edge of paradise, ready to fly, when his mouth sucked my clit. I jumped.

Pushing a little deeper, he broke the suction and said, "You are so tight, I can barely get two fingers in. Relax for me, *malysh*. I promise I will not hurt you."

His words squeezed around my heart. For some inexplicable reason, I believed him.

I looked at his face and I saw something else. A vein throbbed in his damp neck and his eyes were wild green orbs. He was straining, besieged with disturbing thoughts. I didn't want him to regret this, to feel as though I pushed him, so I reached out and searched for his other hand. Finding it, our eyes locked and I put everything into my gaze. I laced my fingers through his and gave him a reassuring squeeze.

He was risking everything.

I'd never seen a man bite his lip from desire, but Kova did. He swallowed hard and entered me again. My thighs clamped around his head and his eyes rolled shut.

"Fuck, I am going to hell for this," he said, curling his fingers inside of me.

"Ahhh," I gasped, my hips bucked. "Oh, God." He pushed deeper, his thumb circled my clit and I cried out.

"Christ Almighty, you are so tight."

"Kova, please." He circled faster, licking his lips. I was so close to an orgasm I could taste it.

My hips rocked against his hand and I couldn't stop. I wanted him to push farther in, but he didn't, and I didn't want to ask for more. If I was being honest, I was kind of scared for more. Not scared of what he was capable of, not scared he would cause me pain, but scared of the unknown, the future, and what he could emit from me.

And make me want again.

On the brink of release, I paused. Kova placed his mouth back on me and sucked, and thank God he did. The dense air suffocated us, my heart beat frantically in my chest while so many thoughts jumped around my head until the rising peak took over and I forgot everything.

I cried out, moaning. My hips propelled back and forth, rocking slowly in pleasure as the waves ripped through me. Clutching Kova's wrist that was around my leg, I held on for dear life as I blew up from the pure rapture of his tongue, never wanting this moment to end. I groaned, and a deep sigh escaped my parted lips.

"That is it, *malysh*, give it to me," he said, circling his thumb and pulling the powerful tremors from me. Once the orgasm faded, my hand loosened and my knees collapsed to the sides. I stared up at the ceiling in bewilderment, wondering how I could get Kova between my legs again. That was quite possibly the best feeling I'd ever had in my entire life.

I was utterly sated. Kova sat back on his hunches. Looking at him, his mouth was covered in my juices. So much so that I was embarrassed. He grabbed my little shorts and began slipping them back onto me. Once they were on, I sat up and scooted closer to him, noticing the massive erection tenting his netted shorts. He had to have blue balls.

When our eyes locked, I expected to see anything other than despair through the black webs surrounding his eyes. My brows furrowed, my stomach dropped. He hadn't wiped his face yet but that didn't stop me from leaning in and kissing him.

Kova held the back of my head to him as our tongues danced erotically slow together. I tasted myself on him this time, and it quickly turned me on. Again. My body warming, yearning for another orgasm.

I scooted over his hips and settled between his legs. I worried Kova would push me away, but he did the opposite. He held me close to his chest, in a lovers caress like he hated the thought of leaving me. He was warmth and comfort and my heart embraced him. As he tightened his arms, his erection strained against us. My hips began moving in slow waves against the hardness. Kova's fingers dug into my head, desperation radiating from them. A growl tore from his throat and I whimpered, rocking harder, grinding until my clit hit him each time. I was almost there, so close again.

Kova leaned back and laid on the floor so I could straddle his hips. My hair caved around us, having come loose long ago. His erection was a different angle, and the tip slipped from his shorts and hit my belly button. He was hot and hard. I nearly melted into him, moaning in his mouth at the feel of his heated skin on mine, moving more frantically, feeling the orgasm burn below. His width hit every inch of my sensitive lips, sending me higher. He moved his hands from the back of my head to grip my hips and helped me rotate and grind into him, rolling my hips hard into his. He slipped a hand into my shorts and grasped my butt cheek, hard, hitching my leg up. The more I moved on him, the more his dick came out. I'd yet to see it and wanted to so desperately. I'd give anything to tear off our clothes and feel the real deal, feel my lubricated slit slide over him.

A whimper of pleasure escaped my lips. Kova growled, his length twitching between us. Little cries released as we feverishly kissed like untamed animals. Kova's hands tightened, squeezing me as my toes curled under his legs. I rode him as an orgasm tore through me again. He rocked into me as a cry of pleasure left both of our lips. Kova groaned deep in the back of his throat, shaking beneath me while I rubbed myself all over his dick greedily.

Perspiration coated my skin as I floated back down to earth.

"Adrianna," came out like he was struggling for air. Adrianna, not Ria. Kova loosened his hold. I responded by pulling back and meeting his pain filled eyes. My brows creased from the pinched looked on his face.

"Go, *please*," was all he said.

I swallowed hard, agreeing. Standing up, I quickly headed for the door. Just before I left, I paused when a draft of cool air brushed my torso.

Glancing down, I saw my sports bra had a damp circle on it. I noticed a drop of liquid the size of a pearl on me. Confused, I touched the sticky substance, and rubbed it between my thumb and index finger.

I looked over my shoulder at Kova. He was seated on his knees, but the position of his body struck a pang in my chest. He was bent over, his elbows on his knees with his face buried in his hands.

His raging erection was gone and I put two and two together. He came, and he was mortified by it.

In that moment, I truly felt the weight of our actions. Looking at him physically hurt me. Any normal person would've ran in the other direction, morally disgusted by his behavior. Probably even tell someone of authority. But I didn't, and I wouldn't. Especially since I didn't think it was disgusting.

After all, my dad was twenty-three years older than my mom. Age was just a number to me.

CHAPTER 41

I couldn't make eye contact with Kova when I walked in the next morning.

It was too awkward. Seeing the way I left him had been on my mind all night.

Broken.

When I pulled up to the gym, cars were already lined in the parking lot. The sun was peeking behind the building, the gloomy gray sky being pushed up. Sunrises used to be my favorite thing to watch when I was feeling down, and it just dawned on me I hadn't seen one in months. A twinge in my chest resonated, a sudden homesick feeling streaming through me once again.

Normally, I was one of the first to arrive, but not today. I'd been a few minutes late, and typically that would've bothered me and earned some rather colorful choice of words from Kova, but I was panicking about facing him, so I sat in my car for a couple of minutes to avoid him. I highly doubted he'd say anything to me anyway.

When I stepped into World Cup, I quickly went to my locker and undressed. I had on a simple black leo today. My hair was already pulled back into a ponytail, but I decided to add a couple swipes of mascara and a thin, black line of eyeliner. Voices drifted down the hall and my heart sped up the closer the footsteps grew. I shoved everything inside the metal locker and waited for them to pass before I closed it. Once they did, I quietly expelled a breath and left the room, heading to the gym.

My feet hit the blue floor and I made a beeline to the warm up area to start my morning stretches, adding in the ones Kova had taught me during our private sessions. I specifically ignored meeting his gaze, but his presence could not be disregarded. It was impossible. The hair on my skin rose and the back of my neck prickled. I knew he was on the other side of the gym talking with another coach from the boys' team. From the corner of my eye, I could see Kova glaring at me, but I didn't look over.

"Hey Adrianna," Holly said, walking up to me. I plastered on a fake smiled.

"Since the coaches gave us tomorrow off, we were thinking about hitting the sand and having a beach day. Did you want to come?"

I paused. "What do you mean we have off?" I couldn't afford to take off time.

"Listen, we don't question our rare vacation days, we use them wisely. A bunch of us are hitting the beach tomorrow and some of our friends outside the gym are coming too. I'd love for you to join us."

I bit my lip. Reagan would be there. After the way she treated me, the last thing I wanted to do was spend any extra time with her. That being said, I missed the beach and normalcy.

"Sure. What time?"

"We're going early to get in as much time as we can. So about eleven?"

"I don't know where any beaches are here. Can I meet you guys so I can follow?"

"Of course. Want to come over to mine and Hayden's place and you can ride with us?"

I smiled big. "That sounds like a plan."

Holly turned to leave, but I stopped her. "Hey, Holly?"

"Yeah?"

"Thanks for inviting me."

Her smile reached her eyes. "Anytime."

⟡ ⟡ ⟡ ⟡ ⟡ ⟡

I SHOULD'VE KNOWN BETTER, READ between the lines. Any time a coach gave time off, they pushed and worked you to the extreme first. I was talking boot camp drills made for Marines kind of extreme. At this point, rest sounded like a better option tomorrow instead of beaching it. Even death.

"Why are they doing this to us?" I asked Holly after doing standing tucks, back and forth across the floor. I climbed the rope in a pike position until my muscles ached, walked across the floor in a handstand multiple times, executed front walkover front tucks until I was dizzy, and performed so many press handstands on beam I'd lost count. And that was only the beginning. We did standing dismounts off the vault, body tension exercises and sprinted until we saw stars in our eyes. We still had bars to work. We'd been at it for hours. Conditioning to the eighty-seventh million power. My stomach muscles were hardened with soreness and I was on the verge of vomiting. There had been no time to think of anything else other than what my body was being put through.

Holly shrugged. "Your guess is as good as mine."

"I bet he's fighting with his girlfriend," Reagan chimed in and I turned to look at her.

"Who, Kova? What do you mean?"

Reagan gave me a droll stare. "Have you not noticed his behavior today? He's been mean and nasty all day, more so than usual. I overheard Madeline tell Kova to calm down and he fired back at her. I actually got scared when he did. I've never seen him speak so harshly to another gymnast, let alone a coach and it surprised me. That's how you know something isn't right."

I had a sinking suspicion I was the root of his issue.

"Yeah, but Madeline isn't any better," Holly added, giving her a sideways glance.

Reagan agreed. "Let's just hope this torture session will be over soon. I'm not sure how much longer I'll be able to stand."

Three hours later, we were allowed to leave. My entire body was in shambles and I couldn't remember a time when I just wanted to crawl into bed and die. My back, arms, and legs hurt. Everything ached so badly.

The worst part of today? My right calf blazed with a searing heat like it was on fire when I ran for miles on the track outside. The pain in my leg was intensifying by the day, but today it made its presence well known. I was close to complaining to the coaches but instead I popped some Motrin and dealt with it. Hopefully an ice bath would help.

Pulling into my complex, Hayden followed closely behind. After he saw me limping, he'd offered to come over and help. I told him it wasn't necessary, but he insisted and suggested an ice bath.

Dropping the bags of ice at my feet, I dug into my pocket for my keys and unlocked the door. I looked over my shoulder as I pushed the door open, "Thanks so much for helping me, Hayden."

"It's no problem," he smiled, holding two bags of ice in his hands.

We walked into my place and I flipped the lights on. He brought the ice into my kitchen and placed it in my sink in case it leaked.

"I suggest making some tea first."

I paused, pursing my lips together. "Tea?"

"Yeah, something hot to drink while you're sitting in the tub. It probably won't make a huge difference at first, but if you focus on the heat of the liquid, it may help a little bit."

I rummaged through my cabinets only to realize I didn't have any tea. It wasn't something I normally drank, so I never bought it. However, I had coffee. Lots and lots of coffee.

I spun around. "Would coffee do the trick? I don't have tea."

"Yeah."

Hayden walked into my bathroom and began filling the tub. As I pulled out a little coffee cup, I thought about how nice it was of him to offer assistance. I was used to being on my own and taking care of my needs, but fortunately Hayden wasn't afraid to speak up and be pushy. So when he firmly told me his plans, I easily agreed to them. Anything to ease the pending soreness.

Just as I finished brewing a cup of coffee, a clattering caught my attention. I glanced down the hall to the bathroom and spotted Hayden bent over, dumping the second bag of ice into the bathtub. I couldn't help notice how tight his sleeves were around his toned biceps or the way his back flexed under the material.

The sound of my cell ringing startled me. I grabbed it from my purse and shook my head at *The One & Only BFFFFFF* on my caller ID before picking up.

"How nice of you to finally grace me with a phone call."

"I could say the same of you. I don't hear from you for two weeks and then you get all pissy on me because I don't answer for a few days? I've been busy."

"Let me guess, you and your new beau," I stated mockingly. "A text would've sufficed, you know. Not the fuck you button eighty-seven times. I thought something happened to you. I was ready to put out an Amber Alert."

Avery chuckled at my exaggeration.

"Where have you been?" I asked, my voice malleable. "I miss talking to you."

"I know, I'm sorry." Avery paused and then said, "I got into a fight with my boyfriend. It's been pretty rough...I think we broke up, Aid."

I was surprised to hear sadness in Avery's voice. "So why didn't you call me and vent? You know I'm always here for you."

"I didn't want to talk about it, I guess. I'm really just upset over it."

"This is totally unlike you to be so down over a guy."

"You mean for me to be a sap?" she laughed sadly. "Yeah."

Then it dawned on me. "For you to be this put off could only mean one thing. You love him. You love him and I don't even know who *him* is." Avery's silence confirmed my deduction.

"Ave? Are you crying?"

"No," she lied. Her throaty voice gave her away.

My heart ached for her. "I can't believe how upset you are and I'm not there to comfort you. I feel like a shitty friend now."

"It's okay, I'll get over it soon...I hope."

An idea sprung to me. "You know, tomorrow I have the day off. I was going to go to the beach with some of the gymnasts here. Why don't you drive over, come to the beach, and stay the night? The next day would be boring since I have practice and all, but you can come and watch for a little."

"Aid, you're like a million miles away."

"Don't be ridic, three hours at most, and that's with traffic. You have to see the guys here and what they look like. Whoever you're pining after will be easily forgotten once you feast your eyes upon the eye candy at my gym. The boys' team." I knew what would entice her.

Avery perked up. "Boys' team? You mean Hayden?"

"Well, there are more boys other than Hayden, I just don't talk to them often. Doesn't mean I don't look though." I laughed, and so did Avery. "So you'll come?" She groaned and I pushed. "Please, Avery?"

"Oh, all right," she agreed, I could hear the smile in her voice. I jumped up and down, grinning from ear to ear.

Hayden appeared at my side, concern written on his face. "You okay?" he mouthed. I nodded frantically. "Yeah! I'm way more than okay!"

"Huh? What?" Avery's voice brought me back to our conversation.

"Oh, sorry. I was talking to Hayden."

Her voice heightened, surprised to hear his name. "Hayden's at your place right now?"

"Yes, he's going to help me soak in ice water."

"Ice water?"

"He's filling my bath tub with bags of ice and adding water. It helps relieve swelling and repair my muscles so I can train at the same rate I've been going at, or so I've been told. Today was brutal, quite possibly the worst day yet. I'll sit for ten to fifteen minutes or so and say a prayer."

"Interesting...and boring. So, I'll leave around seven tomorrow morning?"

"Perfect! I can't wait to see you!" I said excitedly.

"Later, girlfriend."

"I'm so excited! Be right back!" I yelled dramatically walking into my bedroom and shutting the door. I shuffled through my drawers for raggedy clothes. Quickly changing into ones I could wear in the tub, I opened my bedroom door to let Hayden know I was finished. I hadn't seen my best friend in many long months and tomorrow couldn't come fast enough.

"I can't wait for you to meet Avery. I've known her since we were in diapers." I was fixing my shorts and sports bra, waiting for Hayden to respond. When he didn't, I looked up and my cheeks reddened.

"Pick your jaw up, Hayden. You act like you've never seen me in such little clothing."

CHAPTER 42

His mouth moved but nothing came out at first. "I have, but..."

I chuckled, a rosy smile spreading across my face. "Just shut up," I said playfully. "Now come help me out."

"Aid..." I looked over my shoulder at Hayden scratching his head. "You've got a hot body. Seriously, it's rocking."

I knew my body had transformed over the past couple of months from the intensity of the workouts, but I hadn't realized just how much until he mentioned it. Standing in my bathroom, I stared down at the ice filled bathtub and bit the inside of my lip.

"So I just climb in?"

"Basically."

I took a deep breath, my chest rising high and put my hand out blindly behind me, searching for his. He wrapped his hand around my hand as my toe dipped into the frigid water and I squeezed his fingers.

"Shit."

"You just gotta take the plunge."

"I know," I replied, staring at the ice cubes. "It's just the initial step into the water that's going to shock me." I looked at Hayden and expelled a deep breath. "Okay. I'm doing it." I bit the bullet and dropped one foot into the icy waters.

My mouth dropped open. "Oh, my God!"

"Keep going."

So I did, and once I had both legs in the water, I looked at Hayden for strength. Goose bumps broke out across my skin and a shiver wracked my body. "I don't think I can feel my toes."

"Don't be dramatic."

I puckered my lips and crouched down. The worst part was going to be the water hitting my pelvis. Even when I would swim in the ocean, the cold was always so shocking to my hips and boobs. Once

I got that out of the way, it wasn't so bad. But I had a feeling this wasn't going to be the same thing. Not even remotely close.

Holding my breath, I let go of Hayden's hand and slowly eased in. My hands gripped the side of the tub, my knuckles turning white as my butt hit the ice and I squeaked.

"Ahhhh...This is so cold!"

Hayden laughed. "Keep going."

Every muscle in my body constricted from the shock. I was immediately frozen and my teeth chattered. There was no way I'd last five minutes, much less fifteen.

The water hit my stomach and rose to my chest, slipping over my boobs. My stomach clenched. Thank goodness I had on a black sports bra, otherwise Hayden would see my pointed nipples. I drew in an audible breath and tried to lean back, but I didn't want to press my back to the cold ceramic. I was already cold enough and didn't need to add to it.

I swallowed. "Okay—I'm in."

"Now breathe."

"How do you handle this?"

He shrugged. "I don't really have a choice. When I have a hard workout, harder than normal, I'll do cold water therapy. Some say it doesn't work, some swear by it. I truly believe it helps with muscle soreness and inflammation. Today was brutal on all of us, and I saw you limping. You're going to be in bad shape. Maybe this will help you."

My lips were chattering, my jaw vibrating against my will. The goose bumps became part of me. "Yeah, Coach was a dick today."

"Which one?"

"Both." I paused. "Hayden? How come you're so nice to me?"

He tilted his head to the side. "What do you mean?"

"Well, for instance, you're here, helping me. You've gone above and beyond. Why?"

He shrugged. "I don't know...There's just something about you that makes me want to be around you. Girls can be catty. I have Holly, and being here with no one to lean on and training this many hours a day is a lot to handle for one person."

Hayden stunned me. Our eyes were locked while I soaked up the sincerity of his words. An appreciative smile curved my chattering lips. "Thanks," I said softly. "Your friendship means a lot to me." His smile faltered for a split moment and I felt bad. "So you swear this will help?"

"I'm not making any promises, but I have a good feeling it will."

"Hayden, if I tell you something do you promise not to say anything?"

"Of course."

Expelling a serious breath, I confessed. "Something is wrong with my calf. It's been hurting for weeks and today, I was close to asking to take a break."

"I noticed. Have you talked to the coaches about it?"

"No, because I can't afford to take time off to rest and I know it's what they'll have me do."

He tilted his head to the side. "Adrianna, you know you have to speak up now so whatever it is can be dealt with and doesn't turn into something more."

"But if I do, I'll be told to rest it. I can't do that, Hayden."

"Not necessarily. Maybe you just need some muscle therapy, ice and heat application. I don't know, but what I do know is that you have to say something. You're only hurting yourself."

He had a point. "Next time it hurts, I'll see a doctor."

After another three minutes, Hayden stood and held out an over-sized white towel for me. "Drain the tub and step into me."

Nodding, I tried to stand, but my body was crunched tight. It hurt to move and it didn't help that it felt like there was a glacial breeze in my bathroom either. Gymnastics was not always sunshine and roses, I knew that. Pain was inevitable. Gathering the strength to stand up was one of those times when my passion and dedication was tested. I would rather be doing a million other things than dipping my body in subzero temperatures. I'd just have to cross my fingers that all of this would speed up my recovery and one day be worth it.

Glancing down to step over the ledge, my back was hunched over, afraid to take a step without assistance. My nipples were outlined through my sports bra and I had a feeling Hayden could see, but in this moment, I didn't care. I was freezing and wanted to get warm as fast as possible.

I nearly plowed into his arms. "Hold me tight," I begged.

Hayden wound the towel tightly around my body then ran his hands up and down my arms trying to warm me. "I've got you." I dropped my head to his chest, searching for body warmth.

"In about thirty minutes, you can take a warm shower. Until then, let's get you some of that coffee."

"Thirty minutes! I have to stay like this for thirty minutes?"

He was rubbing my back in circles when he said, "You can change clothes, but that's it."

Nodding, I ran into my room and pulled out the warmest clothes I could find—a fluffy pair of velour sweat pants and an oversized hoodie. I peeled off my shorts and sports bra and dropped them on the carpet. I didn't care they were soaking wet, I'd pick them up later. It was too cold to bother with panties and a bra, so I quickly slipped on the hoodie, fluffy socks, pants, and grabbed an extra blanket I had folded at the end of my bed and wrapped it around myself. Taking a deep breath, I was feeling a little warmer on the outside, but I was cold to the bone on the inside.

I was so thankful for the plush carpet as I made my way to the kitchen. Hayden's back was to me, and without thinking, I walked up to him and wrapped my arms around his waist, placing my head between his shoulder blades. He chuckled, turning around. His calming arms and charismatic laugh were honest and real.

There was a certain kind of comfort I found in Hayden I hadn't expected. I wanted to close my eyes and sigh. He made me feel protected and wanted, and I liked that. I wasn't just a concern. Hayden made me his priority. Our schedules were jam-packed and he had just as much going on as I did, but he went out of his way to make an effort to help me. There were no pretenses with him, at least I didn't think there were from what I'd seen so far.

He shook his head and gave me a genuine smile. "Do you want something warm to drink yet?"

"I do, but not yet. Can you just hold me for a bit first?" All I wanted to do was curl up to his side and feed off his warmth.

Without answering, Hayden bent down and scooped me up under my legs, cradling me to his chest. He walked over and sat us down at the end of the couch where I burrowed into his side. I needed this. Hayden tucked the blanket all around and under my feet and held me in his strong arms.

"Thanks, Hayden, for everything," I murmured.

"Anytime, baby," he said, slouching into the couch cushions.

I froze and his hands stopped moving. I had a feeling he slipped and hadn't meant to say what he did. Biting my bottom lip, I took a chance and looked up, propping my chin on his chest. Hayden's jaw flexed as he stared at me. Steel blue eyes were fanned between golden brown lashes. High cheek bones and honey skin. My heart sped up. Hayden dipped his chin down, his lips coming just centimeters away. His breath mingled with mine, hitting my parted lips as I waited to see what would happen.

"I want to kiss you, but I won't," he confessed. Instead, he just held me closer and continued to warm me up.

"HAYDEN? WHERE ARE YOU?"

My eyes flitted open at the muffled, frantic voice in the distance.

"Oh, shit. I must've fallen asleep at Adrianna's." Hayden spoke into his cell phone groggily. He rubbed his eyes with the heel of his hand. "Of course I am. What did you think happened? My phone's been on vibrate." Hayden looked at me. "Nothing happened, Holls. Don't worry." He yawned. "The beach? I thought that was a girls' thing."

I tried not to listen to his conversation but failed miserably.

"Yeah, I'll go. See you then," Hayden said, and hung up.

"You know your volume is turned up so high I heard every word, right?"

He shrugged, his eyes half closed. "I didn't feel like lowering the volume, it's too much work right now."

I laughed and eyed him wearily. "To push a button?"

Hayden snuggled down into the couch and pulled me to him. Resting my head on his chest, he pulled the blanket over us and said, "Yes, it is. I'm beat and I need a little more sleep." He stroked my hair. "Sorry I woke you up."

"It's okay." I curled into his side and said, "I could get used to this."

I felt him smile against me. "So could I," he whispered.

We fell asleep for another hour and then begrudgingly decided he needed to head out if he didn't want to receive another testy phone call from his twin. Avery would be here soon and I wanted to be ready.

I quickly gathered my things, slipping on a bathing suit, putting on a little bit of lip gloss and throwing my hair in a messy bun.

CHAPTER 43

Within the hour, Avery was knocking on my door.

"Ave! I can't believe you're finally here!"

"Oh, my God, I've missed you so much!" she exclaimed. We threw our arms around each other tightly before I hauled her inside.

Avery pulled back and looked at me. "You look really good. A little skinnier than the last time I saw you, but overall good. More muscle or something, like you hit a growth spurt." She paused, tilting her head to the side. "Can we still hit growth spurts? Because I don't think I've grown since I was thirteen."

I chuckled. "Thanks, Ave."

"Just don't get skinner than me. Then we can't be friends."

I gave her a quick tour of my home away from home and placed her bag in the spare bedroom.

"So you ready to talk about the ex?"

Avery's face dropped as she ruffled through her bag. A knot formed in my stomach. She was hiding something and it bothered me.

Raising her anguish filled eyes at me, she shook her head and her voice cracked. "No."

I walked over to Avery and threw an arm around her shoulders. I pulled her to my side and gave her a good squeeze. She let out a heartbroken sigh. I hated not knowing what plagued my friend.

I noticed the time on the clock. "We better get going."

We jumped into Avery's sleek BMW and drove over to Hayden and Holly's apartment, exchanging small talk on the way.

"I didn't know you two were so...cozy," Holly said, eyeing Hayden and me after I pulled up with Avery.

My jaw dropped, and Hayden and I spoke at the same time.

"It's not like that—"

"It's not what you thin—"

We both paused and chuckled. "Really, it's not what you think, Holly. He's been really great, a shoulder to lean on. Nothing more."

A look of hurt crossed Hayden's face, but he quickly masked it. I'd caught it and felt awful at my choice of words.

Hayden's eyes shot to me before he stepped forward. "Holls, please don't make it more than what it is. You know how the gym is about relationships."

"Don't worry, I'd never say a word, even though you guys would make a cute couple," she finished with a smile.

My cheeks flamed and Hayden clapped his hands to change the mood. He slipped on a backwards hat and popped a piece of gum into his mouth. "Let's hit the surf and make the most of today, because tomorrow, it's back to hell."

⚁ ⚁ ⚁ ⚁ ⚁ ⚁

THE SUN WAS SETTING AGAINST an incandescent ocean while soothing shades of pinks and oranges streaked across the sky. I was wrapped in a towel, my feet buried beneath ivory grains of sand as I stared at the roaring waves.

This was my happy place, where I found solace. Where the weight of the world left my shoulders as I breathed in the salty air, exhaling the pressure I was plagued with on a daily basis.

I've missed this so much.

The beach was my serenity, and I was glad I'd asked Avery to come visit. Maybe it would help her sort out whatever was going on in her life. There was something peaceful and calming about the crashing waves and salty air. It was where I used to come to get away from my chaotic world living on the little private island. I'd sit and stare at the ocean for hours, kind of how I was now, and think about nothing.

A small fire had been lit when a few friends of Holly and Hayden's showed up. I'd learned Emily and Gavin were both gymnasts at another gym a few towns over. They met through Hayden in middle school and stayed friends ever since.

They sat with us and someone suggested a game of Truth or Dare. We started off with easy, mindless questions to get acquainted until it progressed into something more.

"Hayden, I dare you to go streaking," Gavin, Hayden's friend suggested with a devious grin.

"Ah, come on," Hayden responded, standing. Stepping away from the fire, he turned his back to us, stripped off his trunks, and took off running, his hands thrown in the air. "Yeah!" he shouted, running down to the ocean.

I laughed, covering my mouth when Avery yelled, "Turn around!"

I looked over at her, feeling her enjoyment. Gone was her sadness and in its place nothing but happiness. Her eyes were huge, and she had the biggest grin I'd ever seen. She smacked my arm and said, "Oh, my God. Look at Hayden!"

Sure enough, Hayden had turned around and was running back. He was too far away to actually see anything, but once he drew closer, he covered himself with his hands. Gavin threw him his board shorts and he caught them with one hand. He turned around and slipped them back on. We all grew silent while we stared at his perfectly rounded ass.

"It's Gavin's turn to go streaking!" Avery yelled jokingly.

Hayden looked at his sister. "Truth or Dare."

Holly rolled her eyes. "Truth."

"Have you ever skipped out on conditioning?"

She gave her brother a droll stare. "Of course I have. Who hasn't?"

"Emily," Holly said. "Truth or Dare."

"Truth."

"Would you rather have rips on both hands or straddle the beam three times?"

I cringed internally at her question. Been there, done that.

"That's a good one," Emily said.

Emily pursued her lips together in thought. She held her hands up, showing her palms, and waved her fingers. "I think I'd rather straddle the beam. That would heal much quicker than my hands."

"Ah, you guys are boring," Gavin said. "Someone do a dare."

Emily looked around at the group. Reagan leaned in and whispered something in her ear. My pulse thumped harder as both sets of eyes made their way to me. A sly smile slowly spread across Reagan's face and her eyes brightened. I knew it.

"Adrianna. Truth or Dare," Emily asked.

No way in hell was I picking dare. She'd dare me to do something that would completely humiliate me. So I went with truth.

"Are you a virgin?"

All eyes were suddenly on me. The only sound was the crackling of the fire and the waves breaking at the shore as she waited for my answer.

"Well?" Reagan pushed.

Picking up a handful of dry sand, I clenched it tightly, wishing I could chuck it at Reagan. She just took the game up a notch at my expense.

"Yes," I said, letting the sand shift through my fingers. She cracked a side grin and raised one brow.

"Is anyone else a virgin?" Reagan asked the group.

Everyone answered at the same time, so the only one to know who was still a virgin was myself.

"Are you a virgin?" I asked Reagan.

"No," she responded, and I was actually surprised by her answer.

"I guess there really is a person out there for everyone," I quipped. Avery sputtered her soda as she laughed and leaned her weight on me.

Reagan's brows lowered, infused with anger and spite. "Ava."

Avery snapped her head over to Reagan and glared at her. "It's Avery."

"Same thing. Truth or Dare."

I chuckled to myself. Avery wasn't afraid of much. "Dare."

A wicked smile spread across her face. "I dare you to make out with Hayden," she said, proud of her dare.

I looked over at Hayden and his eyebrows nearly popped off his head.

I knew what Reagan was doing. She was trying to hurt me. But what she didn't know was having Avery kiss Hayden wouldn't hurt me in the least. I considered Hayden a really great friend and nothing more. Though, it was clearly obvious she didn't see that.

Before anyone could say anything, Avery jumped to her feet and crossed over me to Hayden. She dropped her knees to the sand in front of him, whose blue eyes were filled with shock as he sat motionless. I knew from experience he wasn't a prude, or a virgin, yet he sat stone-faced still.

Avery didn't hesitate and grabbed Hayden's cheeks, pulling his face to hers. Just before she pressed her lips to his, he glanced my way for consent. I knew he was being nice so I smiled in return. Knowing Avery, she was going to put on a show just to piss Reagan off.

His eyes stayed on mine for another second or two longer until they closed shut and he kissed her back. I watched, along with the rest of the group, in silence as the dare went on a little longer than we all expected. Avery climbed onto Hayden's lap, his eyes stayed shut as his brows lifted high on his forehead again. He wrapped an arm around her lower back and threaded the other through her windblown hair and kissed her the way he once kissed me. With passion and intensity.

Someone cleared their throat and the kiss abruptly broke apart. Hayden's lips were flushed and swollen, his eyes wide as Avery climbed off him and resumed her seat next to me, like she didn't have a care in the world.

I shifted my eyes over to Reagan and took joy in her expression. She was seething over her dare backfiring on her.

I smiled from ear to ear.

"All right," Avery said, rubbing her hands together. "Who's my next victim?"

CHAPTER 44

A drianna, come here," Kova said, gesturing me over with two fingers.

I'd been at practice for three hours now working on bars. Only another hour or so before my lunch break and I couldn't wait. I was waterlogged from the beach yesterday, so any break I got was essential.

"Yes?"

He lifted my hand to his face and scowled. "I cannot stand the sight of your wrists. Go in my office and in my desk drawer, there are a pair of wristbands for you." He looked square in my eyes. "Wear them."

I flattened my lips and nodded. Kova had a way of making something so small feel like such a big issue. My wrists were fine.

"Hey, Ave," I said, smiling from ear to ear as I stepped into the cold lobby. She had slept over and came to watch my practice before she had to drive back to Palm Bay. Having her around for the past twenty-four hours had been really good and I was going to miss her dearly when she left.

"What are you doing?" she asked, sitting in a folded metal chair, her cell phone in one hand.

I shook my head and rolled my eyes, holding up my wrists. "Apparently this bothers my coach."

She looked at me, perplexed. "Your hands?"

"*The sight of your wrists offends me greatly*," I said in my best manly Russian inflection. Avery sat motionless for a moment until she erupted with laughter.

"Are you serious?" she asked, grinning.

I raised my brows, nodding. "He doesn't like how I wrap my wrists and has new wristbands for me. I just need to grab them real quick."

Her brows scrunched together, her chocolate eyes zoning in. "Fish Lips has new gym gear for you? He bought them?"

I laughed, shushing her with a finger pressed to my lips. "Don't say that too loud," I whispered.

Avery looked around the bare lobby. "Stop being paranoid, no one else is here. Would you rather I say Coach Kissable instead?" She looked over her shoulder and through the glass at Kova, who was making his way across the gym. "In person, he really does have some nice lips, not to mention, a seriously rocking body. I could almost see his muscles. But does he always look like he's mad at life?"

I glanced in her direction, locking eyes with Kova. "For the most part. How long will you be here for?"

She looked at the time on her phone. "Not much long—"

"Come on, Ria. You are on a roll and I do not want to break it." Kova barged into the lobby, cutting off Avery. Surprisingly, he wasn't mean about it, and his unexpected compliment rendered me speechless. Kova rarely remarked positively on my practice, but I noticed he'd been doing it more and more lately.

The sound of a chair sliding across the floor broke my slacked jaw stare.

"Hi," Avery said, walking over to Kova with her hand outstretched. "I'm Avery, Adrianna's friend from back home."

Kova shook her hand. "A pleasure to meet you, Avery."

"Likewise," she responded. "I was just telling *Ria* here how impressive your gym is compared to the one back home she used to train at."

Ria. The voices faded away, leaving me falling into a black hole. She gave nothing away in her expression, but I knew what that one sentence meant. The beat of my heart thumped wildly in my ears as one word played on repeat in my head.

Ria.

All I could process was how I'd once told Avery my library "crush" was the only one who called me Ria.

Subconsciously, I knew Avery would never utter a word to anyone, but that wasn't the issue. There were so many problems at the moment I couldn't think straight on which one to tackle first.

I wasn't sure how much time passed when I heard Avery mention how she calls me Ria. Dear God. I was going to be sick.

"Nice to meet you, Coach," Avery ended with a megawatt smile.

"Same to you." Turning to me, Kova said, "I have to get something from my car. Grab the wristbands and meet me back in the gym quickly." I nodded blindly as he walked out the front door.

Lifting my apprehensive eyes to Avery's, I prepared for the worst, but I came face-to-face with a Cheshire grin instead.

"You got some 'splainin' to do," she said in her best Ricky Ricardo voice. It was terrible.

"Avery."

She placed a comforting hand on my shoulder. "Shh," she lowered her voice. "Say no more. Your secret is safe with me. But you can bet I'm going to wait until you break for lunch so we can talk."

I gave her a thankful smile.

"Just one question," she said.

My eyes widened. "Yeah?"

"You couldn't go for that cutie, Hayden? You had to go for *him*? Are you trying to get your ass kicked in?"

A low chuckled escaped me and Avery laughed too. "It just happened."

She hitched her thumb over her shoulder and gave me a blank stare. "*That* does not just happen. Hayden happens. Not Fish Lips."

I pursed my lips together, feigning a smile.

Avery's face fell. "Oh, God. What are you hiding?"

"Hayden may have kinda happened."

Her eyes grew wide and she playfully backhanded my arm. "You have some serious 'splainin' to do now!"

The sound of a deep voice caused us both to look over our shoulders at the window. Kova was outside pacing back and forth on his cell phone. He stared at the sky furiously, gripping the phone as a string of Russian left his kissable lips. The only thing I could make out was the name Katja. My heart kicked up a notch and I was starting to sweat.

"I better get back to work. He can be a real dick when he wants to."

Avery nodded and sat back down. "Go."

Walking toward Kova's office, I opened the door and made my way around his cherry wood desk.

Sliding out the center drawer, I fished around for the wristbands, moving pens and paperclips from side to side. I checked the drawer to the left and repeated my steps, but found nothing. Moving on, I opened another drawer, but something stopped it from opening completely. Bending down, I got eye level with the drawer and stuck my hand inside, trying to move whatever was in the way and pulled it open, shuffling things around the deep drawer looking for the wristbands. His drawer was a disaster and in dire need of organizing.

A lightly crumpled piece of paper caught my attention and I could see my name scribbled on it in thick, black marker. I debated whether I wanted to open it or not. I slowly stood with my back straight and the paper balled in my hand.

I mean, it wasn't my business, but curiosity got the best of me.

MY DEAREST RIA,

I FIND MYSELF THINKING OF YOU MORE SO THAN EVER, KNOWING FULL WELL THAT IT IS BEYOND IMMORAL.

MOST DAYS I AM NOT SURE WHAT TO DO WITH MYSELF. I AM SICK, ANGRY, AND MOST OF ALL GUILT RIDDEN FOR WANTING YOU IN WAYS I SHOULD NOT. I HATE MYSELF FOR IT. I AM DISGUSTED BY IT, AND I KNOW THAT IT IS WRONG ON SO MANY LEVELS. THERE SHOULD NOT BE A FIRE THAT SIMMERS WITHIN ME EVERY TIME MY FINGERS GRIP YOUR BODY IN AN EFFORT TO TRAIN YOU. APPALLED OVER MY THOUGHTS DOES NOT EVEN SCRATCH THE SURFACE.

I HAVE TRIED DESPERATELY TO STAY BUSY, TO NOT LOOK IN YOUR DIRECTION WHEN YOU ARE WORKING WITH ANOTHER COACH, BUT I HAVE FAILED MISERABLY. YOU ARE ALWAYS THERE-ON MY MIND, IN MY VIEW.

BUT THE WORST PART OF ALL? SOME DAYS I DO NOT GIVE A SHIT THAT IT IS WRONG. SOME DAYS I ALLOW MY THOUGHTS TO WANDER OFF AND PRETEND YOU ARE NOT MY GYMNAST. BECAUSE I HAVE SEEN THE WAY YOU LOOK AT ME, I FEEL IT IN THE TOUCH OF YOUR HAND ON MY BODY. I KNOW DEEP DOWN YOU WANT ME JUST AS BADLY AS I WANT YOU. MY BODY COMES TO

LIFE WITH A CRAVING SO UNFATHOMABLE AT THE WISHFUL THOUGHT OF YOUR INNOCENT TONGUE CARESSING MY SKIN, YOUR TIMID HANDS ROAMING MY BODY. YOU HAVE CREATED A PROFOUND ACHE I CANNOT SEEM TO SATE. YOUR IRIDESCENT, GREEN EYES CAPTIVATE ME. YOUR DRIVE TO NEVER GIVE UP, NO MATTER HOW MUCH I PUSH YOU DOWN, INSPIRES ME. YOU THRILL ME, RIA. YOU MAKE ME WANT SO MUCH, TO TAKE A CHANCE AND SEE WHAT HAPPENS. SOMETHING AS LITTLE AS A CONVERSATION WITH YOU MAKES ME FORGET OUR SITUATION.

IT WOULD BE THE SWEETEST SIN TO HAVE YOU JUST ONCE. BUT A KISS WOULD LEAD TO ANOTHER, AND ANOTHER, AND THEN MY HANDS WILL ROAM YOUR PERFECT, YOUTHFUL BODY.

JUST LIKE IT HAS ALREADY. AND I AM AFRAID I WILL NOT BE ABLE TO STOP MYSELF NEXT TIME. I WANT TO FEEL YOUR LIPS PRESSED TO MINE, YOUR NAKED FLESH ON ME. OUR HEAT INFUSED SEX SATURATING THE AIR AS I TAKE YOUR TIGHT BODY. THIS DOES NOT EVEN TOUCH ON THE THINGS I FEEL, AND WANT, TO DO TO YOU, ALL THE WHILE KNOWING IT IS SO WRONG. MORALLY WRONG. IMPROPER. NOT TO MENTION, FORBIDDINGLY AGAINST THE RULES. AND LAW.

JESUS CHRIST, YOU MESS WITH MY HEAD WHENEVER YOU ARE NEAR. YOU, MY SWEET ADRIANNA, ARE PURE TEMPTATION. I KNOW I SHOULD NOT WANT YOU. I SHOULD NOT EVEN BE THINKING OF YOU IN THIS CAPACITY, BUT I SEEM TO HAVE NO SELF-CONTROL WHEN IT COMES TO YOU.

OH, BUT THE REPERCUSSIONS WOULD BE SO WORTH IT. I WOULD EVEN LET YOU SET THE PACE. AT FIRST.

SEE WHAT I MEAN, MALYSH? I AM ALL
OVER THE PLACE, I CANNOT THINK
STRAIGHT. AND IF I DO NOT RELEASE
THIS NEED PULSING INSIDE ME,
WHO KNOWS WHAT WILL HAPPEN.

I HATE THAT I THINK OF YOU IN THIS
WAY, THAT YOU DO THIS TO ME. IT IS NOT
ETHICAL. I AM A MAN WHO CAN ONLY
TAKE SO MUCH AND I HOPED GETTING
MY THOUGHTS OUT ON PAPER WOULD
HELP DEAL WITH THE SITUATION.

I WISH I COULD GIVE YOU THIS LETTER SO
YOU COULD SEE THE INNER TURMOIL I AM
HARASSED WITH ON A DAILY BASIS, BUT I
CANNOT TAKE THE CHANCE. I COULD LOSE
EVERYTHING IF SOMEONE FOUND OUT.

FOR NOW, KATJA WILL HAVE TO DO.
BUT I AM NOT SURE HOW LONG I CAN
SUPPRESS THIS NEED I HAVE FOR YOU.

K

Oh.

My.

God.

What the hell did I just read?

Finding this letter was the last thing I expected in a million years. Bewilderment clouded my head as I stood in utter shock staring at the piece of paper between my trembling fingers. Coach Kova had these thoughts of me, and Katja had to curb his needs. The same thoughts I had of him nearly every single day.

Okay, not exactly the same, but similar ones.

Holy fuck.

Kova had deep seeded feelings for me and a state of want only he could fathom, because right now, it was blowing my mind trying to comprehend just how far it went. But the thought of Katja being the one to receive these deep desires didn't sit well with me. Jealously sprouted inside like a tree with roots growing in slow motion. It slithered around my nerves and squeezed my chest tight.

With shaking hands, I returned to searching through the rest of the drawer for the wristbands. I stood up and looked around, thinking maybe they were on the floor or a shelf, but again, I found nothing.

Expelling a thick breath, I walked back into the gym with my eyes trained on the floor and the letter folded tightly in my hand. I didn't want to make it obvious there was something wrong, but I couldn't make eye contact after his secret confession.

I clenched the paper tighter in my hand, frustrated by the fact that he couldn't say these words to my face. He had to write his feelings on paper where anyone could find it. We'd been open and honest and forthcoming with each other numerous times, it's what our connection built on from the start. At least I assumed it had.

Christ. The letter was profoundly personal. But why he left it in his desk at the risk of someone finding it puzzled me. The only logical reason for keeping it here would be due to him and Katja living together and he didn't want to get caught. Still, that wasn't enough in my eyes. The last thing I wanted was to be questioned about my inappropriate relationship with my coach. I wasn't sure how many people went into his office on a daily basis, but if anyone had found that letter, it would be the end of us. Gymnastics. My life. His life.

Opening the door to the sound of someone landing a tumbling pass on the spring floor, I chewed my lip raw as I headed for Kova. My heart was racing, my skin prickled from anxiety. This was going to be the most awkward conversation in the history of the world.

"Kova?" He looked over at me when I neared. "I couldn't find the wristbands."

"Well, then you did not look hard enough because they are there."

I flushed, feeling nauseous. "Um, I did look hard enough, but one of your drawers was stuck and I...um," I began to stammer. "I, um..."

"You, um, what, Adrianna? Spit it out." He mocked, running his hands in circles telling me to hurry up. Lowering my voice to a whisper, I said, "Something was keeping the drawer from opening. When I was finally able to open it and pull it out, I found this."

When I held my hand out, he looked down at the white crumpled paper. "I wouldn't suggest opening it here. You need to get rid of it, burn it, or something, anything." I watched a confused expression slowly form between his eyes. "Please," I begged quietly.

At first he didn't seem to know what it was, then the shock and revelation showed on his face. I looked around, making sure no one could hear our exchange. No one looked our way and if they had, it just appeared like Kova was instructing me on something. His cheeks flushed, but he quickly turned ghostly white and grabbed the paper from my hand, shoving it into his pocket.

"How dare you read this," he gritted through his teeth.

My jaw dropped. "How dare I? Maybe I shouldn't have read it, but I saw my name on it. How dare you leave it in your desk for anyone to find," I hissed. "You're lucky I found it and no one else did," I retorted. Kova looked down at me with an intensity I wasn't used to. "Please, get rid of it."

He took a deep breath and glared at me. "You are sure the wristbands were not in the drawer?"

I shook my head, perplexed once again. He was just going to ignore his little love note? "Positive. I couldn't find them. What are you going to do about this?"

Kova rubbed his jaw with his hand, his eyes distant. "I will take care of this tonight."

CHAPTER 45

xcellent job today, Ria. I am very pleased with you," Kova whispered near my ear.

He placed his hand on my hip and gave me a tap before walking away. I fought not to look in the direction of his hand and I didn't pick up my head to acknowledge his comment. All I could do was nod. I wasn't exactly sure what that meant since the morning practice was just about over, but it was the first thing he'd said to me since finding the letter. Unless he was training me, he never openly touched me like this and it made me wonder if he even realized what he'd done.

"What did he say to you?" Avery asked when I strode into the lobby.

Lost in thought over Kova's praising words and how happy they made me, I stared at my best friend trying to decipher what she said. She was studying my face with a quizzical look then dropped her stare to my chalk covered hands.

"What?" I asked.

"Your coach. What did he say to you just now?"

I continued walking into the locker room and she followed me. "Nothing...that I needed to stick my landing if I want to add another skill to it." I dropped my bag at my feet and opened my locker door. As I went to pull on my pants, Avery placed a hand on my shoulder.

"I find it hard to believe that's all he said for you to have had that little smirk on your face."

My face dropped and my knees shook. Shit. She noticed the grin I thought I concealed. And here I thought I was being slick not looking up. Needing to come up with something quickly, I said the first thing that popped into my head.

"Wouldn't you be excited to hear you're allowed to add a half twist to your vault after working on it for so long?" I finished with a knowing smile. I was petrified someone would hear us.

Avery nodded slowly with an intent stare. She paused and said, "You're lying. I know you're lying."

I closed my eyes. "Not here, Ave. Wait until we get into the car. Okay?"

She agreed and backed off.

I thought about Kova's words and what they could mean as I put on my zip up jacket. *Excellent job today, Ria. I am very pleased with you.* He never complimented me to that degree.

We weren't in my SUV for more than ten seconds when Avery said, "Okay. You better start spilling now. I want to know every little thing that's happened and do not leave out any detail. If I find out you do," she paused and looked ahead, thinking about her next words. "Well, I don't know what I'll do, but I'll do something to you."

Stifling a laugh, I rolled my eyes. She tried to sound so intimidating and she wasn't in the least.

"You want all the juicy details?"

"Fill my cup right up!" she exclaimed, holding out her hand as if she was holding a cup. I shook my head with a faint grin. She pulled her knee up and turned to look at me.

"I don't know where to start," I said, pulling out of World Cup and driving onto the main road.

"How about at the beginning?"

Taking a deep breath, I exhaled. "Nothing really happened...We kissed. Big deal."

"Umm, that's a huge deal. Massive. So anytime you mentioned your library boy, it was really Kova. And considering the fact you withheld library boy for a few months until you caved, this has been going on a lot longer than I know."

I bit the inside of my lip. "Yeah."

"Okay, another lie. More than a kiss happened, then. The orgasms were from him?" I groaned and she smacked my arm. "Stop making me piece it together and do it for me. Did you guys have sex?"

I looked over at her. "No, we did not have sex. Honestly, Ave, I don't even know how it happened. Look how closely we work to-gether, how many hours we spend one-on-one, six days a week. We just started talking one day during a private session and it carried on from there. He's actually a really decent guy when he's not in coach mode. Talking to him feels natural...I like it."

I told her everything that happened while I drove to our destination, not leaving out one detail or word, including the note I just found hours earlier. Deep down, Avery was trustworthy, but telling her was terrifying due to the nature of the situation, another reason why I kept it to myself. I couldn't skate over this slip though. And surprisingly it lifted a weight from my chest.

Pulling into a shopping center, I parked my truck and looked over. Avery sat stone-faced. She didn't move a muscle as she stared through the front windshield.

"Avery? Are you okay?"

She slowly turned my way, exorcist style, and said in a low voice, "You're going to hell for this."

My face dropped and I punched her arm. "No, I'm not. Stop acting like a fool. Let's go eat. I only have so much time."

We both hopped out and walked side by side toward a small outdoor restaurant. After such a grueling workout, I was famished, but my stomach was in knots so a salad was probably best.

"My cup is brimming, Ria, about to spill over. I didn't grab a tall enough glass. Then again, I don't think there's one tall enough for the juice you just poured me. I wasn't prepared for this onslaught of thoughts running a marathon in my head!" she exaggeratedly exclaimed.

"Don't be so dramatic."

"Please tell me you don't have serious feelings for him," she pleaded once we were seated. I looked around for listening ears and was thankful the outdoor tables were somewhat empty.

"Truthfully, I don't know. Do I like him? Yes, more so than I probably should. And before you say another word, believe me, I know how morally wrong it is. But I can't help it."

"You know it could never go anywhere, right? It just isn't possible." I shrugged.

"You're smart, think about it." Distress etched her face. Avery took a sip of water. "Do you plan on having sex with him?"

I told her the truth. "I don't plan on it, but if it just happens, then I guess I will. Yes."

She gave me a comical stare. "It doesn't *just* happen, Adrianna. You can't just accidently fall and a dick slips into you. It doesn't work like that."

"Shh…" I said with a finger pressed to my smiling lips.

"Well, it doesn't!"

Before Avery could continue, a waitress appeared at our table. She took our lunch orders and then turned toward me.

"What kind of dressing would you like with your salad?" She rattled off a list of them when Avery spoke up for me.

"She'll have the Russian! She loves that slightly spicy, thick, creamy consistency in her mouth."

My jaw dropped and my cheeks were hotter than ever. I gave my best friend a murderous glare and wondered where the hell she came from. The waitress gave me a bewildered look and I confirmed it with a tight lipped smile. I asked for the dressing on the side and grilled chicken to be added.

"You're an asshole, you know that," I said when the waitress walked away.

Avery laughed loudly. "I had to! Okay, listen, I'm going to play devil's advocate for a minute."

"Oh, God."

"Even though I'm pretty pissed you didn't tell me, I completely understand why you didn't. I probably would've done the same. Thing is, whatever is going on between the both of you, I'd really consider stopping it now. This isn't just some older guy you randomly met in a giant skyscraper building you both work in. This is a coach who owns a reputable business and has a steady girlfriend. Not to mention, that pesky little age difference. Maybe if you were older, then I wouldn't say anything. But you're not. You need to really think about your actions and the ramifications you both will be faced with if you guys get caught. It could get ugly. It would be wise to stop while you're ahead instead of throwing it all away on some flavor of the month."

"Flavor of the month? Avery, where do you come up with these lines?"

She grinned, shrugging her shoulders. "My mom."

"I know, I know...I just don't know, though. I mean," taking a deep breath, I exhaled and looked at the parking lot. I had so much weighing on my shoulders and despite telling Avery, it was all coming back.

"I don't want to have these feelings for him, and call me crazy, but I don't think he wants them for me either. But after reading that letter, it's clear as day how he feels. It's like we're so aware of each other when we're in the same room, it's hard to ignore. He's my damn coach. A lot of people would be hurt, and regardless of right and wrong, these aren't flavor of the month feelings."

"Aid, you're only a teenager. Nothing serious would happen to you. He's risking his life doing this."

"I know, and I would lose gymnastics, he stands to lose much more." I paused. "Do you think it's all in my head?"

"No, but maybe there's a bit of infatuation that's driving it. Good looks, rocking body, Olympic gymnast..." she trailed off with a raised brow. "What's not to like about that? You'd have to be blind not to be drawn to him. Even in the pictures I looked up when you first met him, I was blown away. In person? There are no words. He's gorgeous."

"He has to know what he's doing and the chance he's taking, right?" I asked.

"That's the thing. You would think he knows...and maybe he does and maybe he just doesn't care. Men don't think with the right head. He knows how old you are, that's for sure. Common sense says red flag stay away, but his dick is like, young, hot girl, right ahead!" Her back straightened and she pointed over my shoulder.

I looked around to see if anyone heard Avery's fake British accent. "You should be a comedian with all the voices and reenactments you do. Was that from the *Titanic* movie?"

"Sure was," she said proudly.

The waitress brought out our lunches. I picked off the croutons and drizzled very little dressing on the salad. There was a lot of fat and shit in this dressing, something my thighs did not need.

Taking a bite, I chewed slowly as I thought about our conversation and my feelings toward Kova. "I'm just going to roll with the tide and see where it takes us. As long as we're discreet, we should be okay."

"Should, being the key word. Just be careful," she said and I nodded. "I don't want to see you get hurt...or him be taken away in handcuffs."

CHAPTER 46

Knock, knock, knock.

Confusion etched my tired face as I tried to figure out who would be knocking on my door at nine at night. Throwing the duvet off me, I looked down at my outfit as my feet padded across the plush carpet. Black bikini panties and a cropped, pale pink, tank top wasn't proper attire to welcome visitors. It was rather thin and if I looked closely, I could see the outline of my breasts.

However, I wasn't planning on answering the door. That was, until I looked through the peephole and spotted Kova.

Dear God. What the hell was he doing here? My heart pounded fiercely against my ribs before it dropped into my gut. Taking a deep breath, I exhaled and unlocked both dead bolts and pulled the door open. The cool air caressed my skin.

Kova stood with one arm propped on the ledge of the door. His face was tilted down, despair written all over him and it hit me like a ton of bricks. My heart hurt for him. He dressed in dark distressed jeans and a jet black shirt. A firm body filled his outfit out and when he picked up his head, my lips parted.

"Kova," I whispered, staring into eyes as dark as the rainforest. "What are you doing here?"

A snarl erupted from his throat, the top of his lip lifting. He peered through his black lashes. "Is that how you always answer the door?" he asked before pushing inside.

"Yes, please do come in." Sarcasm dripped all over my words. "For your information, this is what I wear to bed. I wasn't expecting you, or anyone else." I paused, and gave him a droll stare. "And this really isn't much different than what I wear at the gym," I responded, shutting the door and locking it.

Turning around, Kova raked a heated glance down my body, his eyes landing on my chest. I followed his gaze and noticed my nipples were hard little pebbles from the cool air. I sighed inwardly. I hated when that happened.

Clearing my throat, I crossed my arms over my chest and stood confidently. "Is there a reason you're here?"

"We need to talk and I did not want to do it at the gym. I think you know about what."

I nodded and walked past him to the kitchen. Kova followed closely behind. Pulling open my stainless steel refrigerator, I grabbed a bottle of Aloe water.

"Would you like one?" I asked over my shoulder, but his eyes were on my ass. Seeing that I wielded a little power over him felt good, and I smiled. I knew I shouldn't like his eyes on me, but I secretly loved that they were, so I arched my back and naturally pushed my butt out to give him more of a view while I reached for a drink.

"No."

Turning around, I leaned against the fridge, my knee bending for my foot to rest flat on it. I stayed quiet and waited for him to explain his presence.

"Can you put some clothes on first?"

I sputtered on the water I was drinking, the back of my hand coming up to wipe my chin. "Are you serious?" I barked out a laugh. "Again, this really is no different than what I wear at the gym every day. Not to mention, you've seen other parts of my body no one else does."

He glared at me. "No, it's not. Not even close."

"Yes, it is. I'm not changing. I'm tired, and once you leave I'm going straight to bed. After wearing a suffocating leotard all day in the gym, this is much more comfortable, lightweight and feels like I have nothing on. My body needs to breathe."

Kova appeared to be struggling to breathe himself. "I'm asking you to please put something on."

Taking a deep breath, I rolled my eyes and walked to my bedroom and grabbed an oversized off the shoulder shirt I loved. I slipped it over my head, not bothering to remove the tank top first. When I walked back into the living room, Kova was seated in the middle of my couch. He was leaning back, his eyes clenched shut with his hands propped behind his head and his legs spread wide. He was tense, stressed to the max, and the air was thick with anxiety.

I made my way over to the couch and sat against the arm rest with my knee propped up. Kova glanced over with heavy eyes and sighed loudly, brushing a hand down his face. He reached for his back pocket, pulling out a plastic bag and handed it to me. The wristbands.

A gentle smile eased my face and my heart softened. "Thank you for these."

He nodded. "These should help your wrists much better than all that tape you wear. In fact, you should not need tape with these. They are bigger and longer, more durable with extra padding. Give them a try. If you like how they fit, I will order more for you."

"That was really sweet of you. Thank you..." I paused, swallowing. "Kova?" His eyes, goodness, they hit me hard when he looked at me. Anguish filled them. "Did you bring the letter?"

He shook his head, and for some reason, my heart ached for him. "I took care of it so you will not have to worry anymore. It is gone forever."

Quietly I asked what had been on my mind all afternoon. "Why'd you write it?"

He shrugged, looking at the ceiling.

"Why?" I pressed.

"Moment of weakness? I had been drinking...It was careless of me." Clearing his throat, he said, "After my mother passed away, I saw a therapist for a while. She suggested it may be therapeutic if I wrote my feelings out on paper. At first I thought it was the most ridiculous thing I had ever heard, until one day I gave it a shot and I felt a million times better. I have done it ever since. Habit, I guess."

I became even more conscious of his presence in my condo. I shifted to my knees and sat back, trying to ease the sudden throb between my legs. "Kova, your note could've gotten us caught."

"Believe me, Adrianna, I am well aware of that."

"You don't have any more copies, do you? Like maybe you re-wrote it a few times and threw it in the trash can that's still sitting in your office?"

He gave me an amusing grin. I put up my hands. "Hey, I'm just trying to cover all my bases."

"No, that was the only one. Usually all I need to do is one and it helps."

"Did…did it help you to write about me?"

Looking directly in my eyes, he didn't hesitate. "No."

"Not even a little bit?"

"It just made it worse." He shook his head, baffled. His hands were fisted above his knees. "I see your drive day after day and it fuels me."

"But all the girls have the same drive."

"No, they have a love of the sport and that is what propels them. Not every gymnast wants to go professional. Some are content retiring after high school and not even continuing to compete in college. None of them wanted the Olympics like you do because they know how small the window of opportunity is. That is where we share the same goals, the same spirit. You remind me of myself. I see the determination in your eyes to keep moving despite the obstacles you are up against."

My stomach churned over his admission. Mainly for the fact that this whole time he's seen me in an entirely different light than I thought he did. I had assumed he looked down on me, detested the ground I walked on, when it was actually the complete opposite. It moved something deep inside me and for a moment, I felt guilty about everything.

"I'm sorry."

Kova's eyes narrowed, shock pouring out of them. "Do not ever be sorry for the passion that lives inside of you. It is a gift not everyone is given. It is refreshing to see."

Swallowing back the lump in my throat, I thought about his words in the letter, the sincerity behind them. He wrote his feelings out because he was unable to express them in a manner that allowed him to. It wasn't uncommon to pen one's emotions, but I couldn't get past the fact he hid them so well…or he felt such a way.

With shaky words I asked, "Do you…do you really feel that way about me?"

When Kova looked back at me he didn't conceal his emotions or feelings. "Every word."

My lips parted, a flush of heat hitting my body hard. His conviction rendered me speechless. "Why didn't you just tell me?"

"It is not so simple." Leaning forward with his elbows resting on his knees, he stared at the ground as if he was ashamed of his actions. "If you want to train with another coach, I would completely understand. Just say the word and I will change things around and make it happen."

"No," my voice cracked. "I don't want anyone but you." And I didn't. He was the best coach I'd ever had.

"You will do just as well with someone else at World Cup."

"No," I said, defiantly louder this time.

Kova blew out a remorseful breath and turned toward me. "Ria, I think it would be best. This thing," he shuffled his hands back and forth between us, "this thing has to stop. And with you being so close to me, me training you, I am afraid of what the future holds." The conviction was powerful in his eyes, I knew he meant it. "I need you to know I have never..." he ran his tongue along his bottom lip, "I have never done anything with another gymnast like this. I cheated on the woman I plan to marry someday. I could lose everything that means something to me. I could lose my reputation, my gym." I stayed silent and let him continue. Despite the ache and jealously spreading like wildfire in my chest, hearing he planned to marry Katja hurt more. "I never meant to take advantage of you."

I swallowed hard. "You didn't."

"It is fucking wrong and we both know it."

I got a little sassy because I didn't want him to hold all the weight. "You did way more than just touch if I remember correctly. You gave me two incredible orgasms." I bit my lip, heat tinted my cheeks thinking about how I rode him in the dance room. "It was the most—"

Fire blazed in his eyes as he cut me off. "I am fully aware of what I did," he snapped.

"So, why do we have to stop?"

"Are you serious right now?" Kova stood and began pacing my living room. "Can you not comprehend the magnitude of the situation?"

I stood and challenged him. "I do understand, but it's not wrong if I'm *consenting*. Do you not comprehend that?"

He shook his head and walked toward the door. My heart thumped wildly in my chest. I wasn't ready for him to leave yet, I didn't want him to go.

"Do not say those things to me. It is not the same thing, and it still does not make it right."

"I liked it, Kova, and I wanted it as much as you did. Don't blame yourself for anything."

He stopped dead in his tracks. "Do. Present tense."

I smiled softly at his correction as he turned and made his way toward me. Kova backed me against the wall in my living room. He placed his hand flat to the wall and angled his head down, pressing his forehead to mine. Tension radiated off him, the fight to walk away clear as day in his vacillating eyes.

"That is the problem. I still want you, Ria." He breathed into me and cupped my nape. "I should not, but I do, and it is so fucking wrong and sick. And I love it."

"I love when you say my name like that," I whispered honestly, staring at his lips. "Your accent is so sexy." I placed my hands on his firm chest and slid them up. He tensed, but I paid no attention to it. I wanted to kiss him again, to feel his lips pressed to mine, his tongue tangled with mine. The way he kissed me, so skilled and dominating, I loved the command he took. No one had ever kissed me the way he did. Confidence roared through me, so I grabbed a hold and took a leap.

My heart chased the anticipation as we closed the distance. Faces tilted, we touched lips lightly, and I whimpered into him. My hands tangled in his hair as he placed his hands on my hips and held me still. His thumb drew little circles on my pelvis, eliciting wetness between my thighs. I squeezed my legs together, trying to ease the sudden ache.

He didn't refuse me like I feared he might. Quite the contrary actually.

"Does it make me a pervert for wanting you so desperately?"

CHAPTER 47

N o," I responded immediately.

Because it didn't.

"Good, because if it did, well, I would not give a fuck. I want you."

Getting as close as I could so there was not an inch left between us, I leaned into his strong body. My breasts pressed against his chest and I kissed him passionately. He took the lead and set the pace, and I followed, which rewarded me with a squeeze of his hand. Our tongues swirled provocatively, mounting the desire between us. I knew this was wrong, but I didn't care. I didn't care that Kova could get in trouble, I didn't care he had a girlfriend he planned to marry one day. I didn't care about anything but this moment and seeing where it could take us.

Plus, I liked making him feel good.

One of Kova's hands trailed down my side and around to my back. He lifted the back of my shirt so he could cup my ass. He gave it a good, hard squeeze, biting my bottom lip at the same time. My eyes rolled shut as a light sigh escaped my throat. His touch was incredible, like a million little kisses coating my skin and I melted into him. His hips rose, legs spreading wider as the bulge in his jeans pushed against me.

My hands skimmed over his firm shoulders and chest. I was desperate to feel his skin under my touch. Giving him a slight grasp, my hips surged into his. I pressed hard and before I knew what was happening, Kova removed my oversized shirt and threw it to the floor.

As I went to lean back into him for more, he stopped me abruptly and pulled away by pushing my hands down. His fingers danced delicately over my collarbone to the thin strap of my tank top, slipping it off my shoulder. My breathing deepened, my shirt slowly rising and my nipples were hard little points, while his finger twirled across my chest but not dipping past the thin fabric. His hand slid around my neck, clutching me, his fingers brushing against my sensitive skin.

"Why do you do this to me, Adrianna," he said huskily. "Why do you make me want you so bad? You make me want you in ways that should make me ashamed."

"I don't make you do anything you don't want."

"No, you are right, but you do not make it any easier for me to stop either. You only push for me to take. My pleas backfired on me. You take and I want more, I want to give you more. I can see it, but I cannot stop my actions," he said honestly as the other strap fell off my shoulder with his help. The only thing holding up my shirt were my swollen breasts.

Biting my lip, I asked softly, "Would it be so bad?"

"More than you know."

I took a deep breath and arched my back, my breasts rising slightly into him with my hips. His finger trailed my skin so gently, clearly seeking permission to move lower. I watched the indecision in his eyes, the way a crease formed between them as he fought with himself. He knew right from wrong. A pang of guilt seized my heart for taunting him.

When he hit the plump part of my breast, he ran his tongue along his bottom lip again. The look in his eyes blazed a path of fiery heat across my heated flesh. Kova made me feel desired, wanted, like I was the only thing in the world that mattered.

"I want you," he shook his head, pushing my shirt down so most of my breast was showing except my rosy, pink nipple. His erection strained into my stomach and I found myself growing increasingly wet. There was something so deliciously forbidden about being alone with him in my condo where no one could find us, to do as we desired. My heart raged against my ribs, thumping so hard I wondered if he could see the pulse beating in my neck. My panties were sticking to me and his rough, callused hand sliding up and down my waist wasn't helping. As my chest rose, my areola slipped past the rim of my shirt. Kova paused as I held my breath, and goose bumps pebbled my skin.

"The consequences could be damaging." He slowly pulled down the rest of my shirt, the back of his finger scraping my supple flesh.

"But it is a chance I am willing to take," he growled, then sealed his mouth around my nipple. He sucked so hard my head flew back and hit the wall, I whimpered.

The neck of my shirt sat under my boobs, pushing them up and together, he palmed both and tried to suck my nipples at the same time. My tank top was loose, the straps around my biceps and I wrapped my arms around his waist. I stuck my hands under his shirt and raked my nails down his lower back and sides, bringing my hands around the front of him to his abs.

"Oh, my God," I breathed. "That feels amazing."

"I can tell by the way you are rubbing on my dick." I didn't even realize I was rubbing on him, but the delicious friction was building inside and I wanted more.

With his head tilted to the side, I leaned in and licked a wet trail up his neck. He made me wild with desire, and I couldn't stop the frenzy that tore through me. I attacked his mouth. My hands were everywhere, lifting up his shirt to feel his heated skin against my own as I kneaded and gripped him with everything in me.

Kova froze, swiftly stepping back until he was a foot away from me. "Fuck!" he yelled, making me flinch.

"What's wrong?" I yelled back. Talk about doing a one-eighty. I knew where this was going. Silence enveloped us as we stared at each other. Taking a chance, I acted purely on instinct, "I don't want you to stop. What don't you understand? I want this," I stated, adding emphasis to want. "If I didn't want this, I would be doing the complete opposite."

A tick worked in Kova's jaw. "You do not know what you want!"

"Oh, yeah? Says who?"

"It is nothing for me to make you want these things. I know where to touch you and how." Torture captured his eyes. "You are too young to know what you want. This is nothing more than lust for you."

I shook my head in disagreement. "You did this," I pointed to my bare chest, "to me." Walking up to him with my shoulders back, I reached out and boldly cupped his erection and stroked him through his jeans. His eyes rolled closed, a deep groan escaped him. His body hardened. "And I did this to you. If I didn't want this, if you didn't want this, we wouldn't have let it get this far." He opened his eyes, and I said, "Deny it all you want and go home to fuck your girlfriend, Kova." With a perfectly angled brow, I asked, "Isn't that what your note said anyway? That you have to fuck your girlfriend because you can't fuck me."

My pulse thrummed and I was struggling to keep my hands still and appear confident. Never had I been so provoking when it came to us, but I was tired of being played and it was about time he knew it. All of his back and forth was giving me whiplash.

Kova's eyes were heavy, his lids dropping low. He took a step toward me, and I stepped back. He slapped my hand away.

"You know what? You are right. I want to be so deep inside you until you scream. I want to wrap those nimble, little legs around my hips and get as far in as I can." He stalked toward me until I couldn't back up any more.

"I want to watch your face as you orgasm with my cock buried inside you, your hands above your head so you cannot stop me from pushing all the way in." He gripped the base of my neck, his desperate words floating on my skin. "And the sickest part is that I want you to tell me no, I want you to fight me. But it would not matter, would it? I would take anyway. Because we both know it is what you want, is it not?" He picked me up and stormed to my bedroom, throwing me onto the bed and ripping my panties off with a fast tug before he could rest between my thighs.

"Wait." He didn't seem to process my request as a shadow slipped over his eyes. I tried to close my legs, but Kova had other plans. His thumb found my sex and all common sense left my head.

Kova's eyes were as dark as the night sky as he scanned my body.

"You are so fucking gorgeous it hurts." He shook his head in disbelief. "I have tried to fight it, this urge deep inside me to stay calm, but you are all I think about, all I want." He gripped my inner thigh and I bit my lip. "Your tenacity in the gym, the persistence to not give up no matter how much I wear you down, you are strong, Adrianna. You are a fighter, and that turns me on.

"I am going to show you just what your body needs." He paused, and softly added, "You are my greatest weakness. From the moment I set eyes on you, I have been fighting my attraction."

My heart swelled at his words.

Slowly, he removed his jeans and slipped his shirt off. He climbed onto the bed and settled between my thighs before I got a good look at his length. We groaned in unison at the flesh on flesh contact. My heart bloomed, loving the feel of his body on mine. The pressure, the weight, the heat of our bodies fusing together was a feeling I couldn't describe. Finally.

"Kiss me," I whispered, and he did. God, did he ever. He thrusted his tongue into my mouth, taking me once again for all I had to give. His hands gripped my wrists, keeping them above my head where I was unable to touch him. Being restrained and wrestling against his hold was something I never thought I'd like, but it did things to my head that caused me to surrender to his every whim. Rolling my hips up in a wave, I moved so I could feel his hard length sliding against my inner thigh before it leisurely stroked my sex. I sighed breathlessly at the contact.

"Please, give me more."

"I am trying not to hurt you," he mumbled against my lips. His elbows were propped near my ears, caging me in. I felt safe and secure in his embrace and I couldn't imagine him actually causing me pain.

I whimpered, rolling a bit harder and slower again. I was rewarded with a sexy, deep groan and a thrust against my pussy. Fuck. Kova did this to me. He made my body want him in ways I never thought possible.

"If we are going to do this, we are going to do it my way. Got it?"

I nodded frantically. "Yes."

"Are you sure?"

My heart raged against my chest at the thought of losing my virginity tonight. He slid his bare length over the seam of my vagina and I inhaled with a gasp, nodding. I was soaking wet, and now he was covered in me.

A vibration rattled from Kova's chest against mine. The weight of his body and the muscle underneath his hard frame was exhilarating. To be dominated by such a man took over all rational thoughts.

He placed my hands on the headboard. "Hold on and do not let go. Understand?"

"Yes."

Kova sat back and fisted his cock in his hand. I finally got a real look and saw little trim hairs at his pelvis that lead to a long, thick shaft. He began stroking himself, slowly twisting his wrist up his length and squeezing the tip that was darker than the rest of him. Just when I thought he couldn't get any bigger, I watched his length grow. I could never get tired of looking at Kova's body, it was a work of art. He was sin, a man wild with lust, and I loved that I was the reason for it.

He leaned down and pressed his mouth to mine in a brutally hard kiss, tugging my tongue into his mouth. He slid his dick up and down my slit to coat himself and then pushed in.

I flinched. My legs automatically squeezed his waist in pain from the intrusion.

No preamble. No teasing. No foreplay.

I was ready, but it still burned.

And damn it all to hell, it hurt like a motherfucker.

But I didn't show it.

CHAPTER 48

I couldn't.

He didn't need to know I was a virgin. Men didn't like taking someone's virginity because they assumed emotions were usually attached and that was something I couldn't let Kova think. The moan that vibrated against my chest from him made it all worth it.

This uncomfortable pressure inside me was foreign and not at all what I imagined it would feel like. My hands gripped the headboard tighter as I fought the searing pain of feeling like I'd been split in two, like a thick steel rod penetrated me. As much as I loved the fact we were finally doing this, I kind of wanted it to be over at the same time. The pain was intensifying.

I wanted to tell him to hang on, tell him to give me a minute so I could adjust to his width, but I didn't. The only thing I could think to do was start moving my hips to meet his. Even though I didn't know what I was doing or how, it didn't take a rocket scientist to figure out how to have sex.

Kova's hands were back on my wrists, gripping them so hard it actually hurt. "So. Fucking. Tight."

Believe me, I know.

Kova pulled out and thrusted back in, and I swear he hit my cervix at the same time he hit my clit. It was pain and pleasure combined, and for some odd reason it felt surprisingly good.

"Ria…You feel fucking amazing," he breathed against my neck, spiking my pulse. "Better than I imagined you would."

"So do you." I didn't know what else to say.

"I cannot stop." A vein throbbed from his neck.

"I don't want you to."

"You are so tight," he said, looking down at our joined bodies as his cock slid back in. "And I am not even in all the way."

Kova bent down on his elbows and licked a slow wet trail from my collarbone to my ear before taking my earlobe into his mouth.

"It is almost as if you are a virgin," he whispered before looking at me inquisitively. I froze and clenched around him. He bit my shoulder with a sigh as I tightened more. A hot breath escaped him and his head dropped to my shoulder. Kova growled, squeezing his eyes shut as his pleasure hit me in waves from the vibration in his chest. Our relationship was bound by honesty. I wasn't going to lie and say I wasn't a virgin. And if I had omitted something so important, I couldn't imagine the disappointment he'd feel. So I kissed him seductively hard, putting everything into it. He responded perfectly. There was no way he'd ever know.

Kova groaned when he pulled away. "Fuck, yes."

Instead of focusing on the searing, stretching and tearing pain, I focused on the bliss of the bite, the hold on my wrists, the way he kissed me, and the weight of his magnificent body pressed against mine. It was just enough pressure to make it feel good, like he knew exactly how much to apply. The painful strokes became welcomed ones and I started to soften. My chest rose into his, my hardened nipples grazed his heated skin.

Rising up on his elbows, he looked into my eyes before he cupped my face and leaned in for a kiss. Slanting his mouth over mine, his tongue dipped in as his dick pushed back inside me. The tightness I was struggling with was drifting away and I was finally beginning to enjoy it.

"There you go," he whispered. "You are loosening up."

"You could tell?"

He smirked, giving me a knowing look. Pushing deeper, Kova held it there. My breath caught in my throat and I rolled my bottom lip between my teeth.

"Like right now. I can tell it hurts for me to be this deep inside. You have a vice grip on my cock."

I swallowed. "Does it hurt you?"

He huffed, still wearing the smirk. "Hell no. It feels damn good."

"I've never been with anyone...like you. I'm not use to it." That was the truth, too.

Bringing his mouth to mine, he kissed me deeply. "Just relax and let me do it," he said against my lips, and I agreed. Maybe he sensed my inexperienced nature. I wasn't sure what it was. I was just happy he took control.

Reaching down, Kova hooked his hand under my knee and brought it up, placing it around his back as he reached a little deeper. A breath escaped my throat, somewhere between a sigh and a grunt. It was a different angle, but the smooth, even strokes made me enjoy it more than I thought possible as he hit my clit.

He slid in with ease, erasing the pain and replacing it with euphoria. Pleasure was completely taking me by storm and all I could think about was the fact Kova and I were having sex. My breath hitched in my throat, and I whimpered into his mouth. Quiet gasps escaped my chest. There was no way to stop it. I couldn't. The feeling of him pulling out and thrusting back in took my breath away. Long deep strokes with just the right amount of pressure. The way his fingers laced through mine, how he held my hands to the bed. The way his tongue slid down the column of my throat, tugging on my skin. And the way his hips picked up was a maelstrom of fire brewing inside of me. Every time he surged back in, he hit my clit...And God, it felt fucking amazing.

Pulling back to his knees, Kova gripped my hips. His hands nearly touched each other from the small width of my waist.

He kept the pace steady as his thumb slid over my clit and began rubbing in circles. My knees jumped from the unexpected touch and my hips rose off the bed. It was too much stimulation, too many sensations flying through my body, and I couldn't think straight.

Kova held still inside of me. With his eyes locked with mine, he brought each ankle to rest on each of his shoulders. Each position hit a different spot deep inside of me, so when he began moving again, I clenched my eyes shut and held my breath.

"Focus on the pleasure, Ria. Eyes on me."

I nodded, my body damp with moisture. His hand picked up speed and I felt an orgasm rising. Each time he thrust in, his thumb swirled faster and when he pulled out, he slowed down. Gone was the pain and in its place was sheer bliss. Nothing else. I felt high, like

I was floating, feeling every inch, every sensation streaming through my body. My toes tingled, heat climbed up my spine...

"So, so good..." I moaned. "Right there..."

And before I could get another word out, an orgasm rippled through me and I yelled out. My hips bucked roughly against his, quickly meeting Kova's as I rode out this high. A powerful surge hit me so hard, I swear I saw stars as a blissful wave of sex took over my body and I shuddered around him. I didn't want it to end. The incredible sensation flowing through my veins was an indescribable feeling one must experience to understand.

"I can feel you pulsating around me," he grunted, the veins in his neck straining. He had a rough hold on my hips as he held them to the bed, locking me down. He thrusted over and over, slowly riding me into a state of ecstasy, bringing my orgasm higher and higher.

My legs slipped off his shoulders, falling lifelessly to the bed. Kova collapsed on me, the weight of his body melding to mine was delicious, and I savored it. I gripped his neck and sealed my mouth to his in a brutal kiss. The gratification he brought me only moments ago was something I wanted to feel again.

And soon.

"Make me feel that again and again and again," I begged against his lips.

"Malysh, I am not done with you." Kova's hips thrusted against me, pulling his dick all the way out and slamming back in. My headboard rocked against the wall with each surge. With one arm, he lifted my hips off the bed so they were elevated while my shoulders were still flat on the mattress.

"Fuuuccckkk," a curse tore from Kova's mouth. His dick was twitching inside of me, and I was almost positive it became harder.

God, he was beautiful in the throes of heat.

Arching my back, I shuddered in his grip, feeling my wetness seep from my thighs.

Kova hissed then brought his mouth down to bite my nipple. Hard.

My body bowed and I screamed as he ran his tongue over the throbbing tip only to bite it again. My hands left the headboard and I gripped his strong biceps, my nails digging into his skin. I then pulled on the strands of his hair as pleasure once again ripped through me. I rocked hard against him, drowning in the exhilarated ecstasy that was taking complete control of my body.

"Ria," his Russian accent strong. "I need to come deep inside you."

Hearing his words, I moaned aloud. Before I could muster another thought, he pulled out and flipped me over so I was facing the bed. He pressed my head down and pulled my hips up with a yank.

"Arch your back, face to the bed. Now."

Then, he guided me to spread my legs open by tapping on the inside of my thighs. Gripping my pelvis, he jerked my hips up and angled them so I couldn't move. His dick was still erect and grazing my thigh, and just as I thought he was going to stick it back in, he shocked me to the core. I gasped loudly and tensed.

His warm tongue was flat on my vagina, where he circled my clit.

"Oh, my God," I sighed when he ran down the center and stuck his tongue farther inside me. All modesty out the window, I rocked against his mouth. Unexpectedly I clenched, feeling a heavy amount of fluid seep from me. He had to have me all over his mouth.

With his hand still holding me, I was at his mercy. But I didn't give a fuck so long as he made me blow up from pure rapture again.

Just when I thought I couldn't handle any more, Kova surprised me again by running his tongue all around, flicking my sensitive bud and then pinching my lips together and sucking them into his mouth. The pleasure hit me like a gust of wind and I rocked into his face.

With one last swipe, I thought this time he was done until he went past my sex...and to my ass.

I froze. As far as I was concerned, this was an exit only area. If he thought he was going to stick his massive dick in there when he was done licking me, well, he had another thing coming.

With one hand on each cheek, he spread them open. "Kova?" I asked with a shaky breath.

"Shhh..."

"Kova," I was about to say stop, but when he pressed his tongue to my hole and began rubbing me with his mouth. I just about fucking died.

"What...what are you doing?" I asked breathlessly against my duvet.

I almost cried from the pressure that shook my body. I couldn't believe I was going to admit it, but what he was doing was highly stimulating. My hands gripped the blanket as he hit nerve endings that flickered through my body. Never in my wildest dreams would I have imagined the onslaught of feelings attacking me as he licked my ass.

Kova ignored me. Instead, he sat up and aligned himself with my sore sex.

CHAPTER 49

A drianna?"

"Hmm..."

"Take a deep breath." My chest expanded. "Now, exhale. This is going to hurt but it will be so fucking worth it."

Kova pressed a hand to the swell of my back and surged into me in one long, swift glide. It hurt, he was right. God almighty, did it hurt. Tears sprung to my eyes and as I tried to sit up to relieve the pain, his hand held me down.

"Breathe."

Kova pulled out and a moan erupted from his throat as he slowly pushed back in.

"Are you okay?"

A long breath rolled off my lips. "I'm okay, it just hurts a little bit."

"As much as I love how tight you are, I need for you need to relax for me, *malysh*," he said.

Kova ran his hands up and down my ribs in an effort to soothe me. With him deep inside, he leaned down and dusted kisses to my spine, his hands coming around and cupping my breasts. His chest pressed to my back, he began to slowly rock into me without pulling out. There was something oddly calming with his body on mine the way it was, the buildup, the pressure of his weight. How large he was over me. Kova mounted me like he was trying to mark me. This position hurt so good and despite the pain, the pleasure was finally beginning to override it.

"You feel incredible. I want to stay buried in your pussy for hours." His nose dragged up the side of my neck. "But you know what I love?"

"What?" I whispered.

His hand slid between my breasts to wrap around my throat. He gripped it and I tensed.

"Licking your pussy. When my tongue moved over your clit, you leaked in my mouth." I whimpered, clenching around him. "It tasted better than I could imagine. So sweet and tender, soft and smooth. I could spend hours in your pussy."

I panted, a loud heated breath escaped me. I felt myself grow wet from his words. "Your pussy was made for me, Adrianna." The way he said my name, with so much passion, almost made me orgasm on the spot. "I am going to own it so you never forget what I feel like inside of you, after tonight, you will never forget me," he whispered harshly, grabbing my face and kissing me.

I was pretty sure I was never going to forget.

Sitting back, he quickened the pace and started moving his hands all over my body, squeezing my ass before he gave it a good smack.

I almost came undone.

Before I realized what I was doing, I was pushing back and meeting his hard strokes, silently begging for more. I spread my legs, needing a deeper angle. Kova's fingers wove through my hair, he twisted it around his fist and pulled hard, forcing me to stand on my knees. He pressed his mouth to my neck, his other hand pinching my nipple and holding me to him. My hips drove down on his, and I cried out at the new angle of him inside of me. I was so close to coming again, I wasn't above begging to do anything he'd ask if I could finish.

"Do you like it?" he whispered in my ear, the heat of his breath tingled my neck.

I nodded crazily, then he bit my neck and I shuddered in his arms. "Do you like my cock in your little pussy? Did you dream about it the way I did? Did you imagine me licking right here?" He asked, pressing a finger to my puckering butt.

Never had I felt the sensations pulsing through me as I did in that very moment, and it was then I realized I never wanted this feeling to go away.

"Did you imagine my hand sliding down your stomach and playing with your clit like this?" He asked, following the motion. When I didn't respond, struggling to clear the haze in my head, he asked, "Ria, answer me. Do you like it?"

I was moaning and groaning so much that I don't even know how I managed to get out, "I love it. All of it."

Then in all honesty, I said, "Kova? I want you to give me everything and anything you want to give me."

The moment the words left my lips, Kova unleashed everything he was holding back. Throwing me down to the bed, he grabbed hold of my hips from behind and began thrusting hard. There was no doubt I'd have bruises tomorrow from the way his fingers dug into my skin. I felt all of him, everywhere, and I fucking loved it. I was at his mercy.

Within minutes, I was coming again, rocking against him, feeling his balls slap my clit. My body was damp with sweat as a blast of pleasure shot through me. I was tingling with gratification, my body completely and utterly spent. There was no other feeling I could imagine that was better than this. Nothing could top it.

My vagina was tender and swollen, but Kova began pumping harder and faster. His fingers had to be cutting my skin, but I was too high on sex to notice. His hips smacked my ass so hard that I slid up the bed, and when he pulled out, I immediately felt the loss of him.

Kova's thighs quivered against mine and he made a strangled sound. Moving my hair from my face, I glanced over my shoulder as he came all over my back. His head was thrown back, his eyes were squeezed shut as white, warm fluid shot all over me, the vein in his neck straining. He had a vice grip on his dick, the tip of it purple as more exploded from him. His chest was scarlet as were the muscles in his arms from exertion.

Kova was singlehandedly the most erotic thing I'd ever seen. He leaned over and kissed my neck, his nose nuzzling me.

"*Malysh,* that was incredible, I could not ask for better. Do not move. Let me clean you up."

I was pretty sure I wouldn't be able to walk tomorrow—he didn't have to worry about me moving now.

Kova returned with a damp rag and wiped my back clean, and the inside of my legs. Having him clean me in the manner he was, was slightly awkward but intimate.

"Roll over."

I did as he ordered and he opened my legs and cleaned me there too. A look of relief eased across his face and I asked him, "What's wrong?"

He met my eyes. "I was worried I made you bleed with how rough I got, but there are only a few drops." Dropping the rag to the floor, he climbed into bed and turned me to face him. I curled up into him and stared into those bright green eyes. Kova's skillful fingers toyed with my hair, moving it around. Having someone play with my hair felt divine, but when it was after mind blowing sex, it was even better.

A few minutes of comfortable silence went by when he sat up on one elbow and leaned over me. Rolling onto my back as his hands massaged my scalp, I fell into the intensity his eyes held and submitted myself to him.

He whispered something in Russian as he leaned down, and just inches before my mouth, he spoke in English. "Adrianna, you are so beautiful."

Then he sealed his lips to mine and kissed me slow and deep. His thick tongue wrapped around mine, tugging as his hands never left my hair. He kissed me with passion, he kissed me with skill. Sliding a leg over mine, Kova climbed over my body and hitched my leg up around his hip. His growing length sat against my thigh, his knee pressed against my tender opening as all he did was kiss me senseless. With the weight of his body on mine, my heart was his in that moment. He consumed me, heart and soul.

Breaking the kiss, Kova pulled away and I looked into his grave eyes. Cupping my jaw, he confessed, "I do not know what it is about you, but I want you again and again. I want you all night, to take my time and explore every inch of you. Tell me no, *malysh*. Tell me no."

I didn't know how to tell him no because no was not a thought in my mind. I was guided by the hazy bliss of post sex and all I could do was stare into his eyes. And if this was it—if this was the only night I had with him, I was going to take everything he wanted to give. No was not part of my vocabulary when it came to resisting him, but as far as tonight went, it didn't exist.

I think he knew my answer. His thigh was wet from me rubbing on him. I'd lost count of how many orgasms I had, but I felt one more climbing. My hips gently swiveled on his flesh, my lips parted and my nipples were hardening. I couldn't refuse him, I didn't know how when my body was on the brink of pure rapture.

This time, I went in for a kiss, arching my back and finding his mouth. Kova pulled me to him and rolled to his back, placing me on top of him. With his leg propped up and wide, I panted and kissed his mouth as I rode his leg. I couldn't stop, it felt too good and I began clenching his heavily muscled thigh. I wanted to orgasm just like this, with his thigh pressing against my vagina. Kova's hands were all over me, on my back, in my hair, gripping my hips to him as my gasps became louder and more frequent.

"Come for me, just like this," he said against my mouth before biting my lip. Sex filtered the air and I was drowning in it. My hips bucked and I lost control, but despite being tender, I wanted him in me one last time.

Without asking, I lifted my hips and angled his shaft at my entrance and slid down, taking every inch I could. I was filled to capacity. Kova's fingers dug into my hips, the veins in his muscular arms appearing as he struggled. My back arched, pushing my breasts forward. Kova sat up and wrapped his lips around my nipple, sucking me and penetrating me at the same time. With one hand on the curve of my neck, the other wrapped around the back of my waist, Kova secured me to him. An orgasm quickly came, taking hold of us as we both fell into a state of bliss unlike no other while we rocked slow and steady against one another. It was subliminal. And the slow and steady was by far the best way. I moaned, whimpering in ecstasy. His penis twitched inside me, hitting the walls of my sex. Warmth seeped from between us, the heat of his orgasm coating my skin.

Pulling back, he pressed my forehead to his. My hair was everywhere, shielding the sides of our faces while we breathed in the hot air. We panted into each other, connecting at the seams as awareness coursed through us.

Pulling his soft dick out of me, Kova said gutturally, "Ria, you may be my undoing."

He cleaned me up once again and we lay in silence for a few minutes. My body was completely sated and my eyes were drifting closed when Kova spoke softly. "I could take you all night long and not get tired, but I need to get going."

My head was still a hazy field of desire consumed by lust. I didn't want him to leave, but I knew he couldn't stay.

Getting out of bed, I slipped some clothes on while Kova dressed. Once we were at the door, he turned to me. Gently taking my jaw in his hands, Kova pressed his lips to my forehead, lingering for a few moments. He angled my jaw up and slanted his mouth over mine, giving me his softest kiss yet. He pulled me in closer and I stood on my tiptoes as my hands wound around his back while he kissed me with everything he couldn't say. My heart soared through my chest, my emotions taking hold and grabbing onto him.

"Please, I hate to say this, but tell no one about us," his voice was a broken whisper against my lips.

I shook my head. "I would never," I promised.

Then, he was gone.

Bolting my door shut, my feet padded against the plush carpet until I was back in my room. Climbing between my sheets, I smelled Kova all around me. My mind played like a movie on rewind and fast-forward. Everything processed quickly, starting with how the day began and then ended. If someone would've told me I was going to lose my virginity to my gymnastics coach, never in a million years would I have believed them.

But it wasn't like it was planned. He came to me, waiting and watching for the right set to form. And when it did, I just rode it in with him. Just like the waves at the beach, once you start swimming at the curl, you have no choice but to take it all the way to shore.

Otherwise, you get pulled under and have to claw your way to the top to breathe.

Everyone who lives on the beach knows never to swim against the current.

CHAPTER 50

I hadn't been inside World Cup for more than three minutes before I was surrounded by the sound of the apparatuses springing and the coaches yelling.

Anticipation bubbled in my belly as images passed through my mind of the things we'd done a couple of nights before. I was nervous. I hadn't seen him due to my schedule and his. I had no idea how he was going to act around me, and truthfully, I wish I could've called out just so I could avoid it.

After I switched out of my clothes and into my leo, I put my stuff in my locker. Paranoia flushed through me as I walked down the hall and toward the gym. I tried to act as if nothing was on my mind and keep a straight face. But everything changed. And it was all I thought about.

I lost my virginity to my coach. Though, I didn't actually see him as my coach. I saw him as Kova, a man with buried emotions and a bittersweet past.

A lump of trepidation sat heavy in my stomach. When my emotions and feelings got involved, everything melted away—his age, the fact he was my dad's friend, the consequences of our actions if we were caught. It was just two people connecting. But being back in the place that brought everything into context forced me to come face-to-face with our actions.

"Are you okay?" Holly asked, but I didn't hear her question. "Adrianna?"

I looked up. "Huh?"

"I asked you if you're okay. You look sick." Worry carved her face.

"Oh, I'm good. My lunch isn't meshing with me is all." The lie casually rolled off my tongue.

"Just a warning, Coach Kova is in rare form today."

My heart dropped. "What do you mean?"

"He's been walking around with a scowl on his face and barking orders nonstop. Even Madeline jumped at one point."

"That's not much different than any other day." I gave a nervous laugh. "But thanks for the heads up."

"Adrianna!" Coach Kova yelled, startling me with a loud clap of his hands and grabbing my attention. My eyes locked with his and my stomach tightened. "Two miles. Now."

Fuck. Two miles in this heat, he's insane.

I nodded hastily. I did a couple more stretches, the ones Kova had taught me, and then walked to my locker. I slipped on some shorts and sneakers then grabbed my headphones and iPhone so my run wouldn't be dull. Actually, running wouldn't be so terrible since I needed to get my thoughts under control before I started practice. And getting away from him and everyone noticing my strange behavior was probably best.

Not that anyone noticed. Paranoia at its finest.

Once my feet hit the pavement, I jogged across the street and turned on some music. It wasn't long before I completed one mile and sweat was dripping off of me. A couple more laps and—

My thoughts stopped immediately when a searing blaze of fire traveled up my ankle and caused me to stop in my tracks. The air was robbed from my lungs. Jesus Christ, it hurt and I collapsed on the ground, clutching my calf. The sun was blinding and sweat poured down my temples as my fingers sought relief and massaged the muscle. Aside from practice, it seemed when I did any sort of running for long periods, my calf flared up. Maybe I needed to stretch out more, or maybe I was dealing with shin splints. I wasn't sure what caused it, but I needed to get it under control.

I did a couple of pointing and flexing stretches just on my left leg that hopefully would stretch out my muscle a bit more so I could finish running. Clearing my mind, I stood and wiped the pebbled dirt from my shorts. I started jogging again, ignoring the pain bursting from my ankle to my calf. I bit my lip, applying pressure to my other leg to relieve the impact on the injured side and fought it in spite of wanting to crumple to the floor. I pushed through the rest of the run and made my way back to the gym, limping in agony.

The moment I walked through the doors, the cool air hit my face and I sighed in relief. Georgia heat could be deadly. Between the pain and the humidity, I was lightheaded. I quickly grabbed a bottle of Aloe water my mom got me hooked on and drank half of it while sitting down.

I rummaged through my bag and grabbed a clean leo and went to change in the bathroom. I was sticky and hot. Stripping off my damp clothes, I slipped on a black leotard and then splashed water on my face. I patted the rest of my body with a towel and then applied deodorant. Looking at myself in the mirror, my cheeks were flushed and my green eyes brighter than ever. I fixed my ponytail, the scarlet undertones looked like perfectly placed highlights even though I never dyed my hair.

Luckily the pain at the back of my ankle had begun to subside. Just to be sure it wouldn't come back, or at the very least I didn't feel it, I popped some Motrin and then made my way onto the floor where I'd be practicing today.

Looking for Kova, my heart stammered in my chest when my gaze landed on his finely chiseled body. I chewed the inside of my mouth, taking in every inch of him when our eyes finally locked. He stood waiting for me on the floor, hands propped on his hips and shoulders tight.

"I am not getting any younger, so get moving," he clapped annoyingly.

I exhaled a sigh of relief. He was back to his normal Russian dick self. Maybe my anxiety was over nothing after all.

"Warm up. Sashays, handstand walks, front handspring passes, standing tucks across the floor. You know the drill. I should not have to remind you." He was right—he didn't have to remind me—so I wasn't sure why he was. Maybe if he gave me more than thirty seconds to be back in the gym, he'd see I was capable of doing it on my own like I'd done every other time.

"Then move on and do another pass of two back handsprings, ending in a full. Ten sets each." He added, then stormed off.

My jaw dropped. Ten sets? We normally did three to five sets. Now he wanted one hundred—with fulls? After I just ran two miles, he was trying to kill me.

I shook my head and started up. The first thirty minutes I was good, then as I started my standing tucks across the floor, the ache was back in my lower leg, but so very light I worked through it. It wasn't until I progressed and began the double back handspring fulls that the pain blindsided me.

With both feet landing hard on the floor, I rebounded with a searing agony. Somehow I knew if I didn't land easy it would end badly. So I tightened my body on the way down and landed as gently as I could on my toes to break the impact. I squatted to the floor and clutched my calf in distress, the air knocked from my lungs. I quickly massaged the muscle, kneading the ache, hoping to alleviate some of the burn, but it only aggravated it more. My stomach rolled in knots as I limped back so I could continue my warm up.

It was a stupid idea. The same thing happened after I did another tumbling pass, only this time I fell to the floor clutching my leg and gave out a little yelp.

Madeline rushed over. "What's wrong? What hurts?"

I flattened my lips and looked away. "It's nothing. I just landed wrong."

"It's not nothing when you look like you're about to cry."

I gritted my teeth and sucked it up. "I'm okay."

"Kova!" Madeline yelled across the gym, waving him over. "Take a look."

Kova jogged over, mumbling in Russian. He bent down to get a better look. "Let me see."

I pulled away and he tensed. His eyes darkened and nose flared, perturbed by my blasé attitude. "You seem to forget your place here. Give me your leg."

"I'm fine, I just landed wrong." I insisted.

With two hands, Coach Kova ignored me and began feeling around my ankle, twisting and turning, asking if it hurt. Then he grabbed the back of my ankle and pinched. I gasped in response, acting in reflex and yanked my ankle from his grip. He snapped his eyes to mine, and I panicked, falling back to my elbows because I knew what my reflex meant.

He knew I was lying. "Let us go."

"Where are we going?"

"Therapy room. I need a better look."

Tears sprung to my eyes at the realization I could have a serious injury. My heart pounded as I stared at the ceiling. I wanted to get this over with as fast as possible so I could get back to business. Every minute counted in my world, which meant I didn't have a second to spare.

Kova squatted down and scooped me up. This was the first time we'd touched since we'd had sex and I wondered if he realized it. He cradled me to his solid chest the way you would a baby. I wrapped an arm around his shoulder for support and dropped my head to his chest. He smelled really good and I tried to focus on his cologne over the pain. I was too distraught to make eye contact with anyone, so I kept my head down. His warmth calmed my emotions and brought me ease. An injury in gymnastics could go either of two ways: minor or catastrophic.

I didn't think mine was catastrophic, but I wasn't a doctor either. I knew there was no way in hell I could take a long period off to rest. I'd come too far since starting here for that to happen.

Kova carried me to the therapy room and set me on one of the exam tables with a deep blue, plastic cushion. As I went to scoot back, he stood in front of me and gripped my hips, shifting me gently. I had a hurt calf, I wasn't crippled for Christ's sake.

"Lie back." He stood on the side of the table, arms crossed in front of his chest grimly. "How long has your leg been bothering you?"

I bit my lip, deciding whether I should lie or not.

"And do not lie to me, Adrianna, because I will find out either way."

Shit. Kova lifted my leg. My knee bent as he propped it on the table. He began to examine me with his index finger and thumb. "A few months, I think. I can't remember exactly when it started, just have a roundabout idea."

"What kind of pain do you have?"

"My calf hurts. Certain activities cause it to flare up. It's like a burning sensation, but if I rub it out a little, I'm okay. Most of the time I just push through it."

"That was your first mistake. You never push through the pain, it will only prolong an injury. Keep going."

"Sometimes the pain goes into the back of my ankle. At times, when I point and flex, it hurts."

He began to massage the tender muscle and it took everything in me not to groan from relief. His fingers were magical. I clutched the edge of the exam table.

"Your ankle is swollen."

Looking down, I compared both and realized he was right.

"Did you ever at one time feel like the back of your ankle snapped, or did you hear a snapping?"

"No." He paused, looking at me for clarification. "I really haven't."

"I will call your parents and they will need to take you to the doctor to be further examined since you are underage and cannot be seen without a guardian present. Until then, we will massage it and ice it."

My stomach tightened and I sat up. "There's no need to call them. I can just wrap it up and I'm good to go. Really, I'm okay."

Letting go of my leg, Kova placed both of his hands flat on the table on the sides of my hips. Lowering his voice, he said, "Adrianna, I am not going to risk you being injured more than what you already are. This is my gym, and it is my responsibility to make sure everyone is safe and healthy to practice. From the looks of it, you might have a moderate Achilles injury. But without proper medical attention, I cannot tell exactly what it is or how to treat it, and until then, you will not practice."

My nails dug into my palms as I fought back the tears. Darkness surrounded me. My breathing became labored. There was no way this was happening. Swallowing back my frustration, I asked, "Can I at least ice it and finish today?"

He didn't answer me, just massaged the back of my calf. It felt heavenly, like he knew exactly how to work out my tight muscle with a touch of his fingers. Expelling a heavy sigh, I wiped the one tear that fell from my eye.

After a few minutes of attention to my leg, Kova quietly said, "You should wear shorts for now."

I eyed him, but before I could ask, his fingers grazed my skin. "People might ask what these are." Looking down, I noticed small circles of faint black and blue bruising on my upper thigh. They were close to my bikini line where Kova was feeling. I sucked in a breath and let him continue his gentle touch.

"I didn't notice them before," I said softly. "But I could easily say I bruised them on bars."

Concern carved his sharp jaw. He looked genuinely troubled from the bruises he left on me. "Do you have any more marks?"

I shook my head. "I don't think so."

"I hurt you," he stated more than questioned.

"You didn't hurt me, Kova," I whispered. "If you were hurting me, I would've told you to stop."

He paused, looking at me. "Would you have?"

CHAPTER 51

wanted to say so many things, but I couldn't find the words.

The air thickened as we stared into each other's eyes. Flashes of that night speared through my brain, flushing my cheeks and parting my lips. He knew my answer.

Kova's fingers trailed along my bikini line, dipping a little too far. My breathing slowed. We were in the gym in broad daylight where anyone could see what he was doing. Luckily his back was to the door of the therapy room, shielding his forbidden touch.

"It is hard for me to keep my hands to myself," he whispered so quietly it was almost hard to hear. "I cannot stop thinking about that night—how wrong it was, how good it felt to be inside you. How much I surprisingly did not care about the repercussions." His palm spread across my inner thigh, pushing it open. "Of all the years of coaching," He pulled me up to a sitting position to face him. "The persuasion from the mothers I fought off, the temptation of the gymnasts, then you come along and break it. I have been coaching for many years, had colleagues tell me about relationships with their athletes. I abhorred it."

My eyes widened, my heart stammered. The fiery heat of his touch only made my blood simmer more as I thought back to the night he took my virginity. My legs dangled off the table, his hands remained on my thighs.

The next words he uttered were ones I didn't expect. "It is not safe for me to be alone with you."

"Why not?"

"Adrianna, we cannot get into this here, but you know why."

He paused, then spoke the most devastating words possible.

"That night was a mistake," he confessed. My lips parted with my heart, a shallow breath bursting from my lungs. "On so many levels."

"Don't say that," I whispered, my jaw quivered.

He shrugged. "That is life. Do you realize I cheated on Katja, again? I have never once considered cheating on her, until you. Five years of a relationship down the drain, and I cannot even confess," he hissed softly, "because you are my fucking gymnast."

His fingers were digging into my legs, struggling to stay calm.

"If you regret it so much, then why are you here and not another coach?"

Kova didn't say anything, he just stood there glaring.

Smugly, I smiled and said, "That's what I thought."

I jumped off the table and limped toward the door. Before I could leave, Kova stepped ahead of me and slammed the door shut and locked it. He grabbed my elbow, turned me around and pushed me up against the door. With one hand braced above my head, his other held my thigh hitched around his hip. Thank goodness it was my bad leg, otherwise this straining would hurt.

Kova leaned down. Hovering above my mouth, I stopped him. "I thought you said relationships are banned," I panted.

"I make the rules, remember? I am the coach. You are the gymnast. And who said this was a relationship anyway? You have a lot to learn, Ria."

"This is much more than a relationship. You just don't want to accept the reality of it."

My leg hooked firmly around his hip as my toes struggled to remain on the ground. His hand slid over my thigh, rounding my ass to hold me to him. His erection strained against my center and my eyes flitted shut before I forced them open. His wild eyes looked into mine. Kova tilted his head and rolled his hips, a purr of pleasure escaped my throat.

"You confuse me," I said breathlessly.

"I confuse myself," he countered. "This is the one and only relationship you are allowed to have, if that is what you want to call it. Get rid of Hayden."

My eyes narrowed. "Hayden is just a friend, I really like him."

He gave me an amused stare. "I was not born yesterday. You guys are very close, too close for me."

"I'm not getting rid of him, he's the only true friend I've had since I've been here. I want him in my life."

"I do not like the way he looks at you. Or maybe you want him too?"

"He's just a friend." I reaffirmed.

"The looks you two share appear more than friendly."

Rolling my lip between my teeth, my eyes grew heavy. "We may or may not have kissed."

"You really know how to push my buttons." Kova flared, his lip curled. Revelation of his jealously coiled my belly. "What else happened? Did he touch you?" It was my turn to ignore him. He gripped my chin with his thumb and index finger. "There could be consequences for it, Adrianna. Do not test me."

"You mean test you more than I already have?" I quirked with a half-grin. Two could play at this game. "Hayden is staying in my life."

Kova leaned down and sensually nuzzled my neck, whispering, "When did this happen? Before or after I was deep inside your pussy and fucked you senseless? Did he touch you the way I did? Does he make you come like I can?"

A gush of air burst from my lungs. My entire body was about to combust. "It's none of your damn business."

With his eyes on my mouth, he pulled my face to his and crushed his mouth to mine. This was more than just a kiss. He kissed me with his entire being, surging into me. Kova's hips pressed forcefully into mine and marked his territory, claiming me.

I clutched his shirt in my fist, holding him tight, feeling his solid chest firmly pressed to mine as his mouth devoured me. I wanted Kova so badly, but I could tell he was holding back—and with reason. We were inside World Cup in broad daylight.

Reaching between us, I slid my hand down to his hardness, and grasped him through his shorts. He tensed. "I want this again," I admitted against his mouth, tugging on his length and bottom lip at the same time.

Kova pulled back and smirked, his emerald eyes gleaming with satisfaction. "Greedy little girl. I knew you would want it again."

Blood rose to my cheeks as wetness coated the fabric between my legs. What a cocky Russian he was and I fucking loved it.

"And what is this?" He asked coyly.

I paused, not understanding his question. He saw my confusion and reached down with his hand to cover mine over his growing erection. "What is this, Adrianna?" he repeated, and this time I understood when he squeezed my hand that was holding him.

Nervously, I bit my lip as my gaze wavered to his shoulder. My cheeks flamed in embarrassment once again at his question, unable to meet his gaze. I knew what it was, he knew I knew, but apparently he wanted me to say it.

"A penis," I said quietly.

"Wrong answer. Try again."

His deep, quiet voice had my heart pounding as my breathing intensified.

"Eyes on me, Ria." His commanding tone demanded my attention.

My eyes snapped back up, locking with his. "Dick. I want your dick."

He grinned, and God, was he gorgeous when he did. The kind of grin that soaked panties and made them drop—like mine. It made me wonder if he actually had stayed away from mothers and gymnasts like he said. He squeezed my hand in his again, and I could feel him growing harder.

Kova's head tilted to the side, his eyes flitted across my flesh. Leaning down, he placed his tongue on my collarbone and worked it up the curve of my neck. He pulled my skin into his mouth and continued until he hit my ear. God, what he was capable of making me feel.

"I want your tongue stroking me the way your hand is. Tell me, where is your hand, Ria?"

My lips parted. It was getting harder to breathe. There was no way to stop the shiver that racked my body from the feel of him on me, the way his words pulsated every vein in me.

He took a deep breath and exhaled slowly, the hot air trickling along my skin. "Try one more time." He whispered it ever so slowly right next to my ear and my legs almost gave out. I felt silly saying the word I knew he was waiting for. I hardly ever said it, and not many of my girlfriends back home had either, but then again none of them were in pursuit of an older man.

However, the reaction I drew from him topped it all.

Breathing in, I stood on my tiptoes and boldly whispered in his ear. "Cock. I want your cock, Coach."

He groaned hoarsely in my ear and it made my heart stammer. What was it about him that made me react the way I did to him? Kova's body tightened, his strength felt under the tips of my fingers as he internally struggled with the words I spoke.

A low growl rumbled in his chest, and I loved that I caused it. Being in the grips of a man compared to a teenage boy is something altogether different. It was an awakening.

"Exactly. It is *my* cock. And if you want it, you will have to learn to prove it to me. Do you want my cock?"

"Yes," I answered breathlessly.

Kova pushed into me with his *cock*. "Say it. And this time look me in the eyes."

I purred under my breath and it came out like a moan.

"Adrianna..." he groaned, and then straightened. "Do you really think you are ready for a relationship of this magnitude if you cannot use the word?"

I shook my head contradictorily and used the same line he used on me. "Tell me to stop."

He said nothing, but by the harsh look in his eyes, I knew exactly what his silence meant.

I stroked his cock, adding pressure to the head and said again, "Tell me to stop, Coach."

"Do not..."

My stomach tightened and I could hear my heart pounding in my ears. I didn't want him to end this after we only just started, but I also didn't want him to do anything he was opposed to either.

We stood inches apart, staring into each other's eyes, desiring so much more but not taking what we craved. I could read his internal battle knowing what he should do as my coach, as opposed to what he longed to do to me as a man. One glance at his hard body coiled with restraint and the greedy look in his eyes said everything.

I let go of his length and my shoulders sagged. Fearing I made a huge mistake, my eyes dropped to the ground unable to look at him any longer. I let out an exasperated sigh. I thought I'd read the craving cloaked in the indecision in his eyes correctly. Apparently, I hadn't, and it stung. This was my first real taste of rejection and I didn't know how to handle the onslaught of emotions it came with.

His decision was clear and I needed to get away so I could think straight, but before I could take another step from the invisible cage his presence held me in, Kova wrapped his fingers around my wrist, stilling me instantly.

Snapping my eyes to his face, I was confused when I saw his jaw grind down. He pulled my hand slowly back toward his body and placed it where it was before. On his cock.

"You did not let me finish before. Do not...stop is what I was going to say."

Leaning in, Kova was just inches from my mouth when a knock sounded at the door. We both jumped apart, equal parts of fear and shock matched both of our faces.

"Go to the table," he whispered ever so quietly. I ran, lied down, and crossed my arms over my chest staring at the ceiling. My heart was in my throat, the beat drumming in my ears so loud it was all I could hear. Nausea swirled the knots in my stomach and I fought shaking from panic. My mouth was as dry as the desert. There was no way I could make eye contact with whoever was on the other side of the door. Doing anything in the gym was careless and stupid.

Nervous sweat coated my body when the door opened.

"Madeline," he stated.

Fuck.

"Everything okay in here?" she asked, her eyes landing on me. "Why is the door locked?"

I froze.

"Forgive me. I did not realize it was locked. I have been meaning to replace the knob for that reason alone." The lie rolled swiftly off his delicious lips.

"Kova, Reagan's looking for you."

Kova rubbed his jaw before he spoke. "Ah, I will be out soon. I was just telling Adrianna she has to see a doctor before she can return to train. It seems she has been hiding an injury from us."

It wasn't far from the truth, but I needed to follow his lead so nothing looked out of the ordinary. I continued to stare at the ceiling as I spat, "I don't need to see a doctor. I just need some ice and a wrap."

Madeline turned to Kova and asked, "What's wrong with her?" He gave her a quick rundown.

She walked over to me. "You know, Adrianna, Coach Kova is right. If you don't seek medical attention now, you risk tearing your Achilles tendon completely and putting you out for weeks. I'd hate to see that after how far you've come."

I took in Madeline's heartfelt words and her concerned tone. For some odd reason, tears formed in my eyes. She was right, and in the back of my mind, I knew she had a valid point. I just didn't want to accept it.

Agreeing, I said, "I'll call my dad and let him know."

She brushed my hair back from my forehead. "If they don't want to come all the way over for just one appointment, I'll gladly go with you," Madeline offered.

I looked up at her and smiled gratefully. "Thank you."

"Of course. Just let me know and I'll be there," she returned the smile before she left the room. I may be stubborn, but I wasn't stupid enough to risk everything I've worked for. Being checked out by a doctor was the responsible thing to do, it just took a few moments to accept it. Downplaying an injury wasn't really the best idea. I was better than that.

Kova made sure the door was shut and then walked back over to me. He placed his hand on the table and peered down at me, looking almost nice and calm.

"Now, let me put some ice on you."

CHAPTER 52

It was no surprise Madeline accompanied me to the doctor.

Dad had been out of the state on business, and when I told my mom Madeline offered, she quickly agreed to let her. She said Madeline would be better off anyway because she'd know what to do with the injury and treatment that would follow. She did, however, find a reputable doctor for me, one well-known on this side of Georgia who could see me at the drop of a hat.

Which was where Madeline and I were at the present moment. Dr. DeLang was a fairly young looking Asian doctor only a little taller than me. Her petite frame contradicted her stature and poise. After giving her a brief rundown of my injury, she ordered me to lie on my stomach across the exam table with my legs hanging off. It was an odd position for sure, but who was I to question her.

Holding my foot, she rotated and turned it gently around. I held my breath, nervous about her diagnosis. "Your ankle is a little swollen. How does this feel?"

"Fine. It doesn't hurt too much." She pinched the spot above my heel. "Well, it doesn't seem like you tore your Achilles tendon, I'd be able to feel it." Then she squeezed my calf muscle. "And you have good reflex. When does the pain start to set in? Any specific time?" She patted me to sit up.

"Sometimes in the beginning when I start practice, but after a little while, the pain goes away. I'll feel it come back once I'm home. Or sometimes when I'm running it will hurt."

"And your gymnastics training," she said, writing in the file, "is this a new schedule you started, maybe where your body wasn't used to this type of pressure?"

"I started earlier this year...I went from twenty-five hours a week to nearly fifty hours a week of training. What do you think caused it?"

She looked up. "Hmmm…I'm going to bring in the ultrasound tech to make sure the tendon isn't ruptured. Medically speaking, I'd say your injury is due to overuse, doing things too fast and too soon. However, it could be from landing wrong, the impact, or not warming up enough first. It's a common injury among athletes."

"Is it treatable where I won't have to take time off?"

"Let's see what the scan shows first." Dr. DeLang smiled, and left the room.

Looking at Madeline, I said, "What do you think it is? I can't take time off, I just can't," I pleaded.

She rubbed my back. "Don't get upset. We don't even know what she'll say."

The ultrasound was performed, and another twenty agonizing minutes went by before the doctor finally returned with the results.

"All right," she said, shutting the door behind her. "Good news. You didn't rupture your Achilles." She smiled. "The bad news is that you have a pretty bad strain. There are a few options we have that can heal your injury."

I prayed to God she wouldn't suggest time off.

"Lots of good stretching before and after practice, icing your muscles every few hours, maybe an ice bath to reduce inflammation. Since you have to be on your feet a lot, taping it could help aid protection. Massage therapy is another one that helps. I'll get you in touch with a sports medicine therapist. You'll need to see her before you go back to training so you don't damage your injury any further. Until then, I can prescribe some medicine for inflammation."

Quickly, she scribbled something on a square piece of paper and handed it to me. "If you need anything or have any questions, just call and we'll get you in."

"Thank you," Madeline said.

"Do you think I'll be able to see the sports doctor soon?" I asked Dr. DeLang.

"I'm not sure what her schedule is, you'll have to call and find out." Flattening my lips, I nodded and thanked her.

Once we were in Madeline's car, I expelled a loud sigh and called my mom.

"Mom, it's me. I just left the doctor's."

"And how did it go?" she asked.

"I strained my Achilles tendon and need therapy. The doctor gave me a number for a therapist. Can I give you the number and you set it up for me?"

"No need. I'll find a doctor for you."

I paused, my forehead cinching together in puzzlement as to why my mom would find her own doctor. "Mom, I can't go back to training until I see the physical therapist. When do you think you'll call and make an appointment?"

"I'm pretty booked up today and—"

My heart dropped, my head flopped back. She'd make time when she could for me and not any sooner. Tears sprung to my eyes. "Mom, this is *really* important," I stressed.

"Not everything is about you, Adrianna. The world doesn't stop when you want it to. I said I will call, and I will when I get the chance."

Biting my tongue, I thanked her and hung up. Madeline drove toward World Cup. I stayed quiet while annoyance festered inside of me.

Madeline looked at me with sympathy in her eyes. "It'll all work out. Let's see what Coach Kova has to say."

"Thank you, Madeline, for coming with me."

She patted my leg. "Of course."

Pulling into World Cup, Madeline parked her car and we stepped inside. "Go sit in Kova's office and we'll be there soon."

Nodding, I made my way to the back, running into Holly.

"How'd it go," Holly asked as she shut her locker and faced me.

"Not good at all. I strained my Achilles tendon."

Her eyes widened. "Does that mean you're out?"

"No, luckily no. I have to do therapy though and just be careful not to tear it, I guess. That would put me out for sure."

Her mouth pulled up. "Be careful, with gymnastics that goes together like oil and water."

"Right? I gotta go to Kova's office and wait for him and Madeline. I'll see you later."

Brushing past me, Reagan flew in nudging my shoulder. "Going to the beach?" she asked, opening her locker. Her eyes scanned my attire with a scowl.

I looked down at my hunter-green, Victoria's Secret sundress and Tory Burch sandals. Not wanting to give her the satisfaction, I rolled my eyes, ignored her, and walked away. After my doctor's appointment, I wasn't in the mood to deal with Reagan.

Stepping into Kova's office, I sat down and waited, thinking back on the conversation I had with my mom. Funny how in the span of a few minutes she could make me feel completely inconsequential. I'd asked her for help and she gave it to me. Asking her twice was a whole different story. Calling my dad would be a better alternative, and I decided I'd do it after I left here. I just hoped for once I took priority over whatever project he might have going on.

Within minutes, both coaches were in the office, Kova sat behind his desk. Madeline gave him a detailed update as I stared off, upset over the news. Devastation hit me. Angry tears formed in the back of my eyes. I couldn't believe this was happening after how hard I worked. Any injury, big or small, would hold back any athlete.

"Well, it could be worse," Kova said, gaining my attention after Madeline left, shutting the door behind her. His eyes stayed on my face as he spoke. "Good thing is you will not be out and it is treatable."

"You're not making me stay out until I see the other doctor?" Hope bloomed inside my chest.

"You cannot afford to be out, Adrianna. So you can do extra conditioning and light workouts for now. We will go from there. We may have to scale back some skills though." I knew it was a reach around comment, but I didn't care so long as he'd let me practice. "Since you are here, I should tell you that I signed you up for the Parkettes Invitational meet. We need to get you qualified as an elite, but first, you will compete as a level ten with your new elite skills and see how you do and go from there. This meet has some of the best level ten's and elites in the country competing, so this should be a good test for you."

The smile that spread across my face was ear to ear. Not exactly what I wanted to hear, I wanted to qualify as an elite, but I'd take it since this was a step in the right direction. "When is it?"

"A little less than three months from now—January. Which means we have a lot of work to do. Have you spoken to your parents yet about the injury?"

I groaned. There went my happy mood. Slouching back, I looked away and tucked a lock of hair behind my ear. "My mom, and she said she'll get in touch with a doctor when she has time." My voice softened. "I'd give anything for her to put me first, to show she really cares. She said she was busy, days could go by before she calls anyone. I was going to call my dad when I left here because who knows how busy—"

Kova picked up the phone and dialed away. "I will talk to him."

My eyes snapped back to Kova. We sat in silence, staring at each other with the phone pressed to his ear. I noticed he had a good day's worth of growth on his jaw and his hair was disheveled. Dark circles were prominent under his eyes, and before I could think better of it, I said, "You look exhausted."

His eyes weakened. Kova opened his mouth to speak, but I heard my dad's voice.

"Frank, it is Kova...Yes, she is okay." He told my dad about the doctor visit and treatment. "Adrianna said she spoke to your wife and she would call and make the appointment when she had time. Frank, time is not on our side, and I cannot stress enough how important it is that your daughter be seen soon. "

Kova stared at me, listening to my dad. "That is good, you will call me back and let me know? She cannot be out of the gym too long." He nodded. "Yes, she is right here." Kova held the phone out to me. I stood, reaching for it, but his desk was too wide, so I stepped around and stood next to Kova. Taking the phone from his hand, I leaned against the edge of the desk comfortably and lifted the phone to my ear.

"Hey, Dad."

"My sweet pea, it's good to hear your voice."

I smiled. "Yours too."

"How are you feeling?"

"I feel fine, the pain isn't so bad, and it's not a bad strain at all. I can push through it but no one will listen to me. I know what I'm doing," I said flippantly and he chuckled. "I talked to Mom...Do you think you can take care of everything for me please? I know she says she will, but this really can't wait. Coach said that he signed me up for my first elite meet, so I want to be ready for it."

"Don't worry your pretty little face. I've already got it under control. Kova will hear from me by the end of the day."

"Thanks, Dad." I paused. "I miss you."

"Miss you too, sweetie. I need to get back to work, but I'll talk to you soon. Put him back on."

I said my goodbye, and handed Kova the phone. I picked at my already chipped pale pink nail polish and stayed while he continued talking to my dad. I knew just as much as Kova did I couldn't afford to take time off. After all the long, rigorous hours I put in to get ahead only to take ten steps back? Not going to happen.

There weren't enough hours in the day, but come hell or high water, I planned to be at practice bright and early tomorrow morning.

Kova hung the phone up and angled his chair toward me, leaning back with his legs stretched open. He looked fucking sexy sitting back so casually with his head tilted to the side. His clandestine eyes were on my body. I wanted to know what he was thinking of for his lips to form a slow sexy twist and his eyes to sparkle when they met mine again. The air changed in the room. When we were alone, the intensity of his gaze always undid me, and I knew if I looked at him any longer I'd agree to anything he said.

The cell phone on his desk vibrated. Kova glanced at it only to reach over and silence it.

Staring straight at him, I said quietly, "You have to let me keep practicing."

"I do not have to let you do anything."

Kova was goading me. His phone vibrated again and this time I looked at it. I didn't get a chance to read the name on it before a grimace knotted his face and he sent it to voicemail.

"You and I both know I need to practice as much as possible. Especially if I want to reach my dream of the Olympics one day. I'll scale back on my floor routine if I have to, only practice on beam and bars to take the pressure off my ankle. I'm willing to do anything, just don't force me to take time off."

"Maybe it is not meant to be for you."

I saw red. "What does that even mean? Not meant to be for me? Why do you have to be a jerk all the time?"

He raised a brow. "I am going to let that one slide. Your body was not prepared for the kind of change you underwent and you became injured. Maybe going back to basics is a better idea."

Mumbling under my breath, I cursed him out in my head.

Kova tensed, leaning forward. "What did you say?"

"Nothing. I was talking to myself."

His office phone rang and I jumped not expecting it. When he leaned over his desk to look at the caller ID, his brows were pinched together and his shoulder brushed my thigh. I followed his gaze as he sent the caller to voicemail. It had to be important for whoever was calling and I almost suggested he pick it up.

Sitting back, he said, "Did you purposely wear that dress to taunt me?"

My head snapped in his direction, annoyed he'd think such a thing. His eyes were trained on my chest so I followed his heavy stare. My breasts were pressed together unknowingly by the pressure of my folded arms, giving me ample cleavage in my v neck dress. And by ample, I meant normal sized B cups on a good day. I hadn't given much thought when I slipped it on, but I guess subconsciously I wanted to attract his gaze.

Not surprisingly, the smug look Kova donned suited him. It wasn't often he smiled at gym, or even the few times I'd been alone with him. He was always so serious, so brooding, so...hot.

And let's not forget major asshole, either.

CHAPTER 53

His eyes flickered deviously as he rocked in his chair with his hands clasped casually in his lap.

His smile grew larger, and my heart began to melt. I realized in this moment I liked seeing Kova smile, liked seeing his cheek indent with a dimple and wished he did it more. He was carefree, and it dawned on me he was possibly flirting with me.

"Don't flatter yourself. I wasn't even thinking of you this morning when I got dressed."

His infectious smile only grew larger. I had to fight mine, and the shiver from the goose bumps on my skin. The phone rang again, and this time Kova reached for it.`

"What," he snapped. A moment later he turned to his native tongue. He was short, clipped and angry. Quite the opposite just seconds earlier with me. "No, I do not want to do this," he bit back to the person on the other end. I was curious to know what the conversation was about and why he was abruptly so angry. When I heard the name Katja, I decided against it. Kova had opened up to me about his family life, but nothing about his girlfriend. I was curious to know about his relationship with her and how they'd come together, but decided today was not the day to ask with his sudden change of tone. "I refuse to——" he said, only to be cut off. I could hear her voice and she was just as heated. His eyes widened and a scowl formed on his striking face before he sputtered off in Russian again. His voice rose and his hand tightened on the receiver before he slammed it down with her still talking. He dropped his head to his hand and rubbed his eyes. Whatever happened couldn't be good. His body was rolle`d tight, fury radiating off him. A few moments of uncomfortable silence went by before I spoke up.

"If you think for one second I wore this dress for you, well, then, you're crazy."

Kova picked his head up and angled his body toward me, raking his eyes down my body. His shoulders relaxed and he leaned back in his chair, spreading his legs wider. This made me happy. I didn't like seeing him so bothered and upset. I couldn't help my eyes as they wandered over his broad shoulders down to the thick bulge in his shorts. There was no way to ignore the hard outline laying on his thigh. I tried to picture exactly how he looked under his clothes and my body warmed at the thought. He sat forward. His hand dropped to the side and his fingers danced up the back of my leg. His touch was as soft as a butterfly's fluttering wings and caused a rush of warmth to flow through my body. Expelling a slow breath, I fought it and didn't move, didn't show anything on my face.

"Oh, *malysh,* I am *definitely* crazy," he said in a low voice with a peaked brow.

I playfully slapped his hand away.

He only put it back.

"Stop!" I whispered with a smirk.

Kova chuckled, and God help me, I loved the sound of it, loved the big grin on his face.

"I don't know what you're up to, but stop it."

He shrugged as if he had no idea what I was talking about.

"What if someone walks in here?" His only answer was to skim higher up the back of my thigh. I slapped his hand away again and asked, "What has gotten into you?"

"Let us make a deal," he offered.

My head tilted to the side. "A deal?" I asked skeptically.

Kova clasped his hands together in front of his face like he was praying. He appeared deep in thought for a moment and then spoke, lifting his eyes to meet mine.

"I will let you come in tomorrow and train, do extra conditioning, even if I do not talk to your father or have an appointment set, if tonight I can see you. Of course your routines will have to be downgraded because I cannot risk you getting hurt, but I will not make you take time off. Taking time off really isn't needed. We just need to be cautious."

My jaw dropped. He had me thinking I'd have to take time off! And I think I stopped breathing for a second.

Kova stood up, forcing me to straighten my back as he stepped in front of me. His presence commanded attention and my heart gave it to him completely. This dominating, authoritative side of his is what lured me to him in the first place.

"I want to see you again," Kova admitted.

Dropping my hands, I gripped the edge of his desk as his leg brushed my thigh. He stepped even closer, so close there was hardly any space left to breathe, and I realized what I had felt hadn't been his leg.

The air crackled with tension, the chemistry between us was blatant. I could tell he was still on edge over his conversation with Katja, but I wasn't going to bring it up despite wanting to so badly. My heart raced, my skin prickled with the shiver I fought off. With my eyes cast downward, Kova trailed his hands up my arms, gently over my collarbone and around to cup my neck. He angled my jaw to look up at him where our eyes slowly locked. God, there were no ifs, ands, or butts about it. I was falling for Kova, and I was falling hard. His needy gaze captivated me completely. The swirling desire in his eyes, the way his eyelids lowered and his nose flared, the fullness of his lips. He stared at me like I was the only thing that mattered in the entire world. He was seducing me without saying a word, and I wondered if he felt the same way about me. Our ages forgotten in this moment of silence we shared, the obvious connection could not be denied. The intensity started to smother me. And my heart wrapped around a newfound emotion I couldn't name. I looked down, I had to. Kova had a way of making the world disappear when I was with him.

"Look at me," he said quietly. I shook my head. "Ria, I will not say it again." When I ignored him for the second time, his finger skimmed along my jaw and tilted my head up, but I closed my eyes.

With a breathless murmur, I asked, "What are you doing?"

He ignored my question. "Open your eyes." When I obeyed, his next words whispered across my tepid skin. "I have not finished tasting you." His thumb pressed down on my lip.

"It's not that easy."

"Oh, but it is." The back of his knuckles slid down my neck and over my clavicle. "Agree to my deal."

I hesitated, my mind going over what he offered.

His hand continued down, lightly brushing my breast. "Malysh…"

"What does tasting even mean? It sounds really odd." But hot, I thought.

He chuckled low under his breath. "Exactly why I need to show you."

"You don't need to do anything. You want to. There's a difference."

"If you had not come in here wearing that flimsy little dress and gold sandals, then maybe no deal would have been offered. But seeing you changed my outlook completely."

"But it's not even a real deal!" I retorted jokingly. He shrugged it off knowing I was right.

"So it's my fault you want to…*taste me*? Kova, your choice of words sometimes worry me."

The smirk that formed on his face almost made me smile. In fact, it did, and I laughed. Pressing a hand to his hard chest, I tried to push him back. He didn't budge. "No, "I said again. "Go away," I chuckled.

Kova's hand dropped to my thigh, pushing up the seam of my dress. I half-heartedly slapped his hand away, worried someone could walk in at any given moment, but he quickly moved his hand under mine, going right back to his intended destination. He pushed my dress up higher on my silky smooth thigh, meeting the crease of my hip.

"What has gotten into you today? You're like a dog in heat." I clutched his shirt in an effort to push him away, but all I did was inch him closer. I was breathless, my heart raced as lust and adrenaline pumped through me.

A chuckle rumbled in his chest. "I think *your* choice of words worries me sometimes."

Rolling my eyes, I tried not to smile. "There is nothing wrong with my choice of words, thank you very much. Now, stop." I struggled with fighting his swift fingers as he tried to slip them into my panties. Heat coursed through me and I sighed into him. I really didn't want to stop, but after Madeline almost caught us, it would be wise if we stopped. I gripped his wrist and said, "Go…taste Katja and leave me alone."

"I already have. Many times."

"Getting tired of the same old…flavor?"

He shrugged with a smirk. "Quite the opposite, actually."

I growled, he laughed. His hand dipped past the lacy edge of my panties and I choked out, "Well, go do it again."

"I do not want her right now, I want you." His words caused a maelstrom of emotion and feelings to strum through me. "I bet if I touched you right now your pussy would be wet."

Shit. He was right, my panties were sticking to me, but I couldn't admit that. I tried to roll my hips back so he couldn't reach his destination, but I wasn't having any luck. He was fighting me, pushing me, and truth be told, I found myself smiling and laughing as he did. I tried to force him away again, but the man was built as solid as a boulder.

"Seriously, what does that even mean? Do we all have a specific taste?"

I nearly jumped out of my skin when his tongue licked a wet trail up my neck and his lips captured mine in a searing kiss.

"Do you like when I push you away?"

I shoved at him again and he stayed in place. I didn't want him to move and I was glad he didn't. I liked how he held steady, the strain and struggle between us. I clutched him closer to me and inhaled.

A low growl rumbled in his chest. "You could say that."

I thought about earlier and how he swiftly came back for more, how his hold became stronger. Acting on instinct, I leaned in and bit his bicep. Not too hard, but enough for him to pull back.

"I do not like it, I fucking love when you fight me," he admitted breathlessly, pulling back and nipping at my lips. "I like seeing the indecision in your eyes. It makes my dick hard."

His eyes darkened with desire and my heart flourished seeing his response. My belly fluttered. He looked like a starved animal and it intrigued me. It should have sent me screaming in the other direction, but there was no denying my body and how much I wanted to run to him. Knowing I could draw this reaction from him was exhilarating and empowering.

At the touch of his deft fingers reaching inside my panties, I grew wetter, and a frenzy of fire stormed through my veins, rocking me into him.

"Ah, I knew you would be wet." I tensed and fought a low moan in my throat. "Ah, so tight."

"Does Katja fight you?"

The slippery lubricant allowed him to slide a thick finger easily inside. I gasped and clenched around him. When his finger hit my clit, I trembled, gripping his biceps. My head dropped to his chest.

"Not how I want her to," he whispered against my neck.

For some bizarre reason, that pleased me. I loved how I was able to give him something she couldn't.

"Is she tight like me?"

He didn't answer my question and it burned my chest. Jealously flared through me because his silence was my answer. As much as I wanted to, as much as the heat made me want to agree to his every whim, I didn't think I should. Any time we were alone or intimate, I found myself wanting more from him. It was an emotion I wasn't used to or knew how to deal with just yet.

Now that I had his attention, I needed to bring him to his senses. A few more seconds and this was going to progress rapidly into something that couldn't be stopped, something that was very dangerous for both of us.

"What if someone walks in here?"

Gripping my jaw in his hand, he pulled me forward and held the back of my head to him as he kissed me hard and long, thrusting his tongue in my mouth aggressively enough for me to kiss him back. I wrapped my arms around his neck and held him close to me. He devoured my mouth with a vivacious tenacity I'd never experienced him do before. Full of zeal and hunger, and the tiny thread of control he was barely holding on to was palpable, tangible.

Kova pulled back. He removed his finger and brought it to his lips, licking his finger clean. He looked deeply into my eyes and panted, "Tonight, you are mine."

I slid out of his hold and sauntered away. When I got to the door, I stopped and looked over my shoulder when he called my name.

"Conserve your strength. You will need it for later."

"We'll see about that," I replied before exiting his office and shutting the door in his face.

CHAPTER 54

Sure enough, Kova had kept his word and showed up after dark. I didn't question how he got away from his girlfriend, and truthfully I didn't want to know. I was more than aware an actual relationship between us could never be, at least not any time soon, it still didn't change the fact that I didn't like him going home to Katja every night.

My nerves had been on edge while I waited for him. I wasn't sure he'd truly show at first, but I wanted to make sure I was ready just in case. When I showered after the gym, I carefully shaved every part until I was smooth and silky. I lathered every inch of my naked body in lavender scented lotion and air-dried my hair with a little mousse so the waves were fuller. Picking out clothes wasn't an easy task. I didn't want to appear like I was waiting for him, but I also wanted to wear more than pajamas. I went with a pair of simple rolled up, dark denim shorts and an off the shoulder oversized, ivory shirt. Wanting to be a bit audacious, I skipped the cami and bra I typically wore underneath.

It ended up doing the trick because when I opened the door to Kova, he had his hands threaded in my hair and his lips pressed to mine within seconds. He slammed the door shut with the back of his foot and devoured my mouth as he carried me down the hall to my bedroom.

"I cannot wait another second," he told me, and threw me to the bed. "You drive me crazy." My arms landed above my head and my shirt rose up my belly. My supple breasts tickled the sheer material and I knew my hardened nipples outlined perfect little circles. Heat strummed through my body as he peered at me with a craving so dark my stomach flipped. With a quick tug, he had my shorts off and on the floor, and he stood between my legs.

Kova dragged a hand down my stomach, twisting his wrist so he could cup me over my black panties, caressing my swollen lips begging to be touched.

His large hand slipped into the front and glided down the crease of my folds, one finger entering into me slowly. My hips undulated and Kova groaned. Looking between us, a thick vein was straining down his forearm. Why I found that to be so incredibly hot, I had no idea. He oozed muscular strength and sex appeal. His hips thrusted back and forth as if he was inside of me. He hadn't changed out of his basketball shorts, and his wide erection grew rapidly before me. I groaned, and became even wetter, gripping my bed sheets. It was almost embarrassing to be this wet.

Kova pushed his hips into my center which caused his hand to add pressure, making me moan. His thighs kept my legs open while his finger stroked every inch of me.

God, I could have an orgasm just like this.

I liked his strong touch, his powerful position over me. It was rough yet sensual. Skilled, like he knew exactly what he was doing, which was nice since I had no clue.

Pulling his finger out, my cheeks burned from the sounds accompanying the movement. Kova looked down and our heady gaze mimicked each other's. He slowly added another finger and the pressure was tight, but good. My hips bucked when his thumb landed on my clit and a moan vibrated in my chest. My hips began to move, gyrating on his fingers. More, I needed more, and I wanted it fast.

"Adrianna," he said huskily, pulling his fingers from my core. "I would love nothing more than to make you come like this, but first I have other things in mind," he flattened his hand against me, hard, and I groaned again, his fingers resting past my pussy to my ass.

Fuck. He was teasing me.

The pressure and strength of his hand, his fingers resting low, felt so hot, I wanted him to touch me harder, grind his palm against my throbbing—

"Yes..." I sighed, loving what he was doing. It was like he read my mind. "That feels so good. Just like that."

Kova paused. "What does?"

Breathing heavily, I answered him honestly. "Your hand, how hard you're pushing on me. Soft touches are nice, but this feels a whole lot better. And I like when you hold my legs open." My hips rolled against his hand to show him and I spread my legs wider.

"Do you have any idea what you are saying?" Kova's eyes darkened. They were heavy from arousal, and his body tensed. He shook his head like he was fighting with himself to find the right words. "I like when you tell me what you want me to do. It is intoxicatingly powerful to know I make you feel so good."

I looked deep into his eyes so he'd know my words rang true. "You make me feel better than good, Kova."

"You are playing with fire."

"What do you mean?"

"Oh, *malysh*," he laughed throatily. Kova withdrew his hand, and reached behind his head and pulled off his shirt. "Let me show you."

The mattress dipped as Kova crawled over me on his knees. My fingers traced his granite-like abs, every indentation and every grove that carved his stomach was not missed. He drew an audible breath as my palms skimmed his firm chest and over his nipples. My fingers glided across the sharpness in his shoulders. Dropping his weight on me, Kova looked into my eyes before he kissed me senseless. My body circled around his, locking him in. His warmth spread across my body, our heat fused together. His tongue slowly delved in and out before moving to plant open-mouthed kisses down my neck, around my ear, and pull my lobe into his mouth. My back arched, pushing my chest into him. I was completely under his control and all it did was fan the fire even more.

My hands landed on his muscular back and I gripped him. Kova flexed under my touch and his hips began a slow and steady rock against my center. His erection pressed in and out, and I wondered if somehow he could feel just how damp I was.

Pulling back, he pressed his forehead to mine and squeezed his eyes shut. I was dizzy from his fervent kisses and clutched him tightly. Breaths of hot air blended together as we fought to steady ourselves.

Kova moved to sit back on his heels. His brow lifted, and he gave me the sexiest half-grin I'd ever seen as he pulled my panties off, then pushed my knees back out.

"Let me show you how I want to *taste you*."

Recognition hit and Kova smiled at my expression. *Taste you...* that's what he meant earlier. Fuck, this man was gorgeous and he wanted to do amazing things to me.

"First, I will get acquainted with your lips." He leaned down and ever so gently traced around and through the seam of my pussy with the tip of his tongue. A pleasure filled sigh rolled off my lips as I closed my eyes briefly.

"Does that feel good?"

"Yes," I moaned in agreement.

"After I warm you with my tongue," he looked up, and his eyes gleamed with devious thoughts. "I am going to stretch you out like this." He proceeded by pulling on my folds with force, suckling hard. His tongue speared inside and traced around my core.

I couldn't take it. This man. What he was doing to me.

I groaned, squeezing my eyes shut and thrust my hips into him. My legs wrapped around his strong shoulders. I wanted him.

No, I *needed* him.

All of him.

"Do not move. And keep your hands to yourself. Understand?" I nodded heatedly, not realizing my fingers were in his hair.

Fucking shit. I didn't want him to stop. He could have me any way he wanted when he was demanding like this. I'd do anything he commanded. The hunger for him bubbled, and the desire mounted like a volcano ready to erupt.

"Are you sure?"

"Positive."

"Good girl. Now where were we?" He leaned back down, and continued his wicked torment on my sex.

"After you are warmed up and stretched out, I will show you the steps it takes before you reach your dismount."

My mouth dropped and he grinned.

Dismount. Climax. Same thing.

Having Kova go down on me was both exhilarating and nerve wracking at the same time. While he had for a split second in the dance room that one night, it wasn't very long. I had no idea how much more I could handle this longer pace. The moisture dripping from me was slightly embarrassing and I worried he would find it unappealing.

"We will practice until you get it perfect."

His tongue swirled in and out, dancing all around, feeling every part of me. If he wanted power, I was going to give it to him. Reaching down, I threaded my fingers through his hair and pressed him into me, squeezing his shoulders with my thighs.

Abruptly, he pulled back. His green eyes now the color of a dark jungle. Wild. Untamed. Mysterious. Grabbing my wrists, he planted them by my hips, but I struggled against his hold. His fierce look told me I didn't listen to his no touching rule, and he was turned on by it. The power and strength he wielded was an aphrodisiac and I couldn't get enough.

"Do. Not. Move."

A gush of air rushed out of me as his tongue delved back inside, lapping and pulling at my lips so sensually I melted into the bed, and a moan left my throat. I rotated my hips in a wave against his mouth, completely unabashed by my actions. Each deep, luscious lick sent my head spinning.

Then he was frantic with need. His hands roamed around my body, everywhere. I knew he was holding back by how tense and tight his arms were, and I wished he wouldn't. I wished he'd let go and take me already, give me all of him, everything he had.

"Kova...Oh, my God. I'm so close."

He looked up and my heart stopped when our eyes locked. While we'd had sex, this felt so much more intimate.

The corner of his mouth tugged up with a dare, his eyes glittering with obsession.

"Go ahead and land your dismount."

CHAPTER 55

His mouth returned to my pussy and a moan-filled sigh gushed from me as my eyes rolled back.

This feeling, his tongue on me, licking and sucking, was pure eroticism.

My back arched and I threw my head back as my hips rolled into his greedy mouth while he lapped at me. Kova's hands were firmly wrapped under my thighs, holding me to his mouth. The overwhelming sensations streaming through my veins had me panting loudly, gasping for air. Christ Almighty. I tried to fight Kova, but his tongue worked faster, hitting my clit. He locked me down and licked me with precision.

"Oh, God!" I cried out, my thighs tensing around his head. He slapped my outer thigh for me to loosen up and I quickly did.

"Kova, please, it's too much."

My body was a blaze of fire ready to erupt. My moans couldn't be contained and I cried out. My fingers threaded through his dark hair, clutching it in my fist, pushing my pussy into his mouth even more. Kova became ravenous. His grip on my thighs was powerful, and I wanted to give him everything in this moment. My legs scissored on his shoulders from the force of the pleasure slicing through me as he fought to keep his mouth in place.

Somehow when he came up for air, I managed to pull away and move higher on my bed. I panted, drunk on pleasure. My eyes, I'm sure, were just as glossy and matched Kova's. His mouth was covered in my essence completely, and I knew by the way he crouched low I should not have pulled away.

"Bad move, Adrianna."

He sprang forward and tugged on the hem of my shirt, pulling it off me in a blinding move. I was exposed, completely bare to him. Kneeling before me, he spread my legs open and grabbed them, hauling them over his shoulders. My hips lifted clear off the mattress, hovering in the air.

"No," I lied. What I really meant to say was yes, but telling him no did things to my head, and I couldn't stop.

Kova threw an arm over my waist and locked me in place, my boobs rolled up, and if I wasn't in such a state of crazed need, I would've been embarrassed by their placement. But I wasn't.

Leaning down, he said, "You taste incredible." Then he flattened his tongue and licked me from bottom to top. He flicked my clit and sucked on the swollen, little nub as I squirmed in his arms.

"I don't believe you," I whimpered. My body was flaming hot, my chest burning from pleasure.

"I could eat you every day and not get tired." He penetrated my pussy with his tongue, ignoring my statement. With my hips elevated, an orgasm was quickly rising. Different angle, different position, I wasn't sure why, and I didn't care. I began moaning, succumbing to him in a bliss-filled state unlike any I'd ever experienced before. My hips slowly rolled into his mouth as he suckled and devoured me with momentum and skill. One of his hands shifted and moved to rub my clit. The sensitive, little nerves in my body combusted into a million tiny, silver stars.

"Oh, yes, yes, yes," I moaned. I almost cried from the sheer impact of it all. His thumb rubbed harder and faster as the pleasure zoomed through me, my hips bucked against his mouth.

"Don't stop," I begged. The vibration from his mouth, paired with the tingly heat when his teeth nipped, caused me to blow up. An orgasm erupted, slamming into me hard and tearing through me with pleasure previously unknown.

But Kova didn't let up. He sucked harder, making slurping sounds as he took every last drop to the point where his tongue slid dangerously close to my ass to wipe me up. I couldn't stop making little noises, crying out from feeling such sweet rapture that rocked through my body.

My heart, as my body, was wholly his.

Once the orgasm subsided, Kova carefully lowered my hips to the bed. I was spent, a complete pile of mush with my legs wide open.

My heart, the same.

Coming down from the most incredible high of my life, heated eyes scanned the length of my body and my nipples hardened. A predatory hunger consumed his features while he kneeled between my legs. My eyes leisurely trailed down his torso. Rigid muscle from hours spent honing his physique coiled his stomach, but it was the vein protruding from his abdomen and disappearing beneath his waistband that drew all my attention. He gave me such a look that made me feel sexy when he cupped his shaft and stroked it over his shorts.

I placed my arms out. I wanted him to come to me. I needed him.

Kova gave me the most erotic come hither grin right before he said, "Now let *me* show *you* how *I* land a dismount."

Taunting me with his words and powerful body, his Russian accent blending with his hoarse tone made it almost unbearable. It was beyond physical at this point and had me on edge, nearly begging him to touch me more.

When his nose grazed my neck I whispered, "I like you, Kova." I finally placed my hands on his back only for him to tense.

"What? What's wrong?" When he didn't respond, I could only assume it was from my honesty, and I said, "This isn't fair. I'm getting tired of your hot and cold moods."

He pulled back and raised a brow, his eyes hard and silent.

"Yeah, I get it, but one minute you want me and the next minute a switch flips and you get all weird. You're giving me whiplash."

Kova mumbled in Russian under his breath. His playful, seductive mood was gone and in its place was Coach Kova. Serious. Meticulous. Perfectionist. *Dick.*

Running a hand over his jaw, he said, "Your candor catches me off guard and I do not know why it does since we have been nothing but honest with each other." He heaved a heavy sigh. Kova moved to get off of me, but I sat up quickly and grabbed his arm.

The urge to kick him in his balls, which I was sure were aching and blue, was stronger than ever. His eyes blazed. "You can't get mad when I'm honest with you. It's not fair to me or my emotions, or yours."

"Not fair?" he scoffed. "What is not fair is that I want you when I should not. I want you all to myself," he slapped his chest. "That is the truth. I want you to be mine in every sense of the word. I want to do dirty things to you I should not even be thinking about. The images..." he broke off, and shook his head. "I visualize myself bending you over and taking you as hard as I can, knowing you will bleed and loving it. I want to see your eyes water while you deep throat my cock. Tie your hands behind your back as I take you to new heights you have never even imagined. So you know what I have to do? I have to fuck my girlfriend the way I want to fuck you, I think about *you* while I am deep inside of *her* because I do not want to hurt you." He paused, and said, "And most importantly because it is wrong and yet for some obscene reason, I love that it is. I thrive on the risk of getting caught, thrive on thinking of you while I fuck her. This was a mistake and I should have never let it happen again, yet I am glad it did."

Commence ball kicking. He was purposely taunting me so I would fight him back.

"A mistake? Liar," I spat between clenched teeth, angry that he'd dare utter those words. "You're the one who put this into motion this morning at the gym, not me."

Kova paused, his eerie stare hitting me hard.

"I am a liar?" breathe whispered.

"Yes, you are. I can see it in your blazing green eyes you're worked up, the forbidden thoughts running through your head. It's obvious in this too," Kova sucked in a breath when I reached for his cock. "Tell me you don't want me," I said. His hand immediately gripped my bicep so hard it was possible I'd have a bruise in the morning.

"Worked up?" He bit back. "You do not know what worked up is. And that was only the cocktail hour. That was not even enough to whet my appetite."

Christ, that hurt. If he wanted to play games, fine. I'd fight back how he wanted, anything for him not to leave.

"Oh yeah? Then why can I feel you growing in my hand, huh? I feel your *cock* getting bigger. Harder." Leaning in closer, I lied and said, "Just like when Hayden's cock grew in my hand." Kova's eyes took on an unnatural shade of green. I began moving my hand to rub him. "Tell me you don't want it. That this was a mistake. That each time we were together was a mistake."

"Why do you want this so bad?" his voice cracked. "Why do you push me?"

Biting my lip, my eyes softened with my heart at the despair in his voice. I shrugged. This back and forth was really starting to get to me. I could tell it was getting to Kova just the same.

"I don't know, I just do. It's a feeling I can't explain. I like being around you, Kova. I like talking to you, I like your presence. Don't tell me you don't feel the same way, otherwise you wouldn't be here." I swallowed hard, praying my next words wouldn't be thrown back in my face. "You feel it, don't you? This connection? The chemistry? It's why you keep saying it was a mistake, isn't it?"

"You took the words out of my mouth." He shook his head in disbelief, clenching his eyes shut over his admission.

A gentle smile eased my face when he opened his eyes and looked at me.

"You need to let go of me." He groaned as I began working him through his shorts. His hips thrusting into my hand contradicted his words. "This is a dangerous game we are playing."

His chest began to move—slower, deeper breaths he thought he was hiding from me. His hand loosened on my arm and slowly, very slowly, began to slide down to my wrist that stroked his erection.

"Fuck it."

CHAPTER 56

Kova reached for my chest and palmed my breasts, pinching my nipples.

Groaning from the sharp sting that radiated throughout my body, I soaked it up. Pain and pleasure combined. A hidden desire stirred deep in my belly for more.

Rolling my lip between my teeth, I tugged at the waistband of his shorts and slowly slid them down his tapered hips. His stomach flexed against the backs of my fingers. A light dusting of hair came into view, followed by a thick, heavy shaft.

"Christ," he groaned, fisting my duvet until his knuckles turned white.

I pulled his shorts completely off him and stared in bewilderment. Kova was rock solid, hard like his body, and standing tall. The sight of him splayed out caused a rush of excitement to coat my thighs. Goose bumps broke out over my skin, and it was then that it dawned on me just how much of a man Kova really was.

"How the hell does that thing fit in me?" I blurted out, and slammed a hand over my mouth. Kova chuckled, his shoulders relaxing, and he palmed his naked flesh.

"You would be surprised how easy I can work it in when you are wet."

Reaching out with my hand, my thumb moved on its own accord, rubbing the prominent vein on his dick over and over and watching as it flattened under my pressure then expanded up once I released. Kova sucked in a breath. The sudden image of my tongue doing this had me jutting out my breasts, longing for his touch once again.

While I played with his penis and got familiar with him, I realized my hand was damp. Glancing down, I noticed a droplet at the head and moved to touch it. I slid it through the tips of my fingers, and Kova placed his hand over mine. I looked at him and waited. He began to move my hand over his erection, signaling me to squeeze tighter.

I picked up the pace and stroked him harder and faster.

"Yes..." he mumbled unintelligibly, "like that."

Leaning forward, my lips sucked at his neck. Kova fisted my hair, tugging my head back, and cupped my jaw before leaning in to steal a kiss.

His greedy tongue took my breath away. He released my hair, and his hands traveled down to my breasts where he palmed them both in a rough grip, making me moan. His thumbs ran circles over my puckered nipples, and I continued to stroke him. But it wasn't enough for me—or him. I wanted to make him feel good, the same way he did me, but I'd never actually gone down on a guy before, let alone a man.

"Adrianna..." he panted, "do you have any idea how bad I want this? Want you? I want to slide into you again and fuck you senseless. God, I want you to ride me." His touch was everywhere, almost as if he couldn't get enough. I loved the attention he was giving me. I wanted more, as much as I could take from him.

"You undo me," he confessed. "You have played with yourself before, right?" he asked.

I nodded, unable to find my voice.

Kova jutted his chin up, but looked down through heavy lashes. "Touch yourself while I jack off."

Looking down at the thick erection in my hand, I asked, "Can I do it for you?"

"Do what, Adrianna?"

I bit my lip. "Make you come the way you make me."

His nose flared, and he paused. "No."

"Why not? I want to."

"I would rather you give yourself an orgasm while I watched."

I leaned back and placed my hand on my tender sex.

Kova's stomach flexed as he pumped into his hand. He was a thing of beauty and it wasn't long until I started to feel that newly familiar ache burning in my belly. But I wanted to be the one doing that to him, stroking him. Sitting up, I got to my knees just inches from him. I grabbed Kova's empty hand as he still towered above me and placed it in the V of my drenched thighs. He heaved a sigh. I peered into his lowering eyes and wrapped my hand around his cock, proving just how much I wanted to give him this pleasure. Needing more moisture, I spit into my hand the way I would if I were wearing grips, and returned my hand back to him. A low rumble escaped him and his chest expanded with a deep inhale.

Stroking him hard but slow, Kova's lips parted with an audible sigh. He cupped the back of my head and leaned down to kiss me, plunging his tongue into my mouth. He took control, and I liked it. A lot. More so than I probably should. He was wild, feral, and devoured my mouth with passion. The air was filled with sex and I swear I heard a growl.

"I'm close again...put it in me," I whispered against his lips. His thumb circled my clit and I was desperate to connect with him again, completely.

"God, I want to so badly. Anything to be deep inside your pussy again. To feel you clench around me."

I whimpered, and his dick twitched in my hand. "You can, I said you can."

"It does not work like that."

"Please."

"No...but keep doing that. Keep twisting the head a little tighter."

"I want it."

"With the way I feel right now, I will tear you up. No." Then he said, "Do not stop...fuck, just do not stop."

"Oh, yes," I moaned, riding his hand. My hips began rocking on their own. His palm kept hitting my clit and I couldn't get enough. I grabbed a hold of his bicep and he flexed under my arm. I was on the brink of tears from his taunting. Pure instinct took over and I climbed over his legs, positioning him at my entrance. Our eyes locked, and the moment he touched my opening I slid down. My lips parted as I felt myself stretch. Kova seized my hips to stop me from going down completely.

"This is not a good idea," he held on to me. Biting my bottom lip, I exhaled against his chest. Kova lifted my chin to look at him. He shook his head, his eyes filled with something I'd never seen before.

"You are something else, you know that?"

He kissed me deeply, fueling the fire, and lifted me up and down on him a handful of times before he pulled out and grabbed his shaft.

"Fuck!" he yelled, his penis throbbing. His body shook and it pleased me. White hot liquid hit my stomach. It stuck to me, slowly dripping down my flat tummy. It was the most erotic thing I'd ever seen.

I placed his hand between my thighs again. A gratified smile curved his sensual lips. I didn't know who I was in this moment, or who I had become, only that Kova had brought out a side of me I didn't know existed. I came just moments later.

"Baby," he said so quietly, but I heard it as he wrapped his arm around my lower back and held me against him. I relaxed and sighed into his body, inhaling his sultry scent that was now merged with our sex. My lips pressed to his neck, giving him little satisfied kisses. His dick throbbed against me as he continued to release himself all over me. And I mean, all over my stomach and thighs.

"This is why we cannot fuck again. You are too tight, it would hurt you more than it would feel good. I worried I hurt you last time."

I got serious with him and pushed back. "Way to kill the moment, Kova. How do you expect that to change unless you fuck me again? Your size would hurt anyone." I wasn't actually sure about that since I hadn't seen tons of penises before, I just assumed it, which I think he liked because his brows shot up and he grinned.

I smiled, happy I could draw such a reaction from him. Something shifted in the quiet air as we stared into each other's eyes. I wasn't sure what, but when Kova leaned in to kiss me, it was different this time. He was slower, more careful, and gentler. More methodic. It was a passionate kiss, one filled with more weight than meant to. I found myself falling into him, my heart opening up and holding on to him.

"I am enamored with you," he admitted honestly.

I was beginning to fall hard for this man. And that wasn't a good thing.

Breaking the kiss, Kova said, "Let us get you cleaned up."

My heart stopped. "You're not leaving yet, are you?"

He paused, looking to the side. "I have to leave soon, *malysh*."

"I know, but just stay for a little longer, please." I wasn't ready for him to leave just yet after what we shared.

Kova nodded, and we climbed off my bed and walked into the bathroom. I grabbed two wash cloths, wet them, and handed one to him. As I went to clean myself off, he pushed my hand away and cleaned me himself. For whatever reason, my heart melted as I let him do it. He was gentle and sweet, and the caring look in his eyes tightened something in my stomach. He pressed a kiss to my shoulder and used the same rag to quickly and efficiently clean himself, his eyes never leaving mine. We stood in silence and got dressed. This time I only wore boy short panties and a loose shirt. I pulled my hair into a ponytail when I was done.

Instead of sitting on my bed, Kova made his way to my living room and sat on my couch. I went to sit next to him, but he grabbed my hand and guided me to his front. I climbed up, straddling his thighs and lowered myself onto his lap. Placing my hands flat on his chest, he wrapped his arms around my back and snuggled me to him. Not once had Kova ever held me like this, so relaxed and so very intimate, but without any sexual motive. Almost like a lover's hold.

A few moments of silence passed when Kova spoke up.

"Adrianna, I need to ask you something," he said against me ear. "Are you on birth control?

My heart stopped.

"No."

"Fuck," he muttered under his breath, but I'd heard the disappointment in his tone. His body coiled beneath mine and I felt bad I hadn't even considered it at the time. "I cannot believe how stupid I was."

Pulling back, I looked into his solemn eyes. His hands dropped to my hips. "It's not your fault, Kova. I should've been more responsible, too. I wasn't thinking clearly."

I looked down at his shoulder, lost in thought over the ramifications of our actions. I was smarter than that and yet I made a grave judgment call. It was beyond ignorant of me.

"Well, on the plus side, you didn't finish inside of me."

Kova gave me a sympathetic look, his hands slid to my hips. "I do not have to come inside of you for you to get pregnant, Adrianna. It is called pre-come."

I knew what it was called, I was just trying to give him some hope. "I know, but the possibility is really slim." That, I knew.

I bit my lip. *Come inside you...*My cheeks flushed at his sexy, baritone voice. My hips purposely snuggled into his lap, feeling his length under me. He was warm and comforting, and something about being in his arms was peaceful.

"And yes, I did. The first night we had sex, I came inside of you."

CHAPTER 57

S hit.

The blood drained from my face.

I'd completely forgotten, yet the thought of him coming in me sent a flush of heat down my spine. I'd never been overly interested in sex, but Kova was bringing out the inquisitive side in me, making me want to explore more.

"Anything is a possibility, Ria," he said softly. My fingers traced over his muscular shoulder as I thought about what I could do to lessen my chances of being pregnant. A thought popped in my head.

"What about the morning after pill?" I suggested, brightly. I didn't want to take something such as a morning after pill, who knew what the hell it was made of, but I also wasn't ready to raise a baby, either. I had goals, dreams, and aspirations.

Kova shifted uncomfortably under me and dragged a hand over his mouth. When he stayed silent, I said, "It prevents pregnancy when there is no protection used during sex."

He rolled his eyes back to mine. "I know what it does."

"Oh, well, you didn't say anything."

"I was just thinking about the idea." His distant eyes were staring at something behind me before they swung back to mine. "I cannot force you to take anything, Adrianna. It is your choice and your decision, but I think this would be the best thing for you to do. For us."

I nodded. "I think so—"

He cut me off. "I will tell you right now that if you get pregnant and it somehow comes back to me, I will deny it until the day I die," he said, brushing a fallen lock of hair from my face.

My stomach recoiled at his gentle tone but inconsiderate words. I was just as much at fault as he was, and that was the last thing I wanted. "I don't feel comfortable buying it though...Do you think you could get it for me?"

Kova didn't hesitate. "Yes."

"But what if someone sees you buying it?"

His brows bunched together and then eased apart. "I will go to a pharmacy in the next town over. Problem solved."

We both heaved a heavy sigh at the same time. A relieved look passed over both our faces. The last thing I wanted was to get caught, let alone have a damn baby. And I could guarantee Kova felt the same way.

"When will you go? I think there's an expiration date on how long you have before it's not effective."

He nodded. "I think it is a week or something...Katja—" He stopped, remorse plaguing his face heavily and it bothered me. When he regained himself, he quietly said, "Katja has taken it before. I will go when I leave here and get it. It will be in your locker tomorrow morning, so get to the gym early and take it. I will take it out of the package so no one sees it."

My chest burned. I wasn't crazy about the thought of Katja having to take the pill because Kova couldn't control himself around her. I wanted him like that only for me.

"What does it look like?"

"It is a little white pill. I will put it to the side with a bottle of Aloe water in front of it."

My heart shifted, that unknown feeling coming back. Kova's eyes were on mine as he tugged my hair loose, the thick waves falling down my back. He fluffed it up, pulling a few strands over my shoulder to rest on my chest.

"Your hair is always up. I liked seeing it down today," he admitted somberly. "You looked beautiful when I saw you in my office. I had no intention of doing anything more with you, or that ridiculous deal I had you make, but when I saw you, everything changed."

"I didn't purposely pick that dress out, you know that, right?"

Kova smirked, nodding. "We will agree to disagree on that."

I gave him a playful stern glare. His smile shifted, looking more serious, staring into my eyes with such depth I felt he could see right into my deepest thoughts. "You are different than the others."

I rolled my eyes. "Most clichéd line ever, Kova."

He gripped me a little tighter. "Think what you want, but no matter what I do and say, I find myself drawn to you explicitly. Like a moth to a flame."

My brows lifted.

His nose grazed my cheek sweetly. "It is true, think about it. I am the moth, you are the flame. It is an irresistible attraction that will end in total destruction."

How morbid. "Do you think the moth knows that it's being lured?"

Kova sat quietly, looking at my chest that was parallel to his face. Only he didn't stare with desire, he looked lost in thought, maybe wondering if the moth knew any better. I had on a razorback shirt three times too large that hung loosely on my arms, showing a little skin. The back of his finger came up and unhurriedly grazed the side of my round breast. My nipples puckered in return, showing through the shirt.

"Desire can be deadly. Temptation can be toxic. But do I think it knows it is being lured? No," he said quietly, running his finger in circles on my flesh.

"Like right now, I am tempted to push this thin material aside and press my lips to your tender skin. But I know if I get too close, get a taste of you again," he winked, and I smiled at the devious glint in his eyes, "then I will not be able to stop. I will want more until it is too late to stop. But if I do, do it," he pushed the arm hole over my breast, the back of his finger purposely dusting over my rosy nipple, "it does not mean I have to do anything, but the lust, the hunger, the want, it is all there, pulling with a force so powerful that an ending is not even a thought. It is pure desire."

My fingers continued to thread his hair as he became hard beneath me. His tongue slipped out and licked his bottom lip before he leaned in and delicately flattened it around my nipple. My heart raced, coming alive as he lapped and pulled on my sensitive skin. My back arched seductively as I pressed the back of his head to me. He was taking his time, flicking his tongue over the bud then running it in circles. A moan rolled off my lips and he pulled back with a pop. Looking down through my heavy lids, my nipple was hard and pointed as he stared at it like he wanted to devour me. He covered me back up, and met my gaze.

"You are the bright light that beckons me...And I am okay with it. Thing is, I realized I like talking to you, Adrianna. I like being around you. I have never told any other gymnast or friends about my mother and her secret, only Katja. It feels natural with you. You are a fighter, and no matter how much you get pushed down, no matter what you have against you, you do what you have to do, and you do not complain. You are strong and resilient. You are relentless, and I find that fucking attractive as hell. It is a turn on, but it is also why I treat you the way I do."

"It's why you've been so hot and cold with me."

He nodded. "At first, it was the chase, the sneaking around that all builds it up. As a coach, I know better. There are classes we have to take to be aware of these things—at the end of the day, you are still a minor. But what they do not teach us is it is not always the coach who seduces the athlete. That sometimes, maybe sometimes, it is the other way around."

"You think I seduced you," I stated plainly. "Because at when this first started I knew what I was doing with an older man, so I set out to get you."

He shook his head, his forehead creased with lines. "I think a lot of it has to do with attraction more than anything. Attraction is the root of all evil, not money like some say. It can be everything you have ever imagined and destroy everything at the same time. All relationships begin with attraction that leads to some form of lust. It is a natural reaction that comes from the body. Do I think that you purposely seduced me?" He chuckled with a small smile. "Not exactly." Brushing a lock of hair behind my ear, he said, "The fire that burns inside of you to be better, to prove others wrong about you, is dangerous, and *that* is attraction in itself. It is a hell of an attraction. We will both be our ruin if we do not stop while we are ahead."

He paused and looked deeply in my eyes once again. The guilt woven through his face was strong and it froze me. The knot that formed in my stomach and matched with his features told me his next words would cause damage. A pang in my chest spread through my whole body. My face fell, my heart breaking. "Did I do something wrong?" The tears behind my eyes were steadily climbing.

"You did everything right, but you know as much as I do this has to come to an end. It cannot keep going on. No more skating around the edges. No more chasing. It is not worth losing everything over."

Biting my bottom lip, I studied my fingers as they glided across Kova's collarbone. His words weren't malicious, but they cut deep and I wanted to cry.

"You're right," I agreed with a shaky voice.

"We can never admit anything to anyone, you know this, right?"

Nodding, I said, "I'd never tell anyone."

"But even if anyone suspects it, says that they found out, do not fall for the trap." My brows angled toward each other and he continued. "I will never speak a word of this to anyone, no matter what anyone says. And you cannot either."

Kova's phone vibrated in his pocket. Pulling it out, I saw Katja's name flash across the screen. He scowled. It was close to midnight, and I wondered what he would tell her.

"I have to go." He lifted my hips and moved me off him to stand.

I fixed my shirt and crossed my arms under my chest. "What will you tell Katja the reason why you're so late?"

"She will not question me."

Perplexed, I asked, "Why not?"

"I will not give her the chance," he said, his eyes raking leisurely down my body. My nipples hardened and my cheeks flushed in response. Kova adjusted his shaft, causing me to look in that direction. The bulge in his shorts was blatantly obvious.

My chest tightened, my jaw slackened. He was hard, he wanted sex. And sex would be with Katja.

My heart crumpled at the thought of him having sex with her while thinking of me. I knew it was stupid to feel the way I did, but I couldn't help it.

I followed him to the door. He turned around with his hand on the knob. Kova looked down at me and brought a hand up to cup my cheek. My eyes closed shut as he leaned in and pressed a kiss to my forehead.

I bit my lip as he swiftly stepped out and left, a warm tear slipped down my cheek.

Turning around, I leaned against the door and hugged myself as I slid down and let the tears fall.

CHAPTER 58

It was pitch black when I pulled up to the gym a little earlier than I normally did.

My eyes were swollen, and I was mentally and physically exhausted as I put my truck into park. My face was devoid of its usual makeup and my hair wasn't even brushed today. Climbing out, I grabbed my gym bag from the backseat and shut the door. I slung it over my shoulder and walked into World Cup.

It was eerily quiet this morning. No gymnasts were on the floor, no music was playing, no springboards sounding. Just the scent of chalk and coffee coalesced in the air and the faint sound of papers shuffling as I walked to the locker room and opened my locker door.

I swallowed hard at what was staring me straight in the face on the little shelf. A four pack of coconut water with a Post-It note attached to it, a couple of new bottles of Aloe water, a new package of pre-wrap along with new wristbands, and a little white envelope. Without opening it, I knew it contained the morning after pill.

After Kova left, I climbed into bed and cried myself to sleep. My heart hurt, but the reality of the situation was clear.

There would be no more Kova and me.

Subconsciously, I knew it would never be more than what it was. It could never work in this lifetime. It was just too dangerous. This was for the best, but it didn't make it any easier to deal with the emotional fallout. I still had to see him on a daily basis. I decided I wouldn't engage in any small talk with him, I wouldn't look longingly in his direction, I wouldn't accept gifts from him, nothing. I'd keep it completely platonic. I had bigger things I needed to worry about and focus on, but my heart was broken.

I was falling for him.

Not love, I didn't believe in love. Not at my age at least. I was a realist with goals. Love didn't fit into the equation at this time in my life.

However, I had started to develop feelings for him that crossed the professional level and that worried me.

Yet, seeing his gifts in front of me, gifts I didn't want to accept, for some reason caused my jaw to tremble and my stomach to flutter. Reaching for the yellow sticky note, I read Kova's handwriting.

THOUGHT YOU MIGHT WANT TO TRY THIS OUT. SIMILAR TO YOUR ALOE WATER, BUT IN MY OPINION, BETTER FOR YOU.

K

Of course it was better. Kova knew everything.

I reached for the package, quickly tearing open the cardboard and pulling out a bottle. I uncapped it, brought it to my nose and inhaled. It smelled just like fresh coconuts and my mouth watered. I took a sip, actually liking it more than I expected, and drank nearly half the bottle before I picked up the little envelope and opened it.

Cupping my hand, a little white pill tumbled out into my palm. A pill that reminded me how foolish I had been. My heart began to pump viciously at the sight of it. One tiny pill had the power to irrevocably change a life. I didn't want to give it any more thought, so without hesitation, I threw the pill into my mouth and said a little prayer. I took a swig of the coconut water and swallowed. I may have been careless, but my future was at stake...as well as Kova's. No way was I going to jeopardize it in any way, shape, or form.

I crumpled the note in my hand and dropped it into my bag so I could throw it away when I got home. I wasn't going to be stupid like Kova and risk someone seeing it.

At the end of the day, I came to World Cup for one reason and one reason alone. To train with the best so I could achieve Olympic glory. I wouldn't allow my focus to deter again. I was going to dive into practice and work harder than ever. Gymnastics has an expiration date. And being that I was steadily getting closer to it, I had a lot to accomplish in a short amount of time. I was going to prove them all wrong, and throw every minute I had into the sport that was the first to steal my heart. Mind, body, and soul. I had everything I needed at the tips of my fingers. There was no reason not to have what I wanted.

Self-doubt kicked in while I undressed. It was like that pesky little gnat that just wouldn't go away. I questioned whether I had enough time or if it was even possible to make it to The Games like I once thought.

Unfortunately, I knew I had to downgrade some of my skills because of my stupid little injury. But it would be okay. It would only push me to fight harder.

After I shut my locker and locked it, I strode into the gym where Kova was waiting on the floor with a roll of tape in his hand. My heart jumped, reaching for him. My lips a firm, grim line as our eyes locked. He noticeably tensed, his shoulders bunching as a shadow cast over his eyes, shielding his emotions, giving nothing away.

I stayed quiet as I sat on the ground with my injured leg bent. Kova stood before me with a stoic face. While his eyes were unreadable and his movements professional, the facial hair casting a dark shadow on his jaw, and the puffy circles under his eyes gave him away. The smell of his cologne was faint, but enough to entice me to lean in and inhale the scent into my lungs. Spicy and daring, it made me think of what had happened only a handful of hours ago.

We were both quiet as he placed the white athletic tape in specific places on the back of my calf. This time his hands didn't linger and his fingers didn't stimulate. The sad part was, I desperately want-ed them to.

Once he was finished, he stood and held out a hand to help me up. I couldn't look at his hand without thinking about where it'd been, what it'd done to me. Shaking the thoughts from my head, I pushed off the ground and stood.

"How does it feel?"

The aching organ in my chest? It hurt like hell.

I rolled my ankle around. "Fine, I guess."

"Look at me."

Snapping my eyes up to meet his, he pointed a finger and said, "If you have any kind of pain, anything at all, you need to speak up immediately. Do you understand me?"

"Yes."

"Anything, Adrianna. I am risking my neck for you right now." He gave me a knowing look, and I nodded.

Pulling my lip into my mouth, I chewed on it. I rolled my feet into the blue carpet, cracking my toes nervously. Kova's eyes followed the movement from my mouth to my feet and spat, "Spit it out, Adrianna. What is going on?"

Adrianna. Didn't that just sting. That was twice now.

"I took the pill," I whispered quietly, despite being the only ones in the gym. "And, thank you for the wristbands and coconut water. You didn't have to do that." I was still slightly perplexed at why he had, considering how we ended things.

Kova dipped his chin, then turned and walked away. His back was rigid and stiff and I could tell he was dealing with his own inner demons. It was a little rude for him to do so without so much as a you're welcome, but it was for the best. We really didn't need to speak unless it was gymnastics related.

I trained with my nemesis for a good three hours this morning—the balance beam. In between working with me and the other team girls, Kova helped me water down my routine. He was his typical Russian dick self the entire time, maybe more so to the other girls for once. When we would make eye contact, it was so he could give me an example of what to do. I kept a straight face and nodded when he barked out orders then would follow up and ask me if it hurt to land. This was the first time I didn't actually fear the beam, and that was cause for concern since I wasn't taking chances and risking my neck. A little fear was good.

Or maybe I was just lacking emotion for the day.

As I powdered my hands with chalk to prepare for bars, another event that would take the strain off my calf for now, I overheard Reagan talking to the other girls about a boyfriend she wasn't supposed to have. Not that I cared. It was the dumbest rule I'd ever heard, but I guess it made sense. We'd lose focus if that was the case, and it was. Just look how much time I spent thinking about Kova.

I thought back to the day she didn't want to let me borrow her extra set of grips, as if I had some deadly disease that was going to cost her a limb. I shook my head and huffed as I laced my fingers through my grips and wrapped the Velcro around the new wristbands Kova had given me.

The sound of classical music played in the background, pulling my attention to the floor. Holly was gracefully performing her routine, a routine that had skills I wasn't allowed to do for the time being. And unless my Achilles healed and was strong again, I wouldn't be doing them at all. I wasn't a jealous person, but I was the definition of envious at the moment.

I exhaled and shook my head, my thoughts were jumping everywhere. I didn't need anyone's approval. I wasn't the type to need a lot of friends. I learned living in on Amelia Island that it was better to have a few close friends and keep the rest at arm's length. Everyone was phony and only looked out for themselves. They were what I called *Wonder Bread* people. Fake, gluey, and tasteless.

The definition of Reagan.

God, I sounded like such a cynic.

Hayden strode by with a smile that made my shoulders relax. His charm was contagious and I couldn't help smiling back. Now, he had been a good friend, one I didn't think I could have gone without since coming here.

Rubbing some chalk on my thighs, I overheard Reagan say, "Hayden is so damn hot. Why Adrianna is a virgin is beyond me. Being that she's such good friends with him, it's honestly shocking she hasn't tapped that. Unless she's into girls."

I looked over my shoulder and the girls snickered. *Tapped that?*

"She doesn't know what she's missing."

"Or maybe it's because he wants an athlete at his level, not one who needs serious work and thinks she's better than what she really is," she said cockily. "Not one Daddy has to bribe either."

It got you your stupid café hall that you study in. That was what I considered a win-win situation, but Reagan was so narrow minded she couldn't see it benefitted her too.

Reagan continued. "Adrianna the prude. Miss Moneybags is saving herself for the perfect guy her parents will pay her off too."

The girls laughed again. My blood simmered.

"You know, Reagan," I said sweetly, standing up and walking over to her. "I've about had enough of your shit. I never speak up or say anything about your constant belittling comments, but I am today. I'm sick of your condescending tone and glares. You think you're so much better than every other gymnast here, but I have news for you. You're not. So why don't you just shut the hell up and leave me alone."

My comment didn't seem to faze her. "Oh, you're tired of it?" She batted her eyelashes. I had the urge to punch her teeth out. I nodded, and she kept going. "Isn't that right, Adrianna," Reagan taunted, "You're saving yourself?"

I shook my head. "What are you talking about?"

"You being a virgin," she stated.

"Why does my personal life interest you so much? Unless you're the one into girls and you want me?" It wasn't in my nature to stoop so low, but today was not the day.

"How can you be friends with him," she looked at Hayden, "and not do anything? I would've given up my V card to him any day."

"Not that it's any of your information, but I don't have my V card," I said with air quotes. "There. Will that help you sleep better at night?"

"You don't? Since when?"

I was getting confused. How the hell would she know about my virgin status to begin with? "What do you mean, since when?"

"You don't remember our game of Truth or Dare where you admitted you were a virgin?"

Avery. But that was the least of my concerns right now. My chest heated, blood quickly rose to my cheeks and out to my ears as it dawned on me. Christ Almighty, I had said that! I couldn't remember what I ate for dinner five nights ago let alone what I said to the mean girl squad leader. However, with Reagan reminding me, I certainly had divulged my virginity status and now I just fucked myself admitting I was no longer a virgin.

"Well, I lied. It was none of your business back then and it sure isn't now. Shouldn't you be up on bars perfecting your routine?"

Reagan studied my face, my cheeks blushing even darker.

"You had sex since you've been here," she declared.

"I'm not having this conversation with you. If you're not going to get up on bars, I will." I stepped around her, but she stopped me by gripping my arm.

"You have, haven't you?"

"What does it matter to you?" I yanked my arm away, glaring.

Her mouth curved into a sly grin. "Well, well, well. Carrot top here has been deflowered."

"You know, Reagan, have you ever seen an actual carrot top? Because they're green, not red. So the term carrot top doesn't even make sense. And in case you're color blind, I'm clearly not a solid redhead."

Reagan's cheeks colored and I secretly took joy in it. She was pissed, and I could see the thoughts spinning in her head so fast that a slow smile spread across my face. I rendered her speechless, for once.

"I'm pretty sure I just heard you say you have a boyfriend. What, and who I do, in my spare time is none of your business." I had heard her correctly, right?

Palming the low bar, I swung and mounted it.

"I'll find out who you lost your V card to. Then I'll tell Coach since we're not allowed to have boyfriends," she said with spite. "Can't imagine Daddy can get you out of that one."

Ignoring her, I placed my feet on the bar and stood reaching for the high bar. She was pushing me to crack, but I refused to give in. There was no way she would rat me out, she was just as guilty if that was the case.

Casting to a handstand, I did a series of handstands to warm up and then began adding in connections. I had no pain in my calf yet, though everything I was doing was very light. My body flew seamlessly through the air from one bar to the other. I loved bars. I loved the feeling of shutting out the world and letting go, only relying on myself to catch the bar. It was an adrenaline rush, one I chased often with this sport. When I felt my arms and shoulders tightening, I slowed down to rest on the high bar by angling my hips against it and leaning forward. Up next were pirouettes and a light dismount, where I would start all over and do it again until I felt ready to move on from there.

After I tightened the Velcro on my wrists, I exhaled when my hands gripped the bar and visualized my next move. Awareness kicked through me. My back prickled with heat and I knew without a shadow of a doubt who was glaring at me from behind.

I looked over my shoulders. *Kova.*

He was staring at me furiously, like he wanted to strangle me. The blood drained from my face, my weight slowly descending further on to the bar as trepidation flooded my veins. Kova glared from the sideline, his impenetrable gaze knocking the air from lungs. He'd heard everything, the entire conversation with Reagan.

I was cold to the bone.

Numb.

CHAPTER 59

Holly was there when you said you were a virgin."

I cringed at her words.

"I'll get down to it." She chalked up, lost in her thoughts again as she mounted the set of uneven bars to the left, clearly unaware of Kova standing on the other side of me.

I didn't process what Reagan said. I couldn't. All I could focus on were the veins in Kova's forearms and the tick working in his jaw. His nose flared and I was sure I'd see smoke coming from his ears any minute.

I felt sick.

Nauseous.

He now knew I had been a virgin.

My heart raced so fast from his seething glare, it drummed in my ears. He heard everything. Everything.

And he was pissed. I can't imagine how I didn't see him standing there.

No, he was fucking fuming and looking at me with repulsion, and I detested it. His hands were fisted tightly at his sides, knowing he couldn't comment. So he just stood there, scowling, slicing me open with his loathing glare. The disgust on his face made my stomach churn. After everything we shared between us, the conversations and intimacy, I didn't want him to look that way toward me.

I needed to break the eye contact, so I fell forward and hung on the bar, pretending to fix my grips like they needed to be tighter. I clapped my hands to dust some of the chalk off. Anything I could think of to avoid seeing him when I looked up. My heart was racing so fast it hurt. I needed to get off this apparatus immediately. I needed to get out of here. I had too much on my mind to focus on what he heard, and how I was going to fix this.

No, I needed to tune out bitchy Reagan and pissy Kova and focus on gymnastics. That's what I needed to do.

Shit. Now my legs were quivering. Trying to ignore everything that just ruined my life in a matter of two minutes, I pulled up and continued with my warm up. I finished with a simple back tuck dismount. My mind was all over the place, my stomach was nauseous and I felt sick to the core. I quickly chalked up and tried to get back up on bars. Just before doing a kip, I paused with my hands wrapped around the bar. I couldn't do it. My gut told me not to take the risk. My hands trembled, my heart in my throat. I was off balance. Being around, and training with Kova, was fucking with my head.

Stepping back, my arms dropped lifelessly to my sides. I looked up and spotted Kova across the gym working with a gymnast on the floor. But he was still fiercely staring me down. His incredible eyes saying everything I needed to know.

Jesus, Mary, and Joseph. What the fuck did I do?

"Reagan, leave her alone."

My head snapped at the sound of Hayden's voice. Jesus. I wish he'd been here a few minutes earlier. The inquisitive look in his eyes said he knew there was more to the story than just Reagan being an asshole like she normally was, but luckily he brushed it off. I didn't know when he got here or how much he heard.

Reagan jutted her hip out. "Why? Are you two a thing? Because you know that's not allowed."

"I'm well aware of the rules, Rea. So is Aid. I'm asking you to back down and retract your claws. We're friends—nothing more."

"Aid?"

Hayden uncapped his water bottle and sipped it, never breaking eye contact with her. Replacing the cap, he said, "Yeah—Aid, just like when I call you Rea. It's a nickname, that's what friends do."

Hayden walked away, and I walked in the opposite direction. I couldn't breathe. I needed air. I needed *something*. I was starting to panic and I didn't know how to calm down because I had no one I could talk to. My nerves were lighting up and shaking me to the core. I began ripping my grips off as I exited to the lobby, the whole time I could feel my coach's eyes burning a hole into the side of my face. I didn't look though, because I already knew what they'd say.

Deceit.

Lies.

Trickery.

Loathing.

God, but it was so good. Amazing. And even though I omitted that fact, I still wanted him to want me. I still wanted him to desire me. I'd do it all over again if given the chance. Just thinking about it had my body warming and my heart pounding for all the right reasons. I may have been a virgin, but I knew no one would ever compare to him or the way his body felt against mine, or the pleasure he brought me. There was more to us than just sex and gymnastics, and we both were aware of it.

Shaking it off, I stepped into the bathroom and splashed cold water on my face. I couldn't go home, so I'd just have to act like nothing was wrong, and talk to Kova after practice when everyone left and we were alone.

TWO HOURS LATER, I WAS screwing up my routine left and right.

I may have appeared to have nothing on my mind and only having a bad workout, but that was because I was taught to.

However, if anyone climbed inside my head, they'd see what a hot jumbled mess I was. I couldn't think straight. I couldn't swing neatly. My legs kept coming apart. I stumbled, my feet scraping the ground, and I couldn't land a clean dismount. I was all over the place. It was horrible. People had to see how terribly I was performing. I'm sure Reagan took note.

I wasn't even doing my release moves in fear of messing up and not catching the bar. Or worse, freaking out in mid-air and land on the bar with my hip. I stuck to basic bars and did easy skills, a few simple releases. Truthfully, I had no choice if I wanted to preserve what little sanity I had left.

Reagan and her friends whispered under their breath the whole time. I brushed it off, not caring what they thought. I already had an injury, I didn't need to add to it, so I played it safe for the day. And it didn't help that any time I glanced over my shoulder, I saw

Kova looking at me. Not only was I performing like shit, he was watching me with his beautiful arms tightly crossed in front of his chest, critiquing my every move. He stared so keenly I decided to make an effort to avoid looking in his direction.

Only one more release before I did a copout dismount and would rotate to my last event for the day. I needed to be done with bars, done with practice so I could talk to Kova.

One Giant into a blind change, another Giant to gain momentum, I took a deep breath and released the bar to move into a Jaeger.

Only to fucking miss it.

I panicked, my heart sunk in mid-air, slamming to the ground before I did. A move so simple I'd been doing for years, and because my mind was in a million different places, I messed up royally. I either tapped too early or released too early...or I ducked my head...or I wasn't fully extended. It could be a number of things, and I had no idea which since my mind and body were not in sync with each other.

Falling face down on my stomach, I kept my arms out and in front of me so I wouldn't break any bones on the way down. The dumbest thing a gymnast can do is try to break their fall. *Hello broken bones and goodbye gymnastics career!* At least I had a little common sense left.

A gush of air burst from my lungs as I flopped to the thickly padded blue mat and bounced, chalk flying up around my face. My chest rose and fell heavily as I kissed the mat. My mind ran a million miles a minute trying to figure out how the hell I messed up so badly. While it was a common fall in practice, I was both embarrassed and shocked, and I didn't want to face all the gawking stares I knew I was getting.

Taking a deep breath, I exhaled and opened my eyes only to see Kova hovering above me. He reached down with an opened palm to help me and I grabbed it, not thinking twice.

"Girls," he said, looking directly at me, "rotate to the next event. I will be there in a bit."

A low snicker came from Reagan as she walked past us. I was seriously beginning to fucking hate the air she breathed.

"Get back up on the bar now."

Fuck. Fuck. Fuck. My heart raced, fear exploding through my veins over falling again. To fall so badly and then to get back up and do it again wasn't easy. Fear was suffocating me.

"I...I think I need a break," I stammered.

Coach ignored me as he dragged over a tall, solid mat for him to stand on. A spotting block. He dropped it near the metal post and climbed up, looking at me expectantly and waiting.

"Did I give you a choice? You just screwed up on a simple release move. In fact, I have been watching you screw up all afternoon, Adrianna. You are a sloppy mess and it is embarrassing. I guess we are going to have to take it back to basics since you cannot hit simple skills a twelve year old can master. So get up there now and do it again."

Shaking my head subtly, I slapped some chalk on to my grips and stood in front of the bars. Doing a kip to mount the low bar, I let go and jumped to the high bar.

"Cast to a handstand. Blind change. Jaeger."

I nodded, rotating my hands so they were considered backwards and my knuckles were against my thighs, a half pirouette. Blindly falling forward was not something I was in the mood to perform after the day I've been having, but I took a deep breath and prayed to God I would be able to pull off a Jaeger. Bouncing off the bar with my hips, I cast to a handstand. Coach positioned his hands on my stomach and back, holding me in place, leaving a touch of heat in each fingertip.

"Breathe," he whispered only for my ears. "Calm down, and focus. You got this." I nodded, then I was blindly falling forward into another handstand where he gripped me in the same place again. His hold was firm, secure, and overall, confident. It gave me a sense of comfort knowing he'd catch me if I fell.

"Tighten up." He slapped the back of my thigh lightly. "Squeeze your butt, straighten your legs."

I squeezed every muscle I could in my body and fell back again to hit another handstand.

"Better. Do it again."

I did it again.

"Tap harder," he demanded. "I believe your tap was not hard enough and the reason for your fall."

"Kova," I whispered once I was in a handstand. Coming down, I rested my hips on the bar with my arms locked straight. I turned to look at him.

"Do not," he mumbled.

"We need to talk."

"Adrianna, if you say another word to me, I will put your body through so much conditioning you will not be able to walk tomorrow."

My lips parted and his eyes traveled down to them. The five o'clock shadow paired with his emerald eyes was scorching, and when he looked at me with commanding authority, my body blazed. The bite in his tone was a clear warning to stop, so I listened. I didn't want to push him. It was obvious he wasn't playing around, clearly past the point of pissed off.

"Now is not the time or place to talk about anything. Be smart, Adrianna. Until then, you will land this skill until it is solid and then you are going home. I do not need you breaking bones on me."

I nodded. He was right.

"Now let us go. Do the Jaeger. I will spot you."

Before casting to another damn handstand, I looked at him and whispered, "I'm scared."

His eyes filled with empathy. "Fear is not a bad thing. It is what keeps you alive and trying. Visualize it and then go for it. Be confident. Push for it. I am right here spotting you, I will not let anything happen. I promise."

I believed him. I nodded frantically, picturing the skill in my head. Once in a handstand, I looked for his hands to spot me and when it came time to release again, I arched my back and tapped my feet hard. I released the bar and flipped forward into a pike position. Spotting the bar, I reached for it as if I was about to fall a hundred feet to the ground and gripped it tight. Coach kept his word and heavily spotted by flattening his hand right under my chest and on my back.

He had me.

I followed through with an easy kip and rested on the bar. My heart was racing, adrenaline pouring through my veins as I caught my breath. I looked at him and smiled brightly.

"Again." He tapped the back of my thigh.

He didn't even give me thirty seconds before I was back up. My nerves were shot and only by some miracle did I catch the bar thereafter. I lost count of the number of times I practiced the Jaeger after the initial one. Even with my grips, my palms were on fire, but I blocked out the agonizing pain. My shoulders felt like Jell-O. With each release, the fear dissolved a little more. But it never disappeared. Kova was right about fear, it kept me alive and motivated. Otherwise, I'd lose the thrill of the sport to keep going. He gave me self-belief with his firm touch, the courage to keep going. It was a coach wanting to see his athlete succeed and nothing more.

He ordered one more Jaeger where he said he would spot me, only he didn't. He only stood there to give me piece of mind. I should have expected this, but I was so lost in the moment I didn't.

Panting and out of breath, I bent over the high bar and breathed the chalky air heavily into my lungs.

"Get your stuff and go. Skip tomorrow's practice and do not question my authority." Flipping down, confidence roared through me. Normally I'd be upset over skipping practice, but ending it the way I did made me feel the complete opposite.

I smiled to myself, unwinding my grips and removing my wristbands. I felt good about the Jaegers, about how Kova pushed me to redo them. Had he not, there would be a chance I'd fear them the next time. This practice had started out good, moved to shit, and quickly into a disaster, and then actually ended on a good note for the most part.

I was bent down and shuffling through my bag when Kova strode back over. Standing up, I threw the duffle over my shoulder and looked at his hard face.

His voice was low, only for me to hear. "If you ever perform in the way you just did again, you will be kicked out of here so fast your head will spin. I do not give a shit who your father is. It was reckless and stupid and I never want to see it again."

And then he walked away.

CHAPTER 60

I t'd been a couple of days since the Jaeger fiasco.

I tried not to dwell on it since the past couldn't be changed and nothing good could come from constantly thinking about it. Instead, I blocked it out as much as possible and kept training in the forefront of my mind.

I busied myself and caught up on my homework. I even studied the material I'd be going over with my tutors the next couple of days. When I was done with the boring math I'd never use again in my life, I cleaned and did things around my condo so my mind didn't wander. I went to therapy for my Achilles, and then decided to get take out, something I never did.

The Penne a la Vodka was orgasmic. Too bad I couldn't eat it every day. However, considering it was Thanksgiving weekend and I wasn't with my family, I splurged. Not going home for this holiday wasn't a big deal for me. I'd go home for Christmas, though.

Yawning, I closed my chemistry book shut and dropped it on the couch. My eyes were puffy and swollen, and my hair was damp from the shower I took an hour ago. Relaxed with a full belly, I was ready to cuddle up in bed.

I didn't know what to do, and I had no one to talk to about it. I didn't want to tell Avery I had sex with Kova because I didn't want her to judge me. Not that she would, but after the talk I had with her and how she insisted Kova and I stop, I had a gut feeling she would be disappointed. When the time was right I'd tell her. Until then, it was better this way.

Looking through the sliding glass door, I gazed into the pitch-black sky thinking about what the future held, where I would be a year from now gymnastics wise. The moon hung high and I stared at it when I heard a light knock at my door.

Standing up, I walked across the plush carpet and stood on my tiptoes to peek through the peephole. Taking a deep breath, I unlocked the door and opened it.

All the air left my lungs. God, he was so fucking gorgeous.

He had one arm propped up against the wall as he leaned down and stared at me. His piercing green eyes peaked out from under his thick, black eyelashes, and he had more facial hair than I'd ever seen him with before. It worked in his favor and I wished he'd grow in more. He scanned the length of my body with his heady gaze until our eyes locked again. It seemed every time he stopped by my condo, my outfit was the same—panties and a shirt. In my defense, I wasn't planning on having company.

Kova dropped his arm and sauntered in past me. My heart leaped into my throat and I could feel my body simmering when I got a drift of his clean scent mixed with cologne. He smelled divine. I had a gut feeling he was here to yell at me, and luckily after a few days alone, I had everything planned I wanted to say.

Pushing back the hood of his jacket, I watched Kova unzip it and then remove it. He shook out his tight arms. Fury thickened the air, my heart catapulting in my chest. He was wearing distressed dark jeans and a tight black shirt. Dropping his jacket on the high back chair, Kova stalked toward me. A crease formed between my eyes at his harsh demeanor and I swallowed back the knot in my throat. He stepped toward me and followed me into the kitchen. My heart was wild with anxiety when I felt my back against the wall.

"Are you fucking crazy?" He gritted between clenched teeth. He got right to the point. "Is there something wrong with you?"

"You really had no idea?" I countered.

He snapped his neck to the side like he was cracking it, never leaving my gaze. "You were a *virgin,* a *fucking virgin.* And you let me fuck you the way I did? Let me touch you like that?"

My face scrunched up. He said virgin with a tone of repugnance and it hurt my stomach.

"I didn't let you do anything, you wanted it. We both wanted it, plain and simple. Okay—Maybe I did push you a little too far, but what's the difference, anyway?"

"The difference is you were a virgin, Adrianna. That is the difference. Are you not following the conversation?"

"Well, if it helps, I'm ninety-nine percent positive I broke my hymen on the balance beam, which means in a sense I wasn't a virgin." Kova paused, looking baffled, so I continued. "See, it's actually quite common for a gymnast to break her hymen from a bad fall on the balance beam, and Lord knows I've had plenty of falls. It's probably why I didn't bleed when we had sex."

Kova stepped closer. He placed his forearms on the wall near my head, boxing me in. His eyes narrowed and he was seething.

"Are you really going to school me on straddling the beam and hymens? I know all about that. I have been around the gym world longer than you have been alive. Breaking your hymen does not mean you are not a virgin anymore, Adrianna." Kova dipped his chin and looked deeper into my eyes, fury pouring out of them. "Penetration means you are not a virgin anymore. And while breaking your hymen on beam may be true, I was still your first form of real penetration, and that is fucked up beyond comprehension. I cannot believe you did not tell me."

My chest deflated.

"How is it fucked up?" I asked dejectedly.

"You should have been honest with me." He mirrored my tone and for the first time since he found out about my virginity, I actually felt remorseful.

Kova clenched his eyes shut and stepped away. He began pacing my kitchen frantically. The rage and fury he was casting out was thick and dense, hitting me hard and making me nervous. This was the first time I'd seen or felt real anger from him. It was completely different from the times he yelled at me in the gym, and honestly, I wasn't sure what to do with it.

"I cannot believe how stupid I was. I cannot believe I let myself fuck you, touch you, *drown* in you," he mumbled to himself. "I should have never done it."

I flinched, feeling the regret in his words. "What does it matter, anyway," I yelled, tired of his constant whiplash. "I wanted it. If you had known, would you have stopped?"

He stopped and looked at me, walking to stand close again. "Yes, I would have," he said between clenched teeth. "Because you never had a cock inside you before me no matter how you want to look at it, regardless if your hymen was already broken or not. I was still your first and while it never should have happened, it did. I took your innocence. I took your virginity. Why did you not speak up and say anything? I was always honest with you, Adrianna, always."

I shrugged feeling guilty. "I didn't know how to say it, and I was afraid you would have stopped."

He laughed low, manically. "This is so fucked up."

My heart crumbled. I loved being with Kova. He didn't push me. If anything, I pushed him.

There was no reason we couldn't talk about this situation civilly. He was being deliberately cruel and I didn't like it.

"Kova," I said softly, trying to calm him down. "You did nothing wrong."

His eyes locked on mine, forcing me not to move. "Nothing wrong? I sure as hell did not stop you. I hardly even tried. I saw an opening and took it. The moment I said take and you did, there was not a chance in hell I could hold back. I fucked a virgin. Over and over. Adrianna, I *licked* you, you had multiple orgasms," he said with horror. "An underage virgin at that. My fucking gymnast! There is a lot wrong with this picture. I could have gone to jail."

"You could've gone to jail before it," I muttered.

"What did you say?"

I stuttered when he glared at me. "Nothing..." This wasn't how I planned for this conversation to go.

"You know, this is *your* fault. I should have stopped your advances. I should have been stronger and turned you away like I did the others in the past. I have never," he fumed with rage, "been with a gymnast, let alone someone underage. What the fuck was wrong with me?" He questioned himself, pacing back and forth again. Running a hand through his hair, he repeated, "This could cost us everything."

That gave me an opening. "Are you sure you've never with any other gymnast? I find that hard to believe with how long you've been coaching and how closely you work with them. That can't be possible."

He pulled back like I slapped him, disgust written all over his striking face. "Do you think I am some sort of freak, Adrianna? No, I have never been with any other gymnast, or underage girl in my life. I never desired to. What the hell makes you think that?"

He stalked toward me. "You actually believe I like young girls?" He revolted at his own question. I shrugged. "Answer me."

"I don't know. I guess I don't see how you couldn't have." I shook my head at his question, shrugging it off. "Kova," I said softly, and placed my hand on his shoulder. "It's not like anyone knows, or will ever know."

"Don't touch me."

My eyelids dropped, and I glared at him. Anger simmered inside me, mounting to the top and ready to explode. He acted as if we had gotten caught. The whole virgin thing really wasn't a big deal to me, so I didn't understand why he was so affected by the fact he was my first. I wish he'd just drop it.

"You're overreacting, and to put all the blame on me is absolute bullshit," I fought back. "It takes two to tango. I didn't force you to do anything you didn't want."

The look he pinned me with when he spun around should've scared me, but it didn't. His piercing green eyes were so vibrant and the veins in his neck strained. Deep down, I loved seeing him like this. He was rage and fury rolled into one beautiful package.

"You pursued me! And I let you!" He roared, his eyes racking a heated gaze down my body. His Russian accent was thicker when he was angry.

"I pursued you?" I repeated flatly. "Maybe I did, maybe I didn't. But in the end, it's all the same. You let me get close to you. You opened up to me and let me inside your world," I said, slowly stepping toward him. "You wanted me. And you knew you couldn't touch me, yet you did. You got off on it. Have you ever heard of reverse psychology?" He pulled back in horror but I kept going. "Why didn't you push me away? It's not like you can't overpower me, stop me."

"Adrianna. You are missing the point. It is not about overpowering. It is about removing myself from the situation."

And he was missing my point so I continued advancing on him. I wasn't sure where this courage was coming from, but I went with it.

"We both know you're way stronger than I am and could easily have put an end to anything before it started."

"Adrianna," he warned, a tick starting in his jaw.

"Acknowledge it wasn't just me."

"No," he growled.

"Do it," I whispered, staring up at him. Our chests were so close that if I took a deep breath my boobs would touch him. And I wanted to do it to tempt him and prove him wrong.

"Step back. Now."

"Make me."

CHAPTER 61

Glossy, heavy lidded eyes stared down at me.

I was trying to stay strong, but the look he gave me sent a sensation throughout my entire body. Knowing he liked being told no, and knowing he liked when I fought him, only pushed my drive. It sent another thrill through me. His needs and wants turned me on and I embraced this side he was bringing out in me.

Gripping his wrist, I brought it around to cup my butt. I knew he was lying, he damn well knew he was, and I hated that. His fingers dug into my flesh for a split second before he moved in a blurring speed. He had me pinned to the wall with both of my wrists securely locked behind my back and him pressing into me. My heart skipped into my throat, my eyes went wide, staring into the depths of his.

"Stop fucking with me," he whispered thickly against my neck. "Why are you doing this?"

"To prove it wasn't all me...and I don't want to stop what's between us."

"You are fucking crazy, you know that? You are not right in the head."

"Maybe I am a little crazy in the head, but I think you like it," I whispered. His erection was a hard angle on my lower stomach as I stood on my tiptoes, pushing my hips into him. I couldn't help it, I needed to feel him lower. Wanted to feel him lower.

This was past just physical attraction.

This was animalistic.

And highly forbidden, which just made it that much better

See how easy it was for you to get my hand off you? You have such a tight grip on my wrists there's no way I could've forced anything on you. Now admit it wasn't just me."

His whole body was hard against mine, his breathing ragged. I was pushing him, teasing him…and I liked it. He was bubbling under my fingertips, and for some unknown reason, I wanted to see him snap.

Dragging my foot up the back of his leg, I hooked it around his hip and used my stomach and inner thigh to lift myself to his level, wrapping my other leg around his hip and climbed up his body. I put all that conditioning to good use. I needed to communicate my feelings with my eyes more so than my words since they weren't getting across. But the moment we were eye level with each other, I could feel his lust, his inner turmoil, his utter confusion with right and wrong, and his hunger for more.

"You can't, can you? Admitting it is immoral, and the immoral and wrongness of it makes it that much hotter. But that's not really why it feels so good, is it?" I breathed against his lips, our eyes locked in a gaze so strong neither one of us could break it. Our chests panted against each other, the air thick with tension. My wrists hurt from him squeezing so tightly, but I let him do it without complaint.

"We work well together, Kova," I whispered. "There's an attraction that's more than just chemistry between us."

I was breaking his resolve, I could feel it. This sensual prowess Kova unleashed inside me was untamed and new. My tongue slipped out and traced his lips. He began panting, his erection straining hard against me and the pressure caused my hips to undulate against his. Kova groaned, it was a deep and guttural sound that brought me chills.

"Let go," I pushed.

He didn't move.

He couldn't. Not because I was forcing him, but because he wanted to be here and knew he shouldn't.

Carefully, he maneuvered my wrists to one hand and used the other hand to grip my jaw. We were so close we breathed each other in.

"You are right. I do want you, even right now when you are literally doing everything in your power to seduce me, I want to fuck you senseless. But what you do not see is after this newfound knowledge, I never will again," he said deathly low.

Kova purposely rubbed against me, his cock rock hard and hitting my clit caused little moans to escape my throat. "Starting tomorrow there will be no physical contact unless it is during training. Try it and there will be repercussions. You do not look at me and I will not look at you unless it is gym related. We are through. In fact, I am removing myself as your coach."

He picked up his pace and I could feel an orgasm rising inside of me. The roles had been switched and he was tempting me and pushing me now. I tried to wiggle my arms free, but he smirked and didn't allow it. He had me locked tight and the glimmer in his eyes told me he loved it.

I fought his hold for the sheer purpose of proving my point. But I found being contained brought me higher and higher. I liked the power struggle...His touch seared my skin and I was as hot as an inferno ready to burst.

Locking my legs tighter, I said, "Starting tomorrow...then why are you touching me like this?" I reached for his mouth with mine, but he pulled back quickly, still gripping my jaw. "Why are you still here?" I paused, and then stated, "Unless you really want to fuck." I smiled wickedly. "Is Katja not available to you right now?"

He gave me a scalding glare. If looks could kill.

"Keep going," I sighed, my eyes rolling shut. I was going to have an orgasm any second, and I began thrusting my hips back and forth, grinding on him. He met my pace. My back arched, my nipples straining through my cami as his dick rubbed against my pussy faster and faster. "Right there..."

Kova let go of my jaw and punched the wall so hard with his fist that it startled me. My eyes shot open. His were fierce, pushed past the brink of sanity. Quickly, he let go of my wrists and disengaged my ankles from around his back, forcing me to stand. Keeping his eyes trained on mine, my lips parted when I heard his belt unbuckle and his zipper go down. I reached to help him, but he slapped my hand away. His jeans slid down his muscular thighs, pooling at his feet. With both hands, he ripped off my boy short panties, gripped my hips and lifted me up so my legs circled his waist once again. With one of his hands holding both of my wrists behind my back, he shoved me forcefully against the wall and reached between us to palm his cock, his hand grazing my swollen lips. My body became aware and anxious for his next move. Kova swallowed hard before he positioned himself at my entrance and thrusted in so fast and so hard my back bowed and I squeezed my eyes shut from the force. Fuck, that hurt. He stretched me wide and I squeezed around him, only intensifying the sting. He dropped his head to the curve of my neck and inhaled. "Baby," he murmured over and over and I melted. "Oh, fuck, yes." The groan that came from the back of his throat was filled with conflict, though incredibly sexy. My thighs squeezed his hips from the rough intrusion. Thank goodness I was soaking wet, otherwise this would've felt like I was being ripped apart.

"Is this what you want? To be fucked hard?" He pushed in and out, gripping my hips in a bruising manner and not giving me a second to breathe. I gasped loudly.

"Your body cannot handle me at this rate, Adrianna. I will break you. I am not even in all the way, I have never been in all the way."

"But your girlfriend can? Katja can take all of you like this?" I taunted, and moaned really loud from the intense pleasure he filled me with. I knew there were problems between them and I wanted to use them to my power. I wanted him to tell me no, that she couldn't.

Kova gnashed his teeth together. "Do not mention her right now."

I had to bring her up because she was the one he went home to every night. And deep down, hidden inside, I was jealous of her relationship with him. I wanted what she had.

"Do everything to me you would her. Don't hold back." The back of my head smacked the wall, but I was too lost in the moment to feel it.

"I am not going to think about Katja while I am inside of you."

Kova pushed in deeper at the mention of her name. I clenched around him, growing more aroused from it. Provoking him was surprisingly euphoric and I reveled in satisfaction. I jerked on my arms, trying to free my wrists, but his hold only grew stronger and his erection became harder inside of me.

Kova thrusted back in and held it. I squeezed my inner walls by reflex. "Breathe," he ordered huskily. "Just, breathe." His thumb dug into my hips, forcing me down and I pulsated around him, stretching to accommodate his width.

"This is me deep inside of you just like you begged for. Every inch. You have never had every inch until now." Kova ran his tongue along my neck, leaving a wet trail, nipping my heated flesh. I shivered in his possessive hold. "Can you handle it?"

I almost wanted to say no from being stretched so wide, but I didn't. So I said, "More."

"Such a bad girl. I love it." He countered teasingly, moving his hips harder. The glimmer in his eyes flitted across my skin. I felt a slight tightness but focused on the pleasure instead of the pain.

"You should not want this. *I* should not want this," he said roughly, and kissed me aggressively, showing me who's in charge. I moaned into his mouth, my body ready to let go. "But I do, God, do I ever," he said honestly.

"Oh, God, I'm gonna come." Three more pumps and I was having the most intense orgasm I'd ever had. I yelled out, but Kova stifled my screams with his tongue in my mouth, continuing to push in deep and then revert out, repeating the motion. I sucked on his tongue, fighting the hold on my wrists as the power of the orgasm swept through my body. I never wanted this high to end.

Breathing heavily, I could barely catch the rhythm of my heartbeat when Kova stood tall, hugging me to him. He stepped out of his jeans and then carried me out of the kitchen. I'd forgotten he still had them on. Kova let go of my arms and I wrapped them around his shoulders, resting my head on his chest and inhaling his dark scent. I shivered, my body stretched to the limit but loving the overly full feeling. Cool air kissed my bare skin and it was refreshing against Kova's heated body.

I assumed we were going to my bedroom, but he stopped at the couch and unwound my legs from around his waist. He carefully set me down next to the arm rest and I looked confusingly at his hips. His erection was glistening with my orgasm and I noticed he didn't finish. Glancing up, his deep green eyes peered down at me and his grin was so incredibly sexy it made my heart speed up.

With his hand in my hair, he pulled my head toward him.

"Suck it."

I paused.

"I don't know how," I said softly. It was true, I had no idea how to. Kova lowered his eyelids, an impish smirk formed on his face.

"It is simple. Open your pretty little mouth, roll your lips over your teeth, and suck."

CHAPTER 62

ounded easy enough.

If I could do a double layout on floor, I could do this.

Tentatively, I shifted to my knees, feeling the microfiber softness beneath me and leaned over. My lips parted as I stared at the tip of his penis. Kova moaned quietly. With his hand on the back of my head, he guided me toward him, but he didn't push. There was nothing forceful about it, which I appreciated. I was nervous, but I'd be lying to myself if I said I wasn't eager to see his reaction and what it would feel like.

My tongue slipped out and licked the tip. I wasn't expecting him to be salty and made an effort to hide the dislike on my face. Kova's stomach flexed, his abs hardening as I looked up at him for approval. I reached out and skimmed his pelvis, feeling the rigid muscles and the V on his hips as I took more into my mouth.

Kova groaned. "Wrap your tongue around me like you are sucking on a lollipop."

I stopped and laughed. "A blow pop?"

A deep chuckle came from him. "Yes." I pretended he was a lollipop and astonishingly it worked. His hips moved forward and he held the back of my head to him. "If you want to do what Katja does, you are going to have to suck harder. She loves sucking my cock."

My nose flared and I almost bit down on his cock. That just got my blood roaring. His dick twitched and I clenched my thighs shut. Kova was goading me, I knew he was, and I didn't care because somewhere hidden deep inside me I found joy and satisfaction in it. I picked up the speed and used my tongue, trying to take as much as I could into my mouth. It wasn't easy and my jaw began to ache. Kova moaned when his dick hit the back of my throat and I nearly gagged.

"You have to open the back of your throat."

I didn't even know what opening the back of my throat meant. I didn't want him to know I was clueless, so I nodded. Anytime he thrust his hips, he hit the back of my throat. To avoid him going any deeper, I wrapped my fingers around the base of his penis and held on as I did more of the guiding than him. His arm dropped from my head and I looked up. Kova's head was tipped back, pleasure rocking through him. I smiled to myself. Guess I was doing it right after all. I sucked harder, focusing on the tip.

"Fuck," he said huskily when my tongue wrapped around his length and tugged. My cheeks hollowed. Kova looked down, our eyes locked and something in my heart shifted. It was important to me he enjoy what I was doing to him, just as I had.

His gaze was lethal, protective almost, as if I was the only thing that mattered in his world. Forgotten were moments of uncertainty and inexperience. All I had to do was gauge his reaction and I knew I was doing it right.

He cupped my jaw, his fingers splaying on my neck and into my hair as we both held each other in place with just a look. Our eye contact never broke and his speed picked up. His hips pumped back and forth, the vein in his neck coiling into his shirt twitched. Abruptly, he pushed me away and I fell back onto the plush couch.

Wiping my mouth with the back of my hand, I asked, "Did I do something wrong?"

Kova grunted, holding himself. "No, quite the opposite actually."

A huge smile moved across my face, but then I realized he still didn't orgasm. "But you didn't finish."

"That is because I am not done with you." My eyes tracked him as he took two steps and moved to the end of the couch. He wrapped a strong arm around my waist and hoisted me up. Spinning me around, he bent me over as if I weighed no more than a feather. My knees landed on the armrest and my hands on the couch cushion. Without a second to catch my breath, he took me from behind. It was a different angle, and I wasn't expecting it when he thrusted in. A slight sharpness shot through me and I grunted in pain. I was still tender from the orgasm and I moved to sit up, but he pushed my back down.

"Stay."

I wasn't sure why, but hearing him demand I stayed down caused a flood of wetness between my thighs.

"You asked for it, you are going to get what she gets. Do not say her fucking name again."

Satisfied, I grinned. "Good."

Kova's fingers slipped under my cami, his nails grazed my skin and I shivered. He gave a good tug and ripped my cami off, throwing it to the ground in pieces. He aggressively palmed my breasts and squeezed before pinching my nipples. My back arched and my arms gave out, bending at the elbows. Kova's fingers tightened on my hips as he slid slowly back and forth into me, creating a maelstrom of pleasure. It wasn't hurried or rushed. It was slow and steady—sublime. The only sound was the suction of our conjoined bodies as he pulled out and slid in, holding it for a split second. Just enough time for my clit to throb and greedily beg for more.

"Ahhhh..."

"Tell me you like this, tell me how much you want me to fuck you."

"Yes, you know I do," rolled off my lips. I did, I liked it a lot. Somehow, I found my inner strength. My hips took over and started rocking back into him, meeting him for each thrust. This angle was deeper and slightly painful, but the pain turned to pleasure and the intense feeling streaming through my blood was like a soaring high I never wanted to come down from. A sensation so incredibly powerful I bet nothing could top it.

"Oh, my God." Another orgasm was quickly rising.

But then Kova pulled out before I could find that earth shattering release I knew he could give me. I looked over my shoulder ready to spout off what the hell he was doing when he tapped the inside of my thigh for me to spread my legs wider. He reached over and pushed my head down into the couch, then with a flick of his wrist, he rotated my hips up and back so they were angled high. Of the times Kova and I had been together, this was the most exposed I'd ever been to him. Under normal circumstances, I might have objected to this position due to my vulnerability, but I was in such a daze and lost in his touch, I willingly gave myself to him. No, was never a thought in my mind.

Kova knelt down between my legs and spread my pussy open and ran his tongue along my plump lips. I moaned, my hips arching back even more as my hands gripped as much fabric from the couch as possible. He focused on my clit, sucking and flicking it with his tongue while his finger pressed on my puckered little hole. Tears formed in my eyes from the sheer pleasure that took over my body. I was floating on another planet. I was so sensitive I nearly bucked into his face at the gentleness.

I tried to move but he just gripped me tighter, his fingers digging into me.

"Kova...I...I'm going to..." I couldn't get the thought out before an orgasm racked through me for the second time. Stars clouded my vision and I moaned so loud, rolling my eyes shut while he just kept sucking and sucking, his tongue flicked my sex like he was on a mission. Nothing in the world compared to this moment and his wicked tongue. Sweat dampened my skin, my entire body was on fire. Heat zipped down my spine, blood flushed my cheeks and I was free falling as pleasure tore through me.

I was done. Spent. Exhausted.

My hips melted, no longer able to hold my weight. My knees slipped along the arm of the couch. When the orgasm faded, Kova stood and without hesitation, he jacked my hips back up and drove all the way in.

"Fuck, that hurt."

My face pressed into the couch cushion. Tears prickled the back of my eyes but I wouldn't let them fall. My fingers dug into the cushion while Kova's hand flattened my lower back, arching my hips up. My legs quivered and struggled to hold still.

"I am not done with you. I do not think I could ever be done..." If it was even possible, the thrusts got deeper. At this point, I wasn't going to be able to walk tomorrow.

Kova drove in so hard and fast his balls hit my tender clit. I was sweating—my entire body was a blaze of heat. I almost wanted this to be over.

"You wanted it. You pushed me until my cock was so hard it ached. All I could think of was getting inside of your tight pussy. I am a man with only one focus when that happens."

Kova reached for me and pulled me up so my back was to his chest. My arms reached up and wound his neck from behind. Kova's soft spoken words nuzzled the curve of my neck as he whispered in Russian. I wished to God I knew what he was saying. My legs trembled and he used his strength to hold me upright.

Thankfully, Kova sensed how weak I'd become. I exhaled a sigh of relief when he supported me with his toned arms by wrapping one around my small hips. My head tilted back onto his shoulder when he rolled my nipple between his fingers, his thrusts becoming slower.

"How are you still going? I must not be good if I can't make you come."

His stubble nuzzled my jaw, adding pleasure to the sex, and I shuddered in his embrace. Whispering near my mouth, he said, "I am a man, Ria, not some little boy who cannot last more than a minute. Remember that. I fuck all night long, not three minutes."

I swallowed hard. After tonight, I had no doubt he could.

"Lean over the back of the couch."

I almost whimpered, but did as he demanded. I didn't want to leave the solace of his arms. His thrusts deepened. Long, hard, but slow strokes, like he was trying to feel every inch of me. Kova was close to reaching his pinnacle, I could tell by the frantic way he gripped me and the sexy sounds coming from his throat. I'd have to wear shorts in the gym tomorrow for sure, otherwise his fingerprints would show.

He reached under, and instead of rubbing my clit, he pressed my swollen lips together causing my head to fly back in bliss.

"Right there...that is what I want to feel," he groaned, hitting a new, deeper spot inside, like he had a special spot he wanted to reach.

"Keep that position, I know you can."

"I'll try."

"Not try," he rebutted. "You will do it."

A shiver rolled down my spine and my thighs quivered. Sweet Jesus Mother Mary.

He rubbed my lips faster, increasing the pressure and friction on my clit at the same time. The intense pressure shot straight through me, causing the walls of my sex to spasm, tightening around him.

"Yes, *malysh*, just like that," he mumbled in approval. His hand rubbed warm circles on my back, like he was enjoying this as much as I was, if not more. "I love it, do not stop." Just as my release made its way through my body, Kova removed his hand and slapped my ass cheek so hard that I came before I could even process what happened.

"Omigod." I almost choked. "Yes...More..."

"Ria...just like that," he smacked my ass once more, the orgasm continued to sweep through me at breakneck speed. A burst of electricity exploded from within and I clenched around him. The slapping caught me by surprise and I was a bit confused by how much I enjoyed it. I almost wished he'd do it again.

One last thrust, and Kova squeezed my hips tight as he pulsed inside of me. I was sure I'd have bruises tomorrow. He pushed all the way in and grunted, his hips doing small, slow thrusts as he filled me. He came hard, the warm fluid leaking out and down my inner thigh. Kova's loud moan caused my body to shudder from the remnants of my release. I was coated with him and relished in this moment of unyielding bliss. I loved it. Every minute, every thrust, every touch.

I could easily become addicted to this kind of sex. The tension in the room settled down, and all that was left was heavy panting and the scent of sex lingering in the air.

Kova withdrew and walked to the bathroom, but not before I felt his palm smooth tenderly down my reddened cheek and a gentle kiss was pressed to my spine. I waited until he was out of sight to rollover onto the couch cushion. Reaching higher, I grabbed my ripped cami he threw earlier and covered my chest. I was too exhausted to actually find a new one to put back on just yet.

A few moments later, the bathroom door opened and Kova walked out. My brows furrowed and my lips formed a thin, tight line. Seeing as his release was still on my thigh, I thought he was coming out to clean me up like last time and then spend time with me before he left. Instead, he was completely dressed and he wore a scowl on his beautiful face as he stood before me. His eyes raked down my body, but unlike the heat they usually held, they were completely deflated and it crushed my heart.

A resigned sigh escaped him. Running a hand through his hair, he dropped a damp rag on my leg. I flinched.

"That is what you wanted, right? A good fuck?" When I didn't answer, he said, "Was it as good for you as it was for me?"

And then he stalked off and was out the door like nothing had ever happened.

CHAPTER 63

My alarm blared annoyingly at 5:30 am and I felt like I'd just fallen asleep.

The last thing I wanted was to leave the warmth of my cozy bed. I'd give anything to skip practice today, but I knew I couldn't.

With only three hours of sleep, I was tempted to feign a serious illness just to be admitted to the hospital so I could sleep some more.

Though, I was fairly certain getting a "good fuck" by a Russian dick wasn't a serious illness.

I was sleep deprived for a reason. Reality set in and my stomach flipped in anticipation, making me feel queasy. Kova had treated me like garbage last night. I knew seeing him would be awkward after the night's episode, but I was upset over how callous he'd been. I was still new to all of this and wasn't sure how to process everything. I liked it, I liked the bite of pain, but it hurt at times.

Maybe taunting him hadn't been such a good idea, and maybe withholding my virginity from him wasn't the brightest thing to do, because the more I thought about it, the more wrong it felt. Guilt ate at me. Kova felt lied to and that didn't sit well with me. He was upset because I had kept that little nugget of info to myself, but it really wasn't any of his business. Yet, in the end, I wouldn't change a thing.

Yawning, I stretched my arms above my head before rolling over into my pillow and snuggling up to it. My eyes were as dry as the Sahara Desert. The last time I looked at the clock, it was a little after one. I was beyond exhausted, my body ached all over. I wanted more than anything to go back to sleep, but that wasn't happening anytime soon.

My stupid alarm went off again, and this time I unenthusiastically got out of bed. Soreness resonated between my thighs and I winced.

Fuck, it hurt. I wasn't expecting a sharp sting, like an enormous paper cut down there, but it's exactly what it felt like.

A shower was a must. I was too tired to just head to the gym like I normally did. I needed to wake up.

Grabbing a leo, a sports bra, and some sweatpants, I headed into the bathroom and turned on the shower. While I waited for the water to heat, my bladder made itself known like it was about to explode.

Sighing as if it was an inconvenience to pee, I sat down on the cold toilet to relieve myself only to stop and gasp in pain. Jesus Christ! I tried to pee again by only letting a little out, but my whole body tightened in agony from the sting. It hurt too much to go.

Kova must've torn me up pretty good last night.

Steam filled my bathroom and there I was, leaning over my legs with my arms wrapped around my stomach, holding my breath to the point where my lungs hurt. I could only take so much, so I only let half out.

I'd try again later. Even wiping hurt, so I only dabbed.

I took a fast shower, washing my hair and shaving my legs in record time, careful not to let soap slip to my sex. I once cut my lip down there while shaving. It was a small slice and when soap touched it, it burned like a bitch.

Turning the shower off, I grabbed a towel and stepped out. I wiped the foggy mirror down and then dried myself off quickly. As I did, my brows angled in confusion at the reflection. Standing up, I pivoted around and looked in the mirror so I could see my entire waist and backside. My jaw dropped at what stared back at me.

Kova's fingerprints covered my flesh in tiny little black and blue marks. From the tops of my thighs, to my hips, and the back of my legs. They were everywhere. I could connect the dots if I wanted to. It was hard not to notice them. Bringing my foot up and propping it on the ledge of the counter, I bent over and looked down at my pussy.

My skin was a rosy pink and swollen. I grimaced. I looked closely, moving my flesh around, but I couldn't see anything with the naked eye. Grabbing a small mirror, I placed it between my legs to get a better look. Examining as close as I could get, I noticed a tiny little red mark. I ran my index finger gently over it and I flinched. Kova tore me, which would explain why it hurt to pee. I guess he wasn't lying when he said he hadn't given me everything the first time. He sure had this time.

After I finished dressing, I grabbed an extra pair of gym shorts to cover up any marks and stuffed them into my bag. Typically, I didn't wear shorts unless it was that time of the month for me, though many gymnasts opted to.

I checked the clock and realized I was running behind. Coach was going to kill me. I grabbed a granola bar, approved by my lovely mother of course, and my schoolbooks before dashing out of my condo. It was Monday, which meant I had tutoring, lunch, and then more training later. Plus, therapy on my calf.

Luckily, World Cup was only about ten minutes away. I walked into the gym at five thirty, and all three coaches were already yelling.

It was going to be a long day.

Nearly four hours later, and practice hadn't been easy. Straight up—my vagina hurt. Any kind of split jump on the beam felt like I was ripping in two, and it wasn't like I could choose not to do them, I had to. Not to mention, I was mentally and physically exhausted—it was all the effort I could muster to keep my eyes open, let alone also have to do my routines.

Today, I realized just how many skills I had with my legs spread wide open.

Then came the Tsavdaridou, a round-off back handspring with a full twist to swing down. Those hadn't been pleasant either. As a matter of fact, nothing had been pleasant this morning. The skills terrified me today, and they never had before, but knowing I was going to come down with my legs opened and land with the beam braced between them, I hated it.

For once in my life, I wanted to perfect my turns so I wouldn't aggravate my Achilles.

I'd been extra careful to make sure I didn't straddle the beam as much as I could. I fell a few times, but I was able to catch myself. Dear God, I don't know if I could've handled that splitting pain too. Luckily, beam had passed quickly and now I was on vault.

The urge to pee hit like a ton of bricks. I hadn't gone since this morning because of the stinging pain and feared it would happen again, but now I couldn't hold it any longer. I had to go. If I did one more turn on vault, I was going to burst. And peeing on the vault was not a good look.

I wondered if I could slap some Vaseline on the tears. I figured it would help with peeing and my jumps, but then I also wondered what if I got Vaseline inside. I shuddered at the thought. Never mind. I couldn't take the chance. I'd just have to deal.

To top off my lovely morning, Kova hadn't looked my way once. Madeline had worked with me the entire time and it seemed like no matter where I was in the gym, he was on the opposite side of me. Almost as if he was intentionally keeping us as far apart as possible. Maybe he'd gone through and implemented Madeline as my coach now and not him. I prayed he didn't.

I knew I needed to stay focused on my training, but I couldn't help wonder what he was thinking about, if he was thinking about the night before at all. It was almost as if I wasn't even there. I hated the feeling, like I was invisible and I didn't matter.

I sighed inwardly.

Stepping into the bathroom, I locked the door and stripped out of my leo. This was the one part of gymnastics I detested—being sweaty and having to remove the one piece. It was like peeling off soaking wet, skinny jeans.

Taking a deep breath, I closed my eyes and prayed I could pee without it hurting. I bared down, tightened my insides and only let a trickle out...and paused. Releasing an audible sigh, I let go again only to feel the burning sensation come back full force. My hand slammed against the wall and I leaned against it for support. But I didn't let it all out. It just wasn't achievable. The urine burned the shit out of me!

That was it, all I could manage. I carefully wiped, pulled up my leo and washed my hands. I had one more hour until I broke for lunch and tutoring, then it was back to training for four more hours. After therapy when I got home, I'd soak in the bath.

I had this. I just needed to give myself a pep talk first.

Walking back into the gym, I immediately scanned for Kova. It was more out of habit and addiction than a conscious thought. I craved his glaring eyes and fierce words. They drove me to be better, stronger. To prove myself.

When we finally locked eyes, he didn't break my gaze. His posture was strict, his arms firmly crossed against his taut chest. I walked blindly, unable to focus on my surroundings. He tried to tell me something with his eyes, but I wasn't sure what. All I knew was he was staring like he couldn't stand the sight of me and it hurt.

"Watch out!"

I flinched and put my hands up, ducking.

"Jesus, Big Red. We all know Coach Kova is hot, but pay attention. Don't make it so obvious you're gawking at him. God..."

I closed my eyes and counted to five. Reagan and her stupid redhead comments. I would've corrected her, but I wasn't in the mood. I nearly walked into her dismount, which could've seriously hurt both of us. But she was right, I needed to pay attention.

I didn't apologize, I just ignored her and headed back to vault while she continued on beam.

"You okay?" Hayden asked, concerned. His observant eyes made me edgy.

Or maybe I was just being paranoid.

Nodding, I smiled sweetly and put on a happy face. "Yeah, I'm just exhausted."

Grabbing some chalk for the vault, I rubbed some on my feet, adding a little to my thighs when Hayden walked away. I clapped my hands to remove the excess powder and could taste it in my mouth.

I moved to stand behind the white line and took a deep breath when Kova turned to look at me. He nodded his head, gesturing for me to go. Madeline clapped her hands and yelled, "Get moving, Adrianna. I don't have all day!"

Rising up on my tiptoes, I leaned forward and took off running. I pumped my legs as fast as I could and only focused on the vault. My calf hurt just a bit, but I blocked it out. Everything else faded away and I forgot all the issues in my life as I zoomed in on the apparatus and felt the adrenaline hit me hard.

God, I loved this feeling. My racing heart, burning muscles. The anticipation.

Zoning in on only the springboard, I did a round-off onto it and arched into a back handspring. I popped my shoulders off the vault into a two and a half twist to complete an Amanar. I took a few steps back on my landing and fell.

Fuck my life.

Adding the half twist created a blind landing, so there was no spotting the floor. I had to wish on a prayer I would land it correctly. I could practice it a million and one times, land it at every practice, but it only took a split second where I didn't crank high enough, or my legs were bent, my chest was too low, anything to not land it at competition.

In gymnastics, anything was possible. And considering I was working on the hardest vault for women, that should say something.

Standing up, I heard Madeline sigh loudly. "I'm trying, I really am," I broke in before she could say anything.

She looked at me with pity. "I know you are. Let's do it again."

"Adrianna. Keep your legs straight in the flight, chest up," Kova chimed in, looking at me intently.

"He's right," Madeline acknowledged. "Your legs are sloppy and bent. I noticed your feet were crossed too, which is a big no, Adrianna. Try and set your twist just a tad higher. You need something that will give you points and move you up in the standings, not set you back."

I nodded.

"Is your calf bothering you?" she asked with concern.

"No." I could've lied and said yes, which would be the reason for my shitty landing, but I didn't.

Nothing was worse than being told you couldn't do something after trying so hard to achieve it. Swallowing back my frustration, I stared at the vault and pictured my landing perfectly. I could do this, I told myself. I'd done it before, I just needed to visualize it and be confident in my abilities.

"You got this, Aid," Hayden whispered, tightening his wrist brace with a nod. I smiled at him, my face softening.

Another deep breath, and I took off. Round-off, back handspring onto the vault, popped off and I reached to twist. I mentally noted my legs and straightened them, but it was too late at that point. I opened my arms to balance my landing, but I already knew I was leaning too far back and my hips were too low. It was a feeling inside that was unexplainable, but I knew my body and knew I wasn't going to stick it.

Trying to save it was pointless. I was literally in a seated position and hit the floor just like that, stumbling backwards and falling on the blue mat. Tears welled in my eyes as pain suddenly throbbed viciously through my back. Massaging my side, I felt like crying from being so frustrated and not hitting my marks. Self-doubt was beating me up today and I began to wonder if I was pushing too far.

Madeline sighed. "Go to tutoring and I'll see you later."

"Can I try one more time?"

Madeline nodded, then grabbed a mat to stand on. It was the shape of a box and high, leveled with the vault so she could spot me.

Dear God, please let me land this.

Swallowing, I began running, my feet pounded into the ground. I moved into the entry, and then sprang off the vault. Madeline's hands helped pop the back of my shoulders, lifting me higher in the air to help me set my element. I started rotating, cranking the twist as hard as I could muster to land properly. And by some miracle, I landed—only for another shot of pain to soar through my back, but I sucked it up. Albeit I landed sloppy, my feet hit the floor, not my butt, and that was all that mattered right now. A loud sigh burst from my lips and I closed my eyes in satisfaction, hiding my back pain.

"Again," Madeline said.

I did it again with her help and landed. Yes! Land was a word I used lightly, but the fact that I was standing upright was what motivated me and gave me that little push to keep going.

After three more tries, she pulled the mat away for me to do it on my own. Nerves wracked me hard and I was suddenly worried I wouldn't hit it again. It was an irrational fear that coursed through me, I knew it, but it came with the territory. My heart split between being in my throat and stomach. All eyes were on me. Fear and nerves were part of a gymnast's genetic makeup.

But so was winning.

I had this...I got this...visualize...

Adrenaline pumped through my veins fast as I ran toward the leather apparatus, but apprehension and nerves dominated when I hit the spring board. Fire shot through my back and I panicked in the middle of my rotation and only pulled a full. It was a clean landing, but Madeline glared at me.

Shit.

"You," she said between clenched teeth, and pointed at me, "get your butt back over there and do the Amanar. Now."

My stomach dropped. All I could do was nod and start walking. I didn't have much of a choice.

The urge to pee never really went away, and a wave of pain hit my screaming bladder. It was only ten in the morning, yet this day was going to shit fast. Very little sleep, a burning vagina, and now a raging coach.

And I only had myself to blame.

I did the vault once more and added the stupid twist, but without her push, I barely landed on the tips of my toes. My stomach clenched tight and I gave up and jumped to the side, my calf burning slightly.

Before I could speak, Madeline pointed toward the exit and said, "Go. Come back after tutoring. Maybe you'll be better after you've had a break."

"Can I try it once more?"

"No," she heaved a sigh. "Come back later and we'll work on it again."

My shoulders dropped in defeat. Turning around, I stared at the ground to avoid the gawking stares while I made my way to the locker room. I was beyond embarrassed with my workout and didn't want to see the judgmental look in my peers' eyes.

"Hey Aid," Hayden called out across the gym. I slowly raised my eyes, afraid to be greeted with a look of pity. Surprisingly, I saw encouragement in his eyes as he jogged over to me.

"Give me twenty and I'll be done. We'll ride to tutoring together."

I smiled kindly. After the shit storm morning I had, Hayden's bulldoze through life mentality was exactly what I needed.

Opening my locker, I pulled out my duffle bag and dropped it to the floor, shuffling around for my clothes. I was so upset with myself and wanted to cry. I was better than this, and I let things get in the way of training. I needed to be stronger and overcome my fears, but it was easier said than done. I was training in a sport that could literally paralyze me in one split second by not getting enough air in rotation or landing wrong. And I wasn't at one hundred percent because of my leg. My landings were shit today. If my timing wasn't absolutely perfect, the repercussions could be devastating. There was a reason gymnastics was considered one of the most dangerous sports. It was a risk to take, but my heart was all in. Even with days when I was at my worst, I would never give up.

Changing out of my leotard, I noticed little droplets of blood. Shit. It was a good thing I carried extra leos with me. I dressed quickly then shoved my bag back into the locker and slammed it shut as hard as I could muster. I should've done some stretching to cool my muscles, but I didn't even care to.

Walking into one of the physical therapy rooms, I laid on the blue, plastic table and waited for Hayden. I looked forward to hanging out with him. Throwing an arm over my face, I closed my eyes, thinking about my vault.

"Adrianna...Adrianna, wake up."

Opening my eyes, I was disoriented for a moment and confused at where I was. "H-Hayden?" My voice cracked. Jesus. It felt like I'd been asleep for hours.

He smiled down at me. "Come on, Sleeping Beauty. We've got tutoring."

I groaned. "Did you have to kiss me to wake me up because I feel like I could sleep forever."

His cheeks deepened in color. "I was about to."

"Can I just skip and go home and sleep?" Hayden reached his hand out to help me sit up. I yawned and took it.

"Rough night?"

"If you only knew."

"You look like shit."

A smile tipped my lips. "Be still my heart," I responded flippantly.

"Hey, I just call it like it is."

"I can obviously tell."

We stepped out of the locker room and made our way to the lobby. My brows cinched together when I heard Kova's voice in the distance. The closer we got, the louder it became, and my heart stopped at the soft tone in his voice.

"Hey, what are you doing here?"

I tried not to hold my breath as I listened to the response that met my ears.

"I came to surprise you for lunch." I knew that voice. Katja had one of the most singsong voices I'd ever heard, even with the thick Russian accent that accompanied it.

"You know I keep a schedule, Kat. You should have called me first."

As we rounded the corner, he had her pulled in for a kiss. His fingers were threaded through her chestnut hair in a sensual, possessive lip lock. My stomach dropped at the sight. He never kissed me like that. He never looked at me with love in his eyes. He never embraced me so tenderly.

"What was that for?" she asked breathlessly as they pulled apart.

He tensed and irritably bit out, "Why do I need a reason to kiss you? Can I not kiss you when I want?"

"You do not," she responded with flushed cheeks. "You know you can anytime." She looked at him with hearts in her eyes. "I love you."

I paled at her display of love, my stomach rolled in waves. Hayden was completely blasé to their affection, and luckily completely oblivious to my gut wrenching reaction, as he continued walking to the front door. It took all the strength I had to make my feet continue to move when all I really wanted to do was flop down on the floor and have a pity party.

I didn't want it to bother me, but it did. Watching them in their private moment told me everything I needed to know, and showed me everything I would never have.

With Hayden's keys jangling in his hand, they both turned their heads in our direction. Katja's chin dipped, embarrassment coloring her cheeks.

Hayden held the door open and I brushed against him walking outside. My eyes locked with Katja and then Kova, who held my gaze until I left.

"You okay?" Hayden asked at the sound of my expelled breath as the door shut behind us.

"What?" I glanced at his face distractedly, my mind totally not wanting to function today. I shook myself out of it. "Yeah, I'm just worn out is all. I'm ready for this day to be over."

"You realize it's not even noon yet, right?"

"Don't remind me."

We hopped into Hayden's car and he started the ignition, draping a strong arm over the top of my seat. As he peered over his shoulder to back out, he looked at me and smiled with his warm blue eyes.

"Don't sweat it. We all have off days."

"Off days? I sucked! Badly! I looked like an amateur!"

He chuckled over my exaggerated sigh. "You totally did."

I reached over and punched him. "You don't have to state the obvious!"

"Would you rather I lie?"

"No."

"Hey." He put a finger under my chin at the red light. "Keep your head up. It's just a bad morning practice, not a bad life. This afternoon will be better."

I smiled softly at him. "I hope so. I feel like I'm the only one having bad practices lately."

"It happens sometimes. You'll get through it."

"I know...it just sucks. Regina seems to thrive on my mistakes."

He gave me a perplexed look. "Regina?"

"Reagan, I mean. Have you ever seen *Mean Girls*? She's the Regina George of gymnastics. Loves to see people fail and shit. Like she gets off on it."

"Never heard of it, but why do I have a feeling you're right? Maybe one night we'll watch it together," he said, shifting into another gear.

I pursed my lips together. "You want to watch *Mean Girls*?"

He shrugged, pulling into the library. "Why not?"

"I don't know...because it's a chick flick?"

"So? We'll get some pizza and soda, pig out, and watch a movie one night."

I sighed happily. That sounded like such a great idea.

"I can't remember the last time I turned the television on. Our schedules are so intense and jam packed I fall into bed as soon as I get home. There's no time for fun."

The smirk that slid across Hayden's face told me I was wrong. "There's always time for fun."

I bit my lip. "I'd like that, but can we not tell anyone? Meaning your sister so she doesn't tell Reagan? I don't need any more shit."

"So you mean, I'm your dirty little secret?" He winked.

CHAPTER 64

Three hours later and my brain was fried.

Math was not my strongest subject. When letters got mixed in with numbers, that was it. I was done. Luckily my tutor only made me do it for an hour then moved on to History. Which I loved.

"Want to grab a bite to eat before we head back?" Hayden asked.

I checked my watch and realized I hadn't eaten anything other than a granola bar.

"Eh. I have a salad at the gym, but I'm not really in the mood."

His face scrunched up. "A salad? Aid, you have to eat. You have four hours of practice ahead of you." He had a point, I was running on fumes, but my lack of appetite was due to reasons he was unaware of.

"Honestly, Hayden, I'm just too stressed out to eat right now."

Hayden pulled into a shopping plaza and parked in front. "Gotta eat to keep up that stamina." He winked, and jumped out of his car.

When we walked in, I was instantly reminded of Whole Foods. That place always has a strange odor. The smell assaulted me and I started giggling thinking of something Avery said once.

"What's so funny?"

"It's nothing."

Hayden paused, grinning. "Tell me."

"This place reminds me of Whole Foods. It has the same smell."

He looked confused. "And that's funny to you?"

"Avery swears Whole Foods uses natural cleaning products that are supposed to be orange scented but they actually smell like dirty jock straps. That's why when you walk into one it always has the same gross smell. I agree with her, not that I know what jock straps smell like, it's just a wild guess."

Hayden's eyes were gleaming with laughter.

"What? Don't look at me like that!"

"I didn't say anything," he laughed, putting his hands up.

"You have a look in your eyes. I'm going to punch you!" I raised my fist playfully and he didn't even flinch.

Before I could say anything else, the urge to pee sliced through me. "Can you order me a turkey lettuce wrap please? I need to use the restroom."

"No bread or cheese?"

"Are you insane? Of course not! Just turkey and lettuce. Nothing else."

He knew how strict our diets were. Carbs and dairy were out. I allowed myself carbs once a week, but it sure as hell wasn't from a wrap. Those little flat pieces of nothing were loaded with shit I couldn't afford to put in my body.

Finding the bathrooms, I reached to yank the door open only to find it locked. *Dammit!* I leaned against the opposite wall, counting the seconds and trying desperately not to do the pee dance. My mother would give me the evil eye all the way from Palm Bay if I did. From all the years of being obedient under my mother's watchful eye, I just stood with my legs crossed like a lady, and praying to God this person hurried the hell up.

After what felt like an eternity, a mother holding her son's hand exited the bathroom. As soon as their bodies cleared the doorframe, I dashed in. My bladder burned as I shifted from foot to foot trying to unbutton and unzip my jeans. I tightened my abdomen, feeling ready to explode while I hovered over the toilet.

Taking a deep breath, I closed my eyes and let it trickle out slowly like last time...and felt the burn. I stopped, my teeth biting into my bottom lip as tears threatened behind my eyes.

I hated this pain.

I tried again, but my urine was hot, so it stung even more this time. I expelled a gush of air from my lungs at the little bit I was capable of releasing and then zipped up my pants. I'd much rather straddle the beam than deal with this sort of pain right now.

I flushed, washed my hands, and was out of the bathroom to find Hayden paying for our lunch. I reached into my pocket, but he stopped me.

"Nah, don't worry about it."

I pushed the twenty at him. "Take it."

"No, no," he said, turning around and heading for a table. "I asked you to come to lunch, I can pay for it."

I stood there, dumbfounded with the money in my hand. "I'm not used to people paying for me. I almost don't know what to do."

Hayden whipped his head in my direction and stared at me. "You just stick it back in your pocket and say, 'Gee, Hayden, that was so sweet of you. Thanks,' and sit down and eat."

I tried to suppress the grin that formed across my lips, but it was useless. Hayden was adorable and charming. His dirty blonde hair had a perfect bed head look and he glowed with charisma. I couldn't help but want to be around him.

"You're such a dork. I know how to say thank you," I said, taking a bite of my boring lettuce wrap. "Thank you." Hayden smiled and pushed a small, peachy looking smoothie in front of me. My eyes met his.

"This was part of the special of the day. No carbs—relax. It's organic vegetables and fruit only. I watched her make it. You're allowed to have this."

"There's carbs in fruit and veggies." He just stared at me so I continued. "There was no fruit juice added to make it?" I worried about the amount of sugar in this drink. It looked incredibly good, but I had to be careful and not over indulge.

"She used coconut water. It's all natural so you're safe."

I smiled at Hayden, appreciating his thoughtfulness. He was making an effort by watching out for me.

Picking it up, I sipped the frothy concoction and swallowed. My eyes lit up as the icy drink hit my tongue and I took another sip, this time a larger one.

"Wow! This really is good. Here," I handed it to him. "Try it." Hayden swallowed and grinned, sipping the drink.

"I get the smoothies here a lot, but this was a new one they had today."

"It's really good. I can see why you get it."

After a couple of minutes of eating our lunch in silence, I drank about half of the smoothie and handed the rest to Hayden. "Take it. I'm full from my wrap and this, I can't finish the rest," I lied. I could finish it, and I wanted to, but watching my weight was more important.

Hayden finished with his giant sandwich and chips. He was lucky he could pretty much eat anything. I'd give anything to just eat whatever I wanted. Most of the guys' team could. Being full while at the gym was uncomfortable and I'd rather be a little hungry.

At least it's what I told myself.

Hayden squinted his eyes, and reluctantly took my drink and finished it. "You're lying."

"Fine! I'm lying!" I caved. "Truth is, I'm stressed about gym, so I don't really have an appetite." I bit my lip and then said, "Honestly, sometimes I question myself and why I ever came here. Maybe I'm not cut out for this. "

Hayden tilted his head to the side, studying me. "We all have days like this, Aid. Tomorrow won't be as bad. You're still somewhat new so you're still transitioning into this lifestyle. "

"I'm not new, I've been here for like, a million months now."

"I've been part of World Cup for *years*. I was overwhelmed and almost walked out a few times once I transitioned to elite. The training is way more rigorous, the hours are long. It's draining on so many levels that sometimes I wondered what I got myself into. But at the same time, I couldn't imagine not doing gymnastics. It's in my blood, just like it's in yours. Even when you have days where you hate it and want to walk out, you know you can't. Some days you compare yourself to your teammates and feel inadequate. You're not. You're just having an off day. Some days are really lonely too. It's the hardest when you go home and have no parents or friends to turn to. I have my sister and she understands this life, but that's different." Hayden paused and looked at his hands, thinking about what to say next. "You love the sport too much to give up. And you know you never will. It's just not possible, so you deal with the loneliness, you deal with the bad days, and you truck on."

I swallowed back the lump in my throat. "You're right. You're so right on everything you said." Tears were brimming the back of my eyes. I didn't want to cry, but I had so much on my plate and I felt them ready to spill over at any second. I was bottling it all up and I hadn't realized how lonely I was until that moment. Hayden noticed my change. He grabbed our trash, threw it out, and then took my hand and we walked out to his car.

I didn't say anything about the hand holding, because truthfully, it felt nice. I even leaned into his arm and held on to him. Even though he was only a little older than me, he gave me security in his touch and I soaked it up. He was my comfort, my shoulder to lean on. My heart softened a little for Hayden and I gave him a gentle squeeze.

Hayden pulled open the passenger side door, but before I could climb in, he pulled me into a bear hug. I automatically wrapped my arms around him and buried my head into the crook of his neck, closing my eyes.

"Don't stress about earlier. It's over with," he spoke against my cheek. "Focus on the future."

I nodded, unable to form words. "I'm not sure what I'd do without you, Hayden."

I was being emotional and I hated it. I didn't deal well with emotions, kudos to my mother. These feelings were foreign and unwelcomed and I wanted them gone. All they did was remind me just how human I really was.

Hayden held on to me, rubbing my arms and giving me strength. I hugged him a little tighter, taking everything he offered. "I'm always here for you."

"Thank you." Taking a chance, I asked with a shaky voice, "Do you think you'd want to come over tonight after gym? You know, just to hang out? I could use the company."

Pulling back, Hayden looked down at me. His face was soft and his eyes warm. "Sure. I'd love to." He smiled genuinely, then pressed a kiss to my forehead. "We can even watch *Mean Girls* if you want."

My stomach curled with anticipation. I needed to put my game face on and focus. I was here to train, not worry about what my coach thought about me or how bitchy the girls were.

I climbed into the car, my head flopping back against the leather headrest. I took a deep breath and turned to Hayden. "I got this."

CHAPTER 65

I knew there was something wrong the moment I woke up—two hours early and in complete agony.

Pain tore through my lower belly as a fire ripped through me like an inferno that couldn't be doused. But it didn't just stop there. It went up my side and wrapped around. My back throbbed as if a heavy metal drummer was using my body as practice, the pounding was nonstop.

With my knees pressed to my chest bound by my arms, I curled into a tiny ball, wishing on a star this throbbing sting would go away. I'd never in my life had cramping quite like this before and I wasn't sure what to think of it. I squeezed my eyes tight and chewed my bottom lip raw in a matter of minutes. The only thing that shot through my mind was getting to the hospital immediately.

Thing was, I didn't think I was capable of driving. The pain was that intense. Nausea coiled my stomach and I fought to keep the contents I had for dinner with Hayden down.

Glancing at the clock, it was too early to call anyone, but I needed someone. Madeline was my first thought since she'd come with me to see Dr. DeLang, but something in my gut told me not to call her. The only other person I felt comfortable calling was Hayden. It was either him, or I drove myself.

I shot Hayden a quick text hoping he'd see it when he woke up. I told him I needed help and I was sick. In the meantime, I would take a heavy dose of Motrin—my go to drug—and soak in a hot bath. But trying to stand hurt and it caused me to hunch over and stop. Taking a deep breath, I slowly stood up again, a hand pressed to my stomach this time. As I walked, I could swear my muscles were being ripped to shreds. With this kind of pain, I knew there was no way I could train today. It just wasn't physically possible. That being said, I was terrified to call Kova and tell him, especially with how things left off between us. It was awkward, and I'd be surprised if he'd even answer me anyway.

I turned on the tub and waited for it to fill, I leaned down and pulled out a carton of Epsom Salt and a bottle of Motrin. I dumped a generous amount into the hot water and swirled my fingers around the filling tub. My mom always had this stuff in the house and swore it would heal internal ailments. Once I started training at World Cup, it became a staple in my condo.

Rising up from the tub, a sharp pain shot through my belly. I cringed, gushing out a loud breath. Even leaning over at this angle was agony. Whatever it was, I prayed a doctor could diagnose it and heal me by tonight.

I was a hot mess.

Stripping off my clothes, I looked in the mirror and my eyes widened. I was pale and looked like death. My eyes were hollow and the color weak. There were yellow tinted bruises all around my hips and I was skinnier than ever. Cruella de Vil, also known as my mother, would be proud of my weight loss.

I filled the glass cup I kept in my bathroom with water. The back of the ibuprofen bottle said two pills, but I was going to take four like I typically did. I quickly washed the orange pills down and drank another glass of water before stepping up to the side of the bathtub.

Lifting my knee, I dipped my foot into the water, hating the first steamy touch. I drew in a long, tired breath and exhaled before sinking into the water.

Once my entire body was in, I leaned back on a plastic pillow and propped my knees up, then closed my eyes. The water came up to my neck and I sighed in contentment. I sat completely motionless, trying to relax and allow whatever magic the Epsom Salt contained to do its job. Hopefully the pain relievers would kick in because not being able to move wasn't working for me.

A good five minutes into my bath, and I tightened my stomach as a blaze of fire erupted inside. The throbbing in my back still hadn't gone away. I panted and started a countdown for the pain to actually leave. When I reached one, I slowly stretched out my right leg, then my left. My hips were beginning to feel pinched and I knew I needed to release them to full position.

The hot water and pain relievers were finally loosening up my muscles. Being as tired as I had been lately, my eyes rolled shut and I dozed off in the tub, with the tenderness in my stomach floating away.

Somewhere in the back of my mind my phone was ringing, but it wasn't the right sound. It was faint, and a heavy pounding was waking me up.

"Adrianna!"

I rustled, feeling water splash around me. My eyes popped open and I jumped, realizing I had fallen asleep in the bath.

"Fuck."

Hayden was yelling my name, probably waking my neighbors up, probably petrified something happened to me.

I wrapped a towel around my body and yelled, "I'm coming!" as I headed to the door. A quick glance at the clock and I had my answer as to why Hayden was blowing up my phone and pounding on my door like a lunatic. It'd been over an hour since I sent him the text message. Apparently exhaustion took control whenever it wanted to.

Quickly, I unbolted the locks and opened the door.

"Adrianna, where have you been? I thought something was wrong with you! Are you okay?" He rubbed his forehead after throwing the questions at me. "What happened?"

Once he stepped inside, I locked the door. I wrapped the towel around me tighter and said, "I'm so sorry for worrying you, Hayden. I fell asleep in the tub."

"Do you have any idea how dangerous that is?"

I flinched. "I know. It was reckless of me."

"Everything okay?"

"Not really. My stomach hurts pretty badly. I don't know what's wrong with me, but I need to skip practice today and go to the doctor."

The look on Hayden's face mimicked mine. Distress. He knew missing gym was a huge no. He nodded his head and said, "Go get dressed and I'll call the gym and relay the message for you."

A tender smile eased my face. "Thanks. I appreciate it."

As quickly as possible, my feet padded across the carpet into my room. Before I shut the door, it dawned on me that Hayden himself was late for practice.

"Oh, my God, Hayden! You're going to get in trouble for missing practice!" I yelled. "I'm so sorry!"

"Don't worry about me, let's just get you to the doctor. My coaches aren't hard-asses like yours anyway, so it won't be as big of a deal for me."

Nodding, I closed my bedroom door and dropped my towel. I grabbed a pair of black yoga pants and a hoodie along with a sports bra and panties. I slipped on my clothes as swiftly as possible, the sudden onset of chills caused my teeth to chatter. The only thing I could think of was I had some sort of virus that caused the pain to zip line through my body. Maybe food poisoning. I had been on a carb free diet for weeks and last night when Hayden and I watched *Mean Girls* together, he brought pizza over. This could possibly be my stomach reacting to the junk food and grease. If this was my body's way of revolting against my one night of fun, then I was never touching pizza again.

Even with my door shut, Hayden's voice carried down the hall. Every time he went to speak, he barely got a few words in before he was abruptly cut off. This happened four or five times, the pattern repeating constantly, which was surprising to me. I felt like I was listening to an episode of Maury. No one spoke above the coaches, and when they did, they spoke louder and above people. Whoever was on the other line, they weren't happy with him.

In this moment, I would forever be thankful for Hayden Moore's friendship.

"Ready?" I asked.

His jaw dropped. "Your eyes are blood shot." He walked over and pressed a hand to my head. "You're hot."

I chuckled. "Thanks."

Grabbing my hand, he pulled me to the front door. "That coach of yours is a piece of work. Thank God I only work with him on rings."

The side of my mouth pulled up. "Tell me about it."

"Do you have a doctor or are we going to the emergency room?"

I paused in my tracks. "I don't have a doctor...and I really don't want to go to the ER. Let me do a Google search and find a local twenty-four hour urgent care center."

Hayden cleared his throat. "Ah, you don't have a guardian to sign off on anything should the occasion arise?"

My head snapped up and met his worried look. He was right. I didn't have a parent or a legal guardian while I was here. This could get tricky. Luckily for me, I'd gotten great at lying lately and had the ID Avery made me that made me legal.

"I highly doubt there's going to be an issue. They're most likely going to insist on payment up front, which I have cash I can pay with."

"Where's your insurance card?" he asked as we walked out of my condo. "Do you have it with you?"

"I do, but since I'm paying with cash I don't think I'll need it."

I rattled off the address to a local urgent care center and ten minutes later we pulled into a lit up facility with a big red cross on the front of the building. We were just in time as another wave of cramps hit my stomach. I prayed the wait wouldn't be long as I slowly walked up to the entrance, slightly hunched over with Hayden by my side. The doors slid open, and I looked around at the empty lobby.

Thank God.

A heavyset woman picked her head up and glanced at us as we made our way to the front desk. She sighed irritably and asked, "What can I do for you?" She clearly wasn't a morning person.

"I need to see a doctor, please."

The woman sneered. "What seems to be the problem?"

"My stomach and back are killing me."

She looked at the computer. "Are you pregnant?"

CHAPTER 66

My jaw dropped, and Hayden froze.

"God, no!"

"You'd be surprised how many girls are pregnant by your age, if not younger," she mumbled under her breath, typing away, loud enough for me to hear.

"Ma'am, I'm not pregnant, I'm in serious pain though. I feel like someone is beating on my back and it hurts to stand."

"All right, let's get a few things squared away first." Ms. Attitude pulled out a folder with an impatient look. I handed her my fake ID and informed her I'd be paying with cash. An open chair was positioned next to the counter so I took the liberty of sitting down. I sighed in relief and closed my eyes, grateful Hayden took over filling in the blanks, asking me for the answers. He made a comment about how good the fake ID looked and I mumbled I'd have Avery get him one. That was as much effort as I could handle at the moment.

Thirty-nine agonizing minutes later, I was brought back to an exam room. She checked my vitals and noted a fever. Like every doctor's office, I was freezing and waiting impatiently on the paper-covered table. The pain was so intense in my back, I started rocking to find a way to ease it.

Knock. Knock.

A stout doctor waltzed in wearing bold, black-rimmed glasses pushed up high, resting on the bridge of his nose. He had a warm smile, something I desperately needed after Ms. Attitude in the waiting room and the way I was feeling.

No introduction, the doctor obtained some basic medical information and got down to business.

"All right Adrianna, lie back on the table please. Let's get a feel for what's going on. It says here you're a gymnast," he looked down, then back up at me, squinting his eyes. "And training around fifty hours a week?" He paused, a crease formed between his eyes. "Is that right?"

"Yes, sir." The doctor looked at Hayden like he was looking for confirmation.

He dropped the file onto the gray countertop, slapped on a pair of gloves and turned toward me. Instinctively, I moved my hands higher up on my stomach and the doctor pressed his fingers to my lower belly. I flinched when he gave a solid push, causing him to pause and look at me. I thought he was going to push through my stomach.

"That hurts?"

"A little bit."

"When was your last menstrual cycle?"

Pursing my lips together, I tilted my head to the side and looked at the corner of the ceiling. I had to think about that for a moment. "About three weeks ago? My cycle is usually off, so I don't keep track of it."

"Are you sexually active?"

"No!" I shouted it like a fool. Clearing my throat, I answered again. "No, I'm not."

Hayden threw his hands up. "And that's my cue to step out."

"And who are you, young man?"

"Her brother," he lied smoothly, walking toward the door. "I'll be right outside, Aid."

"Thanks, Hayden."

Once Hayden left, the doctor eyed me suspiciously.

His chin dipped to his chest and looked over his specs. "I'll ask again since your brother isn't here. Are you sexually active?"

"Yes."

"Are you on birth control?"

"No."

"Is there any chance you are pregnant?"

"No. I recently took the morning after pill so I'm good."

"The morning after pill is not always effective. Have you considered going on birth control?"

My heart dropped into my gut at the mention of the pill not being effective. I stared, stone-faced at the doctor as a million thoughts ran through my head. This could not be happening.

"I...I only just became active," I stammered. My jaw quivered and I fought to regain control of my emotions.

His eyes narrowed. "It only takes one time to become pregnant. Unless you intend to become a mother, we have a female doctor you can follow up with once you are feeling better who can perform a Pap smear if you'd like and go from there."

"Thanks, I'll think about it."

The doctor applied more pressure this time, pressing down with both sets of fingers around my abdomen. My body tensed, my stomach flexing under his touch.

"That hurts really bad," I gritted out, crossing my legs as if that would help.

"Sit up." He listened to my heart, my back, and down my sides. As he pushed around near my spine, I grimaced in discomfort. When the doctor pushed on my side near my kidney, I went ramrod straight and sucked in an audible breath, wincing.

"Adrianna, I'm going to need a urine sample to rule out pregnancy and infection."

My stomach dropped. I froze. A pregnancy test? I'd only had sex with Kova twice. There was no way I could be pregnant...I hoped. Fear seized my heart and my breathing became labored as I realized I needed to get my hands on another morning after pill soon.

"I don't have to go, I went before I left," I lied.

He tilted his head to the side. "Luckily I only need a little." He handed me a small cup and gave me instructions before pointing me toward the bathroom.

I grimaced, knowing what was ahead of me.

Walking down the bland, gray hallway to the bathroom, I closed the door behind me and took in the small space. Just thinking about having to pee was causing me fear as the urge struck me. Spreading my legs and squatting over the toilet, making sure not to touch the rim, I positioned the cup under me.

Expelling a heavy breath, I looked down at the cup perplexed. My urine was a murky brown. Definitely not what it should've been. Maybe I was dehydrated and needed to drink more water. Lately, I'd been cutting back so I didn't have to use the bathroom as much. Guess that wasn't such a great idea.

After I put the plastic cup in the cabinet, I washed my hands and walked back to the room. The pressure in my belly had dwelled to a low glow. Despite not wanting to deal with it at all, I'd take this pain over anything else I'd been dealing with recently.

A few minutes later, the doctor came back. I was feeling better and realized I probably could've skipped coming to the doctor's if I had just gone to the bathroom and dealt with the pain instead of acting like a baby.

"Good news—the pregnancy test is negative, but your sample does show bacteria. I'm going to send it to the lab to be cultured. For now, I'd like to perform an abdominal ultrasound and draw some blood."

My brows pushed together. "Why do we need blood work?"

"Just a precautionary. Even though the urine pregnancy is negative, we still like to follow it up with a serum pregnancy test to rule out a false negative. The morning after pill is not always effective," he responded, head down and writing in his folder. My stomach churned at the thought. I knew no form of birth control was one hundred percent, but it never dawned on me until this moment just how big that tiny window could be.

Nearly thirty minutes later, I was stuck with a needle—four times might I add—since the nurse couldn't get it right, and then lathered with warm gel. I had to squeeze the sides of the table as the ultrasound technician pressed on my abdomen and bladder. I was thin, weighing in around one hundred pounds soaking wet, if that. She should've been able to see everything and not need to push as hard as she did. When I asked what she was doing, she said looking for cysts because they can cause major abdominal pain. When she asked me to turn over, she scanned my kidneys.

The doctor walked back in and shut the door. Looking at me, he took a pen out of the pocket of his lab coat and grabbed a prescription pad. "It appears you have a kidney infection. It's a pretty bad one, I might add. You could've had a reaction to the morning after pill that didn't help stop the infection, and the severe cramping in your abdomen is most likely caused by the pill. I suggest refraining from taking the pill in the future and be on a more consistent form of birth control." He paused and pushed his glasses up on the bridge of his nose. "Does it hurt to urinate?"

"It burns like you can't imagine."

"So you hold it in, then," he confirmed.

I nodded.

"That's the worst thing you could do—stop doing it. I'm going to prescribe you some antibiotics and a pain reliever. Take the antibiotics until they're gone and the pain pill as needed." He scribbled on his pad. "I'm also suggesting you take the rest of today and tomorrow off. A heating pad will help too."

"Doctor, there's no way I can take another day off. I just can't."

He ignored me. "If you're not feeling better by the end of the second day, call me."

"But I can't miss another day. I have to go back tomorrow." My heart thumped against my chest, anxiety taking over at the thought of missing another day.

He peered down his nose over his glasses at me. "I'll write you a doctor's note. If your coach has any problem with it, he can call me. Your body needs rest."

I nodded to pacify him, ready to go home.

"Like hell I'm going to take another day off. Coach would have my head on a stick if I did that," I said to Hayden once we were back in his car.

He chuckled. "Maybe it would be a good thing you did. That way you can rest up and not get set back even more. It will give you time off your foot too."

"My Achilles isn't going to heal in two days. It's going to take quitting gymnastics completely for that to happen."

"If that's the case, then why did your coach water down your routines?"

I sighed. "To help heal the strain as much as possible and work back up to that level, I guess. They don't want me making it worse where I have to actually take time off."

He looked over at me. "You must hate that."

"Like you can't even imagine. I've tried so hard, put everything into being here, and I get hurt. That's just my luck."

We pulled up to the drive-up pharmacy and Hayden dropped off my prescription for me. We parked and went inside while it got filled. I picked up a heating blanket, another big bottle of Motrin, then sat down and waited for my medication when Hayden walked off. He was back in minutes handing me a bottle of juice and a box of medicine.

Looking down, I asked, "What is it?"

"Cranberry pills. I read in *Cosmo* they should also help with UTIs and since it's kind of connected, I figured why not. It's all natural stuff so it won't counteract your medication."

My jaw hung open, my brows scrunched together. "Please don't tell anyone you read *Cosmo*, Hayden. That's so...not hot."

He grinned. "It pays to have a sister who reads them. You'd be surprised the stuff you can learn in there." He paused, pulling out his phone and did a quick Google search. "Most outrageous, psychotic tips *Cosmo* has suggested that will put you in the hospital."

Our eyes locked and we smiled. "Let's read it while we're waiting," I said.

CHAPTER 67

The doctor had been right—my body desperately needed the rest. All this training had finally caught up to me.

Overused, overworked, and not resting muscles properly probably added to my body shutting down and not being able to fight the infection. I had a fever all day long and well into the next morning until it finally broke. The painkillers were magical, and the agony I had been dealing with was finally starting to dissipate within twenty-four hours. Even if I had gone to gym, it probably wasn't the brightest idea to train while on them. They made me loopy, which Avery got to enjoy when I face-timed her and filled her in on all that happened, sans the sex.

None of my coaches or teammates had called, except Hayden. Not that they would anyway. And truthfully, I didn't know whether that made me happy or not.

Loneliness struck. Looking around, I liked my space and I was used to my privacy, but for some odd reason the solitude was hitting hard and beginning to upset me. My emotions were scattered about and frayed at the edges. I was going to break if I added one more thing to my fucked up lifestyle. Between training, school, keeping track of all the lies I told, I'd never had this much time to myself to reflect on my current state. Tears welled in my eyes as realization dawned on me at the person I'd become. A habitual liar.

My phone rang, distracting my thoughts. Picking it up, I glanced at the caller ID and a smile broke out across my face.

"Hi, Dad!"

"Hey, baby girl, how are you doing?"

"I'm okay. How are you?"

"Oh, you know, no rest for the wicked."

I grinned. That was his favorite line. "Yeah."

"So, Mom called me..." He trailed off, waiting for me to finish for him.

"I have a little infection, but I'm doing much better now. No need to worry." I really didn't want to go into detail about the kidney infection.

He released a stressful sigh. "Honey, I always worry about you. You're my daughter, and with you not being home it makes me worry even more."

My shoulders relaxed. "I know, but really, I'm okay. My friend, Hayden, took me to the doctor and then we went to the pharmacy afterward to get what I needed."

"The doctor prescribed you some medicine?"

"Yeah, antibiotics and a painkiller. They're helping tremendously."

"Are you getting enough rest, sweetie? I know you're probably used to the schedule by now, but maybe you need a break." He paused. "You can come home any time."

My heart softened at his thoughtfulness. "No rest for the wicked, Dad," I replied quietly.

He chuckled. "Tough little thing. What did Konstantin say about you being home?"

"I actually haven't spoken to him, and I'm honestly surprised the gym isn't blowing up my phone. Hayden did take in my doctor's note so maybe that's why."

"Good. That's because I took care of it for you so you didn't have to worry. I stressed to him that it would be in his best interest to give you time to rest. I had to smooth out his ruffled feathers when he called me," he chuckled lightly. "That piece of paper doesn't hold much water for some people."

I pursed my lips together, puzzled. "You spoke to Kova?"

"I did. We actually talk about every other week. I know you can take care of yourself, but I do worry about you there all alone, so he gives me updates and lets me know how your training is going."

This was news to me. I had no idea he spoke to Kova so often. While I found his concern over my well-being genuine, unlike my mom's, I also was disheartened by the fact he could call Kova and not me. Then again, the phone worked both ways and I didn't call home very often either.

My heart softened. "Thanks, Dad, I appreciate it."

"Get some rest, go to bed early."

"Same with you."

"Your mother sends her love."

I laughed under my breath. "I'm just sure she does," I said sarcastically. "Tell her hi for me."

"Will do, sweetie, talk to you later."

Hanging up the phone, nostalgia struck me. The painkillers were making me emotional. I changed into some pajamas, climbed into bed and switched on Netflix, searching for some mindless teenage drama to watch. As I was dozing off, my phone vibrated and the screen lit up.

COACH

Open the door.

My heart stopped.

Climbing out of bed, I ran to my door and checked the peephole, but saw no one. I sent a text back saying I didn't see him.

COACH

Coming up now.

Turning the lock, I pulled the door open and Kova walked in.

"What are you doing here?" I asked as he dropped his keys and phone on the counter. Before he could open his mouth, I spat, "And if you have one thing to say about my attire, I will lose my shit."

Kova ran a hand through his hair, his eyes raking over my body. My loose top and boy shorts were all I could manage wearing after breaking a fever.

"This was the first minute alone I had to get away from Katja." He let out an exhausted sigh and his eyes traveled down my body. He took two steps and stood before me. Palming my jaw, he tipped my head back and examined me.

"Your eyes are all glossy and red, and you have circles under your eyes," he said quietly. His hands threaded my long hair and fluffed it up. I remembered how much he liked it when I wore it down. "I did not mean to hurt you."

I pulled away and looked at the floor, ashamed he knew my absence was partly due to him. I was a little peeved it took him two days to check on me.

"You didn't though...I really did it to myself."

"Adrianna, do not fool yourself. If it was not for me, you would not be sick."

I swallowed, shrugging. "Partially. But also because I wasn't taking care of myself properly."

"I feel terrible about it, I am very sorry, Adrianna. I was too rough, too careless, I said some mean things, and I put one of my gymnasts at risk. It is just another thing I cannot forgive myself for."

"I won't deny you were rough with me. You were. My body was running on fumes, so it didn't help to fight off any kind of infection either."

Exhaustion took over and I walked to sit on the couch. Leaning over, I placed my elbows on my knees and clasped my hands together.

"This was a big mistake," I admitted, my heart aching with each word. "Catastrophic mistake. I wish nothing had ever happened between us. I wish I could take it all back. I came here to be the best I could and I let myself down." Looking up, I met his eyes. "Maybe I'm not as strong as I think I am." Kova shook his head and came to sit next to me. "I should've told you I was a virgin, it was wrong of me and I'm sorry. We could've ruined so many lives, Kova." Tears welled in my eyes and I hated that I showed any kind of emotion. Damn pain pills!

Kova brushed a strand of hair away from my face, cupping it behind my ear. Our eyes locked and I saw the inner turmoil he was faced with. He hadn't shaved in days, and there were black circles under his eyes too. Gone were the vibrant green eyes I'd come to love, and in their place was a dull shade of olive.

"You look like you haven't slept."

"I have not," he admitted dismally. "You have been on my mind day in and day out. You think you are not strong, but you are. You have taken everything I have thrown at you and ran with it. You are a fighter, Adrianna. Few can handle what you have at the rate you have, and that caused the lines to blur for me. You make me question so many things in my life right now. I wish I could tell you what they were, but I cannot. Just know you are not weak, not even close to it. You are strong, do not ever doubt yourself."

My heart sputtered in my chest. This was one of the nicest things he'd ever said to me. A tear slipped from my eye and he wiped it away with the pad of his thumb.

"But you are right about something."

I tilted my head to the side. "About what?"

"That this was a mammoth mistake. I was unfaithful and I hurt you in the process. I failed both you and Katja. For that, I could not be sorry enough."

I averted my eyes so he couldn't see the pain he caused. "There's a question I want to ask you, and I hope you will answer it." His forehead cinched together. I wasn't sure where this question came from or why I was asking it, but I had to know. Maybe it was the pain relievers talking again.

"I'm asking you one more time. Was I really the only gymnast you've ever been with? Or were there others? Please be honest with me."

My heart thumped wildly against my chest waiting for his answer.

"Ria, I am a lot of things, but I do not desire young girls," he spat with disgust. "I find it repulsive. There has never been another before you, though not for lack of trying on their part. There were some aggressive ones, but I never took it past the professional level."

"So you were never with Reagan?"

He pulled back in horror. "Reagan? Never. Where would you get that idea?"

I shook my head, feeling like an idiot for even asking now. "Just some things she said to me."

"Reagan, while she is an incredible gymnast, lacks the drive and willpower you have. There has never been more than a coach/athlete relationship with her, or anyone else. I can promise you that."

Reaching a hand into his pocket, he pulled out a little box. Flipping it over, my heart sank as I read the front of it. I shook my head, a sad laugh escaped me.

Kova and his stupid little, white fucking pill.

"We've been pretty stupid, haven't we?"

He huffed at my understatement and handed the box to me. "Me more so than you. I knew better."

Opening it up, I popped out the morning after tablet. I stared at the pill and hesitated. I had to decide whether I should just ignore what the doctor recommended and deal with the repercussions later, or hand the box to Kova and explain why I can't take it and how I'd had a pregnancy test already.

I glanced Kova's way. The last thing I needed was a baby or for him to go to jail. I reached for the bottle of water I left on the coffee table earlier. Popping the tablet into my mouth, I swallowed it without dwelling on the situation further. His shoulders relaxed visibly but then something dawned on me. He was more worried about me being pregnant than my well-being. Luckily for him, I didn't have the energy to confront him.

"Problem solved," I said dejectedly.

Standing up, I went to step past Kova, but he placed a hand on my thigh and stopped me. With him sitting on the couch and his height, we were eye level with each other. Turning toward him, I looked into his tempestuous gaze. His hand was high on the back of my leg, cupping the crease of my thigh and butt. His fingers moved in little circles, causing a warmth of heat to course through me. My nipples hardened. I didn't move, I couldn't, as his hand skimmed over my ass and up my back ever so slowly. Goose bumps coated my skin. He placed his other hand on my body and my breath caught in my throat as he pulled me closer. After what he said, I was confused by his actions.

"Kova?" I whispered.

He sat up higher. "I do not know what it is about you, but I have the hardest time keeping my hands to myself when it is just you and me. You understand me as I understand you. We have the same drive."

A pained look resonated on his face. He muttered in Russian as his hands roamed my body. Despite the pain he caused me a few days ago, my body came alive when he touched me.

"What are you doing?"

"Memorizing you with my touch." Kova shuffled me closer between his legs, and I could smell the faint scent of vodka on his lips.

My heart hammered against my chest. This man was so confusing. His words contradicted his actions on a daily basis. But one thing I knew for sure, there was no denying what he felt for me. The look in his eyes as his hands caressed my back, pulling me closer, solidified his feelings. My shirt lifted, baring my back and stomach. His palms grazed my nipples and my back bowed in response. His head dipped to the side, and a breath caught in my throat.

The way he looked at me broke my heart. He was struggling, and what he said earlier was in fact true. After everything, was Kova going to kiss me? I swallowed hard. I wouldn't refuse him if he did. I didn't think there would ever come a time I could refuse anything he offered.

"*Malysh*, I need one last kiss."

He was saying goodbye.

With a small nod, I licked my lips and wound my arms around his neck. Leaning in, my chest pressed to his, my nipples hard. Kova's strong arms wrapped around my lower back, crushing me to him. I loved how strong he was, how he held me and made me feel safe. Our lips grazed each other's, different than any other time. He was gentle and slow, and took his time as he nibbled on my lips.

I took this moment for what it was—he was using his actions to display the things he couldn't say.

When our tongues touched, it wasn't rushed or wild for once. It was deliberate and provocative. My body was a blaze of heat, desire hitting me hard. Our tongues caressed one another's, tangling around and holding on, in the most intense kiss we'd had yet. Wet, warm, and passionate.

My fingers weaved through his hair as I put everything into the kiss, just as he did. I knew after tonight, it was over completely and my heart ached. I had let myself fall completely for someone I could never have.

Kova's hands skimmed up my ribs, his fingers splaying out wide and palming my breasts. I moaned into his mouth, pressing harder into him and devouring him. My body ached even more, but this time for release and nothing more. His kiss made me forget every ounce of pain and replaced it with pleasure.

"I love how responsive you are to my touch," he whispered against my lips, shifting to the edge of the couch. His erection grazed my thigh and I leaned into him as his tongue collided with mine, the same time his forefinger and thumb found my nipple and pinched. A little purr escaped my lips.

Kova's strong hands landed on my hips. His fingers trembled against me as his tongue found my heated skin. My head fell back, I wanted to be the one who eased the pain for him, to give him what he wanted.

The sad reality of the story was I would never be that girl.

And he would never be that man.

His thumbs dug into the crease between my hips and thighs while his long fingers scooped under my ass. He stood and hoisted me up, one arm wound securely around my back, his other hand tangled in my long hair, holding me to him, like he feared I would pull away. I wouldn't. I couldn't. There was no possible way I'd be able to now. I was his for the taking.

I wrapped my nimble legs around his waist. My emotions were climbing and for some reason, tears prickled my eyes. I didn't want this to be over between us, the fire was too wild to contain.

"You can't do this to me and then leave, Kova," I whispered against his lips. "Either stop altogether, or don't stop at all. It's not fair."

I pressed my lips to his, pouring my heart out through my kiss. This fucked up relationship between us was against all morals. He knew it, I knew it, and we didn't care.

Kova pulled back and pressed his forehead to mine. "I need to go." I nodded, agreeing with him. Kova held me as if it was second nature for me to be in his arms. I never wanted him to let me go, but deep down I knew it was time. We'd carried on this affair long enough, because in the end, I knew that everyone gets caught.

Sliding out of his arms, I stood in front of Kova. He cupped my jaw and angled my head back.

"You are so beautiful it hurts. You hold yourself together even during the toughest times. You are a force to be reckoned with, something no one will see coming."

"Kova, why are you telling me this?"

He lifted one shoulder and shrugged like he wasn't sure. "It is just a few of the things I love about you." He placed a kiss to my forehead and held it for a minute. We inhaled at the same time, and I grabbed his wrists, savoring the last intimate contact we would share.

Kova stepped back and walked to the counter, grabbing his keys and phone. Without another glance, he opened the front door and left, leaving my heart shattered in a million tiny pieces.

CHAPTER 68

Unwrapping my wristbands and tape, I dropped my gear into my bag.

I was covered in chalk, tired, and hungry. Just the thought of my bed lulling me to sleep in my quiet condo caused me to move faster. I'd reached past the point of fatigue, I could feel it in my body. Some days I hated being alone, but today I was looking forward to it.

It had taken me a little time to get back in the right mind frame, and I had, but I wasn't sure I fully let go. Working closely with Kova day in day out, I was constantly reminded of what we shared, the things we did in secret. He'd look at me with heat in his eyes, and my body would flush, but not before he quickly masked it. It was still there for him and the lingering of his touch always gave him away. He was struggling just as much as I was.

Today's practice had been an awkward one, but awkward doesn't even begin to describe the past month between Kova and me. I was certain no one noticed the strain between us. We'd been good at keeping things completely platonic. No more late night visits, no indiscretion, nothing reckless. We were never alone together and probably shouldn't have been from the beginning. I was just a gymnast, and he was just a coach, like it should've been. Nothing more.

"All right, team. Once you guys are done, come see me on the floor. We have a few things to go over before the weekend." Kova addressed us all and then left.

Pulling out my hair tie, I fluffed up my thick, auburn locks that were covered with white streaks of chalk before putting it back into a messy bun. I sat down and removed the sports tape from my toes and feet, my calf, freeing my body from all the adhesive. Therapy proved to make a huge difference. I was stronger, more confident. My new routines were solid and I had Kova and Madeline to thank.

They both worked with me and got me where I needed to be. Well, mostly Madeline. Kova had kept his word and hardly coached me.

The qualifying meet was just a couple of short weeks away and every day I was growing more anxious for it. I put everything into gymnastics. I gave it my all. I trained harder, pushed harder, and I never complained. I did what Kova had told me to do—prove myself, make it count.

Taking a seat next to Holly, we all stared up at the coaches and waited. It wasn't uncommon for him to meet with us, but something wasn't right. I could feel it in the air. Kova's eyes dashed around at the group of team girls and boys, but he never made eye contact with me. My stomach knotted, unease swept through me. Something big was coming.

Kova rubbed his hands together, licked his lips and then spoke. "So, we have the holidays coming up, the New Year, and then the Parkettes Invitational. Reagan, Holly, and Adrianna are attending. However, after careful deliberation with the other coaches, we have decided to make a few changes."

An audible gasp surrounded the small group. My heart sank, and my fingers trembled. Somehow, I knew what was coming, but I gave him the benefit of the doubt. I looked around and knew my facial expression matched the others. We were not expecting this sort of news. Changing the lineup had never happened in my last gym, it was whoever was best for the team would compete, and I had a notion it was the same way here.

Kova cleared his throat, and I noticed he refused to make eye contact with me once again.

"This was not an easy decision, but here at World Cup, we feel that your injury is not something we should test just yet." Kova finally glanced my way and locked eyes with me, "I am sorry, Adrianna, but we are pulling you out of the meet."

Silence so thick, it permeated the air. My heartbeat drummed in my ears and my breathing deepened as I stared ahead, astounded at the devastating words I'd just heard. This couldn't be. Not after how hard I worked for this meet.

"I know this is a shock to you, and you should know this was not an easy decision, but it has been made and it is done."

No words, I had no words. My heart was in my throat, all the noise faded away. I was rendered speechless over this shocking decision. How could he do this to me? I was ready. There was no doubt about it that I was ready. I practiced harder and longer than the other girls. I worked my ass off, only for him to take me out of the meet. My heart started to crack, tears formed behind my eyes. But I refused to cry.

"Wha..." I paused, swallowing past my dry throat, "why?"

"Where you may be tighter with jumps and sequences, your dismounts are not solid and your releases are not clean. That is not enough, you need more time. It would only be setting you up for failure."

"I don't know why you're surprised. Your skills are not that difficult or steady," Reagan chimed in. I glared at her, my face conveying every emotion strumming through me

"That's enough, Reagan," Kova snapped.

"That's because I have an injury, you idiot." Turning to Kova, I said angrily, "You made me scale back my skills so I could continue training. Of course my skills are not that complex. This isn't fair."

"It is what is done when anyone is hurt, Adrianna. We did not single you out purposely. We did what we did to avoid any more injury, as we do with any gymnast."

Kova clapped his hands and addressed the group. "All right, girls. That is all. Practice early tomorrow as usual. The next week will be long and grueling before you break for the holidays. We want to get in as much practice time as we can."

Everyone stood up and went on their way as I sat stunned for another minute. I didn't see this coming a mile away, and I couldn't believe he would do this to me after everything. A tear slipped from the corner of my eye as my chest tightened. Not because I was upset, I definitely was, but because I was livid over the change.

"Aid," Hayden said, rubbing my back. "You okay?"

I nodded, not meeting his eyes and stood to walk away. Hayden wasn't the one who I wanted to talk to right now. It was Kova. I was going to rip him a new one.

Walking out of the gym, I made my way down the hall and toward his office. Each step pumped adrenaline through me at a high velocity. I was seeing red, and my blood was boiling. My routines were solid, there were other gymnasts doing skills as I was, I'd seen it on television. So there had to be more to his asinine decision than he alluded to.

I strode into his office and slammed his door shut with as much force as I could muster. Screw the repercussions. I didn't care if anyone heard me, saw me, whatever. I was so stark raving mad I couldn't see straight. My entire body, down to my fingers and toes, were trembling. How dare he do this to me!

Kova's head snapped up, glaring at me with fire in his eyes. I didn't give a fuck. He just told me I wasn't competing in the meet that I worked my ass off for, a meet already paid for by my parents. He had no choice but to hear it from me.

"Adrianna."

"How dare you not allow me to compete, I worked my fucking ass off for that position. You have no right!"

I was so angry I couldn't stop the bite dripping from each word. My hair stuck to my face, my cheeks were beet red. I was already starting to sweat.

Kova stood slowly, flattening his hands on his cherry wood desk and leaned toward me. "I have every right," he spoke slowly. "I am the coach, you are my gymnast. I make the decisions in the end, you do not." He paused, swallowing. "And do not ever come into my office the way you just did ever again, or I will kick you off the team. Now, goodbye."

Goodbye? Fuck that!

"You're jeopardizing my future!"

Kova resumed his seat, picked up his pen, and continued with whatever bullshit he was working on before I stormed in.

"I have already made my choice. End of discussion. And try to refrain from slamming the door on your way out."

I ignored him. "My parents paid for that meet."

"And I already called your mother and explained you are not ready just yet, that you need a little more time. She did not sound surprised at all and said to put someone in your place who has what it takes. Very nice and understanding lady she is." He calmly replied without giving me a glance.

A knot formed in my throat. I was beginning to despise my mother. How could she say that?

"You're lying. You wouldn't do that to me. You know how I feel about her."

He shrugged indifferently. "Call your mom. Though, I would wait a bit. She was not too happy about losing the money."

She'd gloat if I called her. "That money means nothing to her."

"Not my problem, Adrianna."

"Oh, so now I'm Adrianna to you?"

He peered up through his full black lashes, his head barely tipping up. I had gotten better at reading him and could tell I was starting to irritate him by defying his orders. Good.

"You have always been Adrianna to me."

I cocked my head to the side, arching a brow. "That's such a fucking lie and you know it."

"That is beside the point and has nothing to do with right now or my choice. As you can see, I am working here," he waved a hand over his desk, then pointed silently to the door, dismissing me.

Heart pounding, blood roaring through my veins, I walked over to his desk and threw everything off with a swipe of my hand. Kova went rigid, his knuckles a pasty white. His cold demeanor rocked me to the core and I fed off of it.

His jaw flexed and his nose flared. "Very childish, Adrianna. Stop acting immature, it does not suit you."

"Fuck you, *Coach*," I said with sarcasm, walking around to the side of his desk. The last thing I should've been doing was cursing at my coach, but I couldn't control myself. Kova was more than a coach and he knew it. Tears were burning behind my eyes and I was devastated over this change.

"You have no reason to hold me back."

In a blur, Kova stood, hooked a hand around my neck and yanked me to him. He was breathing heavily, his eyes piercing me with a mixture of rage and something I couldn't put my finger on. I shimmied up closer to him and he hadn't loosened his grip on me. Guiding me backward, he pressed me against the wall, his beige filing cabinet cutting into my arm.

Hovering over me he said, "Fine. You want answers, you will get them. Want to know the real reason why you are not going to compete?"

A sugary smile tipped my lips. "I knew it had to be something else with you. There's no way it had to do with my routines."

He fisted my hair, his mouth a mere centimeters from mine. I could feel the heat radiating off him as I stared into untamed eyes, waiting for the truth to spill from his lying lips.

"You broke the rules," he whispered.

I pulled my head back and it hit the wall. Glaring at him, I retorted, "I broke no rules."

Kova tilted his head to the side. "Oh, but you did. In fact, you signed the agreement when you first came here."

I wracked my brain trying to figure out what rule he was talking about as I stared deep into his eyes, but nothing came to mind. He huffed, a sardonic smirk spread across his handsome face.

"No boyfriends. I said there were to be no boyfriends, yet you defied my orders. Therefore, I have more power over you than ever. Your punishment is not to compete at the meet. Maybe next time you will listen."

My mouth dropped with my heart into my gut. I was going to be sick.

"Boyfriend?" I whispered, perplexed. "What boyfriend?" I was so confused. I hadn't been with anyone but him. "But you told my mom I wasn't ready to compete."

"Of course I had to lie to your mom." Coach loosened his hand on my nape, dragging it to my jaw where he slowly caressed my face. "You and Hayden. I told you," his gaze dropped to my mouth, "No boyfriends. I recall telling you to get rid of him."

"But...I..." Caught off guard, I stammered, unable to form words. I gripped his wrist that was still on my face. "He's not my boyfriend."

"Do you think I was born yesterday? I saw him come out of your building. I saw the smile on your face when he pulled away in his car, the way you looked at him. I knew there was more going on when he had to call in for you when you were sick."

"You were spying on me?"

He shrugged.

"He came over to watch a movie and that was it. You can't prove anything."

Hayden helped keep me focused. My friendship with him was really important and any time I was feeling too lonely, he was always there for me. He was the male version of Avery and nothing more, and I didn't know how to get Kova to understand that.

"That is the beauty of it, I do not have to. I am the coach. No one will question my word."

I shoved at his chest, tears filled my eyes and I could barely see clearly. "He's not my boyfriend. I haven't been with anyone other than you. I swear on my life, I haven't. Don't do this to me, please."

"It is done."

"No, it's not." I was going to be sick. "I hate you."

"I would rather you hate me than want me."

"I don't want you." *Lie.*

He shook his head. "You do not get it, do you?"

Confusion set in my face and he answered my question. "I want *you,* that is what you do not seem to understand. But you *never* refuse me. So you hating me will make this easier for you, for both of us. I want you to hate me, so when I do try to come after you, you tell me no."

My jaw dropped, a tear finally slid down my cheek. "So this is about you?" My voice low and crackling. How could he do this to me?

"Oh, *malysh,*" he said, his voice softening. His eyes glazed over and I saw the real truth. "You have what it takes. Your body is in perfect condition," he groaned, his hand skimmed up my thigh and cupping my ass.

CHAPTER 69

On the verge of a breakdown, I dug my nails into him.

"Then let me compete, please. I'm begging."

"No."

"How could he do this to me? Please," I cracked. "I'll do anything. This isn't fair, you're sabotaging my career for the sake of yourself!" Kova ignored me, so I went in for the kill. "Let me compete in the meet or I'll come forward with our relationship." He didn't even flinch.

"No, you will not." His nose skimmed my neck and I shivered. I didn't want to want him, but my body gave me away.

"If you do, it will look bad for you too. You will ruin your career." His breath tickled my neck and I tried desperately not to react to it. I clenched his shirt in my hand, holding him and fighting him at the same time.

"You're ruining it for me by holding me back. What's the difference? Might as well go down in flames and take you with me."

"You will be pulled out of gymnastics and your father's name will be tarnished. Is that what you want after everything he has done for you?"

Guilt struck me. I swallowed hard. I didn't want to shame my parents. Then something dawned on me.

"You forget something huge."

"What is that?" he asked, his lips dusting mine.

I looked directly in his eyes and said, "People don't take lightly to rape. And everyone believes a girl who cries rape."

Kova didn't move, only his eyes widened a smidgen. "That is where you are wrong, malysh. It is consensual between us."

I bit at his lip, taunting him.

"Your fingers penetrated me the way your tongue did. I could easily lie and say you took advantage of me. I could even say it wasn't consensual, and no one would ever know the truth."

Kova said nothing, so I kept going. I knew I should've stopped, but I hurt and I was going for his throat. I was running on adrenaline from his expressions alone.

"We had sexual relations in *your* gym...in the dance room...in front of the rings...the therapy room..." My mother trained me well to smile with my eyes to get my point across. "I'm sure your security camera picked me up. Add me to the list or I'll come forward with our relationship. I will cry rape," I cemented.

Kova's eyes dropped, darkening. "You think you can threaten me?" He gripped my jaw in his hand, his fingers digging into my cheeks. "I am not so easily swayed. Go ahead and try it though, watch how fast you fall. I have never been anything but strictly platonic with every other gymnast I have ever trained. I am sure they will vouch for me. You, on the other hand, I doubt seeing as you do not have many friends here. In fact, I would not be surprised if some of your teammates concoct lies to have you thrown off the team."

"What do I have to lose since you won't let me compete? Nothing." I paused, letting that soak in. "I'm not afraid of you or what could happen. I mean, you took advantage of an innocent minor. A virgin no less. What was I to do?" I asked caustically, batting my eyelashes. "Let's not forget about the morning after pill I'm sure was bought on camera."

Kova ground his teeth, his jaw gnashing together, and I smiled sweetly at him with soft puppy eyes.

"Lies," he whispered harshly. "You pursued me every chance you had, and you know it. A man can only take so much before he loses his fucking mind and caves."

"*No one* will believe you," I bit back. "You know I'm right. After all, I'm just an innocent teenager with a dream and you took advantage of my vulnerability," I said, purposely lying about my age with a pout.

"You made all the first moves—"

"That's a bullshit lie and you know it." I stared hard into his eyes. "If you think I did, then why didn't you stop me, *Coach*?"

He huffed, a half mocking smile displayed across his handsome face. "Not even a priest could have stopped you, or would want to at that, and you know it. You are not as innocent as you come across."

"Excuses, excuses. You should've tried harder." Testing him, I placed a flat hand to his chest, feeling his toned pecs clinging to his torso. My hips shifted into his, his hard length pressed into me as I cupped the back of his neck and angled my mouth in front of his. Taking a deep breath, I released it into his mouth. My tongue slipped out, dancing across his lips, but he didn't move. This was how we worked—the more I fought back and aggravated him, the more he got off on it. The push and pull. It was our foreplay, the tension and indiscretion that brewed between us. Kova stayed stock-still. His fingers strained, desperately trying to stay where they were as they dug deeper into my body. This was way more than just sex between us and he knew it. It was a chemical reaction that couldn't be stopped.

"I can take what I want, right? Isn't that what you once said?" I asked quietly. His eyes narrowed to slits.

Hooking his top lip with the tip of my tongue, I pulled it between my teeth and sucked on it. As I did, my other arm came around his neck as I pressed against him. I nibbled on his luscious lips, slipping my tongue into his mouth.

Four weeks. Four weeks of no touching, no kissing, and now we were at it again. I've dreamed about this, fantasized often. Kova hooked my leg higher, smashing me into the wall as he kissed me like a starved animal. He was rough and raw, taking everything I offered. Momentarily, I forgot why I started this kiss when his hand slid to my throat and applied pressure.

I became instantly aroused from the weight on my neck and moaned in pleasure.

His eyes glazed over. "You like that, Ria?"

I nodded and said, "You're supposed to resist." But he ignored me and hiked up my other leg. My hips pressed into his and I sighed. "What do you want? I'll do it. Anything to compete. Please, just let me compete."

His tongue left a hot, wet trail around my neck and up to my ear. Panting, he said, "Funny thing is, I do not have to ask for anything at this point. I know you will just give it to me. I win either way."

My back bowed, pressing my chest into his. I kissed his hungry, manipulative mouth. His callused hand slid down between us and cupped my pussy hard, painfully hard, but I didn't stop him.

The sad part was that I wanted him to want me, so I took it.

Tongues lapped furiously, delving wildly into each other's mouths. I tightened my thighs around him to hold myself up, he snickered. I needed him. I needed the release I came to crave from him.

"You're the one person who's supposed to be pushing me, and now you're standing in my way." He huffed, and I became desperate. "If I let you have me, will you let me compete?" I asked huskily against his lips, praying he'd change his mind. I was willing to do anything to reach my goal at this point.

Kova fumbled with his shorts between us, his knuckles tapping my sex as he worked feverously to remove them. He pulled at the waistband and pushed it down just enough to pull his cock out, hitting my inner thigh. My legs trembled as a shiver sped down my spine. Hooking his fingers under my leo, he gave a good, hard tug and pulled it to the side. The elastic dug into my skin and I flinched.

"You will let me fuck you either way, and you know it."

He was right, and I hated it.

"Now take a deep breath," he said ever so quietly.

I did as he said. He palmed his length and slid right into me without a second thought to pass. My head whipped back from the rough intrusion and he covered my mouth with his to stifle my loud moan. I almost cried from the pleasure of the pain inflicted on me.

He pulled out and thrust in hard. He groaned, a vein pulsing in his neck. "Once again, you asked for it."

"So what? Maybe I did. And you should've told me no," I panted into him.

Kova pulled out and slid in slower, deeper, hitting the back of me. My lips parted from the ecstasy flowing through me.

"Be honest. Did you want me to refuse you, *malysh?*"

I shook my head, not that I needed to. He knew the answer.

"You want to get fucked, Adrianna, you will. And I have no problem doing it." His hands gripped my hips hard, pushing me down on him. Kova thrust in deep and held it, stretching me wide. My jaw fell open and my eyes squeezed shut. Leaning in next to my ear he whispered, "I know where to touch you, how to make you come, how to make you come back for more."

He was one hundred and fifty percent right. He knew my body, and knew I would come back for more.

Kova yanked down one side of my leotard and pulled my nipple into his mouth. By doing so, it locked my arm to my side. As if it were even possible, I felt myself becoming wetter, his cock sliding so easily into me that it worked me higher and higher, I could barely catch my breath.

"Are you going to try and threaten me again?"

I think he knew in the back of his mind I would never go through with my threat. Not yet at least. Instead of answering him, I said, "I'm close."

"Good, so am I."

"Let me compete, please."

"No."

"I fucking hate you."

"You may hate me, but your pussy doesn't."

"Anyone with a *pussy* would react to you the same way I do."

The climax I so dearly needed with Kova was about to come to a head. We kept going at it like caged animals. A shiver zipped down my spine, heating my body everywhere. Kova sucked on my neck, his tongue lapping and I whimpered, "You feel so good. Don't stop."

Kova seized my lips, nearly sucking the life from me as he fucked me with every ounce of strength he had. Our tongues collided with each other just as fast. I loved the taste of him, the feel of his body on mine, and I wondered if he felt the same about me.

"Feel it, *malysh*, feel it deep inside you," he pulled out and thrusted back in. His cock twitched inside me and I squeezed him with my pussy. "Right there," he groaned into my mouth and I nodded. I felt what he said, and I loved it. His hands came up and tangled in my hair, his breathing became heavy and I knew he was close to losing it. "God, I fucking love being inside of you. Love everything about being with you," he admitted with a moan. His words seized my heart. "I love the pressure around my cock, the way your pussy squeezes me. You make me crazy. All I can think about is fucking you and watching you come. You are gorgeous when you come for me." Chills flitted across my skin, because I loved it too. I loved his touch, his mouth, his arrogant, pushy attitude. I loved so much about him.

"I won't orgasm if you won't let me compete."

"Like I care," he said, then swiveled his pelvis into my clit, proving what a liar I was. "Funny thing is, I can make you come."

"You're nothing but a fucking asshole, you know that?" I panted into his neck as I held on for dear life.

"You are just now figuring that out?"

He knew exactly what my body needed, where to touch me and how to take me. Kova held my hips down on him just how I liked it, and we began to orgasm together when someone knocked on the door twice before barging in.

"Hey, Coach—" Hayden said, then froze, his mouth gaping wide open.

The orgasm ripped through me as I locked eyes with Hayden. I couldn't stop it from happening—and I didn't want to. Kova tried to pull away, but I locked my ankles and squeezed him hard. I needed this orgasm and so did he. "Keep going," I demanded, only for his ears while my eyes were glued to Hayden's. I could only imagine what he saw, what he was thinking. Glossy eyes, rosy cheeks, and a man clearly thrusting into his friend. At least his pants weren't down and it just looked like he was holding me here.

Kova's hand gripped my waist so tight that I knew I'd have a bruise tomorrow. Again. His orgasm flew into me and I took all of it.

Kova looked over his shoulder and gave Hayden a murderous glare, and yelled, "Get out!"

"Ah, oh...my..." Hayden stammered before slamming the door shut and leaving.

My head dropped to Kova's neck. We were breathing so deeply when he asked, "What've we done?"

Kova pulled out and my legs slid weakly down his hips. Thick, warm semen dripped down my inner thigh. I wanted to wipe it away, but I quickly fixed my clothes so I was covered.

"I have to go. I need to find Hayden and make this right."

I didn't have time for anything else.

Kova flattened his hand against the wall, caging me in. I looked up and locked gazes with his steely green eyes.

"You better fix this, Adrianna, this is your goddamn fault. I swear to God, if he utters a word of this to anyone, you will regret it." He was seething with anger but with every right. "Do you understand? I will personally make sure your career is over."

I nodded in understanding.

Quickly, I fled from his office. Luckily no one was in the hallway as I dashed to my locker. I threw on my sweats, jumping into the pant legs and then raced to the parking lot to find Hayden.

"Hayden! Hayden!" He was pulling open the driver's side door when he looked over his shoulder. Disappointment. I saw nothing but disappointment laced in his eyes.

"Hayden," I repeated breathlessly in front of him. "Wait."

"What the fuck are you doing, Aid? Are you seriously sleeping with the coach?" My shoulders dropped. I wanted nothing more than to lie, but I refused. Hayden knew the answer. It was written on his crest fallen face.

He shook his head in disbelief. "Why, Aid? How could you?"

I didn't respond—I couldn't. There were no words for what he saw other than pure abandonment.

"Is he forcing you?" When I didn't answer, he exclaimed, "Jesus, say something!"

I pulled my bottom lip between my teeth and contemplated what to say. Hayden just kept staring at me, waiting for an answer, but I was rendered speechless. I averted my gaze, ashamed of the truth. How did I explain I wanted everything without looking desperate?

Hayden placed both hands on my shoulders. "Answer me."

I shrugged helplessly. "What do you want me to say?"

"You need to come forward and go to the police. This is rape, Aid."

I shook my head frantically, my heart drumming against my ribs. "I can't. It's not rape, Hayden. It's not."

"Yes, it is. You're underage."

"He didn't force me though."

"Regardless if you consented or not, he still took advantage of you. You're under his training, he preyed upon you like a disgusting sick fuck." He ran a hand threw his hair. "I can only imagine who else he's treated this way."

"No, he didn't. It's not what you think. Please, you don't know what you're talking about."

Hayden furiously yanked the car door open. "If you won't do it, then I will."

"No! Please!" I begged, on the verge of tears. "Please don't. I'll deny it if you do."

He looked at me, stunned. "I think you need mental help. He brainwashed you, didn't he? Threatened you if you told anyone?"

"No," I lied. "I'll deny it."

Hayden slammed his door shut and stepped up to me. He cupped my jaw and I stared into his sincere blue eyes, my fingers laced over his.

"Did you do it to get ahead? Because you didn't need to. You have what it takes, babe. You've improved greatly," he said with such sorrow that my heart ached. "You're a different gymnast, you're not what you used to be. You're so much better. Don't be one of those girls who sleeps her way to the top. That's not who you are."

A fat tear slipped from my eye. Hayden saw it and pulled me to his chest, his lips pressed against the top of my head. I sobbed quietly on him, holding him. I needed him to understand the repercussions if he opened his mouth, but fear was taking over.

"Please, Hayden. Don't tell anyone. You can't."

"You're putting me in a tough spot. What he did is wrong. How long has this been going on?"

I swallowed. "Months."

"How many months?"

I went with the truth. "I'm not positive, but about six months or so after I came here."

Hayden cursed under his breath, hissing with anger.

"You don't understand and it's not what you think, I swear. There's so much more to it than you know." A heavy sigh burst from my throat and I said quietly, "He took me out of the meet for his own personal reasons."

His brows bunched together. "What are you talking about?"

"He's taking me out of my first meet, that's what you walked in on. I went in there to yell at him and one thing led to another. He even called my parents and told them I wasn't ready, even though he told me I was. He purposely took me out for his own personal reasons." Tears began falling while I cried into Hayden's chest. He wrapped his arms around me, comforting me and protecting me at the same time.

"He can't do that."

"He can, and he did," I said between hiccups. "There's nothing I can do about it now. At the end of the day, he has the right to take me out of a meet."

Hayden cursed under his breath agreeing with me. "This is a big deal, Adrianna. We need to notify someone."

I sucked in a breath and clutched his shirt in my hands. My heart was broken for two different reasons and I didn't know how to deal with it.

"Please don't get involved, Hayden. I'm begging you. This is my mess, not yours. I'll explain everything to you if you promise not to speak a word of it to anyone."

He groaned, torn between standing by his friend's side and doing the right thing.

"You're killing me here. Don't sleep with him again. Okay? It's not right. You'll get caught eventually," he paused. "We'll figure something out together. Until then, be smart, focus on your love of the sport, nothing else. Fuck him—not literally."

A sad laugh escaped my throat. Easier said than done.

Truth was, I couldn't stop.

I didn't want to...and I wouldn't.

TO BE CONTINUED...

ACKNOWLEDGMENTS

To my husband who went into full attorney mode when I told him my idea for *Balance*. I'll never forget when you pulled out one of your law school books and started flipping through it to answer my questions regarding the storyline. We both knew it was crazy from the get-go. Thank you for jumping on the bandwagon with me and allowing me to do my thing. Your support is most important and means everything.

Lisa Maurer. You're a rare gem. Words could not express how much I appreciate the time and effort you put into *Balance*. The way you pushed me to dig deep and bring this story to life was exactly what I needed. You went above and beyond and tackled this beast with me, and fourteen hundred comments later, you helped bring this novel to fruition. *Balance* came out just how I envisioned. Never in my wildest dreams would I have thought asking you to beta, a virtual stranger at the time, would turn into an incredible friendship full of laughter and lifelong memories. Thank you for everything and more importantly, thanks for being my beta lifer.

Lori Scaman. If you hadn't messaged me that one day, I don't know if I would be writing my acknowledgements right now. I wanted *Balance* to be more about the sport, more than a forbidden romance story, but more about what goes on behind the scenes. Your encouraging words, knowledge of the gymnastics world, and unwavering support made all the difference. You're my fairy-gymnastics-godmother. You heard my cries and reached out, offering your assistance any way you could. Thank you so much for all your help, the countless rereads to make sure every gym term was correct, and putting up with the mountain of questions I asked you.

Nadine Winningham. I'm running out of ways to tell you how incredibly amazing you are as an editor. You're a woman of many talents and never cease to amaze me. Thank you are two words that just aren't enough for you, but I will continue to say them because I am so grateful to have you, not only as my editor, but as my friend. Thank you so much for the time you spent polishing *Balance* and bringing out its true shine.

Alyssa West. You've been by my side since the beginning. You've rooted for me and supported me. You've listened to me vent and cry and have always been there when I needed you. Lord knows I needed you while writing *Balance*. Thank you for your honest and humorous critiquing, and the endless hours of brainstorming you did with me.

Author Micalea Smeltzer. Your inspiring words about writing and not holding back helped push me to write *Balance*. You gave me hope, the courage to write this story how I wanted, and not how I was supposed to. I never forgot them, and I never will. You're still my goal.

Author R.E. Hunter. I asked you many questions regarding the law and you were always so quick to research them. Thank you so much for your help and for being patient with me.

Jill Mac. Thank you for your early feedback. I know it was a disaster at the time but thank you.

Emily Smith-Kidman. Thank you for working so diligently on promoting *Balance*...and putting up with all my questions. Your selflessness does not go unnoticed, nor does all the hard work you put in for the book world. Thank you so, so much!

Thank you to all the avid readers and bloggers who've supported me from the beginning! Thank you! Thank you! Thank you for being patient with the production of this book. It was a long time coming and you guys made it worth it.

And last but not least, Marisa. Like Madonna, Cher, and Wynonna, no last name is needed. You work tirelessly behind the scenes and prefer to remain in the shadows. Thank you for all you do. You are amazing, and I am so grateful for your support. Everyone should have a Marisa in their life.

ABOUT LUCIA FRANCO

Lucia Franco resides in South Florida with her husband and two sons. She was a competitive athlete for over ten years – a gymnast and cheerleader – which heavily inspired the Off Balance series.

Her novel Hush Hush was a finalist in the 2019 Stiletto Contest hosted by Contemporary Romance Writers, a chapter of Romance Writers of America. Her novels are being translated into several languages.

She's written over a dozen books and plans many more for the future. When she's not writing, she can be found swimming in the ocean or getting lost in her butterfly garden.

Find out more at authorluciafranco.com